Black Guild

Second book from the tales of the Black Powder Wars

J P Ashman

"Once again, a relentless, emotional, heart pounding journey…"
LJ Waguespack – Goodreads

"Dark and gritty at times and yet infused with humor and witty banter."
Shawn Wickersheim
Author of The Penitent Assassin

Black Guild

Second book from the tales of the Black Powder Wars

J P Ashman

This Paperback Edition
IS – 1

Published by J P Ashman through
Ingram Spark's POD Service.

Date of Publication
April 2018

Cover art by Pen Astridge

Series map by J P Ashman – illustrated by Charles Richardson

Edited by Jeff Gardiner

Dedications

I want to dedicate Black Guild to the memory of my father, Phil, but also to Taya, Pen, Mihir and all those amazing fantasy fans and friends that stayed with me, supported me and helped me get through the shittiest of times; The Fantasy Five, The Fantasy Hive and The Terrible Ten are all a huge part of this. I cannot rave about the online fantasy community enough. From bestselling authors to readers, bloggers to editors, the community I am a part of is the most welcoming I have ever known. Truly. This is for all of you, because you have been with me throughout.

Thank you, my friends. Thank you!

Author's Note

I want to give my readers the heads-up on Black Guild, because it's not your usual sequel.

Black Guild and Black Arrow (due for release in summer 2018) were originally one book. One. Big. Book. If you'll believe it, Black Guild was bigger than Black Cross, which proved only just viable to print without pricing it out of the market. Second to that, the original Black Guild had so many twisting and turning and crossing storylines, my editor and beta readers suggested I split it in two. So I did!

Unlike the usual 'Part One' and 'Part Two' halves of such a tome (*GRRM* springs to mind), Black Guild and Black Arrow actually run side by side. I know, it's unusual, but it's how I felt the split worked best. In fact, the splitting of storylines worked so well, there was little for me to do afterwards. It's almost as if I had purposely written two books set at the same time, but from different points of view and geological areas.

Of course, this means there are many characters from Black Cross who will not make an appearance in Black Guild. There'll also be new characters appearing in both. Hell, some Black Cross characters won't reappear until Black Prince, the fourth book in the Black Powder Wars series. But please be patient. This is a building war that encompasses several kingdoms, after all, and early reviews and beta reads have reassured me that there is plenty here to sate your Black Powder Wars thirst.

I'll keep you no longer, folks. Now you know what to expect, I hope you enjoy new characters and old, and many new places throughout Brisance in this, the second instalment of the Black Powder Wars. I hope you enjoy Black Guild. I certainly enjoyed writing it.

J P Ashman

Map of Brisance

Dramatis Personae

Caravaneers

Couig, Master of the Caravaneers
Collett, Mistress of the Caravaneers
Belcher & **Legg,** caravan guards
Jevratt, lead caravan guard
Sir Xand, hedge knight
Souch Sader, sorcerer
Cheung, assassin

***

Altolnan Nobility & Households

Will Morton
Duke of Yewdale, Lord High Constable of Alton;
brother-in-law to King Barrison

Sir Merrel & **Sir Fell,** Captains to the Duke of Yewdale
Severun, Morton's agent,
former Master of the Wizards & Sorcery Guild
Egan Dundaven, Morton's agent,
former Samorlian Witchunter
Sean, Ten, Graehm & **Rough Paul,**
men-at-arms to the Duke of Yewdale

Ward Strickland
Master of the Wizards & Sorcery Guild,
Lord High Chancellor of Altoln

Morri, infirmary cleric
Orix, former Master Cleric
Effrin, City Guard cleric

***

Goblin War Galley

Charlzberg, Admiral of the goblin fleet
Bosun, bosun
Spyde, navigator
Cooker, cook
Tull, stern dangler
Ptarmigan Twins, tiller-crew

***

Sessio

Captain Mannino
Hitchmogh, first mate
Parry, blade master

***

Black Guild & Dockside

Master Poi Son
Mistress Bronwen
Master Alden-Fenn
Pangan, lead assassin for Master Poi Son
Blanck, former assassin
Terrina, assassin
Rapeel, street-assassin
Longoss, former assassin
Coppin, former whore of Mother's brothel
Keep, former assassin turned inn-keeper

***

Others about Brisance

Crackador, the legendary great-dragon
Dignaaln, emissary

Prologue

Brisance
Summer - 492nd year of the Alliance

The Caravaneers' camp stretched out to the east of the road like a town of wheeled hovels. On the western side of the road stretched Lake Beddoe, its green shores and shallows swarming with splashing children, adults and animals alike. Birds circled the smoke-blackened sky. Corvids mainly, but vultures were always present around the edges of the permanent camp. Taking in the scene from beneath his hood, Cheung silently recited his guild's assassination orders before plunging into the mass of merchants, tradesmen and drovers. He passed unseen in his disguise; the stall holders didn't call to him and the caravan guards he passed didn't eye him once. He, to their eyes, was a priest of the Temple of Tears, and no one from that temple was worth talking to, for talk they did not.

All manner of people from various kingdoms called out in the trader tongue, hawking their wares of spices and cloths, foodstuffs and tools, martial services and slaves. Cheung glanced over the chain-folk: humans, goblins and adlets of all ages. He eyed some of the adlets, knowing the dog-legged clansmen made good scouts and soldiers once broken and trained.

Leaving the chain-folk behind and working his way through the passageways created by the colourful vardos, carts and traps, Cheung headed towards an area of the camp he knew caravans leaving for Altoln gathered. Sailing Lake Beddoe was an option he'd considered. Alas, Cheung could not swim and the thought of bobbing along on the depthless lake was too much even for him.

Passing a pungent spice stall, vivid colours arrayed in enticing circles of shifting shades, Cheung neared his destination: a six-wheeled armoured vardo with a rampart-like roof.

'Ah, a priest of tears, if I'm not mistaken?' A bare-chested man emerged from the back of the vardo, tattooed arms folded.

Cheung nodded before stretching out his foot and roughly writing the word 'Altoln' in the dirt.

Biting his bottom lip, the guard answered the written request. 'Aye, priest, we're off there. Ye have coinage for the passing?'

Cheung nodded once more and held out both gloved hands, weighing them like scales.

'For dat, ye'll have to speak to me ma. Pay her yer dues and ye'll be all set.'

Cheung bowed low in demonstrated appreciation.

'Me name's Jevratt. Do ye have one yerself, priest?'

Cheung purposely scrawled a line of illegible nonsense in the dirt.

Jevratt screwed his face up, then grinned. 'Right ye are, Priest it is.' Jevratt pointed to a gaudy vardo further down the column. 'Me ma's in dat one. Go pay her yer dues, Priest, and we'll find yer own vardo and settle ye in, nice and sweet like dat.'

Cheung bowed and shuffled across the rubbish-strewn camp to the vardo in question. Weighing the money pouches beneath his robes, he chose one of the larger ones and pulled it free; he needed to make them believe it was all he had.

Muffled, hacking coughs came from inside the vardo as Cheung climbed the steps to knock on the yellow door.

'What?'

Cheung nearly answered, before biting his tongue and knocking once more.

More coughing. 'Bollocks to ye for makin' me get up, but I'm on me way so have yer bloody coins ready, ye bleeding welt of a cock...' The haggard woman's curses stopped as she opened the door and stared at the hooded priest.

'My apologies, Priest.' She offered a nervous smile and fingered a net of red petals around her neck. 'Travel, is it?'

Cheung nodded once.

'We end in Altoln,' she said. 'Rowberry to be precise. Nod once for there, twice for somewhere along the way.'

A single nod was followed by a bag of coins.

Jevratt's mother snatched the coins and weighed them, eyes closed.

'Aye, that'll do.'

Cheung shuffled, as if agitated.

'All ye have, Priest?'

Another nod.

The woman sighed, emptied the majority of the coins into a bag about her waist before returning the rest to Cheung. Without another word, she turned back and slammed the door on him.

Amused by the exchange, Cheung couldn't help but smile, before returning to Jevratt, who'd been watching. The tattooed man had three lads of similar build stood around him, although none of them wore rat tails – genuine rats' tails – woven into their otherwise cropped hair as he did.

Cheung approached the grinning trio and was pulled along to the nearest campfire, a stream of seemingly nonsensical chatter marking the way. It was all the assassin could do not to shrug off the confident hands on his arms and back.

Chapter 1 – Pride and prejudice

Cheung rocked gently in the shade of the cab as it rumbled along the road. The caravan was heading more east than north, and far more east than west.

There was trouble in Sirreta according to Master Couig, who led the caravan. Troops were moving and armies were massing. People were being attacked on good roads by brigands and goblins, and caravans were being attacked by Sirretan troops of all things. Cheung had thought hard on the news for the past couple of days. It wasn't unusual for Marcher Lords to skirmish along their borders, but word was the whole kingdom of Sirreta was up in arms.

Unsure what to make of it, Cheung moved it from his mind as much as possible and cleaned his bone-handled kamas again and again in an attempt to calm himself about the deviation. He was glad to have a vardo largely to himself, at least.

Chickens can't talk, he'd mused, when revealing his black-bladed weapons opposite the caged poultry. He'd also thought he was losing his mind, thinking such things. Cheung was used to a solitary life, but the buzz of the Caravaneers all around him made his silence and quiet nature feel unfamiliar.

He struggled with the lack of training, the lack of motion. Sitting in meditation was one thing, surrounded by the rooftop gardens of his home, but the constant rocking and boredom was something else. Whenever the caravan stopped and made camp, the caravan guards would take part in hunts, wrestling matches and bare knuckle fighting. Cheung felt ashamed at his lack of control, but he'd wanted to throw off his robes and step into the dirt-drawn rings they used, to stretch his muscles, if nothing else.

Cheung thought about the fights he'd already witnessed. *They're good, the guards, but I believe them to be better than they let on. The children are the same. They strut around as if guards themselves, a look of pure contempt on their grubby faces whenever they pass anyone who isn't bare-chested. The masters would do well to recruit from those little bastards.*

Sudden singing from the roof above, as seemed to be the norm.

Masters release me. Cheung threw his hood over his scarred head and attempted to meditate.

The singing was taken up by every one of the dozens of vardos and carts and traps along the road, followed by the bass groans of camels and oxen.

Cheung's exasperated growl was the first noise he'd made since leaving his rooftop home.

After several days stretched along the road, the caravan made camp outside a walled town on the edge of the Toye Hills. The following morning, as the sun crested the peaks of a small mountain range known as The Sprigg, the gates opened and the townspeople of Nameless came forth. Carts of their own, some empty, some laden with produce, descended on the Caravaneers. Men and women bartered for this and that, whilst some Caravaneers entered the town to seek wares not sold from the back of a cart.

Cheung heard a boastful crowing as he rounded an armoured vardo, and wasn't surprised to see Jevratt as its source. Cheung stopped, leaned against the vardo and enjoyed the entertainment.

'I'll fight any man!' The half-dressed caravan guard slapped his right hand on his left forearm and mirrored the action with the other as he spoke. 'For we can all do dis, can't we, eh?' he went on, slapping his forearms in repetition. 'We can all do dis.' He flung his tattooed arms about his bare chest and rolled his head as he danced around in front of a poorly armoured, but armoured nonetheless, knight.

'Yes,' the knight said, unamused. 'I'm sure you would, and yes we can, but I'm not here to fight. I'm here to pay passage back to Altoln.'

'Ah come on. Take yer metal off yer back and we'll have a bout. I bet ye'll like it. Hey, hear dis, I'll even wager ye five silver coins. Silver! How about dat, me man?'

The knight shook his head and made to move past.

'Ah-ah,' Jevratt said, holding up his scarred hands. 'Not before ye pay yer dues to me ma.' He pointed to Mistress Collett's vardo. 'If ye want to travel, ye need see her.'

'I thought it was Master Couig that ran this caravan?'

Jevratt filled his cheeks and put his arm around the knight's maille-clad shoulder, before releasing the breath and replying. 'Aye, me man, ye're right there...'

'But?'

Jevratt smiled. 'Ye know the right of it, don't ye? Ye see, Collett, me ma that is, well she'd be the one to handle the comings and the goings. Whether dat be people or money—'

'And the Master Caravaneer? Master Couig?'

'Well, he be the one who guides us. He be the one who rules us. He be the one...' Jevratt pulled the frustrated knight in closer, 'who decides what's to be done when someone breaks the rules of the caravan. But me ma—'

'Handles payment.'

Jevratt moved backed to arms-length, grinning. 'Ye know ye bloody stuff, don't ye? Eh? Ye know ye bloody stuff.' Jevratt let go of the knight, but not before taking the man's iron-encased hand and shaking it vigorously. 'Ye're a fighter and a scholar, of that I'm sure. Now, off ye pop to me ma. She'll love to be meeting such a noble as yerself.'

'I'm a hedge knight, as far as you'd call it. Not a noble.'

Arms wide, Jevratt moved in and hugged the surprised man. 'Whilst ye're here,' he said, face pressed against the knight's own, 'ye're nowt but family.' Jevratt pulled away again and seemingly missed the look of disgust on the knight's face. 'Now, as I tell ye, off ye pop to see me ma.'

Releasing a heavy breath, the knight shook his head in disbelief and moved across to Collett's gaudy cab. Once at the top of the rear steps, he rapped his plate knuckles on the yellow wood and awaited a response. From inside, Collett called out.

'What?'

'I am here to… pay my dues, milady.'

A cackling laugh from inside. 'Milady?' More laughter, followed by a stream of throaty coughs.

Frowning, the knight looked back to Jevratt, who was now flanked by three lads, all young, with shaved heads and bare chests. All four grinned, as did Cheung, before moving on towards Nameless.

Shouting and cursing greeted Cheung upon his return. Before the familiar fire and cauldron came into sight, he saw one of the many bare-chested young lads, squatting by the wheel of Cheung's own vardo, braes round his ankles. The lad eyed the assumed priest of tears warily as he held his breath and forced out a shit.

Clenching his teeth under the shade of his hood, Cheung merely walked past and into the space surrounding the fire.

'Dash him!' Jevratt shouted. 'Dash him in the face, ye shit.'

A lad dodged left and right as a man twice his girth threw heavy punches his way. More lads, and young girls wearing very little, their skin darkened by the bright sun, shouted and swore as the two combatants circled each other within a larger circle of toe-scraped dirt.

'Dash him, Legg,' Jevratt called again, to the amusement of the younger ones.

'Legg, Legg, Legg!' Several began to chant.

He doesn't like that, Cheung thought of the larger man, who he knew to be called Belcher, and could see the red-faced anger as the youths chanted his opponent's name.

'Stop yer feckin' dancing, ye pricks,' a girl shouted from the other side of the ring. Laughter followed, and Cheung noticed the other hood, behind the girl.

Where did you come from? Cheung struggled to see more of the man, what with the voluminous robes he wore. The figure moved and Cheung watched closely.

A capable man, by the way he carries himself.

A collective intake of breath brought Cheung's attention back to the duelling pair, in time to see Belcher double over in pain.

Don't hesitate, boy, Cheung thought, but Legg did, and through the hesitation, Belcher lashed out with surprising speed and clocked Legg on the chin with a well-aimed uppercut.

Dust lifted as Legg hit the ground. Belcher cheered, as did the crowd.

Fickle. Cheung smirked as the 'Legg' chanting youths switched to 'Belcher' instead.

Looking back for the hooded man, Cheung cursed himself. *Gone.*

***

'Is it reliable, Strickland?' Morton said, walking into Tyndurris' lounge and dropping into a comfortable chair, his sheathed bastard-sword now resting across the chair's arms.

'Good day, my lord Yewdale,' Ward Strickland said, lowering his book and removing his horn-rimmed spectacles. 'And yes, the source is reliable. I'm not the guild master for nothing.'

Morton pursed his lips and nodded at that. He waved away an approaching servant.

'What will you do with my report?' Ward asked.

'What can I do? Other than send word to border forces and place chosen men on the roads.'

'And do you think that will stop an assassin entering Altoln? One man or woman?'

Morton sighed and rubbed at his lined face. 'Honestly? I don't know.' He spoke through his hands.

Ward offered a tight smile.

'We've doubled the guard at the palace,' Morton said, hands now back on his bridging sword. 'As clichéd as that sounds.'

Ward offered a warmer smile and the bob of a silent laugh. 'Yes, that does always seem prudent, given such dilemmas in fairy tale or song.'

'All it will do is slow an assassin down,' Morton admitted. 'If they're determined, they'll get through. Whether it's to lace food with poison or spring from a bloody curtain with knife in hand.'

'I may have an answer to the former. As for the latter, are Barrison's servants loyal?' Ward reached for the wine on the low table between them, placing his book and spectacles down at the same time.

'Of course they're bloody loyal,' Morton said, although the magician knew him well enough to know he meant no offence. 'Those folk and their families have lived and worked in the palace for generations. Some for centuries, believe it or not.'

'You had their humble lineage traced?'

'I did.' Morton changed his mind at that point and waved over a servant, who brought wine.

'That must have taken some doing?'

'There's a scribe. Spent time here a while back, after his sojourn with the Samorlian bastards,' Morton said, eyes everywhere but Ward's as he took in the surrounds. 'First time I've been inside Tyndurris, Grand Master.' Morton looked at Ward, a sincere and rare smile on his face. 'Can you believe that? All my years in and out of Wesson, and I've never visited.'

'You've never cared much for what we do here...' Ward raised a hand to stop Morton's protest, '...and I can understand that, truly.'

'Never stopped me going to that damned cathedral though, did it?' Morton snatched the goblet from the servant when he came close. 'And *those* fuckers I hated the most.'

'Past tense?'

'Eh?' Morton paused, goblet hovering at his bottom lip.

'They'll still be operating, here and there. The Samorlian witchunters and inquisitors.'

Morton took a swig of the wine then rested it on his sword. He pursed his lips again and nodded. 'True.'

'Back to this scribe, my lord.'

'He was tortured,' Morton said, falling back into the tale, 'by an inquisitor.'

Ward's eyes widened a touch. 'And survived the questioning?'

Morton chewed his bottom lip before answering. 'We got him out of the cathedral. Well, Bagnall Stowold and the City Guard did, with my enthusiastic consent.'

The magician's eyes widened fully at that. He placed his own wine back on the table. 'The scribe who told the Samorlians how to breach this tower, you mean?'

'Yes, Lord Strickland, the very same. I doubt you could have avoided talking—'

'I didn't mean that,' Ward said quickly, holding his hand up to apologise for the interruption. 'I was merely surprised he was still… working for you, for anyone after such an ordeal.'

Morton nodded before swallowing more wine. 'It's… how should I put it… made him more inclined to do all he can to help his King. Not that he wouldn't have done beforehand, but now? Now he works feverishly to help in any way he can. He feels responsible for what happened here.'

'He mustn't.'

Morton nodded. 'I know. Damn, but we all know. His mind, after what he went through…'

'You've talked to him?' Ward asked, surprised at the answer he thought he already knew.

'Yes,' Morton said sharply. 'Why wouldn't I?'

Morton continued, saving Ward the need to answer. 'He's done well in tracing the servants. He leads a good team of scribes and ensured me that all in the palace are loyal. And I trust him in that.'

'In that?' Ward asked, knowingly.

Another gulp of wine and the goblet met the table. 'He's having troubles at home. His team tell me. He fears he is being watched, followed even.'

'Could he be?'

Morton moved his head from side to side. 'It's possible. He escaped them, after all, albeit by our hands. They won't like that, the witchunters. They're disbanded, but as you said, they'll still operate. Equally it could be in his head, after what he went through. I've seen such a thing before, more than once, from trauma physical or witnessed.' Ward made to speak, but Morton waved it away. 'I've not the time nor resources to solve Brisance's problems and those of all the men and women alive.'

'Not one man?'

'Yes, one!' Morton said, voice rising. 'Barrison, my bloody King and brother-in-law is that one, Strickland. I have a duty to see him

16

safe and well. Ellis Frane, the scribe, will do what is needed to see we have no adders in the nest. My men will do what is needed to ensure one doesn't easily slither into that nest, and my peers and below will do what is needed to hinder if not stop one of those shites getting across our borders from Eatri!'

Ward raised both hands as guild members around the room looked over. He also noticed two armoured knights appear in the doorway. Morton waved a hand above his head without looking and his retainers repaired to the hallway.

'Apologies, Ward,' Morton said eventually, back to rubbing his face. 'It's all getting a little much.' He laughed. 'Even for an old wolf like me.'

Ward smiled. 'I do understand. It's not that long ago since my own nest was an unknown entity, with arcane magic being enacted above my very head, in the chamber I now reside in.' He shuddered before going on, the thought of what Severun did too much to bear. 'We do what we must when faced with difficult circumstances. You have a lot to think about and a lot to do. All you need do is ask, and I'll help in any way I can.'

Morton clasped his hands and looked up, an intense stare replacing the weary look.

'Do you have men out there, Ward? On the borders? Men or women; mages, working or experimenting or whatnot?'

Ward took a deep breath and nodded. 'The guild does, yes.'

'I need them, Ward. Barrison needs them.'

Ward's slow nodding continued.

'Have them search the ports of Lake Beddoe. Have them search riders and the camel trains and Caravaneers, beyond the borders if they must. I'm having ships searched when they dock in Wesson, but put word out, tell your mages what to look for. Even if it's to let us know the assassin has crossed the border, so we can flood our own roads with men. If I do that now, send armed men here and there before I even know there's a foreign assassin in Altoln, I'll have barons marching on barons for a swift land grab. I'll have earls harrumphing and putting their own men on the roads, those men fighting one another for no other reason than pride and prejudice.'

'Will,' Ward said, using the Duke's first name like he did only rarely, like he did when he really wanted the Lord High Constable to listen to him. 'Will,' he said again, as Morton made to talk on, 'I already have.'

Chapter 2 – A deadly race

A pony trap raced past the crawling caravan, followed by another, then another, with at least four lads sat on the benches of each trap. The drivers were flanked by recurve-bow and spear wielding youths with faces set stern. Something was amiss.

Opening the cab's door and leaning out as much as he'd expect a priest to dare, Cheung tried to see the front of the column, to where the pony traps were heading.

'Don't be worrying none, Priest,' Jevratt shouted down from the vardo's ramparts above. 'The lads're racing. There's nowt in it. No danger.'

Cheung waved an acknowledgement and ducked back into his cab. Closing the door, he drew the cloth across the window, removed his gloves to reveal the scars beneath, and rested his head back against the board.

Racing… Cheung stared at the caged chickens opposite. *Yet they wear their war-like expressions.* He heard two more traps rattle past, down the other side of the vardo. *Not once have I seen the boys smile and yet Jevratt and his kin do nothing but.* The armoured caravan guards around the Caravaneers' camp on Lake Beddoe sprung to mind and Cheung smiled to himself. *Now it's the boys that seem like guards, whereas Jevratt and his bare-chested lads?* Cheung grunted a laugh. He sighed after that and closed his eyes, tracing the scars of his face and head with a finger. *Who am I to judge them? I've seen these men and boys' prowess with their fists and feet, and it's impressive.*

And if we're attacked by someone that doesn't want to fight in a dirt-drawn ring? Cheung drew in a long breath and held it. *I'm not sure how they'd fair against a real foe.* He let the breath out slowly. Measured. Controlled. His right cheek rose from another smile. *And yet they've lived as nomads for centuries. You don't survive such a life without being able to defend yourself.*

A sudden clucking from the chickens opened Cheung's eyes. *Ah, eggs.* He left his thoughts behind as he helped himself to breakfast.

Although Master Couig's snaking caravan hugged the road besides Ghauni Forest, rather than venturing into the Toye Hills, the old caravan master shuddered at the thought of what lived out there. He knew Jevratt and the other guards would be extra vigilant on this stretch of the journey, but couldn't help squinting to the north himself. He hoped he didn't see anything, but if they were out there, he'd feel better knowing he'd seen them as soon as possible.

'Are ye well, uncle?' Legg appeared and climbed up next to Couig, his young eyes locked on the horizon like his late father's brother.

Couig turned and winked at Legg. 'Aye, me boy, I'm well. Nervous, but well.'

'Adlets?'

A sniff and a nod.

Sudden singing came from further back along the caravan and Couig cursed those responsible.

Hissing, Legg turned on the bench and stared back, trying to see which vardo or cart it came from. A group of boys rumbled up the side of the column on a pony trap, faces set stern whilst singing the solemn nomad song.

'I'll hush 'em—'

'Leave it, Legg. Let 'em sing. If adlets were to know we were about, they'd know. A trap of noisy turds wouldn't change that.'

The pony trap came alongside and the boys looked up to the caravan master and his nephew. None said a word, but the singing stopped and the trap raced off ahead.

'We have scouts out a-ways,' Legg said, seeing his uncle's eyes locked north once more. Couig nodded and smiled, although it was half hearted.

'You'll feel better when we're at Grounding, won't you?'

Couig reached across and squeezed Legg's hand, eyes on the hills to the north. 'I always do.'

The boys in the trap came racing back towards the caravan from a bend in the road, hidden by the trees of Ghauni Forest, faces still set as if to murder, as always, but Couig braced himself all the same. As the lads clattered back down the caravan without a word, he released the breath he'd held and rubbed at his running nose.

'If only the little bastards would act like they're *not* going to war for once, my nerves might settle a bit.'

Legg smiled and nodded, although he didn't speak, squinting as he was at a point on the horizon.

'How're ye fairing after that bout with Belcher?' Couig asked, wanting the subject changing. 'I heard ye gave him a run for his coin?'

Moving his hands to his ribs, Legg grimaced. 'Hardly. Bastard had me, as he always does.'

'He's a big lad,' Couig said, re-assuring one nephew over another.

'Doesn't stop Jevratt from one-punching him.'

Couig laughed at that and turned to Legg. 'Nothing would stop Jevratt one-punching any man, and you know it. Ye got to fight against yerself, not the opponent.'

'How's that?'

'Ye keep trying to beat Belcher, but ye haven't beat yerself.' Couig tapped his temple with his index finger and laughed again as Legg looked on, confused.

'Listen, me boy, ye got skills, ye got good skills, but ye tell yerself, every time, that Belcher'll win. Ye tell yerself enough and it'll be the truth. And it has been!'

Legg looked back to the horizon.

'Ye get me? Eh? Ye get me?'

A nod.

'Ah, come on, don't be giving me the silence now.'

Legg stood.

'Ye jumping vardo for that? It's the damned truth—'

Couig stopped as he saw the look on his nephew's face. A look followed by a called warning from several guards at once. As he turned his head to the Toye Hills, Couig's heart began to hammer a beat. All the more when he saw what approached.

An empty pony trap crested the nearest hill, one of its two wheels damaged and wobbling, the piebald pony leaking blood from an obvious wound on its flank.

More shouts and curses followed as two traps raced out towards the injured pony.

'Stop them!' Couig shouted, standing alongside Legg, reins gripped tight.

Legg shook his head and strung his recurve-bow. 'It's too late. They'd never make it back...'

A haunting howl announced the arrival of scores of hound-like humanoids as they crested the hill near the pony traps.

'And I'm not sure we will, either.'

Eyes wide, Couig turned back to face the rest of the caravan. 'Onward!' he shouted, as loud as he could. 'Onward! A fighting run to Grounding!'

A roar of agreement and of shock and anger followed as the adlets charged down the hill and crashed into the traps and their grim-faced boys.

Chapter 3 – Resonate

Men screamed and adlets howled, arrows thumped and the dead voided their bowels.

Master Couig's caravan continued on towards its goal, Ghauni Forest to the left, death to the right. Pony traps ran the line, the lads riding them, launching arrows and spears and stones from slings. The majority of those missiles struck true, although the adlets hit by them often continued, thick skinned and frenzied as they were.

'Come on, me beauties, keep yer pace,' Couig called to the oxen before him. Despite their size, the beasts of burden could shift when he wished them to.

A couple of cuir bouilli clad adlets loped across in front of the oxen and round to Couig's left. Before he could react, they leapt up at him, canines bared.

Flinching away, Couig only just caught Legg's intervention. The lad dropped down onto the bench from the roof of the vardo, smashing the man-dogs away with brass covered knuckles. He deftly evaded their hasty lunges and swipes with crude sword and sickle, before crunching his fists into their faces numerous times. They fell away to the moving ground below, but Legg didn't hesitate. Hearing a call from behind, he climbed back onto the roof and rushed to aid his fellow guards.

'Gods, boy, but ye don't know how good ye are,' Couig managed under his breath. He risked a glance around and behind, to see adlets throwing themselves at the vardos and carts, and caravan guards throwing whatever they had back at them; fists mostly, but arrows licked out now and then, as did the odd spear. Couig saw Jevratt yelling orders up and down the line and couldn't help but smile at the lad's confidence, despite such a heavy assault.

Looking back to the road ahead, Couig grimaced. *I've known them hit us hard before… but never well-planned, like this.*

The log across the road was deliberate, of that Couig was sure, and his stomach twisted at the thought. *Such a simple trick, yet nothing more is needed to halt us.* 'Legg!'

Couig's nephew was quick to jump back down to the bench besides his uncle. Legg's fists were bloodied, as was his torso, although from his own wounds, or his enemies, Couig had no idea.

'Oh,' Legg said flatly, looking ahead.

'Aye lad. Now we need to move it, and quickly.' Couig began to slow the caravan. He heard the cries of alarm and outrage that followed. Legg jumped back on the roof to pass the word on.

Before Couig could stop the caravan, three pony traps overtook him, towards the log. Reaching it swiftly, the dozen lads dismounted and made short work of rolling the log around in an arc, off the road.

'Good lads—'

Couig stopped at the sight of the adlets running from the trees. Arrows left them, as did throwing axes. Only one trap made it away and that one with less lads on it than before. Cursing and swallowing the lump in his throat, Couig snapped his reins and cracked his whip. He followed that with a yell and the oxen accelerated once more.

'Legg, I need men front!'

Someone screamed from not too far back, but before Couig could think on it, Legg dropped down, accompanied by a lad with a bow.

'We'll need more'n that, boy.'

Legg swallowed hard and nodded. 'Aye, uncle.'

An arrow left the boy next to Legg, followed by another, but more came back their way from the adlets on the road.

Pony traps once more shot past. Four this time, with Jevratt and Belcher aboard the trailing one.

'Ye stay there, Legg,' Belcher called. 'Us men'll handle this lot.' His wink was lost on Legg, for the lad had dropped to the road and set off at a run. A tremendous run.

Couig cursed.

The archer looked to Couig, a grin on his face. 'He'll 'ave the dog bastards, Master Couig. Don't ye worry none.'

Biting his bottom lip, Couig said nothing as he watched his nephew leave the caravan behind. He was followed by an arrow that whipped past him and slammed into an approaching adlet. The one behind that fell to the weight of Belcher as the large man threw himself from the moving trap and flattened the raider. Before the adlet could react, its head crumpled to the meaty fists of Couig's eldest nephew. Looking up for another threat, Belcher laughed as Legg ran past, dust rising from his feet.

'Go get 'em, lad! Just don't let 'em thrash ye like I do!'

Couig couldn't hear Legg's retort, for the traps had reached the adlets and the raiders were howling and the caravan guards were roaring.

Climbing to his feet and making for the scrap, Belcher clearly felt the rumble of the caravan reach his back. Moving to one side, he waited until Couig was alongside before jumping up with some effort to sit next to the old man. They both watched Jevratt and his boys go to work.

An adlet lashed out with a spear, but Jevratt sidestepped the weapon, grabbed it by the shaft and yanked it from the raider's clawed hands. Dropping the weapon and stepping in close, Jevratt knocked his opponent out with a single blow, before rushing to his next target.

Legg arrived to take a young lad's killer from his feet. Landing atop the thrashing adlet, he received a nasty gash from the clawed feet kicking out at him as his brass knuckles finished it. He jumped up and turned to face another adlet, but a young caravan guard with blood across his face took out the raider's long legs and fell about it, slashing with a knife.

Turning again, Legg saw Jevratt battling two adlets. Their weapons seemed useless against the fast-moving man, who dispatched both with fists alone.

The immediate danger was over, the remaining adlets about them turning and running for the hills, but as Legg turned to take in the nearing caravan, his heart reached for his mouth. He cursed, then spat. 'We're all for the pyre.'

Eerie horns preceded more howls as well over a hundred adlets crested the nearest hill.

'Don't be so feckin' sure about that, Legg.'

Legg turned to Jevratt, eyebrows raised.

Jevratt pointed to a hooded figure stood on one of the vardo roofs. 'That man's more than he seems to be. Of that I'm sure.'

Legg wiped sweat from his eyes and nodded. 'I hope you're right, for we're gonna need somethin' special to see that lot off.' *And no mistake.*

As adlets raced down the hill towards the caravan, the hooded figure dropped from the vardo and ran to meet them.

Filling his cheeks and letting it out in one, Legg nodded again. 'Jevratt,' he said, 'I think ye might be right.'

Jevratt grinned. 'Come on, let's not leave him to it.'

Jumping onto the nearest trap, followed by Legg and two others, Jevratt whooped and the pony launched forward, followed by the other traps, lads and guards.

As they passed Couig, the old man waved at them, face ashen. Belcher shouted a curse and climbed atop Couig's vardo for a better look. More traps left the caravan to chase the hooded runner as arrows overtook him, slamming into the first adlets down the hill.

Whatever that man's going to do, Legg thought, *he better do it fast… and it better be good.*

Stopping, the hooded figure raised his arms and looked up to the sky. The grass about him wavered, the sky darkened. The adlets faltered and the traps behind the figure slowed. With a bass thud which seemed to come from the man's open mouth, the adlets nearest to him dropped to the floor, weapons forgotten. They clutched their ears and shrieked as the stranger released another three concussive thuds that resonated through the bones of all present. The traps stopped, but the archers and slingers continued. Their missiles found their marks, many of which were prone, and the remainder of the adlets faltered as many dropped to another resounding thud.

'He's feckin' impressive,' Jevratt shouted to Legg and the other lads on his trap. They all nodded. One let another arrow fly.

A chest pounding thud and yet more adlets dropped.

'He's doing it with his mouth, this man?' Jevratt turned to Legg, then back to the strange happening before him. 'Isn't he, Legg? The bastard's doing it with his mouth?'

Legg said nothing as the man released another thump from his impossibly wide mouth.

'Eh? Isn't he?'

'Yes, Jevratt,' one of the lads said, eyes wide.

'Ha!' Jevratt slapped Legg on the back. 'The bitches are running.' He turned to the moving caravan and shouted. 'The bitches are running!'

He's saved us all, Legg thought, eyes on the robed man more than the fleeing adlets.

A cheer went up from the caravan and two pony traps set out towards the hills.

'Hold, ye little shites!' Jevratt shouted, moving his own trap towards them. 'Hold or I'll smash ye, ye little bastards.'

The traps came about and clattered back past Jevratt. The boys on board were bloody, but their eyes were hard and their faces set in their usual angry visages. Jevratt gesticulated to them and they steered clear of his trap as he brought it to a halt near the impressive man.

'Who'd ye suppose he is, Jevratt?' Legg asked, eyeing the strange traveller.

'I dunno, but he's feckin' something else, isn't he? Also, he's paid his due to me ma, so I don't give a bollocks who he is.'

Legg nodded and looked to the Toye Hills. The adlets were gone, apart from those who had dropped to missiles and the mysterious thudding; of those, none stirred.

'We'll lift ye back to the caravan, me man,' Jevratt called to the approaching figure, who nodded his thanks and climbed aboard. Everyone stared at him openly as he took a seat.

Jevratt tore his eyes away to flash a dangerous look to Legg and the others. 'Don't be burning him with yer gazes, boys. Ye hear?'

All three nodded and looked away from the man, and away from Jevratt. Legg's stomach twisted in fear from Jevratt's look, almost as much as it'd twisted when the adlets had crested the hill.

'Let's go, me man. Back to yer vardo and back to our journey, and at Grounding ye can talk me through that fancy shit ye pulled there. Eh?'

The hooded man turned to Jevratt. 'Absolutely,' he said, voice softer than any would believe.

From the window of a rocking vardo, Cheung watched with interest as Jevratt's trap rode back to the line, hooded stranger on board. *Now who the masters are you? Never mind…* Cheung pulled the cloth across the opening and returned his unused kamas to their satchel. *You saved me having to reveal myself and for that, I'm grateful. As should the Caravaneers be.*

Chapter 4 – Another scar

The young woman groaned as the vardo rode over a bump in the road. She was unconscious but alive thanks to Cheung's ministrations. After the adlets retreated, Jevratt came looking for Cheung, to ask him for help. There were people with severe injuries throughout the length of the caravan, and many more with minor wounds. The girl Cheung saved was close to passing before he tended to her trauma. He couldn't let her die. He may have been taught basic healing by his tutors, and gained more experience since, but it was his cover that was important; priests of the Temple of Tears knew healing very well, and if he was to refuse Jevratt's request to have the girl brought to his vardo, it would have raised suspicions. As it was, Cheung knew enough to save the girl, through poultice and wrappings. He was surprised no one else was able to help her, until he hung from the vardo's door, heard the cries of pain and saw the multitude of persons tending to the wounded.

As the caravan moved on, Ghauni Forest clinging to its left, unwrapped bodies were tossed from the moving column. There was no room for sentiment within the families of the Caravaneers.

They free themselves of the burden of the dead, Cheung thought, watching a former child bounce as it hit the ground. A woman wailed and a man stood stock still, gripping his partner in a seemingly emotionless state. Cheung knew better. *He holds it inside, I'm sure, so she can let it out. Time will pass and roles will reverse. Although his release could come in many ways, not all of them good for her.* Licking dry lips, Cheung pulled back inside the vardo and sat back, eyes locked on the slowly rising and falling chest of the girl he'd saved. *Your kin would have left you behind too. Left for the kites, for the crows and the foxes and the worms. All things along this road gain the taste for human flesh because of this tradition. Your people think they release a burden, but they create one; predators… adlets.*

Cheung wasn't sure whether adlets ate human flesh, after all, they were part human themselves, but he'd heard rumours, and rumours tended to come from some truth, at least.

A song began outside Cheung's vardo. Low at first, before building in strength. Many voices added their own uniqueness to the lament, which stretched the length of the caravan. The words were muffled in places, and without knowing them, Cheung struggled to understand, although the gist was clear to him. It was sorrow and farewell in one, both to those lost and to Ghauni Forest herself. The caravan was leaving Eatri behind to cross the River Beddoe. Beyond that, multiple mountain passes led through to The Marches. The caravan would skirt up and around the forests that made up those ever-contested borderlands, to pass below Chapparro Minor and the Altolnan gnomes that lived there.

At least we will be free of adlets and the like. Cheung leaned forward and checked on the dressings of the girl. *And you will likely be able to leave my vardo.*

She groaned again as his hands left her bandaged side and Cheung hesitated; his hood was down. Eyes fluttering, corners creasing and cheeks lifting with pain, the girl turned her head and looked up into the dark eyes of her saviour. Her eyes widened as she took in the scarred face for the first time. They widened yet more as Cheung's henna-patterned hand pressed across her opening mouth.

'I'm sorry,' he whispered, leaning into his hand and restraining her with his other. His stomach turned as she struggled, but a few deep breaths calmed him until she fell still and quiet.

Taking a deep breath, holding it a while before releasing it, Cheung rubbed hard at his face and sat back once more, this time with his hood up.

Why did you have to wake so soon? Why did you have to see my head, my scars? Your body will bounce now. I only hope to the masters this doesn't cause more of your kin to fall to the side of the road.

Cheung closed his eyes and listened to the chickens cluck, and the song of the Caravaneers.

I have but one mark, that is all. I will travel leagues to see that life end and it could even cost me my own. I do not wish it to cost any more, but if that is what it takes, that is what I will do.

Masters forgive me, but my toll on this path has already begun.

Eyes locked on the girl's lifeless orbs, Cheung pulled one of his kamas from his satchel and drew the depthless blade across the back of his unblemished neck.

I will not forget you.

Chapter 5 - Grounding

Not long after Couig's battered caravan crossed the wide bridge over the River Beddoe, did Grounding come into view. Nestled between the foothills of the Chapparro Mountains, the grassland plateau stretched out to either side of the road.

Pony traps rode left and right, followed by dogs of varying sizes and the vardos and carts themselves, pulled by horses and camels and oxen. The sudden breaking of the caravan seemed random, but as Couig watched on, he knew each family led their wheeled homes to specific pitches on the featureless but fertile grassland.

Leading his own family on, Couig guided his vardo to an unmarked spot; he knew it well, since his family and ancestors had pitched there for centuries. Once in position, Couig waited for his family to form a circle of vardos and carts, his in the centre. Other families did the same, some close, some much further away.

It took a while of manoeuvring, shouting, cursing and some singing before all the families were settled. When they were, the previously plain plateau was spattered with circles of gaudily painted wood and faded canvas, and should any of them have been able to fly, Couig knew, they would see that Grounding resembled a giant eye, with Couig's family the pupil.

Dusk arrived by the time beasts were tethered and fires were lit. There was little wind and less cloud and the first bright dots appeared in the eastern sky. Couig lay on the long grass, a stem sprouting from his mouth. He listened to far off singing, accompanied by quiet groans and whimpers. There were many injured and many more grieving.

'We shall have a wake,' he said, staring up into the darkening sky. 'Tonight?'

'Aye, Legg, tonight will be remembered, and through it, our felled cousins and siblings and parents and children. All of them.'

Legg put more wood on the fire and nodded. 'All of them.' He sat back to admire his work and turned to his uncle. 'Is it time?'

Couig watched the orange sparks lift with the smoke, sniffed and wiped his nose with the back of his hand. 'No. Not yet.'

Jevratt and Belcher arrived and crouched opposite their cousin and uncle.

Couig looked over to the two lads, then back to the glowing spots of orange mingling with the shining spots of silver far above. 'Tonight, the wake comes before Grounding.'

All three nodded at their uncle's words. They stared into the fire for a while, watching the wood darken and lighten in shimmering oranges and yellows. It was mesmerising, as always. Such a simple thing, fire, and yet to look at it was to be drawn in. To look at it was to feel its heat, its light; life and death, joy and pain.

'That hooded stranger's a one, ain't he?' Belcher said.

Legg nodded and Couig said nothing. It was Jevratt who replied.

'Oh he's the boy alright. A tip-top boy by my thinking, and I wanna know what he knows. I wanna know what it were, what he done.'

'Where's he to?' Legg asked.

Jevratt wrinkled his nose and shrugged. 'Dunno. He said Altoln to me ma. No specific place though. He's the boy though, that's for sure. Powers like that, he be a wizard or the likes, eh Couig?'

The stem of grass launched from the old man's mouth in an impressive arc.

'He's of magic, for sure,' Couig said. 'But a wizard? I dunno, lad.'

'Well whatever he is or isn't, he's top boy in my mind.' Jevratt surged to his feet and cursed at the pain. 'Anyways, it's time for the wake. Ye agree?'

Legg and Belcher both said 'Aye' and Couig rolled and pushed himself up to stand with them.

'Right ye are, Jevratt, me boy. Right ye are. Let's get to it.'

Belcher made to move and stumbled. 'Feck me leg and feck it twice.'

'It's that bad?' Legg asked. 'What was it? Spear? Sword?'

Belcher bent at the knee, sucked in air and shook his head. 'Nah, a knife. Didn't hurt at the time. Never noticed it until after the scrap with the bitches. It'll be good though, don't ye worry.' He managed to dance about a bit, although the pain was evident on his face. 'Good enough to smash you again, Legg. Good enough to smash you.'

'Not until later, ye shites,' Jevratt said, pulling on Belcher's arm. 'Off we go to rouse the families. We've folk to remember.'

Couig winced at the thought of those lost. 'Off ye go, lads. I'll catch ye.'

'Ye sure, uncle?'

Couig shoved Legg on and the lad chased after his departing cousins.

'I'm getting too old for dis,' Couig said to himself, as he climbed atop his vardo. Once on the roof, he rummaged in some of the chests and withdrew a dented, curled horn. After spitting on the mouthpiece, he drew in his lips, pressed them to the cold metal and blew a long, sorrowful note that lasted long after he'd stopped blowing.

Tonight's for remembering. And I'll be staked and stamped if we don't wake the gnomes of Chapparro Minor whilst doing it.

As soon as the horn finished its remembrance call, the shouts, cheers, wails and singing started, and increased in volume… and increased some more. Smiling to himself, Couig returned the horn to its chest and stood to take in the view. Turning, with the star-filled sky above and the smoke of his fire catching his nose, he looked on at the ring of rings with fires at the centre of each. It was a special sight and one he never tired of, even when a wake preceded Grounding.

Ah, but Grounding is all the better for such things. Makes us remember what we have, what's ours and what we could have lost, rather than what we did. Couig pulled his lips into a tight smile and turned around again, fingers tapping on his leg to one of the many songs he could hear. *For we could've lost it all today. It really came that close. And what would become of Grounding then?*

Breathing in the smoke-tainted air and sighing with satisfaction, Couig took one last look around and climbed down from his vardo. *Now to find the lads, before they start a fight.* Couig wandered from the centre of his circle and off into the night, into the eye, a multitude of family circles to choose from.

The beat was kept with a goat-skinned drum, but dozens of feet about Couig's circle followed and increased the beat until it resonated within the muffled heads of all present.

On top of Couig's vardo stood Jevratt, a cow-horn of ale in each hand. At the top of his voice he continued the song he'd sung three times already that night, but despite his hoarse voice, the crowd couldn't help but scream for more and sing the chorus when it came.

We turn our wheels and we set our course
Dues are paid by the traveller's purse
Me ma takes coin that's business done

And that's the life on the road and run!

The ground gets thumped and the laughs are long
The instruments played and the spirits strong

The life we lead is both hard and fun

And that's the life on the road and run!

The raiders try and slow us down
We fight our way to the nearest town
We all go down when our time is done...

And that's the life on the road and run!

Scores of people cheered after the last chorus and despite Jevratt's attempt at continuing, the people demanded he drank both horns at once instead. He obliged.

Another cheer and many followed his example, grabbing horns from one another so they could try two at once. It was said later that Grounding drank more ale than the Caravaneers that night. It was also said that the gnomes of Chapparro Minor could not sleep and a song was written of that very thing. But before the night could end, it was time for Grounding.

'Families!' Couig shouted over the chants for Jevratt to drink more. They all fell quiet at the sound of their caravan master's voice.

'Families,' he shouted again, taking all those in that he could see. The crowd tried to push in from outside the circle, from the darkness and the light of circles farther afield, but there was no way they could all fit in. Dozens of travellers mixed amongst the Caravaneers, many suffering from wounds, most from drink. There were those who were sober: a hedge knight and two robed and hooded men.

'It is time!' Couig shouted as loud as his spinning head would allow.

A tremendous roar erupted and before Couig could shout another word, the families exploded from the centre of the great eye and raced to their own circles and wheeled homes.

Couig laughed, lost in the din of his running and cheering kin. 'Well,' he said to Legg, who moved alongside him, 'that saved me a speech.' Legg slapped him on the back before moving off to prepare their own vardos for Grounding.

Couig felt a gentle tap on the shoulder and turned to see the priest of tears stood behind him. The hooded man pointed to the Caravaneers rushing here and there, attending to the vardos, but not the carts; he shrugged.

'Ye want to know what we're about, Priest?'

The priest's hood dipped low; a nod.

Pulling the man in close, Couig hesitated, surprised at the hard muscle beneath the robes. Shaking it away, the old man proceeded to explain Grounding to the quiet priest.

Listening intently, Cheung's eyes widened under his hood as he saw the explanation in practice mere moments later. All the vardos in Couig's circle were surrounded by swiftly erected bamboo scaffolding, their wheels removed. No carts were touched, but with practised ease and efficiency, despite the amount of ale each man and woman had consumed, the wheel-less vardos were lowered on pulleys to the grass below. The circle now resembled a miniature hamlet of gaudy, box-like structures, many with the rampart-like roofs of Cheung's own.

What possible benefit is this? Cheung thought, bemused. He was pulled around the circle by Couig, who talked him through each vardo; which family lived in which, how they were related to him and how old that particular 'home' was.

If we're attacked, Cheung thought, hardly listening to the man, *there's no escape. The camp is spread wide and thin… defenceless.*

Well, apart from that mage.

Cheung's eyes locked on the hooded figure stood opposite him, but before he could pull away from Couig, the mage was lost to the shadows beyond the circle.

Before he knew it, Cheung was introduced to various families and any travellers they had with them for the journey. The knight who Cheung had already seen, greeted him with suspicion, but others greeted Cheung with the respect a priest would expect. Most of the travellers knew each other from the journey, but Cheung had kept himself to himself, even during the wake.

By the time Couig and Cheung made the rounds, with Couig saying several times how proud he was to have a priest of tears travelling with them and how grateful he was for the priest's attempts to save the girl in his vardo, despite her not pulling through, Cheung was startled by the silent arrival of an eagle-owl. The barred and mottled bird appeared as if from nowhere and approached a woman's leather-clad arm. That arm dipped as the large bird alighted on it. Craning its head around at impossible angles, the owl took in all present before pulling a dead chick from the woman's gloved hand and swallowing it whole.

I'm suffering from a lack of training, Cheung thought. *I should have known of the bird's approach, especially one that big.*

'What news?' Couig asked, moving across to the bird handler. She leaned into the owl and her eyes glazed over for a moment, before clearing again.

Stroking the back of the eagle-owl's head, the woman grinned at Couig. 'The eye is complete,' she said. 'It's time for Grounding.' She heaved the bird up into the air, and after a low swoop that left its wings brushing the grass, the majestic bird disappeared into the night like a spectre.

Shaking his head in amazement at the true silence of the creature's flight, Cheung cringed as the Caravaneers began to shout and cheer once more. They spread like ants from a disturbed nest. All about they ran and leapt, before encouraging their guests to follow them into their grounded homes. Cheung was wary as Jevratt appeared and pulled him towards the chicken-filled vardo he'd been travelling in. He could see the same trepidation on other travellers' faces, including the hedge knight, Sir Xand's.

Steeling himself against the strange ritual, Cheung allowed the tattooed arms of Jevratt to drag him up the steps and into the now familiar vardo. Once inside, Cheung was taken aback by what he saw.

A gaping hole opened out where the inner floor of the vardo had been, stone steps leading into the depths below.

Cheung had one thought as the transformation sank in.

Where is my satchel? Where are my kamas?

Chapter 6 – Silence broken

Cheung felt his way down the steep steps below his vardo, the air about him damp. His soft-soled boots gripped the stone well, but he would have felt better knowing where Jevratt was leading him.

Do Caravaneers bring travellers to Grounding to lead them into... what? Dungeons? Worse? Cheung clenched his teeth, nostrils flaring. *Is there any unrest in Sirreta at all, or was that a lie to drive us north?*

'A little way more, Priest, and we're there,' Jevratt said from behind and above Cheung.

And where is there? Cheung wanted to ask. Gods, a growl or hiss would have satisfied him. *I am losing myself,* he thought, aware of how his temper was flaring quicker and easier of late. *I suffer from my lack of true meditation and training.* Swallowing and taking a deep breath, Cheung forged on, down the steps into the darkness below.

'Ah, see ye'll love this, Priest. I know ye will.'

Cheung ran his gloved hands along the rough stone walls either side of him. He hit the bottom. He'd moved to step down again and his right leg buckled as he struck the flat stone floor.

Before he could do anything, Jevratt brushed past him and there were half a dozen flashes of flint on steel and several curses before a torch flared to life. The yellow light illuminated a yellow door at the end of a short corridor.

'Down here, me man. Follow me.' Jevratt strode down the short space, torch in hand, before wrapping his bare-bone knuckles on the yellow wood.

Cheung balked at those knuckles, those fists topped in polished bone, illuminated by the torch as they were. He'd taken Jevratt's knuckles for dusters, much like the brass ones Legg used. But no, Cheung realised that Jevratt's knuckles were literally bare bone. *His* bone. Cheung swallowed as bile rose. He'd seen a lot of grim sights, caused some, but for some reason Jevratt's knuckle-bones, like snow-capped mountains lifting from a fog of flesh, knocked the assassin sick.

A hacking cough came from the far side of the door.

'Ma! It's me!'

Cheung forced the nausea away and shook his head in disbelief as a latch clicked and the bright yellow door swung inward. In its place stood a red-faced Collett, a tallow candle in hand. The smell of the tallow hit Cheung as the light of both torch and candle danced across Collett's lined face and the grimace she maintained. That grimace dropped as soon as she saw Cheung.

'Ah, Priest,' she said with glee. 'Ye bless us with yer presence. Come, come.' She waved Cheung forward and shoved Jevratt to one side. Bowing respectfully, Cheung moved past Jevratt and into his mother's... whatever the place was.

On the other side of the door, a plush expanse of fur rugs, wooden chairs, dressers and gaudy totems stretched left and right. Opposite Cheung stood another yellow door identical to the one he was passing through. He glanced left from beneath his hood and noticed a couple of much younger children playing in a large stone basin, carved from the floor itself. The water steamed as the children played and Cheung realised the warmth of his feet.

'They call it thermal something or other,' Collett said, following Cheung's hooded gaze. 'Keeps the water and floor warm, from below.' She laughed. 'But don't be expecting more explaining than that, for I don't have a mind for telling ye the details.'

Jevratt entered the chamber behind Cheung and his mother closed the door behind them.

'Welcome,' Jevratt said, tattooed arms wide, 'to Grounding.'

Cheung turned to Jevratt and bowed low. *These Caravaneers are full of surprises.*

'And now we eat,' Collett said, before coughing up something wretched and reaching for a long pipe in one. 'Follow me,' she added, packing the bone pipe with tobacco. Cheung followed the woman right, away from the bathing children and round a right-hand corner, where a cavernous space opened out before them. The stone ceiling rose up conically, making way for a large chandelier of candle topped antlers. The light the magnificent piece gave off created a warm glow that made Cheung smile involuntarily. *This place is truly magical,* he thought, taking in the scene and smell of cooking meat. Frowning, the assassin looked about for a fire. *I smell cooking... but not the burning of wood?*

As if sensing his thoughts, Jevratt rushed across to a glowing alcove where he pointed with excitement. 'Hot coals,' he said. Cheung looked to Collett, who was lighting her impressive pipe. The woman nodded for him to go on. Cheung bowed to her and crossed the fur covered floor of the hall-like space. Reaching Jevratt's side, he saw the white-hot coals in question. There was no wood about the fire, nor was there much smoke, but the oven glowed red in the centre. Above them sat a large pot and the smell was wondrous.

'The ground heat is enough on that spot there,' Jevratt explained, 'to allow the coals to get cooking hot.' The hardy man folded his arms and grinned at Cheung, before unfolding them again and motioning for the assassin to take a place at the large stone-hewn table below the chandelier. Obliging the man, Cheung sat on one of the few wooden chairs.

Collett placed a dozen or so half-horns for drinking, pouring a good measure of mead into each. She did it all whilst pulling and puffing on her pipe.

Cheung motioned around the round table, much of which was surrounded by curved benches, if not chairs. Grinning again, Jevratt indicated the way they had entered by lifting his chin.

'Some of the family will be joining us, once their own Groundings are set—'

A door banged open and children shouted out in pleasure.

'Good timing,' Jevratt said, taking a seat next to his guest.

Before Cheung could do or think anything, Couig, Legg, Belcher and several others piled into the hall. And before the assassin could rise, they all came to him in turn, telling him what an honour and pleasure it was having a priest of tears come to Grounding. He was pleased they expected little from him, knowing, as they did, that the priests of that order never spoke, and so as the food was placed before him and the drink supplied, Cheung enjoyed some rare relaxation and enjoyment as he did his best to play the role of priest, guest and friend.

The food proved plentiful, as did the mead, and once Cheung took his fill of both, Jevratt showed him to a small alcove with a shelf-like bed carved out of the wall of a dark tunnel. On the bed lay furs and down-filled pillows of linen. The luxury was beyond the assassin, used to the roof of a house as he was. He bowed his thanks several times, before climbing up onto the bed and pulling the heavy drapes across the opening. Cheung removed his hood and gloves, before running his pale fingers across the stone above and to the side of him. It wasn't long until he discovered the hole running perpendicular to his knees. Reaching into it carefully, he was relieved to feel the familiar satchel and kamas within. Reassured all was where he had packed it, and unopened, Cheung stretched out, yawned and closed his eyes. If nothing else, he had experienced a wonderful evening at the hands of the Caravaneers, and that would be something he would cherish whenever he allowed himself the time to truly relax.

Relax? Cheung's eyes opened, although it made no difference in the black alcove. *I've let my weapons leave my side. I've drunk far more than I should. I have a mark... and here I am thinking of relaxation and pleasant evenings with, what? Friends?* He rubbed his scarred face with both hands. *I hardly know anything about this Grounding I have descended into.* Steeling himself from the weariness of the road, and the comfort of the bed that begged him to close his eyes and succumb to its embrace, Cheung retrieved his satchel, donned his gloves and pulled up his hood. He drew the drapes aside and lowered himself down into a crouch, taking in the feint outlines of the tunnel. Torches were lit somewhere beyond a corner and it gave him enough ambient light for his eyes to soak up. Moving quietly, Cheung set off in the opposite direction to Collett's subterranean home.

Voices reached him, from back in the hall, but Cheung crept on, curious as to what else lay about him; beneath the expansive plateau above. More alcoves opened up on both sides of the passageway as he moved along, although all seemed open and empty from the little he could see. Following the winding path, the light brightened until he came across another yellow door, much like the one he entered Collett's Grounding via. Pulling back his heavy hood and pressing his ear to the wood, Cheung listened for signs of life on the other side.

Nothing.

Testing the handle, he found it unlocked, and so opened the door. Slowly. Quietly. Hood covering his face.

Beyond lay... nothing. Another tunnel with another torch. He passed into the space and closed the door behind before moving along the new path. There were no alcoves here, no features whatsoever, but it led somewhere of importance, the stone floor worn smooth. As he travelled further along, the darkness crept back in, the torch left far behind. Eventually, another light became apparent, albeit around a sharp bend. Checking behind him before moving on, Cheung heard muffled shouts and cheers as he came closer to the light source.

Unable to do anything about it, Cheung, whilst continuing to move cautiously, came face to face with a young, bare-chested boy walking barefooted the other way.

Both jumped, startled. Both stared wide eyed, although Cheung's eyes weren't visible to the boy. It was the stern-faced lad who spoke – priests of tears do not speak, after all.

'What the shite're you doing here, Priest?'

Cheung looked behind him, struggling for what to do. His first instinct was to silence the boy, but that would do him no good, surrounded as he was; trapped as he was. Fortunately, it was his silence and inactivity that saved him any action at all.

The boy grinned – a strange sight coming from one of the Caravaneer lads – and wagged his finger at the perceived priest.

'Ah! I know ye, Priest. I know yer mind.' He clenched his fists and rolled them in front of him, hopping from foot to foot several times. 'Ye wanna see some scrappin', don't ye? Eh? Ye wanna see it, ye do. I know it.'

Cheung nodded, bowed, thankful for any excuse to distract the lad from Cheung's snooping. Cheung punched the damp air half-heartedly with his gloved fists, nodding once more.

'Ha! I have the right of it, don't I?' The lad beckoned Cheung forward, the grin plastered across his face. 'Follow me, Priest. Follow me for the show ye've been searching for.'

Not wanting to do anything to make the boy suspicious, and more than a little curious besides, Cheung followed the wiry boy round the bend and into the torchlight before a blood-red door. Knocking on the wood several times, the boy grinned at Cheung one last time, before resuming his murderous expression and stepping through the opening portal.

The noise that burst forth assaulted Cheung after the near silence he'd experienced since Jevratt left him. Shifting his satchel so his kamas were easily retrievable should he need them, Cheung set his jaw firm and strode through the doorway after the boy, into the enormous, cuboid space beyond.

Scores of people shouted, roared and cheered all about Cheung as he followed his guide onto the steep stepped sides of the tremendous subterranean amphitheatre above and below him. The sudden height was dizzying. He looked down to the sunken fighting pits below, several of which were occupied by grappling and fist-fighting duos of men, women, goblins and adlets. Turning full circle, Cheung looked up and took in rows of stone steps above him, of which less than half were occupied. He looked up further to the flat roof and its dozens of antler chandeliers like those in Collett's hall. Below ran more stone steps and scattered groups of cheering men and women, each watching their preferred fight.

'Well, Priest? What ye think?' the boy asked, this time without the grin or mirth.

Cheung merely nodded. Truth was, he was stunned. He'd never heard of such a place and that surprised him, considering the amount of talking and bragging the Caravaneers did along the road. *They have barely survived a raid by adlets, yet they come here to fight some more.* Cheung's shoulders bobbed with a silent laugh as the scene sunk in. *These people are insane.*

'Come, Priest. I'll show ye about, I will.' The lad pulled on Cheung's sleeve and the assassin followed, down steep steps to the nearest sunken pit. The top of the square hole was topped with crude iron spikes and bits of broken pottery and glass. The floor was covered in sand. Sand and smatterings of blood.

'Here, sit.' The young Caravaneer motioned for Cheung to sit on the step behind him, and so he did, with the lad dropping down alongside whilst pointing to a tall adlet who was snarling and baring its fangs. 'He's a good'un, for sure he is, but he'll be going down in this bout. You watch, Priest. I'd put coin on it if I hadn't already lost it.' He laughed at that and whacked Cheung on the back. His eyes never left the adlet.

Cheung watched the creature. Its bare chest and arms weren't too dissimilar to that of the man circling it, but its legs were like those of a large wolf-hound stood upright, as was its tail and elongated face, despite its semi-human features. Cheung cringed. He'd seen plenty of the raiders before, but never had he had the opportunity to study one for so long. Alas, before he could fully take in the adlet, it launched itself at the man opposite and the fight began.

Shouts and inventive curses exploded around Cheung as quickly as the adlet sprung forward.

The boy was already on his feet, shaking his right fist about in imagined punches as he shouted down at the now wrestling duo. 'Smash him, don't hug him, ye prick!'

Unable to tear his eyes away, Cheung watched on as the adlet spun the caravan guard up and over, slamming him down. The sand clouded upon the man's impact, but no sooner had he hit was he rolling away and pushing himself to his feet. He looked stunned, swaying, but as the adlet came on again he stepped to one side and struck the creature on the temple with a well-aimed punch.

The adlet went down hard.

Turning to look up at the crowd's cheers and boos, the man missed the adlet's counter attack. Several people laughed aloud as the Caravaneer was smashed from his feet and crunched into the stone wall. He received several hits to the side, the adlet punching him again and again. Arms bent and down, trying to protect himself from the powerful blows, the man eventually dropped to one knee. The adlet clenched its fists together and brought them down onto the head of its opponent.

Several onlookers cheered as the man collapsed, but most groaned and swore, handing over coins and other goods in the process.

The adlet was ordered back into a corner as the crowd argued amongst themselves, the unconscious Caravaneer being lifted out of the pit.

Cheung looked to the lad next to him who merely shrugged. 'Told ye I lost me money, didn't I? Wouldn't bet on what I say.' He stood, patted Cheung on both shoulders and turned to leave. Looking back, he winked once. 'Enjoy! Ye can find yer own way back to Mistress Collett's, can't ye?'

He was gone before Cheung could nod.

Cheung thought it best to make his way back to his alcove. He felt exhausted, slightly drunk and although part of him wanted to climb down into a pit and stretch his muscles and skills, he knew he should save his strength and not risk himself. After all, he had a job to do and he was determined to do it and return home afterwards, despite the odds. The most important thought, that he was supposed to be a priest not a fighter, never entered his head.

Standing, Cheung turned away from the pits and looked up to the dizzying heights of the amphitheatre. As he did, he heard the biggest roar and cheer yet. Many of the people around him filed across to another pit as the crowds pushed and shoved to get closer to the action.

Reaching up and pressing through his hooded robes to the fresh scar on the back of his neck, Cheung tilted his head and wondered who or what was fighting to draw in such a crowd. *Masters forgive me, but one more won't hurt.* Cheung checked his satchel by his side and hurried after the spectators.

As the people cheered again, Cheung made his way around and down the steps to get a closer look at the fight that was under way. His priestly robes allowed him passage through the throng, something he was getting used to, and when he looked down to the sandy floor below, he nearly made a sound through shock alone.

Jevratt!

The lead caravan guard was sporting a bloody lip and a black eye, yet he looked in much better shape than his opponent. The older man staggering around Jevratt was holding his left arm at an awkward angle, the skin about his ribs darkening.

'Finish it, Jevratt,' a woman next to Cheung said, before shouting the very same at the top of her shrill voice. Cheung groaned and moved a few places as more of the same followed.

'Do him!'

'Don't be going down now, ye fecker!'

'Me ma could do better!'

'Quit dancin' and get in there!'

Cheung settled again and watched as the older man staggered in towards Jevratt. *He's done,* Cheung thought, before seeing the speed with which the man launched his attack.

Jevratt ducked left and right, stepped back and in. He accepted the left hook to the jaw, spat out a tooth and came around with a punch of his own.

The older man took the hit in the kidney and staggered before lashing out with his right foot to connect with Jevratt's right knee. Cheung's host went down.

It wasn't hard to hear Collett's voice, cough and voice again, despite the rising din. Cheung saw the woman higher up, behind him, pipe in hand. She saw her guest priest, nodded, winked and motioned for him to look back to the pit, a grin on her wrinkled face.

Cheung spun as the crowd sucked in stale air as a single entity.

Jevratt stood over the older man, who'd been knocked out, and who'd pissed himself in the process.

Looking up to all those looking down, Jevratt raised his bloody, bone-bare knuckles high.

The crowd chanted Jevratt's name and went wild.

As did Cheung...

Chapter 7 – A painful belch

Following Jevratt's victory in the fighting pit, and Cheung's vocal celebration, near silence fell across the amphitheatre like the gradual cessation of a torrential downpour. Scores of eyes turned to the supposed priest of tears – the should-be mute – and those eyes were either wide or, mostly, narrowed.

Cheung's heart quickened, his gloved hands moving towards his comforting satchel and kamas; what good would they do him against scores of capable fighters? Looking around in genuine fear, more for the failure of his mission than his own life, Cheung saw movement. Movement towards him. He scanned for a way through the closing crowd, for the blood-red door he'd passed through with the boy. For any door.

And will I make it out of Grounding even if I do make it to a door? Cheung cursed his stupidity and lapse. He cursed his intrigue and curiosity. But most of all he cursed the fear clouding his judgement, and in doing so, pushed it aside, sobering in an instant.

They know I can speak, so speak.

Before he could, Collett rushed down the steps towards him. Cheung braced himself and slipped one hand into his satchel, but Collett turned her back on him and held up her hands, smoking pipe held out in one.

'What's the business here?' she said, voice carrying an air of authority that stayed everyone present. 'So the feckin' priest cheered for my son, so what?' Her eyes darted here and there, daring anyone to move or question her. 'Are ye all so proper that ye can't believe it possible? That ye can't believe one such as he...'

Cheung pulled his head back as the long pipe whipped around and hovered in front of his shadowed face.

'...might be travelling in secret?'

Mumbles and whispers spread throughout the crowd, but Collett continued regardless. 'Is that not what we offer our guests? Travel without question? Travel without judgement; judgement such as we suffer ourselves at the hands of many!'

A nod and shout of agreement from some.

'But a priest?' A woman stepped forward. She was similar in age to Collett, but far less haggard in appearance. 'He hasn't the right! He could be open about himself and we wouldn't question, as you well know, Collett. So why pretend to be a priest? Of the Temple of Tears, no less.'

The pipe returned to Collett's mouth as she turned and looked upon the robes of Cheung.

'Because I *am* a priest,' Cheung said, surprising himself.

Collett drew on her pipe and frowned as many called Cheung a liar.

'How so, me man?' Jevratt appeared by Cheung's side and placed one of his hands on Cheung's shoulder. Cheung glanced sidelong at that hand, body tense. There was blood on the hand, both Jevratt's own and his opponent's. The off-white of Jevratt's knuckles poked through the damaged skin, like the snow tipped peaks of before, but from a sea of gore.

'Well?' Jevratt asked. 'Priests of the Temple of Tears cannot speak, we all of us know that. There's no need to continue with this line, Prie—' Jevratt grunted a laugh at that, and again someone called Cheung a liar.

'Offer up the truth,' Collett added. 'We'll not judge why ye travel or who ye be. But… leave the priest title alone now, for yer own sake.'

There were whispers and murmurs again and people shuffled closer.

'Because…' Cheung said, more to Jevratt and Collett than any other present, 'it's not a lie. I am a priest… but I ran.'

Collett released a plume of smoke from her lips, took a deep breath and nodded. 'He ran before they took his tongue,' she said, loud enough for all to hear.

'Take him back!' Someone shouted from higher up, followed by agreements by others.

'For what purpose?' Jevratt shouted towards the general direction of whoever had spoken. 'Eh?' he pressed. 'For what purpose? Do we take escaped prisoners back? Do we take travelling thieves and murderers and outlawed knights back?' Jevratt pointed one of his tattooed arms to Sir Xand, the hedge knight who'd been watching from across the fighting pits. Cheung hadn't even noticed him standing there.

I cannot remember a time I failed myself in so many ways, Cheung thought, jaw muscles bunching. *I'm not sure my body will cope with the punishments I shall lay upon it.*

Several people shook their heads and some remained angry. Cheung didn't miss that.

'It's different,' the woman close to Collett said. 'A priest, Jevratt. A bleedin' priest of tears of all things. He took a vow—'

43

'And he paid his bloody dues to me!' Collett shouted. Her face reddened more than normal and she shook with rage. 'I'll not be preached to about preachers by you, Serny!'

Cheung felt Jevratt's hand tighten on his shoulder. 'Me ma's got the right of it.' His eyes bored into those around him. 'He's paid his dues like that knight over there, like that merchant over there...' His finger pointed out these people, previously hidden in the crowd of Caravaneers. 'That child rapist over there; if there were any bastard we took back, or worse, it'd be that fecker.' The man shrunk back into the crowd. 'But no,' said Jevratt, pointing his swollen hand to those around him, 'we don't do we? We take their coin and we travel them across Brisance. We feed their bellies and we offer them a dance. We pour them mead and we sing them songs, because that's the life...'

'On the road and run!' The chorus echoed from the flat walls of the subterranean amphitheatre and was followed by cheers and chanting and fists in the air.

'Now leave this be!' Collett shouted over the racket. 'Leave it be and throw in yer coin, for me son's to fight again!'

A bigger cheer rose to that and the Caravaneers and travellers alike filtered down to Jevratt's pit. A handful remained, glaring at the robed priest of tears; it was clear to them that Cheung was not what he seemed, but the crowd was content and for that Cheung owed his hosts his mission, possibly his life. If one or two came at him during the journey, or in Grounding, Cheung knew he could handle it. What he couldn't have done was fight off an army. Especially one made up of folk born and raised to fight. Turning to the man whose bare-knuckled hand remained on his shoulder, Cheung said but one thing: 'Thank you, friend.'

Jevratt grinned.

A while later and Cheung was eyeing a tubular earn.

'I'm not sure how this works?' he asked Jevratt. It felt strange to be talking around the Caravaneers, but he was content enough in the knowledge that they seemed to care about little past their own lives.

'I told ye, Priest,' Jevratt said, hopping about and flexing his scarred fingers, seemingly still fresh after yet another bout fought and won. 'I put me hand in there, like it is, see?' He held his hands palm out, palm in. Palm out. Palm in. 'And the rat's thrown in; hungry.' The man's hands showed signs of damage from the amphitheatre.

Cheung looked to the onlookers, most of which were talking too quickly for him to understand. He did understand enough to know they were betting on the outcome of the other two men stood about the large urn, and enough to know none of them bet against Jevratt.

'Why bother, Jevratt, if no one bets against you?'

Jevratt grinned and slapped his forearms. 'Pride, me friend. Pride it is. These pricks here…'

Both men made to protest, until Jevratt looked at them. Their silence was followed by sniggers and jibes from the gathering crowd.

'As I say to ye, these pricks here are hit'n'miss. Hit'n'miss they are. So they're worth the bet. Me?' He turned slowly, hands held high to the sudden chanting of his name. 'I do it…' A well timed pause. '…because I can!'

The crowd cheered, a sound felt in the chest of everyone in the subterranean amphitheatre.

Cheung filled pale cheeks and nodded. 'Go on,' he said, after releasing the breath. His place at the front was of Jevratt's making. To his left stood Belcher, to his right Collett. Jevratt's mother took bets in an impressive run of speech that blended into one long stream of gibberish. As far as Cheung was concerned.

Without warning, Collett's hands shot high and the bets stopped. As did the voices.

The amphitheatre was eerie in the near silence. Two women came forward with a wooden box stretching between them. They hefted it atop the urn, opened hatches along its length and stood aside as a man with maille mitts reached in.

A squeal announced the apprehension of an inhabitant and before Cheung knew what was happening, a large brown rat was yanked from the hatch and shoved into one of the urn's holes. This happened two more times before the box was removed.

The crowd yelled and three hands plunged into holes, two more hesitantly than the other.

Names were shouted and people laughed as grim faces were pulled. Two of the three contestants sucked in air and spat out curses, grimaced through pain, twisting their bodies. They gripped the sides of their holes with free hands as they reached further inside.

Jevratt seemed calm as his tattooed arm jerked about in the blackness of the urn. A rat squealed and there was a loud thump from within the thick ceramic container.

'Feck off!' one of the three shouted, pulling away from the urn, his bloody hand following. He was dragged away just as quick and followed by boos and hisses.

The next man lasted but heartbeats longer before he cried out and was pulled back by two women, his thumb nothing but a mangled mess of bright bone and red flesh.

Jevratt laughed aloud and practically lay on the urn, his shoulder working so furiously the rat tails resting on his neck danced. His other hand went up, index finger pointing to the ceiling.

The crowd whooped and called his name.

A second finger went up as a muffled screech came from the urn; more cheering.

On the raising of Jevratt's third finger, all hell broke loose. People jumped atop each other. Others fell to their knees. Some ran, just ran, from here to there and back, their faces lit with glee.

Cheung turned to Collett, who was pulling on her pipe and taking coins from people, one eye on her son.

Cheung looked to Jevratt, who pulled a torn hand from the hole. His biceps worked to lift the three large rats he held aloft. Their heads lolled, wobbling as he shook his catch for all to see.

The cheering was the loudest yet and Cheung couldn't help but join in.

Jumping along with everyone else, whilst hands patted backs and losing gamblers forgot their woes, Cheung's breath caught in his throat as Jevratt bit the tails from each rat in turn, throwing the bodies to the crowd and passing the tokens to his mother. He turned, eyed Cheung and tugged on the bunch of rat tails woven into his hair with his damaged hand.

'The most I ever done kill in one bout!' he shouted to Cheung.

Cheung couldn't help but laugh at that, and offered the man a low bow of congratulations. As he rose, Jevratt was there, grabbing him and hoisting him atop a dais of upturned hands.

'This is me luck bringer,' Jevratt shouted. 'Me luck bringer and me friend!'

The crowd's chant turned from one name to another, and Cheung rode the human platform across the amphitheatre to the chant of 'Priest', his friend raised and riding at his back.

***

As the blade scraped across his scalp, removing all traces of stubble, Souch Sader thought about what he had seen in the Caravaneer's amphitheatre the night before; the priest who he'd previously thought nothing of. And he thought, with frustration, of the magic

46

he'd been forced to release whilst protecting the hard-pressed caravan from the adlet raiders.

I revealed myself to him, as he revealed himself to me, Souch thought, as the boy finished his job and rubbed a balm into the sorcerer's scalp and face.

'All good, me man?' the boy asked, throwing the cloth down onto the shelf beside him. He reached for a square of polished brass and moved it swiftly about the back of Souch's head, before returning it to its place.

I wouldn't know if it weren't, after that. 'Yes, a steady hand indeed.'

The boy's usual frown turned into a wide grin as Souch handed over two Altolnan farthings. The boy winked his thanks and popped the coins into a pouch, before calling for his next client.

Brushing himself down, Souch climbed from the simple wooden chair and out through the small door, pulling up his hood and stepping down from the grounded vardo. Another traveller, the hedge knight known as Sir Xand, nodded as he entered the vardo.

Definitely not an assassin, Souch thought, heading off towards Couig's camp at the centre of the caravan's giant eye. *He's far too...* The sorcerer pursed his lips for the right explanation as he walked amongst the grazing beasts of burden. *Full of hubris,* he thought, smiling at the conclusion. *No, that one has something else to hide for sure, but it's likely debts, or a casual murder – if there is such a thing.*

Oxen shifted from Souch's path as he strode across the grassland. One of the beast's groaned as it was forced to move and Souch couldn't help but smile at the complaints of the large animal. *If you'd stayed still, it would have been me doing the moving around you.*

Souch stopped, turning back to look at the circle of wheel-less vardos he'd come from. He wasn't sure why it dawned on him, but he realised that Xand had no need of a shave. He was as clean-shaved as Souch was now, and Xand's hair was already cropped.

So why is he visiting...?

Souch scattered oxen, camels and ponies alike as he charged back across Grounding, heading for the vardo he'd left. His heart pounded and his mind struggled to focus on what he might need once there. The opening of the vardo's door was out of sight, but as he approached, he could see the edge of the open door, moving in the breeze.

Reaching the vardo and rounding on the opening, static-filled robes crackling, Souch prepared himself for a fight and looked inside.

A barely visible flickering of light scattered across the grass around Souch's feet and knees as he slouched to the ground. The boy was lying on the floor, level with Souch's chest, his throat open and his bloodied razor resting on the wood next to him.

Souch's breaths came quickly. He stared at the scene, at the cut thong of leather on the boy's belt that'd held his coin pouch, at the mess of his neck; at the opening to Grounding itself.

Grinding his teeth, Souch climbed to his feet and stepped up into the vardo. The stone steps that descended next to the lad had a drop or two of blood on them.

The bastard knight went down.

Hurrying, Souch moved down the steps, static once more building about him. He hummed ever so quietly, causing the nearest animals to keen, groan and whinny.

Torches lit the bottom steps and the open door. Moving through, Souch listened for sounds of movement.

Nothing.

He entered, taking in the calm scene about him. Furs lined the floor and walls of the small space. Another door, bright green, was ajar to the right so he made for that.

A rustle and curses from beyond.

The humming emanating from Souch's mouth increased and the curses stopped. Preparing himself, Souch spread his hands and gritted his teeth; they tingled as the humming persisted, increased, built to a crescendo, and when the door before him opened, Souch released the vibrations he felt within and opened a small portal in his mouth.

Xand rushed out, rondel dagger in hand. He hesitated as he realised who confronted him, yet he thrust his dagger forward nonetheless.

It did no good.

Souch threw out what felt like a painful belch that grated his throat and churned his stomach. That belch-like action projected the effects of the tiny portal, unleashing a concentrated burst of stale air that punched Sir Xand from his feet.

Static energy flickered and illuminated the walls of the chamber as Souch took another breath, but before he could replicate what he'd unleashed, the experienced knight kicked the door between them shut.

The action caused Souch to swallow and he doubled over from the agonising spasms that followed. He'd luckily failed to keep the tiny portal open, but the build-up of pressure and power he'd created within was enough to drop him to the floor, and within heartbeats he fell unconscious.

Chapter 8 - Accusations

Souch felt soft grass beneath him and tight bindings on his wrists and ankles before he opened his eyes. It was light, he knew that much, for it illuminated his eyelids. His stomach knotted and twisted from the aftermath of what he'd intended to unleash on the hedge knight.

Sir Xand!

Opening his eyes, Souch cursed, the sun momentarily blinding him. He closed them again, turned his head and re-opened them to look at the scene coming into focus: dozens of booted and bare feet.

'The killing shite's awake!' a woman shouted, followed by several curses and accusations.

Killer? Souch tried to pull at his bindings but they held his arms and legs firmly to the soft ground. An awful smell struck him and along with the dampness to his back, he realised he was lying amongst dung.

A familiar face came into view as the caravan master crouched beside Souch.

'Master Couig,' Souch said, with relief. But when he looked upon Couig's face, his relief left him. 'There's been some mistake,' he said.

'Oh, is that so, mage? Is that so?' Couig shook his head. 'Because ye see, to us lot here,' he waved his arm about, encompassing the gathering, 'it seems pretty clear.

'Ye killed a boy!' Couig shouted. 'Me friend's son!'

'My boy!' a woman screamed. She was held back by a stern-faced brute of a man, who glared at the sorcerer tethered to the ground.

Souch shook his head in disbelief. 'No,' he said, taking in the parents. Gods but his heart thumped, gut churned, bladder swelled. 'No. It wasn't me, I swear it.'

'Ye just happened down there, did ye?' the boy's father said. He was surprisingly calm, but his wife was straining to get at their son's presumed murderer.

'I chased the killer—'

'Bollocks!' someone shouted from another side, and Souch realised he was the centre of a large circle of people.

'It's the truth,' Souch pleaded, eyes back on Couig. *Believe me!*

'There was no one else down there. And you'd been seen going in stubbled; now you're not.'

'Well, of course I'm not. He shaved my head and I left.'

'Down, not out?' someone asked, off to the side.

'No, out,' Souch said, exasperated. 'I left and... Sir Xand!' He couldn't believe he hadn't said it straight away. 'It was him!'

'The hedge knight?' Couig asked, unconvinced.

'Yes.'

'Liar!' the dead boy's mother shouted, tears streaking her face.

'I'm not lying, you have to believe me. Master Couig, you must believe me.'

'I mustn't anything.' Couig shook his head. 'It's you who must give proof of your accusation against Sir Xand.'

'How am I to do that?' Souch dropped his head back to the grass. 'Sir Xand went in after me,' he said, speaking to the sky, 'and needed no shaving from what I saw. But I walked away, not thinking anything of it until—'

'When?' the father asked. 'Until you made this rot up?'

'No!'

'He's talking shite,' a girl said and Souch turned his head to take her in. She was pretty, but young. 'Xand wouldn't do that to anyone.'

Xand? 'He's a knight, girl,' Souch said. 'He's trained to kill.'

'Shut yer pissin' mouth, mage,' she said, stepping forward, fists clenched. Souch saw him, stood behind the girl, brazen as a bull.

Souch struggled against his bindings, eyes locked on Xand. 'He's right there!' he shouted. 'Take him, take him and let me go. Gods above.' All the thrashing in the world wouldn't have loosened the ropes or stakes, and Souch knew it. He did see the look in Couig's eyes though; the old man turned to Sir Xand, questions clear on his face. His eyebrows raised and he lifted his chin to the man.

'Take him.'

'No!' the girl shouted, widening her stance and raising her small fists.

Two men moved to take the knight, but they stopped before the girl.

'What're ye for?' Belcher said to the girl, eyes not leaving Sir Xand's, who'd rested one hand on his sword.

'He's with me, ye fat shit.'

Belcher swung for the girl, but she ducked his fist and slammed her own into his gut in rapid succession. Belcher grunted but took the hits, grabbing her by the hair and swinging her round and to the floor.

'Ye'll stay down, ye little bitch,' he said, reaching for Xand, Legg approaching the knight from the other side.

51

'Disarm, Sir Xand,' Couig said, standing. 'There's no evidence against ye but this man's word, so if ye've nowt to hide, ye'll leave that sword be and come quietly.'

'Come quietly for what purpose? So that magic man can slander me? So you can bind me to the ground? I've done nothing wrong—'

'You killed that boy!' Souch shouted.

'I did no such thing.'

'Maybe not...' Several people moved out of the way as Jevratt walked into the ring. '...but ye bedded that girl, didn't ye?'

Xand couldn't help the smirk that played across his mouth. 'What if I did?' he said, winking at the girl, who smiled up at him from the floor.

'Because,' Jevratt said, a sickening calm falling across him, 'she's my wife's kid sister. She's family.'

Xand swallowed hard. He gripped the hilt of his sword all the more, hubris forgotten.

Souch felt a spark of hope. 'He's—'

'Close that mouth, mage,' Jevratt said, pointing a battered hand towards him. 'I'm not talking about the murder, we've yet to decide on that.' Jevratt looked back to Sir Xand as Souch closed his mouth. 'I'm talking about this cocky bastard taking one of me own into his bed.'

'It were my choi—'

The girl stopped as Belcher dropped towards her. He didn't strike her, but could have and she knew it.

'We can sort this here and now,' Jevratt said, again with an air of calm that was terrifying. 'In a dirt circle. I'll give ye that chance, Sir Xand. I know ye to be a fighting man, ain't that right? So I'll give ye this one chance. Ye beat me, fair and square, and the girl's yours, ye can marry her today. Na-ha!' Jevratt held up one of his bone-crested hands, stopping Xand's protest. 'Ye wanted her, ye fight for her. Ye wanted her, ye marry her. And then it'll be accepted and ye'll be part of the family. Agreed?'

Xand looked furious. His chest was rising and falling, visible as it was without his coat-of-plates, or any other armour, for that matter. His hand wrung his sword hilt all the more, but with scores of angry Caravaneers eyeing him up, he nodded his agreement.

They take more offence to this than the boy's bloody murder, Souch thought, incredulous. 'And his murdering of your boy?' he dared, to the parents whose eyes hadn't left him.

The woman broke free of her husband and rushed forward, murder in her own eyes. She was tackled to the floor by Legg, but not before she launched a gobbet of spit that landed on Souch's closing eye.

'Bastard!' she screamed, falling into heavy sobs. Her husband came to her and pulled her to her feet, doing the same for Legg.

'Proof,' the man said to Souch. 'Where's your proof?'

Souch opened his mouth, but nothing came out. He shook his head and looked on in horror as all turned away from him. Several men dragged their feet to make a fighting ring off to one side and Xand was undoing his arming belt and handing it and his sword to his potential wife. He looked far from pleased, but when he caught Souch's defeated eyes, he managed a smile and a wink before turning away.

As the proof Souch had so desperately needed struck him, rough hands pulled his head around and forced a linen gag into his mouth. Souch threw everything he had into screaming at the two men who were securing the gag in place. He needed them to know that Xand had a line of blood below his ear, caused by the dead boy's bloody razor. But when one of the men dropped his elbow into Souch's stomach and laughed, it was all Souch could do not to throw up from the impact, and the magic churning in his gut, for that would have choked him to death on the grasslands of Grounding.

I cannot die... he thought, albeit hopelessly. *My mission is too important. Master Strickland forgive me, I may have discovered the assassin, but my interfering has once again landed me in trouble and, this time, more trouble than I can handle.*

The circle of grass was flat in many places, the two men circling each other as they'd done for some time. Jevratt sported far more bruises and cuts than Sir Xand, but the knight hadn't gone unscathed; a split lip, possible broken eye socket and several bruised ribs and knuckles, and a deep cut below his ear.

Xand's potential wife looked at those wounds and her face lit up. 'See how he fights for me?' she said, to anyone who'd listen. But none did, too engrossed as they were in the ongoing bout before them.

Xand took a deep breath, rolled his head on his weary shoulders and moved forward, hands relaxed.

Jevratt allowed Xand to come in at his waist, knowing he was trying to lock him in close where Jevratt's punches wouldn't be as dangerous. Jevratt also knew, from experience, how deadly knights were at close quarters. He'd once seen a knight wrestle another off a moving horse with nothing but his bare hands, only to dispatch the rider with the rider's own dagger.

Xand cursed as Jevratt deftly sidestepped the attempted tackle, but the knight was prepared and managed to throw himself at the tattooed brawler again. This time he connected.

Jevratt cursed as Xand wrapped his powerful arms about his knees and brought him down. Jevratt thought he'd have gone for his waist, but Xand wanted Jevratt grounded, and tackling a man's knees from the side would certainly do that. Jevratt hit the ground and attempted to roll, but Xand held on, thwarting the attempted retreat. Thrashing, Jevratt attempted to shake the man off, but Xand's grip was solid and his head tucked in, preventing any potential connections with Jevratt's jerking knees.

Xand, whilst hugging Jevratt's thrashing legs, bit down into the soft flesh of Jevratt's thigh. Jevratt screamed.

A roar of anger erupted around the circle of men and women as they saw Xand's move, but it was followed by much mirth as he came away with missing teeth. Jevratt had sat up in a sudden rage and managed to throw one of his bone-bare knuckles into the knight's mouth whilst Xand pulled away from the bite. It was all Jevratt needed to shake Xand free.

Pushing himself to a crouch, Jevratt glanced at the bloodied braes he wore, and pulled back his right fist for what he knew would be a finishing blow.

A horn sounded from the east. Jevratt hesitated before falling backwards as people scattered and Xand lashed out. Wasting no time, Jevratt rolled away from the attack, stood, turned and casually knocked Xand out in one.

'Fun's over!' he shouted to the stragglers stood watching. 'To your camps! To arms, ye feckers!'

The remaining men and women fled, curses on their lips, followed by warning shouts to everyone and anyone they passed.

'Adlets?' Couig shouted to Jevratt, a frown creasing the old man's face.

Jevratt rolled his painful right arm and stared off to the east as another horn sounded. 'Surely not this side of the river?' he said, a bloody frown creasing his forehead.

'It's rare, lad, but not impossible.' Couig moved to Jevratt's side. 'Are ye well?'

'Well enough.' Jevratt began walking towards the centre of the great eye, Couig close behind.

'What of Sir Xand?'

'Send Legg back to wake him,' Jevratt said. 'He's a good fighter and gave a good account of himself. He can wed the girl when this has blown over, and join the family, but first, he's to help us defend Grounding when he wakes. If he wakes.' Jevratt grinned as they walked, mouth leaking blood.

Nodding his agreement, Couig waved towards an incoming trap, which bounced across the grasslands towards them.

'What news?' Couig asked the boys as they neared.

'Dog bastards, Master Couig,' the archer of the group said. 'From the Toye Hills.'

'How many?' Jevratt didn't look at the boys, nor slow, so the pony trap rolled alongside the duo, all eyes on the older men.

'Least as many as before,' another boy said.

Jevratt spat blood on the floor and nodded. 'Away with ye and go keep watch.'

The boy with the reins flicked them and yelled at the pony, which surged forward, pulling them back the way they'd come.

'We need everyone up and the caravan mobile. Agreed?'

Couig nodded. 'We'll need to be quick.'

'Aye.' Jevratt stopped and took hold of his uncle. 'Pounder?'

Couig smiled. 'I like ye thinking,' he said, before continuing towards the centre of the eye.

Jevratt ran off to the nearest camp circle, where men were stringing recurve bows and readying spears, and women were fetching and tethering animals.

'Pounder!' Jevratt shouted as he ran. 'Fetch Pounder!'

Chapter 9 - Pounder

The ground shook and dirt fell from the ceiling. The resounding thud, thud, thud, continued as Cheung rushed through the tunnels of Grounding, trying to learn what was afoot. He'd heard shouts echoing through the chambers and tunnels, but hadn't seen anyone to question.

They know I can speak now, so there's no harm in asking, he thought, whilst turning a corner and continuing down another stretch of featureless tunnel. *It's a maze down here.* He'd taken the opportunity since his vocal outing to talk to Jevratt about the mysterious home the Caravaneers, nomad by definition, made for themselves underground. The subterranean complex was centuries old, according to Jevratt. It'd been built bit by bit, added to each time the Caravaneers camped there. Cheung was more surprised to learn that Grounding wasn't unique. There were other subterranean settlements, one for all the caravan routes that snaked through the landscapes of Brisance, from the Eastern Planes to The Orphanides.

As Cheung thought about all he'd learnt, a young woman ran out in front of him, babe in arms. She jumped, startled, as Cheung collided with her. She tried to backtrack, pulling her baby round to the side, away from Cheung, but the assassin took hold of her.

'What's happening? What's the thumping?'

'It's Pounder,' she said, eyes wild.

Cheung pulled back a little and asked what that was.

'We're being attacked,' she said, before pulling away and running down the tunnel. Cheung followed her, knowing she'd head to others. Following the now crying baby and its mother, Cheung ducked instinctively as the pounding caused debris to fall from the ceiling. He thought about the weight of earth above him and cringed.

As they rounded a corner, the woman kicked open a door and continued through, Cheung close on her heels.

The thumping turned into a real pounding as Cheung followed the woman up stone steps to the light above. Reaching the top, he ran through the vardo and out into the sunlight beyond. The woman was lost in the crowd of people.

'Anyone behind ye?' a man asked, looking past Cheung.

'No, I don't think so.'

'Good enough. Heave!' the man shouted lastly. Cheung turned to see the vardo he'd exited Grounding through lift off the ground. Beneath the vardo was… nothing but grass.

Shaking it away, Cheung caught his bearings and ran towards Couig's camp. Vardos were being lifted everywhere. Some with wheels on, others having them fitted. Camels and oxen were harnessed and pony traps darted about, the lads atop them shouting news in a rapid slang Cheung could barely understand.

The pounding continued and when Cheung traced the source of the sound, his run faltered and he came to a stop. Across the grassland, situated on the outside of a readying circle of vardos and carts, stood a giant of a man with a huge, stone-headed mattock. The man was swinging the mattock around, over and slamming it onto a flat stone, which shook the very ground Cheung stood upon.

I would have thought it a gnomish machine making that noise.

Rubbing at the back of his healing neck, Cheung forced his eyes away as the mattock struck once more, and took up his run towards the middle camp and the caravan master.

Cheung heard Couig before he saw him. The old man was shouting orders at folk, his own vardo having its wheels fitted. Several others were ready, their scaffolds being removed, bundled and loaded onto carts.

A boy ran past and Cheung grabbed him by the arm. 'Adlets?'

The bare-chested lad nodded, shrugging off Cheung's grip.

'Is that Pounder?' Cheung asked, pointing to the giant hammering the rock.

'Aye, Priest, but not the man. The mattock.'

'The mattock's called Pounder?'

With a nod, the lad raced off, followed by three others, all of which jumped onto a pony trap and sped away from the centre of the great eye.

'Ah, Priest,' Couig said, Cheung reaching his side. 'Yer healing may be needed soon enough.'

'I'll do what I can, Master Couig.'

Couig managed a smile at that. 'Gods, it must be easier to be able to talk once more?'

Cheung smiled back, although it was hidden by his hood. 'It is indeed. Am I best in my own vardo?'

Couig nodded. 'Aye, ye stay there, where we can find ye, and protect ye. We'll be pulling out soon by my reckoning, rather than sticking around.'

'You won't defend Grounding?'

'Our best defence is those dog bastards not knowing it's here. Once we're gone, there'll be no discovering it.'

Another horn sounded from a way off, followed by another.

Couig looked about the camp, worried. 'They're closer than I thought.'

'I'll let you get on,' Cheung said, moving away.

'Thank you, Priest, you're a friend to us and I won't forget it.'

I'd rather you did, Cheung thought, finding and climbing into his wheeled vardo.

Master Couig's caravan managed to pull out of Grounding before the adlet raiders arrived on the plateau, although one vardo was left behind, its wheel damaged with no time to fix it. It was set alight by lads with a pony trap, to ensure adlets couldn't steal anything or glean anything from that left behind.

Most of Jevratt's men were ordered to the rear of the caravan as Couig drove his vardo off the plateau and through the confusing passes towards the River Minor, host in tow.

'I've rarely known the adlets to be so bold,' Couig said to Legg, who sat on the bench beside him. 'And never to cross the river after us.'

'Nor me,' Legg admitted, looking behind. 'I should be back there, with Jevratt and Belcher.'

Couig planted a hand on his nephew's shoulder, bringing the lad's attention back to the road.

'I need ye with me, nephew. I need a good head and good hands up front, as well as behind.'

'There's to be no adlets ahead.'

'Maybe not, but there could be brigands or goblins. We don't want to get stuck between a shit and a turd now, do we?'

Legg couldn't help but smile. 'Nope, we don't want that.'

Shouting followed another horn blast from way back down the column, and Legg turned again, this time standing. 'I can't see a thing.'

'Ye won't,' Couig said, cracking the reins and urging his oxen on. 'We're spread thin with the ragged retreat from Grounding. There'll be hastily loaded carts lagging behind, but Jevratt and his boys will keep the adlets at bay.'

Legg sat down and cracked his knuckles. 'He will, I know it. Doesn't make sitting here any...'

Couig turned to Legg and frowned. 'What is it, lad?'

Legg looked back. 'Souch Sader.'

'Shit.'

'We left him tethered.'

'Someone will have lifted him.' Couig cracked his reins once more. The oxen lowed, complaining, but continued on at quite the pace.

'That sounded convincing, uncle. Mind,' Legg went on, 'he did kill a lad. The adlets can have him.'

Couig bit his bottom lip and said nothing.

Legg stared at him a moment or two, as another horn sounded. His eyes widened. 'Ye think him innocent, don't ye?'

Couig continued to look ahead.

'Uncle?'

'Yes!' Couig snapped. 'I did think it, at the end, alright?' He turned to Legg. 'But there's nothing for it now. He'll be dead.'

Legg sat back and sighed hard before sitting bolt upright. 'Wait, that means—'

'Sir Xand, aye.'

'And he'll be with—'

'The girl? No. He's with Jevratt and Belcher at the rear. At least he should be.'

'And that's where I'll be, before going for the poor bastard sorcerer.' Legg jumped off the vardo and ran back down the column.

'Damn ye, Legg!' Couig shouted backwards. *Damn him for his conscience.* Breathing heavily before calling out to his oxen, Couig turned his mind to the task at hand. Outrunning the adlet raiders.

It didn't take Legg long to reach the back of the caravan. Several Caravaneers cheered him as he ran, and two pony traps turned and followed; grim-faced lads keeping pace alongside.

He could see the raiders now, hot on the heels of the trailing carts. He saw traps flanking their scouts and Jevratt, Belcher and the lads loosing arrow after arrow and spear after spear at the closing enemy.

Reaching the carts, Legg deviated off to the side. He ran away from the fighting and up, up onto the goat tracks of the surrounding hills. He knew them well, for when the Caravaneers were at Grounding he would run them, and fast.

It was said that Legg could outrun a pony, and the traps he'd left behind before accelerating up the side of the pass' flanking hill was testament to that.

He leapt over loose scree, before dodging right around a bolder. An adlet appeared on the other side of the obstacle, but before it could react, Legg laid it out with the palm of his right hand, which he'd slammed into its temple.

Continuing at speed, Legg dodged another adlet. This one saw him coming, but failed to react in time to the swiftly moving Caravaneer. It managed a howl though, and Legg cursed his luck and ran all the harder.

The carts were lost. They'd fallen too far back from the caravan and more and more adlet appeared. Some ran down from the hills either side of the path, but most came from behind. The numbers were growing and Jevratt knew the speed and stamina of the dog-legged raiders. He'd ordered his men to move to the fortified vardos now at the rear of the column, where they could effect a proper defence. It was there where he now stood, throwing his fists at the leaping adlets that started to catch the caravan proper.

'I've never seen so many,' Belcher shouted. He grunted as he threw a bag of iron scraps. When the bag hit the ground, the pieces of iron clattered out, tripping running adlets and causing others to yelp, drop and roll, snapping legs and shredding bare feet.

The two men stood on a low platform of the last vardo. Above them, archers and spear-wielding guards stood behind wooden crenellations, like the defenders of a baron's keep. Arrows flicked out often, as did stones and spears. Many adlets fell to them, but many more were catching the vardo and leaping onto its sides, only to be skewered by spears or struck off by dropped stones. Jevratt and Belcher continued to thump those that climbed the rear platform, knocking all back and killing some through fist or fall.

'Where's yer man, Jevratt? The fancy sorcerer, eh? Where's he now?'

Jevratt cursed as an adlet caught his shin with a crude blade. The cut was shallow, but the impact numbed his leg. He dropped into a crouch and head-butted the raider's long snout as it attempted to climb aboard.

'Ye know where he is, ye prick.' Another adlet fell to one of Jevratt's fists. 'He's tethered where we left him. It's the damned knight I wanna see. He's supposed to be lending us his skills, here.'

'He came round when I slapped him,' Belcher said, as an arrow took the adlet closest to him. 'He were mine!' Belcher shouted to the archer above. 'Xand were awake,' he continued to Jevratt, 'so no excuse there, although he were messed up pretty good by yerself.'

Jevratt's grin showed blood on his remaining teeth. 'Never mind. Ye see Legg run off, before?'

Adlet arrows came in, thudding against the side of the vardo.

'Shites are further up, on the hills,' one of the archers above shouted.

'So stick 'em back, will ye?'

Jevratt laughed at Belcher, before moving to the side and opening a hatch behind him. The gathering adlets, fast on their feet, fell about themselves to dive away from the jagged stones that tumbled from the open hatch. Most made it to the side of the road, or dropped back out of harm's way, but some fell, ankles twisted or snapped on the rubble underfoot.

'Ha! Bastards!' Jevratt danced about, painful leg forgotten, and slapped his forearms, one after the other. 'We can all do dis, can't we? We can all do dis, ye flea bitten feckers!'

Belcher joined in the curses, before remembering Jevratt's question. 'Oh shit, aye, Legg.' Belcher looked to Jevratt. 'He took off, didn't he? Up the hill on his goat tracks. Back to Grounding?'

'Aye, but for what?'

They both cursed. 'Souch Sader.'

'Stupid bastard,' Belcher said, grabbing a bag of pottery shards and broken glass and emptying it out before the re-approaching adlets.

'Or clever,' Jevratt said, noticing yet more coming down from the hills. 'What's making 'em so determined, eh? What's driving 'em?'

'I dunno, Jevratt, but whatever it is, Legg's gonna be running straight into it.'

Jevratt spat at that, and killed a leaping adlet with a single punch.

He'd more close calls than he'd want to count, but the dense clumps of gorse on the hills allowed Legg to hide and avoid most of them. Several encounters saw him come to blows with iron-armoured adlets, and he'd thought that strange, since the raiders normally wore no more than boiled leather, if that. Those encounters pushed him to the limits of his skill, but he'd won out, each and every time. He'd ducked blows, side-stepped thrusts and pummelled faces to get past. His fists throbbed like never before — adlet faces were harder than humans'.

Reaching the edge of Grounding's plateau, Legg did his best to slow his breathing. He'd crawled through skin-scuffing gorse to look across the hastily left camp-rings, and by one of them, where he'd been left, was the tethered sorcerer, Souch Sader. He wasn't alone.

Legg crawled closer, bit by bit, clenching his teeth at the thorns snagging his linen braes and skin beneath. His underside took the worst; bloody chest, arms, legs and... he barely bit back curses as certain areas caught and scratched.

Why the feck am I doing this? He might be a murderer. Legg grunted a laugh and shook his head. *He might be our saviour.*

Coming to a stop, Legg saw more of the maille and plate armoured adlets. They carried clean weapons and walked with an air of vicious confidence that sent a shudder through Legg.

A runner came in, not far from where Legg was lying. The bare-chested adlet loped across the grassland to the group of armoured raiders, who parted, allowing the scout an audience with the biggest adlet Legg had ever seen. The beast was a head taller than the rest, and much broader, although it was possible his padding and pouldrons made him appear so.

The warlord reveals himself. Couig was right, there was no way all of this was random...

Legg stopped crawling as another figure stepped forward from the throng of raiders, previously obscured by the smoke from the burning wreck of the one vardo left behind.

A human? Legg shuffled that bit closer and squinted, but the distance remained great. *If only I could hear.*

The human looked his way.

Legg didn't duck, for he feared the movement would betray his exact position. His lungs burnt after his recent exertion, but the man looked away again and Legg managed to release the breath he'd held and suck in a lungful of warm air.

An argument? Interesting, he thought, the adlet warlord pointing his bardiche at the tethered sorcerer before him whilst shouting at his human ally. Several of what could only be the warlord's bodyguard turned on the stranger, but he didn't show any fear, not from what Legg could see; the man's relaxed posture never changed. He did, eventually, bow low to the warlord, who shouldered his pole-mounted blade before moving to and crouching over Souch. Again, Legg wished he knew what was being said, but as he thought it, the warlord swung his shouldered weapon down in four clean chops, severing each of Souch's bonds.

Legg pulled his head back in surprise. *Didn't see that one coming,* he thought, brow creased. He twitched his nose as a spider crawled across it, and watched as two of the adlets dragged the gagged mage to his feet. As Souch hung from their grasp, the warlord gave an order and a third adlet moved about the prisoner, tying what looked like wire snares above Souch's knees. Legg could see Souch struggle as the adlet wound the wire tighter and tighter. Satisfied with its work, the adlet moved away and the other two pulled Souch across the grass towards another dog-legged raider. This one wasn't quite as tall as the warlord, but he wasn't far off. Legg's eyes flicked to the warlord and human, who were talking again, before looking back to Souch. The sorcerer was being strapped to the back of the tall adlet, who, as soon as Souch was secure, took off at a steady pace in the direction of the fleeing caravan.

Soon after, the rest of the raiders followed, warlord included. The only one left behind was the human. Legg considered sprinting towards him, and almost did when the man dropped into a crouch and inspected the earth near to where Souch had been tethered. Legg thought it likely the fighting ring Jevratt had defeated Sir Xand in.

No, Legg thought, heart in mouth, *it's a pathway to Grounding he's found. But how?*

Before the stranger uncovered anything, Legg jumped to his feet, making his presence known. Anything to distract the stranger from Grounding.

It was as if winter's breath had returned when the man looked back.

Legg couldn't move. He'd froze. Not literally of course, despite the chill he felt when adlets appeared by his side and took hold of him. He never even struggled. Eyes locked on the stranger, Legg was walked forward, his stare returned in equal measures. The sun warmed his skin, the light made him squint, but the chill took hold of his soul.

Soul, Legg thought, although doing so was like waking from a fast fading dream. *That's what chills me so. His eyes bear no soul.*

Closing on the man, adlet to each side, Legg's heart began to pound. The stranger hardly moved, hardly changed his locked expression, which seemed of intrigue more than anything.

Such dark eyes, Legg thought. He was released by the adlets, but stood unmoving. *Empty eyes. Is he young or old? Altolnan or Eatrian? Sirretan or... I can't make out any recognisable features...*

The smile could have been a slap, for it had much the same effect on Legg. He pulled back, stepped back further still. The adlets made no move to restrain him. They seemed, elsewhere. Their eyes were glazed and their expressions vague as if the stranger affected them as much as he affected Legg.

'You're of the caravan?' It was more of a statement than a question, but Legg nodded all the same.

His voice is soft, incredibly soft. Oh to hear him sing would be...

'I apologise for what has happened to your people,' the stranger said. It seemed sincere. 'It was not my intention for my allies to hound you so.' Dark eyes flicked from Legg to the adlets either side and back. They turned and walked away. 'As soon as I arrived, I asked their clan master to call off the horrific attack. Alas, adlets do not take kindly to orders from the likes of me. It was all I could do to stop him from killing the one you returned for.'

That snapped Legg back to attention. 'Souch Sader?' he asked, looking about for the sorcerer.

'Is that his name?' The man pursed his lips, and Legg remembered.

'You had him taken!'

'No, I had him forgiven.'

Legg frowned, but before he could ask, the man before him held his hands out wide, slender fingers parted. 'My apologies, friend. I have failed to introduce myself.'

Any thought of Souch Sader faded as Legg rushed to reassure the man that no offence had been taken.

'My name is Dignaaln.' He swept into a low bow. Legg's cheeks flushed at the show of respect, and he tried to emulate the impressive flourish.

'Legg, at yer service.'

Dignaaln smiled and came forward, wrapping an arm around Legg and turning him west.

'We should talk, Legg, you and I. We are friends now, are we not?'

Legg smiled back at his new friend and nodded.

'Excellent. Let us walk and talk, undisturbed. We can talk of retrieving the sorcerer you came back for and of an offer I would like to make you, with regards to your people. I am, after all, an emissary, and an emissary must make offers if he is to make friends for his master.' Dignaaln squeezed Legg in close and began walking, following the trail of destruction.

'I'd very much like that,' Legg said, wrapping his own arm around his new friend in return. *How lucky I have been to be accepted.*

'Good,' Dignaaln said, not much more than a whisper. 'For there is a lot we can do for one another, Legg of the Caravaneers.'

Despite the hushed tones, Legg heard every word as if it was all that mattered in all of Brisance. 'Name it,' Legg said, his immense eagerness lacking enough enthusiasm to please his new friend, as far as Legg was concerned. He needed to do as much as he possible could to make up for it. 'Name it, Dignaaln, and I shall see it done.'

Dignaaln beamed and Legg practically melted inside.

Chapter 10 – Stonebridge

The square of daylight revealed the flanking adlets that ran tirelessly alongside the moving caravan. Cheung traced the scars on his face round to prod the newest one on the back of his neck as he watched the running battle.

The fast pace was paying a heavy toll on the beasts pulling the vardos and remaining carts. As the caravan slowed, the adlets caught and flanked the moving column, keeping pace with it whilst launching sporadic attacks here and there along the line, looking for weaknesses.

This is measured. This is planned. Cheung watched the co-ordination in the attack taking place.

Arrows and atlatl launched spears – of all things – came first, the short and long missiles sailing in from the hills to one side, then the other. Shortly after came the runners, blades held high. They ran in at sharp angles, heading straight for a small stretch of vardos towards the front of the caravan. Horns blew and pony traps clattered by, arcing out from the line to meet the raiders.

The pass they now travelled was shallow but wide, and this gave the traps a chance to intercept flanking groups of adlets. Cheung watched on in appreciation as the young lads launched arrows, and stones from slings, at the approaching raiders. Many struck, as they always did, but this time was different. Cheung slowed his breathing and tried to calm himself as he saw the maille and plate armoured adlets that approached. They emerged from gullies winding through the hills, with polearms and falchions and hatchets, and shields. *I've never seen adlets use shields,* he thought, pulling down his hood and tracing the scars under his black hair.

An arrow struck the door of Cheung's vardo and he pulled back, replacing his hood. A head lowered itself into view and the boy asked if Cheung was well.

'Yes, thank you,' he shouted as someone from above screamed. A raider's arrow had found its mark. The boy nodded then tumbled soundlessly from the vardo, an arrow taking him too.

They're going for this section, Cheung thought. He moved back to the window and watched as a trap overturned on poor ground. The lads rolled free; fell to the brutal efficiency of the armoured adlets amongst them. Heavy bladed weapons rose and fell once or twice before the raiders continued, closing on Cheung's vardo.

Arrows flew from the line, but even those that struck now had thick padding and plate to contend with. Some of the adlets even wore looted helms; all of their armour was looted, that was now clear to Cheung. *They've taken somewhere bigger than the norm, or won against those sent to hunt them, to be wearing such armour.* A thrown spear split the wood to the side of the window and the chickens were all flapping and feathers at the loud impact, but Cheung didn't flinch this time, he'd seen the atlatl-hurled spear coming.

A pony trap came alongside before turning out, heading straight for the nearest armoured adlets. On its back stood an older Caravaneer, his back broad and his arms thick. With roars and streams of curses, the man swung Pounder about his head, letting the heavy mattock thud and clang into every adlet he passed, pulverising insides with each impact. He took many down, some literally leaving the ground through Pounder's impacts, but as the biggest threat away from the caravan itself, it wasn't long before Pounder's wielder was brought low by arrows. When he fell, so did the surrounding adlets; they fell upon him with blades and hammers of their own.

Moments before the rest of the visible raiders reached the caravan, the incoming arrows stopped. The outgoing arrows continued though, one punching through iron links to drop the adlet nearest to Cheung.

Cheung reached for his kamas as a body swung through the window on the other side, but he knew from the movement of the cab that it was one of his protectors from above.

'We need move ye to the trap out here, Priest,' the boy said, opening the door on his side.

'I can't leave my things,' Cheung said, but the boy had already snatched the satchel and thrown it onto the bouncing trap alongside. Cheung followed it without another word. Landing on the shifting wooden bench besides another boy, Cheung turned back for the lad inside. He barely saw the lad disappear as the adlet entering the far side of the cab pulled him back in. The guttural cry that followed tore at Cheung's insides.

I can't fight, he reminded himself as the trap slowed and let the defending section pull forward and peel off to the left, three vardos in total. *I can't reveal myself, no matter what. Those are my orders.*

As the adlets leapt aboard, climbed on top of and slaughtered the remaining Caravaneers of the three vardos Cheung had been part of, the rest of the caravan accelerated to fill the gap, and Cheung's trap accelerated too, heading towards the front of the column, and Master Couig.

Cheung managed to look back before they reached the front, and what he saw stunned him. The pass was long and wide, and as far as he could see, vardos and carts were scattered here and there, many on their sides, many more swarming with adlets. Screams and howls filled the shallow pass.

Slowing his breathing and retrieving his satchel from the back of the trap, Cheung took in the faces of all those he and the lads about him passed by. Many stood on the rampart-like roofs of the remaining vardos, many more hung out of windows, stood on platforms or clung to the sides or backs of whatever vehicle they could.

The caravan had been halved in the time it had taken to travel the length of the pass. Looking forward, Cheung saw the River Minor and the fortified bridge that spanned it, and potential safety from the relentless onslaught that continued behind him.

Reaching the front, he saw the blood-stained faces of Belcher and Jevratt turn to him. They'd taken many wounds by the looks of things, but they looked back as if wanting more. As Cheung's trap came alongside the vardo they perched on the back of, Cheung asked the lad guiding the pony to pull as close as possible. He didn't know why, but satchel in hand, Cheung hopped across onto the platform, next to the two men, and all three sat there, glaring at the bloody scene the caravan was finally leaving behind.

The last thing they saw as they approached Stonebridge – the Altolnan fortifications that guarded the River Minor – was a beast of an armoured adlet holding a bardiche high. Next to him stood a tall, unarmoured adlet, with what looked like a man strapped to his back.

Belcher spat off the back of the rocking vardo. 'If you'd killed that big fecker, Jevratt, the bitches would've fled for sure.'

Jevratt turned to the battered man by his side and pushed him off the platform. Bouncing once and rolling, Belcher managed to dive out of the way of the next oxen pulled vardo before shouting his threats and curses Jevratt's way.

Jevratt sighed. 'Ye don't think I know that, Belcher,' he said, to no one in particular.

Cheung watched Belcher climb onto a slowing trap, but the assassin's eyes turned back to those colourful but broken-wheeled homes and the people left behind. He wasn't familiar with the feeling assailing him, but he was quite sure it was called guilt.

A swollen and bloody hand took his shoulder. 'You'll shed the tears, Priest, it's what you do, for us all.' Jevratt paused, his hand remaining. 'But don't let it pull ye down, for there was nothing ye could've done for any of 'em.'

The hood moved up and down as the hand moved away, and the tears fell for real.

If only that were true.

The initial pain of wire cutting into flesh was overtaken by a constant throb and numbness. Souch didn't know how long he'd been strapped to the back of the stinking adlet, but it had been long enough for him to fear for the recovery of his legs. The beastly raider carrying him stopped along with its companions when the sight of the fortified bridge came into view. The tail end of the caravan were crossing it as the adlets massed. Shortly after, Stonebridge's garrison sallied forth. They wore the green and black of the Marquess of Suttel and were seasoned veterans, that much was known to all; the adlets moved no closer.

Souch willed the adlets to advance, knowing they stood little chance against the fortified bridge and its Altolnan defenders. He felt sick from the constant pain the adlets' movements caused him. He held no hope of an escape. And he feared what was to come.

The grunts of the guttural language was lost on Souch, but he could tell arguing when he heard it. The armoured warlord and his bodyguard stood nearby. Weapons were pointed to the men forming across the road, whilst others pointed back the way they had come. Souch knew the raiders were intelligent, to a certain degree. They weren't the mindless beasts many made them out to be. Never had he heard of such numbers though. It was clear clans had come together, judging by the mixed markings and natural groups that seemed to gather when they stopped.

Altolnan archers with tall war bows filtered out into scrub to the north of the road, whilst two score mounted men-at-arms formed up on the road itself. They were headed by three knights, one of them richly armoured and caparisoned. Souch squinted over the fur covered shoulder of his carrier, but couldn't make out the device on the commander's shield or surcoat.

One of Earl Bratby's sons? Souch thought, trying to forget the pain enough to concentrate on the man shouting orders. *Possibly, although—*

Souch gasped as the adlet slapped both clawed hands back, onto Souch's swollen legs. The raider grunted something and turned, following adlets who were running from the scene. Each bounce brought burning and lancing pain alike. Souch screwed up his face and squeezed his eyes shut, doing all he could to fight the fear and helplessness the pain accompanied. A human cheer went up behind him, and it hurt more than anything he had experienced thus far.

Howls followed the cheering, but even they faded as Souch allowed himself to fall from consciousness once more.

Chapter 11 – Silent flight

The gag was dry. Souch's saliva was so thick it did little to wet the wool stuffed into his mouth. He opened his eyes and attempted to blink the dryness away. They ached, the balls in his sockets; they ached along with his jaw which he tried to stretch to little effect, and the throbbing hit him once more. The wire dug into his flesh of his legs now, matted with dried blood. He looked past the side of the adlet's head that carried him, but failed to see anything but the faded green of the hill his mount was now crossing. Each jerk hammered another throb through his legs, although below the knee was numb. Small mercies, if he didn't think to the future of those limbs. The pain across his back remained, his arms unable to move to ease it, but it paled when compared to everything else.

The adlet crested the hill and stood before a column of its kin, trotting along as they do. Souch watched them pass, taking in the myriad of weapons and armour they carried. A group passed him pulling sleds full of cut wood. If he had been himself, he would have seen it for the siege equipment it was.

Over the barked orders and distant howls, Souch heard softer voices, approaching from behind as his carrier joined the column. He did his best to block it all out, the noise and the pain and the wet dog smell from the sweaty, matted fur he clung to, so he could listen to those voices.

'You think you can do this for me?' The higher voice said. He was either very tall, or mounted on a beast bigger than an adlet.

'Oh aye, Dignaaln, I reckon so.' A familiar voice came from lower down.

'That would please me, and my master, of course.'

'Well that's what counts now, isn't it, me friend?'

'It is, yes. We have an accord, you and I.'

'And how shall I be moving the sorcerer, with his legs bound as they are?'

Souch stiffened and tried to turn, which pulled at his back and legs. The gag disallowed the cry of pain that movement sought.

'You may take the adlet carrying him, I am sure. After I have spoken to the warlord.'

A clap of hands. 'That's that, me man, we have it sorted.'

'Indeed we do, Legg. You have negotiated the protection of your caravan and the freedom of Souch Sader. You should be proud of yourself. I am sure your caravan master will be.'

There was a pause, filled with shifting feet and grunting adlets before Legg replied.

'Aye, well, me uncle may well need some sense talking into him on the matter, but I'll be sure to do that without a fuss. And I'll be doing it before anyone else knows the plans.'

The adlet carrying Souch jolted as he jumped over a rock on the path. Souch missed what was said next, but as the pain subsided to the usual, a rider passed on the left, the white tail and golden flanks of his horse a glorious sight in the sun; if it weren't for the pain and situation.

Souch tried to look around his adlet, to catch a glimpse of the rider rather than the eye drawing palomino. The height of the column's adlets scuppered that, and all it did for Souch was to pain the strained muscles bunching and stretching around his neck and shoulders. He could feel mucus in the back of his throat, after sniffing back his tears countless times since his capture. He swallowed, which made little difference, and rested his head back on a shoulder that was becoming all too familiar as a pillow.

'How fair ye, Master Sader?'

Souch jumped. More pain. Opening his aching eyes from the wince forced over him, he turned his head to look at the young man by his side.

'Egg?' It was more of a grunt through wool than anything else.

The young man grinned. 'Aye, it's me. I came back for ye, so I did.'

And secured a deal it seems. I dread to think.

'Here, me man, let me take this from ye mouth. The emissary gave me a water skin.' He laughed. 'Can ye believe it?' Legg eased the woollen rag from Souch's mouth, who coughed as he tried to swallow one too many times.

'Here, here,' Legg said, holding the skin up to the dry opening. 'Stop bouncing so, will ye?' he said to the adlet carrying Souch. The raider growled, but pulled to the side of the moving column and stopped. Legg poured some of the surprisingly cold water into Souch's mouth, little by little.

'Just a bit for now, Master Sader. Just a bit.'

The taste was incredible. How he'd taken such a necessity as water for granted all these years. And real water too, not small-beer or watered wine. Clean, drinkable water like that found in the upper districts of Wesson. *Tastes like home,* Souch thought as it cooled his throat, despite failing to clear the mucus. *Tastes like... Tyndurris.*

'Lush, eh? Lush water is that. Not tasted the likes for a long while.' Legg grinned some more and moved the skin away, taking a swig for himself. Letting the skin drop to his side on its cord, Legg prodded the adlet beside him in the ribs. 'Off we pop, dog. We've yer warlord to hear from.'

The 'dog' growled. Legg grinned. Souch grimaced and the adlet set off at speed to make up the ground it'd lost.

'Won't be long now and we'll have ye across the River Minor and to me people,' Legg said effortlessly, whilst running alongside. 'Ye can answer for yer crime then.'

Gods above, Souch thought, moving his jaw around and listening to the crunching below his ears. *He's come all this way, risked everything, to take me back for more of the same.* Souch didn't respond, apart from the involuntary grunt and groan as the adlet jumped over another rock.

'Nope,' Legg said, from the side, 'won't be long now.'

Safely on the Altolnan side of the River Minor, Cheung knelt on the hard-packed earth the caravan circled. He closed his eyes, relying on his other senses. He took in the wood-smoke, earth, dung, blood, sweat and fear, as groans and shouts of men and women and animals in pain created a symphony of agony all about him. He blocked the sounds out as a voice he now knew well came from close by.

'No sign of him,' Jevratt said.

'He's a dead man,' another said, before grunting.

'Ye watch it or I'll hit ye full on next time, eh?'

'Sorry, Jevratt, but come on will ye. He ran off into adlets galore for a feckin' murdering magic man, and for what?'

Another grunt and a curse.

'He's me cousin, I don't care for what. But ye know, I'm for sure it were to save us, ye prick.'

A wailing of sobs and denial filled the camp.

'There's another fecker dead,' Jevratt said. He was approaching Cheung now.

'Priest,' he said, reaching the assassin's side. 'Ye meditatin' or what? We need ye for healing, not praying.'

Cheung rose in one fluid motion, hooded eyes opening before Jevratt. He bowed his head.

'There's people smashed and fucked all over the camp, I need ye to get on it. Can ye do that?'

'Yes, of course.' As Cheung turned to head towards the loudest groans, an eruption of anger drew his attention to a nearby vardo, its leather clad sides scarred and stuck with arrows.

'Ye're a feckin' coward, not a knight!'

A dog barked, following the commotion. Several more dogs joined in across the camp.

Cheung watched the young girl stepping down from the vardo, linen sheet pulled about her.

'If ye're too beaten to fight the bitches killin' me folk, ye're too beaten fer a poke!'

Despite his spatial awareness, Cheung was nearly knocked aside as Jevratt stormed past, another bare-chested lad with muck and blood across half his body in tow.

'What's the craic?' Jevratt said, voice loud enough to hear across half the camp. The dogs stopped barking and people raised heads from tending their wounded kin, their fires and their animals, and weren't disappointed when the girl turned on Jevratt and flicked him two fingers.

'Mind yer own,' she said, before being dragged away from the vardo's steps. She didn't need asking again after the slap she received.

Glaring defiantly at Jevratt, the girl spat before answering. 'Me husband to be couldn't defend the caravan.' She laughed. 'Wouldn't though, that's the right of it. Soft twat wouldn't! Not couldn't. I know that now. He wouldn't stick his iron length in a dog bastard, but he'll try and stick his own prick in me.' Her fists were bunched, one to hold her coverings, the other out in front of her. 'I'm not marrying a little bitch like that, Jevratt. I'm not!'

Jevratt shoved her aside and hammered his blood-blackened fist on the side of the vardo. If Cheung didn't know any better, he'd have said the vardo was made of paper the way it moved.

'Ye get out here, Xand!' Jevratt shouted. He held a finger up at his sister-in-law before she could add anything.

'He's a coward!' the lad accompanying Jevratt said.

'Shut it.' Jevratt hammered again on the leather clad wooden cab.

The lad swallowed hard, but managed to puff his chest out behind Jevratt's back.

A crowd was gathering now, chores forgotten. The smell of a fight will do that to people.

'He's hiding,' a woman alongside Cheung said, to another. The assassin moved forward with the others now, unable to take himself away from what was to come.

'If he were a real knight, he'd be back out and fightin', wounds or no,' Collett said.

Cheung smiled beneath his hood, unsurprised the Caravan Mistress had been drawn to the commotion. It surprised him less when she started taking bets on the fight to come.

'I said come out!' Jevratt hammered some more on the vardo and several men began dragging their feet in the customary circle, clearing folk out of the way as they did so.

Cheung noticed Altolnan men-at-arms wandering into the camp. The Caravaneers didn't bat an eyelid as the men in the Marquess of Suttel's colours rested on their polearms to watch the show. It wasn't long until Collett was taking their bets too.

Heads turned and a cheer rose as the vardo door filled with the man in question. The following voices carried nought but anger at the maille and partial plate about his body, and the sword in his hand.

As well as Sir Xand's armour, he wore a sneer on his face, directed at his wife-to-be, then at the man calling him out.

Cheung didn't miss Jevratt's smirk. Slapping his hands on his forearms, Jevratt rolled head and feet, loosening his joints.

'No ring,' he shouted, backing away from Xand, who jabbed his sword at the nearing girl he'd been set to wed. She dodged away as the crowd shouted, and parried his half-hearted stab with inventive insults.

Stretching his arms behind him, Jevratt turned his back on the knight approaching him and winked to the crowd; the cheers renewed, as did the bets.

Cheung noticed Xand's eyes hover on the men-at-arms a while longer than anyone else.

He thinks he has a chance. He thinks, here, more than on the road, he can walk away should he win. Cheung shook his head a little. *I think you've gravely mistaken your worth to these soldiers of Suttel, Sir Xand. They're here to guard a border crossing, not an unknown knight.*

With the lead caravan guard's back to him, Sir Xand rushed forward.

Even if the rustling iron links weren't blocked by the sounds of the crowd, Jevratt wouldn't have needed to hear them to know of the man's approach. The dozens of eyes looking his way told him all he needed to know.

Leaving it until Xand's maille shushing and plate scraping was audible, Jevratt moved enough to the side to see the tip of the knight's sword pass his midriff, dangerously close.

Cheung expected Jevratt to move away from the attack. A smile played across his lips when Jevratt did the opposite, taking hold of the blade as it came by, moving with Xand's lunge and planting his opposite elbow into the face of the man behind it.

Cartilage crunched and Xand's head rocked back. Before he could recover, Jevratt released the blade, turned and crunched bone-bare knuckles into the side of the knight's head.

Sir Xand's lifeless body fell to the ground, his maille tinkling for half a heartbeat, like the pouring of a banker's coins.

The near silence lasted mere moments before men and women danced about, laughed and cheered. Men-at-arms stomped away poorer than when they'd arrived and a pretty girl in nothing but a linen sheet crossed to, spat on, and then proceeded to strip all value from her previously promised husband.

As the crowd departed, back to the wounded, fires and animals that needed them, Cheung crossed to the half-naked corpse of Sir Xand. He crouched and took in the razor-cut below the man's ear. Drawing a deep breath and releasing it slowly, Cheung spared a thought for the sorcerer left tethered at Grounding, for a crime he didn't commit.

Three men came to knock Sir Xand's white teeth out and Cheung watched on, unsurprised.

There will be a few that will need those teeth, after the running battle these people have been through, he thought, before turning away to the nearest moans and groans of the broken Caravaneers.

Chapter 12 – Impossible escapism

Darkness punctuated by camp fires gave way to darkness punctuated by braziers and torches. There was little in the way of total darkness in-between, but what little there was, Cheung found it. He was thankful for the cloud-filled sky and the black blades of his kamas, which he held lightly in his gloved hands. He longed to feel the bone against the skin of his palms, but couldn't risk his pale skin being seen as he moved through a series of stretches and manoeuvres with the familiar weapons.

His hood remained up, hiding his face from eyes that may be looking, although he was quite sure the men-at-arms of Stonebridge were looking across the river, not to the camp of Caravaneers that regularly crossed borders throughout Brisance.

An owl made itself known, its call coming from somewhere on the edge of the camp to Cheung's left. He wondered whether it was the large bird he'd seen at Grounding and he stopped moving, breath held.

If it is, he thought, *can it pass on what it sees?* He risked a glance left and cursed his stupidity. *Why do I soften so, my awareness and my mind? Is it the travel, the company… both?* Cheung dropped softly to his knees and slid forward onto his stomach, stretching out into a star. He pressed the side of his head to the ground and blocked out all sound of the camp and the keep, of the people and the dogs, the rushing water and the owl; listening to nothing but his breathing.

I have spent so long alone, as is my way. Is it my immersion in the day to day lives surrounding me that distracts and draws me from my… myself? Cheung was finding it harder to escape from the world, from thoughts. He used to sit for hours, staring at the unfurling of a flower or the shifting shadows cast by a horizon-approaching sun. He used to go days without talking to another soul. Even contact with his guild was rare, apart from the receipt of marks via his head. He didn't even know how they did that, whether it was a constant connection or a temporary one. His breathing faltered. *Can they hear me now, the masters?* He swallowed and licked dry lips. *I don't even know how you do it,* he thought, directing it towards the masters that could very well be listening. *An ancient magic, I know that much, but nothing more. I don't remember the connection's first touch… I don't remember my first mark; there's been so many within Eatri. I think this is the first beyond our borders, but I'm no longer sure even of that.* Cheung rolled onto his back and looked up into a sky that held nothing but the faintest reflection of the fires below.

He controlled his breathing once more and lifted his kamas over and across, then back again. He repeated the movement several times, focusing on the nothingness of his blades as they passed one another. *My only thought other than the mission was my plants.* Breathing gave way to a grunted laugh. *I worried... No. I knew, that they would perish without me. That I would have to start afresh upon my return.* Passing the kamas across once more, Cheung surrendered himself to the reality of what he had been tasked to do. *I'm not going back.* He brought his weapons down and rested them on his chest, close to his heart, which beat quicker than before. *They don't mean for me to come back,* he thought, the unseen masters nothing but shadows in his memory.

Cheung never thought about much past his training and his surrounds. Nothing much past his masters and their will, whichever one contacted him on any given request. The marks had come and gone, his training too. His memories stretched back to nothingness. He had no recollection of childhood. Cheung had no recollection of anything beyond training and killing. His life had been for the moment, whether honing his skills, meditating, watching his plants grow or eliminating marks for his masters. *And now... now for the Black Guild of Altoln?*

He frowned and rolled onto his side, facing the camp. He raised his legs together, holding them there until they began to shake, his stomach pained, before lowering them to the ground again.

Is it that which has pulled at me, which has brought me from the present, to think more to the future? Or is it Jevratt and my other friends...?

Cheung rolled and sat up. He feared the word, the thought. He feared it when he lied about it, when he acted it, and he feared it all the more when he believed it, as he just had.

He shook his hooded head and let the light of the distant camp fires dance before his unblinking eyes.

'They're not my friends,' he whispered, 'and I'm not theirs. I act it. That is my part in this. To act it until I leave. To act it to avoid suspicion.' *I'm not even sure I know what it truly is.*

An owl called again – a shriek of a noise.

Taking a deep breath, Cheung stood effortlessly and continued stretching. *And there I go again, thinking, wondering.* He moved quickly, cutting left, right, turning and slicing the air with blades as black as a dilated pupil, darker still.

The owl again, from above this time, leaving the camp and heading out over the grey stone of the fortified bridge.

Perhaps these Caravaneers poison me through their food. He crouched, bringing the points of the kamas back past his legs, skimming the ground. Springing up, he tensed his abdominal muscles and curled, flipping back, feet sailing overhead before hitting the grass, knees bending to take him back to a crouch. *Or is it them, their personalities? Their humour and their caring, despite their daily aggression and violence towards one another.*

Cheung sighed. *They're more than that. They're more than fighters and...*

The owl flew back from Stonebridge, silent if not for its shrieking call.

A shout went up in camp. Cheung looked from the camp fires to the sky, where he heard the owl call again. His head rocked back, hood falling as he followed the growing light on the underbelly of the clouds. Turning to look at Stonebridge, he saw the source of the sky's orange hue.

Stonebridge's keep was alight, its wooden roof blazing as a ball of pitch streaked through the air from the far side of the River Minor to slam with a flash into a wooden structure below the burning keep.

Horses screamed.

Stables...

The sound was horrific, but no other sounds came from the keep and its outbuildings. No cries of alarm, no bells, no horns, no shouting men. When Cheung saw what was coming from those walls, he pulled his hood up, shoved his kamas into his satchel and ran for the rousing camp.

Hooves pounded the ground behind as he ran. Horns followed that sound, coming from the now bustling camp ahead.

'Who's that?' a lad shouted from the wooden crenellations of the nearest vardo's roof.

'Priest!' Cheung shouted back. 'I'm the priest of tears.'

The hooves were closing.

'Hurry!' the lad shouted. 'There's a feckin' golden horse behind ye!'

No shit, Cheung thought, surprising himself. He slid under the vardo as the rider reached it, and heard the man's voice call out behind him.

'To arms! To arms!' the rider cried. 'The adlets have infiltrated Stonebridge and opened its gates. They're crossing the river!'

As Cheung looked back out from beneath the vardo, he saw the rider moving off on the rare palomino, calling the warning to all who'd listen. And before Cheung could react, he saw the truth of the man's warning.

A line of torch carrying adlets crossed the dark expanse at speed, with a fast-moving man with an awkward gait ahead of them. Cheung strained to see what the man was carrying, for there was a bundle of something heavy on his back.

Cursing, Cheung pulled himself from under the vardo and climbed to the top.

'Jevratt!' he shouted. 'It's Legg! They're chasing Legg!'

Chapter 13 – Warning

Vardos were pulled into hasty circular forts, dotted across the chaotic Caravaneer's camp outside the flame ridden keep and outbuildings of Stonebridge. Those who failed to circle their wheeled homes lay dead or dying on the ground, their belongings scattered about them as adlets scavenged.

The Caravaneers who defended their makeshift forts were tiring. They'd received no help from Stonebridge. It had been taken from within, so the palomino rider said, before taking refuge in the same vardo-fort as Cheung.

Legg laid Souch Sader down as the vehicles were maneuvered, the sorcerer's legs a mess of swollen, lacerated flesh and dried blood.

Jevratt and Belcher appeared from the darkness, shoving Legg about with a mix of scorn for his stupidity and joy for his return. The lad seemed quite well, mere cuts and bruises, considering his dangerous rescue of the sorcerer. There was no time for explanations, with the adlets so close.

All three climbed atop an armoured vardo, after Jevratt ordered Cheung inside, ordering him to stay safe whilst attempting to revive the unconscious sorcerer.

'Ye can't do no good, me friend, not out here,' Jevratt said to Cheung. 'Try and rouse him, try and have him help us.' The assassin's chest tightened, hands itching to hold the bone handles of his kamas and stand alongside Jevratt and his kin. Rough hands shoved him in the end, into the vardo, but not before Cheung saw the palomino rider disappear into the darkness on his golden mount. There was something about him. Something… familiar? Cheung didn't know. Had no time to ponder.

Howls, shouts, screams and the clash of metal went on for some time. Arrows thumped against the side of the thick-walled vardo and Cheung unwound the wire from Souch's legs, whilst glancing at the door repeatedly.

It's only a matter of time, he thought, hesitating at his work as the patient groaned.

Iron struck iron in all directions, and the shouting of the living mixed with the wails of the dying. Souch's eyes opened and widened all the more when he saw who was tending him. He sucked in a breath and tensed.

'Fear not,' Cheung said, holding his gloved hands up to show he meant no harm. 'I haven't been able to tell them, but I know you didn't kill that boy.'

Souch's visible relief was short lived, the sounds outside the vardo registering. Pain hit Souch again and he tensed again at Cheung's renewed touch.

'I need to remove this wire, but you're lucky they didn't kill you.' The fear on Souch's face remained. His eyes were locked on Cheung, despite another thud of an arrow on the side of the vardo followed by a scream from above.

Souch opened his mouth to speak, but nothing came out. It was clear to Cheung that the man waged a war within himself, but about what, Cheung could not know. He looked scared though, of that Cheung was sure; not surprising with the adlets surrounding them and what had happened to him by their clawed hands.

Working away, pulling bloodied wire from torn legs, Cheung felt Souch's eyes on him. The sorcerer studied him more intently than anyone else since he'd joined the caravan.

'Sir Xand,' Souch managed, through a grating throat.

'Dead.' Cheung's eyes remained on his work. 'He tried to lay too low after what he did; tried to lay with the wrong girl.' *And still his stare fails to break.* Cheung glanced up and saw Souch's throat move once, twice. *Is it me he fears?*

Jevratt's voice came from above. Loud, aggressive, accompanied by Belcher's and Legg's.

A brief respite, Cheung thought, proceeding to mop exposed flesh with a cloth soaked in wine. It was all he had to hand.

Although Souch winced, clenched his fists and tensed at the cloth's touch, his eyes remained on Cheung.

A knock at the vardo's door. Cheung looked up, Souch didn't.

The palomino rider entered, clothes and sword bloody. He sported a wound to his right shin, bad enough to have cut through the boots he wore, but other than that he seemed unharmed.

His face… Cheung frowned. *I can't place his origins?* Cheung continued, lost in the man's unusual features. *And those eyes, so—*

'He knows,' the man said, his tone urgent but hushed.

Cheung sat back, head tilted within its covering.

'Souch Sader knows, damn it!'

Before Cheung could wonder who the man was, his words and the sudden look of horror on Souch's face struck home.

A renewed attack became obvious, as howls, horns and curses filled the air beyond the open doorway. The man looked behind him, worried. 'Do what must be done,' he said. 'You are at risk, Cheung, and I can only hold a path for your escape so long. Your masters would not want you to tarry. My name is Dignaaln and you need to trust me.'

Cheung's heart hammered, matching the fresh clashes of weapons and thump of arrows. Someone cried out and landed heavily behind Dignaaln, who pulled back from the vardo and out into the night once more.

A horse whinnied.

Two pairs of eyes met. Fear present in both. One for his life, and maybe a great deal more than that; large stakes were at risk to the man and the man's king should he fail, both knew that. The other for the loss of what he had found on the road; friendship.

You know what I am, Cheung thought. He rocked back as the man before him nodded.

Yes, Souch thought in return, doing all he could and using all he knew to read the hooded man's thoughts. The effort drained what little he had, but he needed to leave enough in reserve, despite what was to come. The assassin's eyes gave more away in that moment than Souch would have believed possible; barriers had been willingly dropped. *He's reluctant to do what he needs to do*, Souch thought. The realisation that the dropped barriers allowed Cheung to hear Souch's thoughts as much as he could hear Cheung's own came too late for Souch.

He looked down at what seemed to be a nothingness, pressing into his chest. He tried to take a breath but the sharp pain made it difficult. He attempted to make sense of the bone handle hovering before him, but couldn't.

Cheung dropped his hood.

Looking up, Souch felt none of the hate he would have imagined would come from looking into his killer's eyes. *Sorrow*, he thought, as what little light there was in the vardo began to fade. *He feels sorrow, and regret...*

Cheung tensed at that, swallowed hard. Nodded.

The vardo shook and fresh shouts came from above.

'Where's that sorcerer, Priest?' Jevratt followed his question with a string of inventive curses.

Souch used the sorrow he felt pouring from the man before him, the sorrow he felt *within* the man before him, as another depth-less blade appeared, drawing a crimson line below the assassin's right eye. The cut was deep, parting flesh to bone, and Souch felt Cheung's pain on top of his own, the connection was so thorough. Souch's final thought was all the more powerful for all of that, feeding off the emotion that fell within Cheung's bloody tear; passing leagues in a final heartbeat, in the only way a thought could.

Souch Sader passed peacefully, despite the horror beyond the vardo. He'd managed to fulfil what he'd been asked to do. He'd managed to send a warning all the way to the top of Tyndurris and he'd managed, with what little he had left at the end, to do it without the assassin's knowledge.

Cheung slid his kamas free and stared at the body of the sorcerer, ignoring Jevratt's renewed shouts for that very man's aid in the horrific fight outside. Thoughts and fears and possibilities lost and found whirled around Cheung's head like a zephyr of confusion.

Pulling his eyes from Souch Sader's immobile form and looking to the fire-flecked darkness outside the couch, Cheung made his gut wrenching decision.

***

Damp from a cold sweat despite a warm summer's night, Ward Strickland woke, heart racing, fists clutching his blanket... eyes wide, seeing *beyond*.

The assassin has crossed the border.

Souch Sader's transmitted thought accompanied an image of a pale, scarred face and a tear of blood.

Chapter 14 – Road to Rowberry

Anger surged within Cheung. His head spun, his teeth ground and his calm, his control… was gone. He knew too little. He'd spent weeks with the Caravaneers; the most he'd spent with any people in as long as he could remember. He'd eaten and drunk with them, talked and sang with them, laughed and… lied to them. His fists gripped the bone of his kamas tight as he thought about how easily he'd thrust one of those weapons into the man he'd been treating moments before.

Surging to his feet, Cheung stormed from the vardo, looking about the flame-lit darkness. Vardos, carts and traps burnt in all directions. People ran and adlets cut them down. Lit arrows flitted through the night, most landing on the ground, some taking fleeing people or animals. The ground thundered as beasts of burden were set free by caring owners, only for those freedom fighters to be hacked down by iron wielding raiders. Oxen and camels groaned and ponies whinnied. Traps raced to-and-fro, with too few bare-chested lads aboard them.

Cheung turned and looked up, to the backs of Jevratt, Legg and Belcher. Two other men stood atop the armoured vardo. One fell to an arrow as Cheung looked on.

Jevratt shouted curses as he loosed arrows in return. Belcher threw rocks like the shot putters of the Eatrian Games and Legg flung stones from a sling with tremendous speed.

Hooves thundered behind Cheung. He turned to see the golden mount of Dignaaln approaching.

'You must flee!' Dignaaln shouted as he neared.

'Run, Priest!' Jevratt called down, without turning. 'Go with the rider, he'll take ye to safety. I can't protect ye here.'

Breaths came quickly and as a guttural cry turned Cheung to the next vardo along, adlets appeared atop it, the defenders fallen.

The palomino shifted beside him, pawing the ground, snorting.

'Cover your weapons and come, now,' Dignaaln said, his voice barely more than a rasping hiss of anger.

Cheung looked back to Jevratt, who leapt across the gap between vardos and tackled the first adlet he came to, throwing bare knuckles into the raider's face before attacking the next. Cheung sucked in a breath and almost rushed forward as another adlet climbed up behind Jevratt, drawing a blade, ready to thrust.

From the darkness above, a silent flyer screeched before impact, knife-like talons outstretched. The adlet behind Jevratt arched its back and roared as the talons sunk in. Dropping to one knee and turning, the raider took hold of the eagle-owl and pulled its huge wings from its body. The shriek was horrific. Jevratt turned too late to save the bird, but was quick enough to avenge it.

'I can't leave them!' Cheung shouted back to Dignaaln, anger pulling at his scarred face.

Dignaaln looked genuinely surprised. Dark eyes narrowed on Cheung. Leaning from his saddle, he pulled Cheung by his robes. Cheung let him, although he didn't know why.

Feeling the wetness of blood beneath his eye, following his latest kill, Cheung listened to the words backed by a cold breath. 'This is not your mission, assassin. Your masters command you to flee, to finish what you set out to do. Much rests on King Barrison's death.'

Cheung turned back to the vardos, watching as adlets made the top where Belcher and Legg fought with fists. They handled themselves well, as always, yet they were hard pressed. Legg nearly fell to an adlet's axe, but Belcher stepped in, taking the blow on the arm and losing much of it in the process.

Dignaaln pulled again on Cheung's robes. This time his hold was shrugged off.

Cheung looked about frantically, listening to the curses, shouts, howls and grunts whilst the flying of lit arrows continued. A ball of burning pitch joined the lighting of the clouds above, its successful target a vardo off to the side, which erupted in a sky reaching fireball. The residents' screams faded instantly.

A man's loud grunt, a cry from another and a dull thud behind Cheung turned his head as the emissary's words sunk in and took control. *Your masters command you...*

Belcher lay motionless on the ground, his half-arm twitching, an arrow embedded in his face.

Adlets appeared from somewhere off to the side, whooping as they ran. They came at Cheung and Dignaaln. A heavy ended goedendag swung in at Cheung and thrust back at him after he'd stepped aside. The iron point of the goedendag jabbed back as another adlet sliced down with a large cleaver. Cheung avoided both weapons. He embedded a black blade in each adlet before they could come at him again. Metal crashed behind as Dignaaln parried an adlet's blow and gave several back in return. Dignaaln finished the adlet alongside his mount before the golden horse kicked out and finished the remaining raider.

Before Cheung could look back to Dignaaln, he caught Jevratt's eye. Jevratt hesitated as he saw the hoodless priest, kamas bared. The look of disbelief, of betrayal, that Cheung witnessed and felt in that brief moment was bested only by the feeling that twisted his gut and stung his heart as a length of iron forced itself violently, bloodily, from the chest of the Caravaneer staring back.

As Jevratt's eyes dropped to the crude sword point sucking back into his flesh, Cheung heard Collett scream from somewhere in the flame filled night.

Legg leapt across to his cousin whilst Cheung turned away, to be pulled atop the palomino.

As they rode through the burning camp, Cheung looked past the lads charging to the failing defences of Jevratt's vardo. Past the staggering, arrow-stuck form of Master Couig, who slumped to the floor, and on to Collett, her wide eyes staring, disbelieving, at the man who she'd defended when his voice had been heard. The man she had accepted into her home within Grounding. The man her son had called friend.

Burning vardos and carts broke that stare as Dignaaln guided his horse through the dying remains of the Caravaneers' camp and along the road to Rowberry; towards King Barrison, the mark and reason for Cheung's journey.

With the sounds of the caravan's death throws chasing him, after all he had sacrificed, Cheung knew what he had to do; knew what he could do. An incredible confidence settled over him. It didn't come from improved focus or training, if anything, they had worsened. It came from the knowledge that the mission was all he had left.

Cheung no longer thought he would return to the rooftops of Eatri. He no longer believed he deserved to.

Legg carried his wounded cousin across uneven ground at great speed, risking putting a foot wrong, tripping, falling.

Falling would mean dying, for both Jevratt and Legg.

'Hurry!' Collett shouted from the back of a bouncing trap, looking at the silhouette of her son being carried, backed by the remains of their camp licking up in yellow flames. Adlets pursued, of course, but not many. Most fell about the dead and dying, finishing off the latter and looting the rest. The last wheeled homes were torched and belongings scattered as the raiders sought what they would.

'Slow a little,' Collett said, loud enough for the boy at the reins to hear. The pony slowed and Legg gained ground, nearing the back of the unsteady trap. They were travelling at speed, yet another risk, this time to the pony's ankles in the dark, but Legg caught up enough to heft the weight of his cousin into Collett's trembling arms. She fell back with her son, helping hands coming from another woman besides her, and two more young lads. None of them were family; Jevratt's wife and children were lost to them both. She hoped they'd escaped on one of the many traps she'd seen flee, but didn't hold out much hope. They'd been in the first vardo-fort to be hit.

What if he wakes and asks for them? She thought, cheeks wet and streaked from the tears she'd already shed. *What if he doesn't?* She swallowed hard and looked at the hole in her son's chest. Dark blood oozed from the wound, which bore a little hope, for she'd seen the pumping a heart could do.

Collett looked up. Legg was gone. She raised herself up a little, eyes working hard to try and see her nephew. *Where are ye, Legg? Where's the idiot gone now?* Her fear for her son brought her eyes back down and her tears fell again, mixing with the bag of red petals she'd pulled from around her neck. Working them together in the leather pouch, with some of Jevratt's own blood, Collett spat into the bag for good measure and turned the contents out onto Jevratt's wound, smearing the balm in before sitting him up with help and doing the same on his back.

The light of the fires and the screams and howls faded as the trap continued on, jerking about all those on board as they headed along the road to Rowberry, binding Jevratt's wounds as they went.

Chapter 15 - Overcooked

Cheung could feel the large muscles working beneath his legs. The beast was walking, but the power of the animal remained impressive.

Immaculate cloak before him, Cheung couldn't recall when Dignaaln had donned the garment; he couldn't remember stopping since the flight from Stonebridge. They passed tall trees on the left, whilst mountains reared to their right. Cheung followed the landscape up into those peaks. Snow decorated the tops, days' worth of travel distant. He twisted in the saddle, looking back along the road. They'd travelled throughout the night. The sun had risen behind them, casting shrinking shadows before reaching its zenith above their heads.

'We will stop up ahead,' Dignaaln said, without turning.

Cheung nodded, in no mood to talk to the emissary sent by his masters.

'I said—'

'I heard you.'

'You are not wondering why we are stopping here?'

'I don't care.'

A laugh, soft, but clear. 'You should, Cheung. You should.'

Cheung sighed. He rubbed his face, hands pulling away when the line below his eye re-opened. Fresh blood ran warm down his cheek.

'There is an inn ahead. You need to rest and we need to part company.' Dignaaln did not turn.

Looking back towards the distant mountains, Cheung said nothing.

'You are not surprised I am leaving you?' Dignaaln asked, and he did turn a little at that, taking Cheung in with one dark eye.

'I don't—'

'Care. Yes, I am beginning to understand that.' He looked forward once more. 'Your masters—'

'*My* masters?'

'Ah, a proper response. Yes, *your* masters, Cheung. Did you think I am *their* emissary?'

No answer.

'Your masters are working for my master, and my master wanted you back on track.'

'I was on track,' Cheung said, pressing a gloveless, pale finger to his cheek and bringing it away red. He wiped it on his robes.

'You were losing your perspective and I was ordered to remind you of it. You think I do not have better things to attend to, other than steering one assassin back on track?'

One assassin? Cheung thought, eyes narrowed. There was something in the way Dignaaln said that. 'I told you, I don't care.' Cheung watched the back of Dignaaln's head shake slowly from side to side.

'Much is changing in Brisance, and you are an integral part of it. As is your guild.'

'I was never trained to think of the bigger picture,' Cheung said, looking left, to the trees. 'The opposite is true, in fact.'

'You think they were your friends, don't you?'

No answer.

'You forget you paid them your dues. You gave them coins to be fed and led to Rowberry. That is all.'

'I gave them more than that, and they gave even more in return.'

Immaculate shoulders bobbed.

'I wouldn't expect you to understand, emissary.'

'Because you do not understand it yourself?'

It would have been silent but for the palomino's hooves on hard-packed earth, and the calls of woodland birds to their left.

Cheung watched smoke lift, merging with the grey sky. 'We part ways soon, you say? I am glad.'

'As am I, Cheung. As am I.'

A buzzard called from high above as the horse walked its two riders towards the growing inn. That call was joined by another. Cheung's eyes widened when he looked up to see five of the raptors circling their position.

'They will hang there, hoping for scraps from the people at the inn,' Dignaaln said, looking up, along with Cheung. 'The gibbet tree opposite often bears them fruit.'

Cheung looked back down, and over to the mountains again; better that than Dignaaln's back. 'They'd do better flying along the road to Stonebridge. I leave more fruit in my wake.'

Dignaaln turned and smiled, but said nothing.

They moved on, coming closer to their parting. The inn was sprawling, with outbuildings, stables and a barn. Goats and chickens walked the surrounds, and a pond stretched out alongside the inn like a poorly designed moat. By the flat waters sat a boy, pole and line in hand. The child looked up to the road as they closed in, then back to the end of his pole; it was no strange sight, horses bearing two riders;

90

horses bearing armed and bloody men. Even a golden horse like the palomino.

Cheung glanced opposite the inn, to a tree with more ropes than foliage. Two corpses hung there, picked clean. A murder of crows sat watching the new arrivals, but even they seemed unimpressed, and continued to bicker and squabble over the remains hung out for them.

Dignaaln pulled up to a tying stump, paused and waited for Cheung to dismount. The assassin didn't see the wry smile on Dignaaln's face as the black blade of a kama pressed cold against Dignaaln's exposed throat.

'We *are* parting here, Dignaaln, but it is I who will ride on, and you who will find other transportation.'

Dignaaln made to talk, but the blade prevented it; his smile remained, unbeknown to Cheung.

The boy watched now, fishing forgotten. Many people came to the inn, some fought during or after their stay. Few did it before they even entered, before they drank. Despite the situation, Dignaaln was aware of the boy's eyes on them. He was aware, to a certain extent, of the boy's thoughts on the scene. He suppressed a laugh but not the broadening of his smile.

Sighing dramatically, Dignaaln stretched his arms wide as his passenger drew the sword at his hip and threw it towards the gibbet tree. Crows took to the air, their complaints numerous.

'Now climb down and fetch your sword,' Cheung said. 'And know this, Dignaaln, should you—'

'Fear not,' Dignaaln interrupted, noticing the sudden space to talk he was given by the subtle shifting of the blade at his throat. 'I am a mere emissary, Cheung. I am not foolish enough to tackle an assassin, even if it costs me my valuable steed.'

'Don't think I'm glad to hear that.' Cheung let Dignaaln climb down, and shuffled forward into the saddle proper.

Dignaaln watched the scarred assassin and laughed. 'Oh, I am not. Your feelings towards me, your saviour, are not—'

Cheung's booted foot lashed out and Dignaaln fell back. 'I grew tired of your voice the moment I heard it.'

Before Dignaaln could rise, the dust of the road did just that. Hooves struck earth and the white and gold of his horse left with the assassin he had been sent to guide back on track. A smile was all Dignaaln offered; a smile through the blood about his mouth. He looked across to the fisher boy, who found sudden interest in the pond once more.

My work is done, Dignaaln said to another; far away to the south-west, in Orismar. After a pause and no reply, he rose effortlessly. *And on I go. On to my next thankless task.*

Dignaaln wore his smirk like a mask as he retrieved his sword, walked over to the inn and pushed his way through the door.

Chapter 16 – An unlikely duo

The high-low call of buzzards mixed with the complaining of crows as Legg stumbled along towards the inn at the side of the road. The sun was disappearing behind the forest of The Marches, but there was enough light for him to see half a dozen horses tied up outside. He looked over to the gibbet tree opposite the inn's door, shuddered, then moved to and entered the inn itself.

It was dark inside. A fire-pit in the middle of the room gave off more light than the clay oil burners on each table, but it was the shadows that won out around the edges, their darkness impenetrable. Closing the door behind, Legg turned back to the people looking at him with more than a little suspicion in their eyes. Yellow light played on those faces. Legg took in every one, for there were only a dozen, sat in the light, anyway.

'Welcome,' the inn keeper said, from behind a table-bar. He tapped one of the barrels on the table and held his other hand up, fingers rubbing together.

Legg patted his torn and bloody braes down and shook his head, eyes moving across the faces looking his way. He noticed hands on belted knives and other weapons. Chest bare, but for the blood and dirt, Legg felt very out of place, and vulnerable. Running from Collett and the others seemed right at the time. He'd wanted to catch Priest and Dignaaln. He wanted to punish them both; Priest for his betrayal and Dignaaln for his… what? Legg shook his head, opened the door and walked back through. He heard stools scrape as the door closed behind him, but made nothing of it.

What did Dignaaln do to me? Legg thought, legs softening below him. He staggered forward and fell against the tying stump. Horses huffed and shifted as he slid down to the floor.

The weight of what had happened washed over Legg. Images flashed before him. Sights mixed with smells of smoke, sweat and shit. Familiar faces fell as he watched on, through his mind's eye. Flames licked up and family members screamed, their deaths running through his head, faster and faster. *Belcher, gone. Endell, gone; Peens, gone, Tollimer gone, Brommel gone Jenn gone Uncle Couig gone…*

'Dead… all of them, by my hand.'

Legg's breaths came fast, eyes moving rapidly from side to side, heart thumping in his chest. Cramp hit like a claw digging away at the back of his left leg. He rolled sideways and doubled up, leg stretching and bending as he worked through the pain and sobbed shamelessly, tears marking the earth beneath him. *I let him charm me. I walked with him and watched him turn men on men with his words alone in Stonebridge. I watched him open the gates to the bridge and I led him into our camp. I should have warned them...* Fingernails caught on stones as Legg grasped at the earth about him. *I killed them all...*

As the warm breath and bristles of a horse brushed the side of his face, coming to rest and nuzzle, a door opened and six men walked out, hobnailed boots scraping. The horse's head moved away as swords were drawn.

Legg failed to move. Failed to accept his life was worth moving for.

As the men moved forward, the last light of the dropping sun back-lit the forest opposite them.

'I see no more,' one man said.

'There's always more Caravaneers,' another said, bitterness tainting his voice.

'The message was clear.' This one was well spoken, his tone commanding. A knight? 'The assassin travels with the Caravaneers.'

'So we question him?' the first asked.

Legg could hear it all, but failed to move; he didn't even attempt to.

'Aye, we need to know what's happened to his caravan.'

'Gentlemen?'

Legg's eyes opened. Dignaaln!

'Mind yer own, traveller.'

'No need to be like—'

'He said mind your own business and you'd do well to listen, sir,' the well-spoken one said. 'We mean you no trouble, so go back into the inn.'

'I think I may be able to assist, good knight.' Dignaaln's smile was clear in his tone.

Legg turned his head and saw the immaculately dressed emissary, framed by the dark doorway of the inn and lit by fading, orange sunlight as the door closed behind him.

'Listen, go back—'

'Wait,' the knight said, holding his hand up to his man. Legg looked at the knight and his men-at-arms. 'What do you know, good sir?'

Legg caught the white of Dignaaln's smile and the gleam of steel being drawn.

'Cheeky bastard,' one of the men said, moving forward.

'Run,' Legg tried, but his voice caught and broke. The knight turned to him as his man closed on the smiling emissary.

'What was that?'

'I said run!'

The last slip of light caught on steel as it cut the air before Dignaaln. The soldier before him fell without a sound, dead before he hit the ground.

There was a surge of movement, of boots on stone, blades held out, others held high. The knight turned to see his men charge the smiling swordsman.

They each fell in turn, as quickly as the first.

Breaths came hard for the knight following that. Face lined, teeth bared and eyes narrowed, he turned and moved to his horse. The beast snorted as he swung up into the saddle. Steel cleaved rope and the knight deftly guided the animal around the tying stump as the killer of his men stepped forward.

'Assassin!' the knight accused, pointing his sword forward, his snarl lost to the darkness. He turned to look down on Legg. 'You brought this filth upon us.'

Legg stood, wearily, and nodded. 'I did, aye...'

The knight looked back to the approaching killer. As he dug his heels in, he heard one last thing.

'But he's no assassin.' *He's much worse.*

Muscles bunched and stretched and powerful legs propelled the knight towards his quarry.

Dignaaln dropped as the horse reached him. Out came his arm, sword an extension of his limb and will. Horses' legs gave way to steel. The beast screamed and the other horses stomped and pulled at their tethers, one breaking away and fleeing into the night.

Dust lifted as the destrier collapsed and slid past Dignaaln, its spraying blood covering the emissary's boots and hose. The knight rolled forward, head over his horse's thrashing neck. His maille hauberk did little to protect him as the blood-slick sword punched through the surcoat covered links and padding, finding vital organs within.

The horse continued to thrash and project its guttural scream and blood alike.

Fresh tears smeared Legg's face as he looked on. *Finish the horse, damn you. Finish it!*

Dignaaln stood. Eyes met.

Dignaaln wiped his blade on the dead knight's back, which bucked atop the struggling horse's neck. He sheathed his sword and smiled at Legg, before walking back into the inn to the sound of equine screams, his clothes immaculate once more.

***

'You cannot be serious, my lord,' Severun said, pacing the palace chamber the Duke of Yewdale had invited him to.

Egan Dundaven grunted. 'I'm not fond of the idea myself, wizard.'

Severun spun on the former witchunter, a snarl pulling at his top lip.

'Master Dundaven, I will have your silence,' Morton said, rubbing his temples with the tips of his fingers. 'Severun,' he added, looking to the former lord, 'Egan Dundaven has sworn his allegiance to King Barrison, and me. As, may I remind you, have you.' Severun made to speak, but Morton held his hand aloft. 'You dislike what the Samorlian church has done.' Severun clenched his teeth, stole a sideways glance at Egan and nodded. Morton smiled. 'It wasn't a question, Severun. So too do I. But...' he crossed to a chair and dropped into it before rolling up his linen sleeves. 'Nor did I particularly like what you did to this city.' He looked back up to the source of Wesson's recent plague.

Egan smirked.

Severun opened his mouth to speak, then closed it again.

Morton smiled and absent-mindedly traced one of his facial scars before clasping his hands together.

'So it is,' Morton said, to them both, 'that we come to this. You two, together, working as one.'

The two men before the Duke scowled.

'Now, you know what we ask of you—'

'And King Barrison knows this time, does he, my lord Yewdale?' Severun said, eyebrows raised.

Egan frowned and turned to Severun, then back to Morton, who sighed.

'We've been through this, Sever—'

'Lord—'

'No.' Morton shook his head, expelling a breath. 'No, Severun, you lost that title.'

Egan smirked once more.

'Your recent actions in that park were necessary,' Morton reassured, eyes locked on Severun's. 'Those two individuals needed burying, for all our sakes, but Barrison needn't ever know by whom, despite what you told the two of them that night.'

Egan frowned again, his confusion clear.

'And it's none of your business what we talk of,' Morton said, finger pointed at the former witchunter. *Despite their failings, they were your own archbishop and Grand Inquisitor, and Severun best keep his killing of them from you, for both your sakes.*

'But this, what you ask of us?' Severun went on. 'Barrison knows about this?'

'Of course he bloody does,' Morton said, exasperated. 'The bastards have sent someone to kill him, made of him a mark to be struck off. He may be benevolent, our King, but he's no mewling fool. He wants the Black Guild bringing to account.'

Both men nodded at that.

Well that's a start, Morton thought. He rose from his chair and crossed to a small door. Opening it, he turned back to the unlikely duo.

'By gods above, below or wherever, I wish you well with this, gentlemen. I wish you success and I wish it fast. Yesterday was too long to have waited for news on Barrison's assassin.'

'Or assassins,' Egan interrupted.

Severun's eyes widened and Morton took in a lungful of air and nodded. Letting it out he said, 'Aye, there could well be more than one. Of that, I will await what you find.

'Good day to you both.' Morton left the room, wondering, but briefly, whether he should have told them what Ward Strickland had just told him; the assassin is coming from Eatri, and he's already crossed the border.

Chapter 17 - Palomino

The animal lacked any sense of loyalty, to Dignaaln anyway. For Cheung, the palomino did whatever he asked. If events leading up to that point weren't weighing so heavy on him, he might have enjoyed the ride. As it was, his mind was torn in two, between what had happened and what would happen. His warring emotions nearly led Cheung into a party of Altolnan soldiers on the road. It was the horse that saved him, or them, perhaps. The golden horse walked off the road, Cheung in no mood to stop it. Now, the two of them rode under heavy branches, following seldom used, overgrown forest tracks. It was tough going.

The palomino pushed through low branches, many of which snagged on Cheung's robes in their attempt to pull him from the saddle. He did little to fight it, little to avoid the scratches those branches inflicted upon his face and hands. More than once the two of them came across startled deer and even a boar. Cheung made no move to ride the animals down, despite his hunger. It would likely be impossible anyway, but with what was to come, he knew he should be trying to build his strength, trying to catch food. He hadn't even foraged, and carried no supplies.

What is to come? he thought, ducking a thick branch. *I have lost the conviction I once had, or rather it comes in fits and starts before leaving me just as quick. But have I gained freedom?* Cheung laughed bitterly. *Hardly. I have lost my way, that is the truth of it. I have lost my way physically and mentally. My time with the Caravaneers...*

The next branch caught Cheung by surprise, nearly taking him from the saddle. He cursed as colourfully as any Caravaneer.

Was I ever their friend? Does it even matter? I journeyed with them for one purpose, for an outcome I need not know more about other than the need to see it done, for my masters. 'For myself.' He shook his head. *Perhaps I should be wanting to know why they want this latest mark attending to? I have blindly followed, always, but now I question.* Cheung snarled. *Where is my control, my calm? Where is my resolve? I am weakening, becoming something I am not, something I cannot be. I am as inconsistent in my thoughts as a... I can't even think of a bastard analogy.*

Strange words flowed from the scarred lips of a mouth previously unused to much else. Cheung recited a phrase uttered countless times. Its meaning was unknown to him, but that was the point. He didn't need to know, he only needed to recite. The breathless string of words flowed into one, the mantra relaxing, calming. When it finished, he felt warmer, despite the chilly evening air. He straightened his back, clenched his teeth and nodded along with the movement of the horse.

I need think no more of this, of anything, until the morrow. A fresh perspective is all I need. I am as I was, yet I am more. I have grown... and perhaps that is what's needed for me to succeed; the masters forever have their plans, and I am but a part of them.

It was dark now, the forest filled with eerie noises and the hoot of tawny owls. Whenever he heard the birds call to one another, his mind drifted back to their large cousin as it flew silently above him outside the camp, moments before its warning of the adlets' assault. He thought, with regret, of the great bird's demise at the hand of the adlet raiders. Cheung shuddered at the image of that instant, and all the images that came with it.

The palomino stopped, threw its head up and down several times and lowered itself to the ground.

'You want me off?'

Flinging its head sideways, Cheung took the answer for what it was and stepped off the saddle.

'I can't see well enough to undo the saddle, your bridle... any of it. I'm not experienced with such things, alas.'

A soft whinny and the head lowered to a floor invisible in the murk.

I thought horses slept on their feet?

The animal huffed and stood, its tail flicking against Cheung, before settling once more.

'Don't stand on me in the night.'

A snort and a shake of the head.

Cheung gingerly moved around in the blackness until he found a tree and slid down to its base. Clutching his satchel and attempting to clear his mind, he stared into the night of the northern most tip of The Marches, until exhaustion took him.

***

The inn was deserted. The bodies out front had been lifted up and hung on the gibbet tree by Legg. It had been hard work, but Dignaaln had asked nicely, so how could he have refused? Inside, the two men sat, ate and drank. Dignaaln had insisted his friend washed in the horse trough outside, and had found clothes for him. The eldest son of the inn keeper hung naked on the tree out front, along with the rest of his family. The young fisherman had been the easiest for Legg to raise, so he'd hung the boy the highest, much to the delight of buzzards and crows.

Smoke filled the inn, the hole in the thatched roof of little use as the central fire pit blazed. A spit reached over it, chunks of horse meat skewered along its length. Legg could hardly remember the last time he'd eaten so well.

He stopped chewing. *Grounding...* Licking his lips, Legg looked about the dark room, confusion settling in. When his eyes settled on the emissary besides him, he drew in a quick breath, stood, backed away.

'Legg, my friend,' Dignaaln said, arms wide, dark eyes sinking away to nothing. 'What startles you so?'

Legg tried to blink the smoke from his eyes. Head swimming, he took a deep breath and held his hands out low, palms down. 'I stood too fast, methinks.'

Dignaaln smiled. 'Yes, yes I think you did. Take a seat, have some more wine. It is not grand, but it will do us, for now.'

Nodding, Legg sat back down and took the clay pot offered to him.

'Such crude containers,' Dignaaln mused aloud, studying the pottery in his own hand. 'I miss glass.' His eyes turned to Legg. 'Have you drunk from glass, my friend?'

Legg shook his head before drinking the wine.

'No, I did not think so.' Dignaaln sighed and slumped lower in the chair. 'You have missed out there, Legg. It makes such a...'

Wheels clattered outside.

Dignaaln frowned. 'Now who would be travelling at night?'

Legg shrugged, before leaning forward to cut more meat from the spit.

Dignaaln straightened in his chair and pulled on Legg's arm. 'Go and see, will you?'

Legg turned on Dignaaln and nodded eagerly, before tossing fat onto the fire to spit and sizzle. Rising, he crossed to the door, smoothing down his gifted, red woollen tunic and adjusting his matching cap as he went. *How fine I look,* he thought, smile broad. Before he reached it, the door opened onto a scene not much darker than the one behind him.

'Aunt Collett!' Legg shouted. His face was a picture of surprise and delight. 'You made it!'

The woman rocked back on her heels, unsure how to take the enthusiastic greeting.

'Where's Uncle Couig? Where's the caravan?' he said, face dropping as he looked past her angry visage.

'Shit,' Dignaaln said from behind.

Legg staggered from the slap he took.

'Ye're drunk, ye shit. We're fightin' for Jevratt's life and yer here, drunk.' She shoved her nephew into the inn, following him to shove some more. 'And dressed like a prise cock, to boot.'

'Woah, Collett, stop that.' Legg backed off, pointing to Dignaaln, who stood. Legg missed the cuts, bruises and torn clothes the emissary now sported.

'Mistress Collett,' Dignaaln said, bowing low. He winced as he did so.

Fists balled as the woman surged across the room, shouting all the way. 'Where's the bastard priest, eh? Where's the traitor?'

Legg interposed, forcing himself between the two. 'Priest forced Dignaaln away, Collett. He forced him to carry him from Stonebridge, to flee. He beat him and left him on the road. Left him for dead and stole his beautiful horse.'

Collett's eyes never left Dignaaln's as her breaths came ragged and hard. She coughed and reached for her pipe.

'Come,' Legg said, dragging her back to the door. 'Did ye see? Did ye see the men, women and boy Priest strung up in the tree? Did ye see those he slaughtered?'

Suspicious eyes left a nodding Dignaaln, before looking out towards a pointed-out tree she couldn't possibly see in the dark. 'Enough,' she said, as Legg went on. 'Enough I say!'

'He helped me, your nephew,' Dignaaln said smoothly, coming forward.

Collett rounded on the man. 'I'm not sure what he's done, that boy.' She pointed, yellowed finger inches from Legg's face. 'But I know what he's to do now.'

'Anything,' Legg said, moving between Collett and Dignaaln again.

'Ye're to help carry yer cousin in here, and fast. He's on the mend through skill, and luck in abundance, but he needs more than I can do for him on the road if he's to continue mending and not die... like everyone else.' The words visibly pained Collett. 'Now get him in, Legg, and maybe I'll forgive ye for running from us.'

Nodding eagerly, Legg rushed out of the inn. Collett watched him go, packing her pipe as she did so. She never saw Dignaaln's dark eyes smile, whilst he popped a piece of horse flesh into his mouth. And somehow Legg felt that smile, despite being out of sight. He felt it and matched it with one of his own.

***

An iron-shod hoof pressed on Cheung's cheek. The cold touch opened eyes that followed a golden leg up to a broad-chested beast. Eyes met and horse and human huffed. Removing the foot, the palomino nodded its head. Cheung closed his eyes and groaned.

Those eyes opened wide and quick as a weighty thud preceded several more. The impacts of hoof on ground were followed by a gush of warm liquid. Cheung rolled away fast, climbing to his feet whilst pulling his wet and steaming robes from his body; the horse had been faster.

'Of all the places,' Cheung said, throwing his soiled robes to the floor and glaring at the offending animal, the smell of the horse piss overwhelming.

The horse whinnied.

'I was waking, in my own time.'

The horse moved away.

'You are insufferable.' Turning away from the animal, Cheung relieved himself then followed, robes retrieved, shook off and thrown over the golden rump of the palomino. A grunt of complaint was all he received as he climbed into the saddle.

'I'm not myself, horse,' he said, *which is clear by my talking to you.*

The palomino pushed on, without a sound.

'I war within. The old me fights the new, and the new struggles to care.' No reply from the animal pushing its way through the undergrowth. 'I feel a strong sense of duty. I must seek my mark and end him, like all those that came before him, but…'

Cheung lay flat against the horse's white mane, allowing a branch to pass over him.

'But I also want to go back; back to see how the Caravaneers fare.'

Cheung rubbed the fresh scar on the back of his neck and ran a finger down the poorly healing line beneath his eye.

'How many more will fall to my blades before I reach the man they are intended for? Answer me that, horse.' Cheung grunted a laugh to himself. The horse grunted back.

Dark green faded to lighter shades; paler and paler until warm sunlight touched skin and hide. Cheung laughed aloud when he saw the road stretching into the distance, Chapparro Minor rising up to the right of the road, to the north.

'You're saner than I am right now, and smarter it would seem.' Nudging the animal with his knees, Cheung took the reins and urged his mount on.

'Take me to Rowberry. Take me there and beyond, to Wesson. I'm sure you'll see me right along the way, and who knows? Perhaps I shall be who I need to be by the time we get there.'

The palomino and its rider hit the long road to Rowberry at a steady canter, whilst Cheung repeated the mantra he'd attempted the night before. This time, the words were less forced. This time, he almost believed in the unknown, as he once had.

Chapter 18 – Look out below

The night, once again, was made longer by the sullen atmosphere the two men endured throughout their three days in Dockside. Severun took a dramatically deep breath and strode from the lay house and out onto the muddy cobbled street beyond, which stunk only a little worse than their night's accommodation. Egan Dundaven rolled his eyes and reluctantly followed.

'Where now?' Severun asked, without turning.

Egan shrugged. Severun turned, eyebrows high. Egan shrugged again and Severun sighed.

'Is this not your area of expertise, witchunter?'

'I've exhausted my expertise since we entered this Samorl forsaken district,' Egan said, whilst placing his hat firmly on his head. 'I have no leads. You've done little as of yet, wizard.' *Very little, in fact.*

'If I were able to summon the Black Guild like a sorcerer summons a... spirit or some such, I'd have no use for you. And trust me, I wish that were so.'

Egan grunted. 'Trust you?' He set off down the hill, a single glance behind after a couple of gull-call accompanied steps. Severun followed, white staff in hand, robes flowing ridiculously.

'Yes, for this task you must trust me, Egan, as I do you.'

Egan stopped. He turned to face Severun, who looked down on him.

'You trust me? We barely know one another, and we're an unlikely paring, especially with our particular histories.'

Severun was nodding before Egan finished. 'Yes,' he said, 'we are, but I've heard what you did below the city, whilst fleeing Tyndurris. I know you saved my friend's life: Master Orix.'

Egan's stomach lurched and a shiver ran through him, despite the sun. 'The gnome,' he said, his words barely more than a whisper. His eyes focused past Severun, to the memory of killing his superior to save that gnome. It remained as vivid as when it happened and he feared it always would.

'You made a great sacrifice to save him,' Severun said, his tone softening for the first time since they'd been forced together by Will Morton.

Egan swallowed hard. 'I couldn't see him murdered before me. It wasn't what I joined the order for.' Egan focused back on Severun before continuing down the road. 'Past is past,' he said, as Severun came alongside, easily matching the smaller man's pace. 'We have a job to do now. A job I relish much more than the one I was tasked with upon my arrival to Wesson.'

'Yes, we have,' Severun agreed, looking about the shabby buildings surrounding them. He stopped suddenly.

'Severun?' Egan said over his shoulder, stopping a couple of paces further on and watching the wizard with narrowed eyes. *What's he about?*

Shaking the 'whatever it was' away, blank expression losing out to alertness, Severun offered a weak smile and continued on down the hill, Egan now following him.

'Come on,' Severun said, stride long, 'we've work to do. The Black Guild won't make themselves known to us.'

Egan nodded as he followed. 'Not if we're blessed,' he said, catching Severun up. 'For if they do, it'll be on their terms, and I don't like the thought of an impromptu meeting with assassins on their terms.'

'We agree on something else,' Severun said, eyes back to scanning the crooked buildings either side.

'Fellas!' a heavily tattooed gnome – of all things – shouted, from a slither of a dark alleyway – despite the sunny morning. The two men stopped, looked to the outlandish gnome, then to one another.

'Yes?' Egan said, hand finding the hilt of his cloak-covered rapier. The familiar feel of the weapon calmed him, but a little.

'I might be havin' some information for ye both,' the gnome said, a cocky grin lifting one cheek high.

'Might you?' Egan looked to Severun, who shrugged, then back to the offeror of information, who grinned all the more and nodded. Egan tipped the brim of his hat to the gnome. 'And what might that be?'

'You two be lookin' for the Black Guild, ain't ye?'

Severun said yes as Egan said no. Both closed their eyes and sighed as the gnome laughed.

'Sure enough ye are. Now follow me down here, and I'll tell ye what ye need to know.' Severun made to speak, but the gnome cut him off. 'Should ye offer the right price that is.' He winked with a twist of the head at the two men, before disappearing back down the alley.

'Isn't this what we wanted?' Severun asked, eyes on the gap between hovels.

'Like I said before,' Egan said, hand wringing the hilt of his rapier, 'not on their terms.'

Severun pursed his lips and nodded.

'Off you pop, wizard.' Egan held his free hand out for Severun to lead.

'What? Oh. Yes, well, let's get on with it, eh?' Severun strode into the alley with a level of confidence that niggled at Egan's pride; he followed with a lungful of air; chest broad.

'As long as his confidence is more genuine than mine,' Egan whispered to himself, eyes attempting to adjust to the shadows enveloping the duo.

Half the morning later and Severun and Egan were continuing on their way through the shit-filled streets of Dockside. Following the gnome led to nought but an informal chat with a human lad. Whereas the lad's information seemed invaluable, Egan decided it would be prudent to take it all with a pinch of salt, despite their lighter purses.

They continued to discuss the boy as they walked down the narrow, sloping road, mud sucking at their boots. Reaching a junction of sorts, where two alleys lead off, either side of the road, Egan pulled Severun to one side, half under an overhanging first floor, perched precariously atop a ramshackle house.

'Listen, Severun—'

'Lord Severun.'

'Severun. You're not a lord any longer, *Lord* Yewdale said as much.'

Severun frowned.

'What you need to understand, about that boy and the gnome before him, about this place – Dockside – is that we stand out like an inept carpenter's thumb. They knew what we were. Samorl, Severun, he knew *who* you were!' Severun made to say something, but Egan held up his hand and the publicly executed and officially deceased wizard held his tongue. 'My bet is that he was set to watch us—'

'And slipped up when we spotted him, thankfully for us,' Severun said, but Egan was shaking his head.

'No,' Egan said flatly. 'I think you remember that event differently. He knew what we were about and his asking if the Black Guild was what we were looking for was meant to gauge us, don't you see? We're being watched, followed, measured up, as either potential enemies or... clients.' He said the latter slowly, emphasising the word.

'But by whom?'

'I thought mages were intelligent? The Black Guild themselves!' Egan added, before Severun could fire off a retort.

Severun scoffed. 'That's ridiculous. The very guild we seek, out of all those working throughout this city, just happen to be watching us? Whilst we try to watch them?'

'Exactly! Although they're doing a better job at it than we are, aren't they?'

'Well, I'm not so sure, since I'm not sure I believe you. That lad wanted coins across his palm and he got it, for good, usable information.'

'Listen, Severun, everything that's happened since we entered Dockside, everything that's going to happen, within reason, is by design. By their design, believe you me. They don't have a big wooden door in a fancy old building in Guild District with a brass knocker on and a sign saying "to book assassinations, knock here" do they? So how do you think clients find them?'

'They ask.'

Egan lifted his hat to scratch at his scalp in frustration. 'Where?'

'Taverns, inns and brothels. You know, seedy places.'

Egan sighed with frustration at what was, to him at least, obvious. *Samorl give me strength.*

'No, Severun, all that will do is get you laughed at or killed, or both.'

'Go on,' Severun said, clearly playing along, but unconvinced, 'what do you do to get in touch with the Black Guild?'

'You do what we're doing. Why do you think I've had us traipsing around Dockside for three days? Certainly not for the fresh air and scenery. We've made subtle enquiries. We've let people know we have money and will pay for information, but we're not to be pushed around, enough so the Thieves Guild won't have anyone touch us. We've not had an attempted mugging for over a day, have we? Despite your jewel-eyed bloody staff.'

Severun thought about that for a moment, bringing his staff in close. 'Which means?' he said, eventually.

'We've been passed up the food chain,' Egan said, raising his hand level with his wide brimmed hat. 'I have no doubt that the gnome and boy were watchers for the Black Guild, although I don't believe any of the information the lad gave us.'

'Why would they have him talk to us?' Severun rubbed at his face with his free hand, then looked up and down the road, shifting from foot to foot through impatience. 'I've enacted simpler spells,' he said through his fingers, which continued to rub his face some more.

'Because they want to see what we do with that information. We follow it to the letter and they're scared off, they don't want to work for anyone so obvious. They need us to have a certain level of tact and stealth about us. Should they take our contract on, they want to know we won't go blabbing about it to anyone and everyone.'

'If what you're saying is true, what next?' Severun asked, hands and staff out to the sides.

'That, we need to think on, but hurtling off to act on the information the boy gave us is certainly not what we should do. I think other signs will present themselves as time goes on, and we'll use them to move forward from here on in.'

A creak from the wooden shutters above their heads caused both men to look up. Egan's hand moved to his rapier's hilt. It was too little too late, not that it would have saved either of them.

The old woman screeched an apology and slammed the shutters with a loud clatter as the contents of her chamber pot splashed across the two men in the street below, both of which cried out in a mix of surprise and disgust as they began heaving and retching against the wall beside them. They were now safely, if a little too late, hidden under the overhang of the building's upper floor.

'And I suppose,' Severun said, picking a lump of excrement from his face and throwing it at his companion whilst heaving some more, 'that was all part of their plan to gauge us too, was it?'

'No,' Egan said. He spat, trying to remove the taste of piss from his mouth. *Samorl hydrate that woman...* 'I expect that's a case of us,' he spat again, 'standing in the wrong place at the wrong time. Although I'm sure,' another throaty spit, 'it's given them something to laugh at, reducing their suspicion of us as potential enemies.'

'Oh, I am pleased.' Severun closed his eyes and mumbled under his breath before pointing the unicorn's head of his staff at his face, which erupted in a jet of cool water.

Egan squeezed his eyes shut in front of Severun and waited his turn, the continuing smell overpowering.

'Come on,' he forced through tight lips, 'use that conspicuous walking stick on me.'

After a couple of moments, Egan opened his eyes to see the wall of the house, but no wizard. He turned to the sucking footsteps of Severun walking down the road, further into Dockside. Wiping at his face again, gagging again, Egan shook his head, sighed and followed.

'The damned guild has nothing to fear from us two at this rate.'

'What?' Severun shouted back.

'Nothing!' Egan replied, heaving yet again.

Chapter 19 – Nose of a dog

A studded door with a polished brass knocker filled Severun and Egan's view as they turned the corner the third lad they'd now dealt with led them to. Surrounding the door was a chipped and soiled marble arch, a large keystone at the top. At the side of the door more brass, this time in the oblong shape of a plate, like the rich guilds in Guild District used. On that brass plate, letters had been etched.

To book assassinations, knock here.

The lad turned around and grinned. 'Like it? He said you would.' Before they could respond, he disappeared down a side passage neither of them had noticed, their attentions stolen by the doorway.

'Great,' Severun said. Egan nodded. 'It seems they heard us.'

'Every word,' Egan added, 'and I'm not so sure the chamber pot incident was a total accident now, either.' It was Severun's turn to nod, nose wrinkled at the continuous smell coming from them both. Mainly from Egan, but from them both nonetheless.

'I agree,' Severun said, 'although I see no relevance in doing that to us.'

'Well…' Egan smirked. 'At least they have a sense of humour.'

'Great,' Severun said again. 'Do you wish to knock? Or do I have the honour?'

'By all means.' Egan held his arm out in invitation for Severun to step forward and strike the brass knocker.

Severun did so, and when he did, the knocker made a pitiful tapping sound.

Severun turned to Egan, who shrugged, whilst one hand moved to hover over his rapier hilt and the other over a hand-held crossbow strapped to his harness.

Childish laughter came from the dark path beside the door and the watcher boy appeared again. 'Down here,' he said, barely suppressing his laughter. 'That door isn't real, it's for your entertainment. And ours.' He grinned and motioned for them to follow.

Severun scoffed. 'Yes, very entertaining.'

Egan laughed. 'Lead on, my lord Severun.'

'Oh no, Master Dundaven, after you. It is I that insist.'

Laughing again, Egan followed the boy down the passage he'd had to turn sideways to get down, and Severun followed, cursing under his breath.

As they proceeded down the passageway, which was nothing more than two tall buildings set extremely close together, Severun stumbled several times, over what, he had no idea and no wish to know, much to the amusement, it seemed, of both the watcher and Egan.

Several heartbeats later they came to a recent hole in the left-hand wall. The boy led them inside. Severun had to duck to miss the makeshift wooden lintel spanning the small gap, and although Egan didn't have to stoop quite so low, he had to remove his hat. Once inside what they realised was a courtyard, and quite a plush one at that considering the district they were in, the two men were able to straighten.

'Take a seat and Master Son will be with you shortly,' the lad said, before disappearing through an opening covered by a heavy drape.

Looking around the ivy-covered walls, Severun surmised there were probably spy holes, if not arrow slits hidden in each wall, and even now they were being watched.

'Alright,' Egan said, 'we might as well take a seat and relax.' He moved his sheathed rapier out of the way and took a seat on the nearest bench, behind Severun, who walked the perimeter of the yard.

'Relax, are you serious?' Severun hissed. 'We could be anywhere and our hosts anyone. A ganger haunt at the mercy of a vicious murdering gang master, or even better, we could actually be where we want to be, in the blasted Black Guild! Neither of which fill me with a sudden urge to put my feet up, take out my pipe and think about pleasantries past or future, endeavours new or—'

'I get the picture.'

'Do you, Egan? Do you really? I seriously doubt that.' *Lords above, this man...*

'Severun, sit down. If this is the Black Guild, this is what we wanted and if they wanted us dead, we would be by now, so what are you worried about?'

'Of course, how silly of me to worry at all about any of this, when all we're trying to do here is...'

Egan was out of his seat, across the yard and up against Severun in a heartbeat, his left hand pressing against Severun's mouth and his right hand holding the top of the ornate staff. His eyes did all the talking needed and Severun nodded before relaxing. Egan removed both hands and walked back to the bench. Before he could sit, the watcher pulled the heavy drapes aside and a woman with green hair appeared holding two goblets filled with a ruby wine. She attempted a half-hearted curtsy and offered the drinks.

Egan smiled, took his goblet and walked back, with the woman, to Severun, who accepted his with a genuine smile. The woman curtsied again and hurried back through the curtained doorway, where the watcher stood, grinning.

'It's good stuff,' the lad said, indicating the drinks both men held. 'Master Son let me taste it, for doing good. He'll be ready for you shortly.' He was gone before they could reply.

Egan sniffed the liquid and threw it back in one go. Severun's eyes widened and rolled as Egan smacked his lips in appreciation.

Severun sipped the drink. *Not bad,* he thought.

'I've tasted that before, but don't recall the name,' Egan said, licking his lips. 'From my neck of the woods I would think. Southern wine is the best.'

'I can't say I've had it before, but I know what you mean… a familiar taste to it. Can't quite put my finger on it though. Knowing our luck, it's laced with something.'

Egan shook his head. 'No, I'd have smelt it. Even the unscented ones,' he added before Severun could say anything. 'There might be a lot you know and can do, wizard, but there are hidden talents within me too you know.'

'A dog's nose?'

'Droll.'

'Then what? How could you smell an unscented substance?'

'I was blessed with it when I joined the order.'

Severun nearly spat the contents of his mouth.

'Laugh all you like, but there are things far more powerful than magic in this world, and just because you or your precious guild can't explain them, doesn't mean they're less real.'

'If you say so, Egan,' Severun said, unconvinced. He finished the goblet.

Before either could say another word, the young watcher pulled the drapes back again and called for them to follow him through. They kept hold of their goblets, even though both were empty, and followed the boy into a smoky, oil-lamp lit room, which led to more heavy drapes.

'He's through here,' the lad said, holding the second lot of drapes aside.

'Thank you,' Egan said as he ruffled the lad's hair. The boy screwed up his face and ruffled it back again. It looked no different to Severun, who smiled and followed Egan through.

The room beyond had a low ceiling, with oak beams reaching from near to far wall, where a small window let a minimal amount of sunlight through. Under the window sat a large man with a hat set low over his pronounced brow. A thick set jaw matched his burly arms and ham-sized fists, which held a small lute he poorly plucked with his left hand. Two stools sat in front of a low table, where a quill and several sheaves of rough paper lay. The man stopped plucking the strings long enough to point at the stools and nod to the watcher, who pushed in between the two men, snatched the goblets from their hands and disappeared through the drapes.

Egan and Severun took a stool each and stared at the beast of a man, awaiting an introduction.

He offered a tight-lipped smile and continued to pluck at strings, nothing musical forthcoming.

Before Egan or Severun could say anything to break the awkward silence, the green haired woman appeared with the two goblets, full again with a green liquid this time.

After accepting them, Severun noticed Egan subtly sniffing the liquid before sipping it. Severun followed suit.

'Good?' Master Son had a surprisingly soft voice, a child-like innocence to the way he asked the question. Although for some reason, Severun felt it to be false; an act.

'Yes, thank you,' Egan said, before drinking some more.

'Absolutely,' Severun agreed, 'thank you, Master Son.' The man's right eye twitched at the mention of his name.

'Please,' he said, again with an innocence that didn't fit his face, 'call me Poi.'

'Thank you, Poi…' Severun swallowed, his mouth suddenly dry.

Egan smiled briefly, before lifting the goblet and sniffing what was left of the liquid. The large man's attention seemed to drift down to the lute, which he began strumming incredibly badly indeed. Severun found himself entranced by the shocking music, if it could be called that, and had to concentrate on the table to put the goblet down. He noticed the goblet was empty. *I drank it all?*

So had Egan, who also put his goblet down on the table in front. 'Ha,' he cried. 'Poi Son, I get it. Oh, how very funny. What's your real name?' Egan had a silly grin on his face that Severun wanted to disapprove of, but he found himself grinning.

Their host looked up at the question. The awful music stopped. 'That is hi— my name. Poi Son. My... father was called Poi.'

'Oh really?' Egan said, his disbelief plain to see. 'Well, if that's your name and trade also, I can tell you now...' Egan was now slurring his words and swaying, much to the vocal amusement of Severun. '...you've a lot to learn! You can't spike my drinks, oh no, I would smell it, you see?'

'Blessed he is,' Severun said rather loudly. 'Blessed by Sir Samorl himself... with the nose of a dog no less!'

'Yes, nose of a damned dog I say, he says, we all say, so say all of us!'

'Well, of course,' the man sat opposite said, his voice taking on a bass tone. He put down his lute and sat forward on his chair. 'That's why I didn't poison your drinks.'

'Ha! I knew it! See, wizard? I told you!'

'You did, dog nose. Ha ha!'

'It's why I poisoned the contents of the chamber pot this morning. Slow acting poison I used, or should I say, poisons. Doubt ye smelt them did ye? Too much shit comin' out yer mouth. Much like now. Which will teach ye for seeking the bastard Black Guild's services. Cunts that they are.'

Egan's smile faded at the revelation, but Severun laughed out loud again, slapping his knee, then his companion, who fell off his stool.

'Old dog nose here could smell through your shit, couldn't you, dog nose? Dog nose? You awake?'

'No, he's not,' the large man said, his grin spreading, golden. 'And neither will *you* be in a moment's time.'

'I very much doubt...' Severun landed in a heap atop Egan.

Longoss retrieved the stolen lute and started playing again.

'Gods below, Longoss,' Coppin said, from behind the heavy drapes. 'Cut that din out will ye and drag them two through here.'

Sighing, Longoss whipped the hat off his earless head and threw it and the lute across the room.

'Aye,' the former assassin said, 'I'm on it. We best be off anyway, lass, before the owners of this here house return.'

Chapter 20 – There's gold in that

Dark became murk; murk became haze, a haze including a green smudge and a gold… grin.

Egan tried to shuffle away from the two, no, three solidifying people stood before him. The back of his head struck stone. He looked left, his vision delayed in following the movement. Nothing. He risked the pain and the ache behind his eyes to look right. Severun. Out cold.

'Can you hear me?' the green haired woman said, voice soft.

'Well, ye bastard?' the one who'd called himself Poi Son said.

Egan reeled at that rough voice. 'Yes, yes,' he managed, although his throat disliked it.

'Your friend will wake soon enough,' the woman said. 'Or so we hope. The poison turned out to be more potent than we'd expected.' She grimaced. 'It's a new day, you might like to know.' She crouched before Egan and slapped away the big man's hand. 'He's tied up, Longoss. Quit worrying for me.'

'He's a witchunter, lass,' the third, older man said.' He stood the furthest away, an old but well-kept crossbow cradled in his thick arms.

'I *was* a witchunter,' Egan corrected, scanning the room for clues as to where they were. *Barrels, crates… A cellar,* he decided.

'Was?' Longoss asked, heavy brow furrowing and revealing a myriad of silvery scars previously hidden amongst lines and larger scars.

'Yes, was,' Egan snapped, not wanting to talk more than he had to.

Longoss crouched now, leaning in to look Egan up and down.

'Ye dress and arm like one?' he said. 'Ain't that right, Keep?' The older man nodded.

'And you dress and smell like a piss-stained drunkard,' Egan retorted. 'Is that what you—?'

This Longoss moves quick for his size, Egan thought whilst groaning on the stone tiles. His aching eyes and throbbing head had a new friend, which dribbled blood onto his top lip.

'I guess I deserved that,' Egan said, nose throbbing whilst being pulled to a sitting position once more by the woman, who he realised was the one that'd hit him. He nodded in appreciation at that and sniffed at the free-flowing blood. She pressed a dirty cloth to his nose. It stunk of piss. *Guess I deserve that too.*

'Ye smell like a chamber pot yerself,' she said, with a wink.

Egan couldn't help but smile, despite the situation.

'All they want to know,' Keep said, casually aiming his loaded crossbow at Egan, 'is why you sought out the Black Guild? Why you sought out Poi Son specifically?'

Severun groaned, but remained unconscious.

Licking the metallic taste from his top lip, Egan nodded.

'That question would have saved a lot of time, and pain our end, if you'd bothered to ask it before you drugged us.'

Coppin frowned. Longoss snarled and Egan went on quickly.

'I know who you two are,' he said, nodding to the two crouched before him, 'and assume you, sir, are in league with them?' he said of the man with the crossbow.

'That doesn't answer my question,' Keep said.

'You're trying to hinder the guild,' Egan went on. 'Poi Son especially. Hence why you took us, thinking us his potential clients.'

'And ye're not?' Coppin asked, widening her eyes.

Egan shook his head. 'No.'

'This is taking too long.' Longoss drew a small knife.

'We're here to hinder them too,' Egan practically spat. The knife hovered before him and Longoss nodded for him to go on. 'The Lord High Constable ordered us to track down Poi Son, to track him down and find all we could about the planned assassination of—'

'King Barrison,' Longoss finished, his voice but a hoarse whisper.

Egan nodded eagerly. The knife lowered.

'Not many people know about that,' Keep said, lowering his crossbow. 'Most of them're in this cellar.'

'Aye,' Longoss said, as if trying the word for the first time. His eyes drifted past Egan's for a moment, before focusing back on the former witchunter. 'Tell us more.'

'See to the wizard first—'

'See,' Coppin said, spinning to look upon Keep, 'I told ye he were a mage.'

Keep took a deep breath, placed the crossbow on the ground, rooted in a pouch at his belt and threw the woman a coin. Longoss snatched it before she could whisk it away.

'Mine for telling ye both these two were too stupid on the street to be real clients.'

Egan frowned and glanced at Severun on the floor next to him.

'Aye, witchunter, it were the wizard who gave ye both away.'

'I knew it.'

'So ye're really here to help?' Coppin asked, eager for it to be true.

'Oh, I don't know about that,' Egan said.

'But ye're here to take down the Black Guild? Ye said it yerself,' she said, leaning forward that bit more.

'We're here to stop Barrison's assassination, nothing more.'

'Same thing,' Longoss said. Coppin nodded.

'And we're to do nothing whilst we're in this state.' Egan shuffled and pulled against his bonds.

'Not sure we can trust ye, yet,' Keep said, picking his crossbow back up.

'Well, what will that take?' Egan asked, incredulous. 'We can hardly prove it whilst tied down here, can we?'

'We'll think on it,' Keep offered. He removed the bolt from the crossbow, relaxed the string and headed up the steps to the door. 'I've a tavern to run. You two, give the wizard some water, and his pet witchunter. Then come up to me, we've talking to do.'

Both Coppin and Longoss nodded as they continued to stare at Egan.

Sighing hard, Egan rested his head back against the wall. 'We're running out of time,' he said, eyes on the dank ceiling.

'There's time yet,' Longoss countered whilst standing.

Egan's head lowered as he looked to the man. Fresh blood trickled from his nose.

'What do you know?'

'I was the one who helped warn the authorities, witchunter,' Longoss said, slapping a hand against his chest.

'I know that! Hence why he and I are here, for Samorl's sake. But what more do you know? We were given no specifics.'

Gold shone as the big man smiled. 'Might have learnt me some more about it all, whilst the three of us have been cocking things up for Poi Son.'

Coppin chose that moment to go and retrieve some water for the two bound men.

'And that is?' Egan asked.

'All in good time,' Longoss said, 'all in good time. We're to talk to Keep before deciding what to do with you two.'

Egan's head dropped backwards and once again hit stone. He didn't even wince.

'I'm glad we found 'em,' Coppin said, whilst bending to pour water into Egan's open mouth.

'And why's that, lass?' Longoss poured himself an ale.

She allowed herself a smile. 'It means Sears made it out of Dockside alive.'

Longoss' clay jug stopped before it reached his mouth. 'I hadn't thought of that,' he said, before quaffing it in one. Gold shone when the jug lowered, and both of them shared a look of genuine relief.

Egan felt no relief at all. In fact, all he felt was a vulnerability he was unused to. Both for himself and, with surprise, for Severun.

'Are we in agreement?' Keep said, looking to Coppin and Longoss, the latter for longer. Both looked to one another then nodded to Keep.

'I don't like it, but ye seem to think it's the only way?' Longoss said.

'Aye lad, I do. Now, go see it done and I'll tend the bar. I've been out there less and less lately and folk will talk. Now go.' Keep turned and moved out into the tavern proper, his booming voice drowning out the patrons' din.

'Who's to do it?' Coppin asked Longoss. The man took a deep breath.

'You,' he said, holding her gaze. 'I don't trust 'em enough as it is, so I'd struggle to keep me head about me. I'll come with ye though.'

Coppin nodded and moved for the stairs. Longoss caught her arm, firm but painless.

'Be careful though, wizards are dangerous folk, and with a witchunter as a companion... well...' he screwed his face up, scars creasing, and shook his head. '...I ain't ever seen the like. Be careful.'

'I will.' She reached up and placed a delicate kiss on his lips. 'I've more to live for than ever, Longoss,' she said before turning for the door.

Longoss' contented, gold-less smiles were rare, although lately they'd made appearances more often.

Coppin heard him following a few steps behind. *I've come a long way since you saved me,* she thought, the kiss lingering on her lips. *I dread to think where I'd be now? Dead, probably, or worse. For there is worse. But I hope you know, Longoss, how much I'm with you, for you, and not out of gratitude for what you did, although I have an abundance of that too.*

She opened the door and peered down into the shadow-filled cellar. The two men remained, although the wizard was awake and their conversation quick, muffled; heated. They both looked up, both relaxed when they saw it was her.

118

I hate that, Coppin thought. *I hate that the sight of me relaxes men, rather than keeping them on their guard, as does the sight of Longoss or Keep.*

Longoss' words came to her, his advice, to use that fact to her advantage. She nodded to herself, imperceptible to anyone watching, but nodded all the same. That nod came as those words met with the face of the wizard looking up at her. He was powerful, of that she was sure, but he seemed, pleasant. He seemed harmless to look at. Oh, he was tall and she imagined with his grandeur and robes anew he could emit an intimidation few could match, but right there, he looked harmless. *As do I. But I'm not. Not anymore.*

Coppin descended the stairs and weathered the stares with an obvious air of caution, fear even, although she felt less of it than she had when she opened the door. *They have no idea who I am, what I'm capable of,* she thought as she reached the bottom of the cool cellar and smiled meekly. *And that is my power.* Their eyes drifted past hers to take in Longoss, who appeared at the top of the steps, all anger and tensed muscle.

Oh, he won't kill ye, Coppin thought, *but I will, if ye put a foot wrong.*

'Gentlemen,' she said, voice soothing, 'let us discuss what we're to do with you, shall we?'

Both men rocked back at the flash of gold above and behind the woman.

Chapter 21 – The Tri Isles

With incredible strength, two score hobyahs heaved their war galley forward, it's bladed prow slicing through the choppy sea as the brutish hobyahs pulled at their oars, attempting, as ever, to reach their reward. Tull, the goblin dangling off the stern of the ship, squirmed. He looked at the hungry mouths of the oar pulling beasts, all of whom heaved themselves towards him, or so they thought. He knew the futility of their eager actions, but it didn't make the eyes locked on him seem any less scary, any less deadly. The hobyahs heaved on, pulling their oars to the sound of the only human crewman, who called 'Pull' in his monotonous tone. Even if Tull had dangled over the prow, the hobyahs' rowing would never have brought them any closer to him, but from the stern? That made it all the more hilarious… to the admiral anyway, not to the goblin who hung there; not to Tull.

'Pull pull pull pull,' Charlzberg called as he climbed from beneath his awning. 'Pull pull, all of you pull,' the goblin admiral continued, 'and soon you'll get to eat poor Tull!' He erupted in a high-pitched laugh, to which most of the crew followed suit. All except the 'pull' calling Bosun, and the dangling Tull.

'Where're we about, helmsmen?' Charlzberg asked, as he approached the Ptarmigan twins, both of whom wrestled with the tiller. Charlzberg winked at Tull, who now hung motionless, his scrawny arms folded across his bare chest. He refused to wink back, or smile, and so looked past the admiral and on to the rows of hobyahs staring hungrily at him.

Admiral, pfft. He has two vessels and dares call himself admiral.

Charlzberg removed his tri-cornered hat and scratched at the off-white wig beneath, before replacing the hat and impatiently tapping his foot on the grubby deck.

Ha! Tull thought. *Even the twins ignore him.*

'I said where're we about?' Charlzberg screeched, causing Bosun to miss a 'pull' and the hobyahs to do the same. The twins jumped in unison.

'Ah, well, Admiral…' Brother said, looking to his sister for help. Sister shrugged and looked away, seemingly tending to the workings of the tiller, although Tull knew nothing needed tending.

Charlzberg filled his pallid green cheeks and released the breath quickly, again and again, his head beginning to visibly shake.

'Uh oh,' Tull whispered. 'He's gonna blow.'

'Northbound!' Spyde shouted from above.

Charlzberg, fists clenched, looked up to the black-clad goblin clinging to the middle of the netted sail.

Tull rolled his eyes as he hung and swung and watched on. *We might be somewhere specific if the rotting admiral used canvas as a sail, rather than a damned fishing net.*

Spyde pointed past the prow. 'Land, Admiral. Land, I say!'

Charlzberg shook some more. He hissed before shouting, 'What ripping land, Spyde? What land? That's what I wanna know from you, you freak bully bastard!' A high-pitched keening came from Charlzberg's clenched teeth and he crouched as low as he could go, before shaking with the purest rage. The keening built whilst everyone winced, and when it seemed he couldn't go any more without taking a breath, Charlzberg jumped up and screamed like a banshee. Bosun stopped his calling, the hobyahs stopped their rowing, and cringed on their benches; all hands cringed. All, that was, except Tull, who sniggered at the impressive tantrum.

Looking up once more, Charlzberg bared his filed-flat teeth and tilted his head so a corner of his hat rested on his bony shoulder.

Spyde pointed again. 'Tri Isles, Admiral. We're towards the Tri Isles as planned.'

Charlzberg took a deep breath and nodded. He glanced sidelong and up at Bosun, who returned to his droning call. With a groan from both the hobyahs and the galley itself, they shifted towards the mountainous island and the gargantuan weighing scales that reached from the horizon to touch the sky.

'Bird!' Spyde shouted, and all eyes lifted as he scrambled across the giant net to retrieve the tangled tern, squawking as it thrashed in panic and fear.

'Mine!' Charlzberg demanded, to Spyde's poorly hidden dismay. 'All the cats are gone. I'm eating no more fish or rats, you all hear? No more! If there's to be no cats until dock, birds it'll be for me.' Pleased with himself, Charlzberg ordered a signal sent to his second boat, which trailed somewhat behind the galley. After that was done, he had Spyde bring down the throttled tern, which Spyde handed over reluctantly. Snatching it without a word, Charlzberg returned to his awning and slid beneath, followed by the audible crunching of bones.

'On we go, ye pimpled pricks. On we go!' Spyde shouted, moving to the centre of his web, and Bosun called 'Pull' as Tull squirmed some more.

Not long after the crunching of bones had ceased, Tull contemplated the Tri-Isles before him, albeit upside down.

Hundreds of white cubes filled the steep side of the mountain, the buildings' blue tiles flecking the white like a mosaic. Solid towers rose from amongst the cubes, with conical roofs coloured to match the rest of the city's rooftops. Thicker smoke than the majority rose here and there, from bakers and taverns and inns, and Tull salivated at the thought of what that meant.

'Pull.'

Charlzberg appeared from his awning and adjusted his hat. He turned his shaded face to the hulking bosun, and sneered.

'Pull.'

'Enough!' Charlzberg shouted. 'Enough, enough, enough!' He flung his arms about and stamped up the deck towards the blunt-faced man. 'They're pulling, ye piss. They're pulling and I'm having enough of the pull pull bloody pull.'

'Pull.'

Charlzberg screeched up at Bosun, who paid Charlzberg little heed, even when the goblin threw his tender fists against the man's stomach.

'Ouch,' Bosun said flatly. 'No, Admiral, please. Please don't. Pull. It hurts so bad.'

Tull, dangling from the stern, watched in utter disbelief as Charlzberg continued to pound on Bosun's abdomen. Rolling his eyes at Charlzberg's grunts of effort, Tull decided to squirm vigorously, in case the banks of rowing hobyahs lost interest in him and started to get mischievous ideas whilst Bosun was slightly distracted.

'Ouch. No more,' Bosun continued, as Charlzberg shrieked and continued to punch him. 'Pull.'

The Ptarmigan twins by the tiller winced at the commotion.

'Someone needs stop this before he gets hurt,' Sister said.

Brother turned to her, confused. 'Bosun?'

Sister laughed. 'No, silly. Charlzberg.'

Brother chewed his rubbery lips and nodded.

'Pull.'

Another scream erupted from Charlzberg, this one in triumph, as Bosun finally went down, slowly; casually. Spyde looked on from above, half tangled in his web-like sail as the man being bullied laid down on the deck and feigned injury.

'Enough, Admiral,' Bosun said. 'You've hurt me bad. Ouch. Pull. You're too much for me, Admiral.'

Standing with one boot placed triumphantly on Bosun's broad chest, Charlzberg looked to his crew, eyes narrowed.

'Pull,' Bosun said from his prone position.

'You see, bastard-shits?' Charlzberg shouted. 'See what I unleash when you disobey me?'

'Pull.'

'Such wicked fury to behold, Admiral,' Spyde said from above. 'But moving on—'

'Care, Spyde.' Charlzberg glared up from beneath his ridiculous dwarven hat at his navigator. 'Take care now. I have more left in me. I hardly tire, you know?'

'Pull.'

Nodding, with a vacant expression, Spyde cleared his throat and went on. 'Apologies, Admiral, but we're coming close to dock. The port's pilot is approaching, with troops aboard. Should we not run up the whites?'

Charlzberg, foot planted on Bosun still, licked his cold-sore infested lips and nodded. Without a word, he removed his foot from the man saying 'pull' and made for the twins at the tiller.

'Up with the whites,' Spyde shouted, and two goblin sailors attended to it.

'Yes, on with it,' Charlzberg ordered, once the white flags were already hoisted. 'And you two piss puddles, guide her in nice this time, eh?'

The twins froze as Charlzberg turned to them, suspicion in his eyes. They'd both muttered nasties, but neither thought he'd heard them.

'Pull.'

Turning back to face the prow and the incoming pilot, Charlzberg continued his ridiculousness. 'Take her in nice, Ptarmigans, as I said. Not like last time we were here.'

Neither twin dared explain that the pilot was inbound to come aboard and guide the galley in himself, as it had been last time, and the time before, and… They said nothing. Not through fear of Charlzberg's pathetic wrath, Tull knew, but through fear he'd talk some more and hang about on deck for the affair. Thankfully though, as soon as they acknowledged him Charlzberg returned to his awning and scurried beneath it, leaving the rest to his capable crew.

As Bosun climbed to his feet and straightened himself out, Charlzberg's head popped out once more. 'Don't forget to inform the rest of the fleet to prepare to make port.'

'Aye aye, Admiral,' Spyde called down. 'Tull! Do us the honours, would you?'

Tull nodded, swung about on his rope and spoke to the towed longboat behind.

'Eh up lads,' Tull said. 'The pilot's inbound.'

The longboat's trio of a crew looked up to Tull from their game of bones and nodded. 'Understood,' the closest of the three goblins said, before looking back to the game.

'Fleet's informed,' Tull shouted back to Spyde.

'Good, now wriggle some more, Tull. The hobyahs are slowing and Bosun ain't calling.'

Bosun jumped at the realisation he'd stopped, to look at the titanic set of scales rearing up out of the sea opposite the mountainside city they approached. The tips of those scales scraped the clouds above. Bosun couldn't quite believe the enormity of the structure, that much was clear from his gaping mouth.

Turning back to the rows of beastly hobyahs falling out of rhythm, Bosun said what he was paid handsomely by Charlzberg to say, 'pull', and the war galley glided on.

Chapter 22 – The bells, the bells

Spyde felt unsteady on the solid quayside. The stone underfoot hurt his feet, his ankles and his knees. If he'd thought about it and stopped himself before making the stupid offer to hunt for food, he would've been able to stay in his web of a sail. But as it stood, Charlzberg had used Spyde's offer to order him off the galley as a companion, rather than a hunter.

'I want something on the galley's prow,' Charlzberg said in his ever-whiny tone.

Spyde rolled his eyes and glanced to the gaudily dressed goblin beside him.

'Such as what, Admiral?' Spyde asked, eyes back to the bustling square they set off towards.

Charlzberg flung his arms wide. 'For Squall's sake, Spyde, I don't know? I can't be expected to think of everything.'

Spyde nodded a quick apology as Charlzberg pushed past a couple of brutish sailors.

'Like the Northfolk's longships have, perhaps?' Spyde offered before Charlzberg could comment on the nodded apology Spyde had offered the affronted sailors. 'Dragons and such?'

Charlzberg puckered his lumpy lips in thought. 'No, a woman. I want a carved woman on the prow. A mermaid or some such beauty.'

Spyde frowned. 'And how are we to pay for such an item?'

A high-pitched whine started in Charlzberg's throat. Spyde acted quickly.

'It wouldn't survive our next ramming action anyway, Admiral.' Spyde sped forward and rounded on Charlzberg, hands held up placatingly as the whine built in volume and pitch. 'It'd be such a waste, is all I'm saying. Such a glorious addition to your flagship, to have it destroyed when you next wreck your enemies upon our ram. Eh?'

Charlzberg's face was thunderous. His beady eyes narrowed and his flat teeth gnashed. Through those grinding teeth, he managed, 'I. Want. One.'

Spyde's shoulders sagged and his hands dropped by his sides. He nodded. 'I'll make it happen, Admiral. One way or another, I'll make it happen.'

Without a word, Charlzberg pushed past Spyde, teeth bared in glee. Turning to follow, Spyde cringed as he saw Charlzberg's new focus.

'Mannino,' Spyde whispered, before hurrying after Charlzberg. 'Captain? Captain!'

Could this be any more embarrassing, Spyde thought as he caught Charlzberg, who was fast approaching the renowned *Sessio's* captain and, by the looks of it, the equally infamous Master Hitchmogh, Mannino's first mate. Spyde allowed himself a smirk as he saw Mannino's head sag before he composed himself.

'Ah, Captain Charlzberg, how lovely to see you once again,' Mannino managed, although he was clearly in a hurry. His grizzled first mate snarled by his side.

Spyde tensed, ready for the inevitable tantrum that was bound to follow the incorrect title. It never came.

'Actually, Captain Mannino,' Charlzberg said, stopping uncomfortably close to Mannino and beaming all the while, 'it's admiral now, but you weren't to know that, friend.'

Friend? Spyde wanted to melt back into the shifting crowd.

Mannino's nostrils flared, but he offered a tight smile. Hitchmogh's snarl turned to a barely contained smirk.

'I won't go into the details of how I gained such a lofty title, Captain,' Charlzberg went on, 'but suffice to say, I now command my own fleet.'

Mannino bowed. 'My congratulations to you, Admiral Charlzberg. I trust you did not kill anyone we know to gain said fleet?' There was a sparkle in Mannino's eye, to which Charlzberg released an incredibly loud laugh. He looked to Spyde, frowned, and Spyde followed suit. Mannino's mirth was short lived as the two goblins before him continued on with their attention drawing laughter.

Once the awkwardness had passed and the stares had found new curiosities, Charlzberg asked of Mannino a question Spyde thought even his dim-witted commander wouldn't have the nerve to ask.

Mannino rocked back. Hitchmogh's slack jaw was less subtle.

'You want me to join your fleet, Admiral?' Mannino asked incredulously.

Spyde swallowed hard, eyes locked on Master Hitchmogh, who was now fingering his cutlass' hilt.

Charlzberg nodded eagerly, leaning forward in anticipation.

'I see,' Mannino said, looking to Hitchmogh for support. Hitchmogh caught Mannino's pleading look, turned and disappeared into the crowd. It was Mannino's turn to drop his shoulders.

'Alas, Admiral Charlzberg,' Mannino said, back straightening with conviction, 'it is with incredible regret that I must decline... for now!' he added, as Charlzberg's smile fell into a frown, and on into a scowl.

'Perhaps it's time to look for that bow decoration, Admiral?' Spyde offered, hoping to draw Charlzberg away from a situation that his temper would turn sour, deadly even. Spyde knew Captain Mannino's reputation. He was a fair man, but a brutal one should you cross or make a move on him or his crew. "Brisance is a safer place without Mannino as a pirate" was a common saying.

'I shall hope to continue this conversation another time, Admiral,' Mannino said, bowing low. 'I wish not to keep such a busy commander as you any longer. I am, indeed, humbled you sought me out.'

Teeth grinding yet again, Charlzberg did nothing but stare at Mannino, who looked to Spyde, nodded, accepted Spyde's apologetic nod in return and departed into the crowd.

'Spyde.'

'Admiral?'

'A real woman.'

A group of filthy children pushed past Charlzberg, practically knocking him to the floor.

Real woman? Spyde thought, sidestepping the children's mad dash away from the shrieking goblin, who drew a knife and waved it at the backs of the disappearing youngsters. Noticing Spyde's lack of support, Charlzberg drew a second blade, incredibly slowly.

Spyde caught on in time, managing to move himself so his throat was in a good position for the closing weapon. Once the dull iron pressed against the sickly green skin of Spyde's throat, he feigned fear.

'No, Admiral, please! I didn't see the ruffians coming—'

'Silence! I could gut you here and now, Spyde.'

Not unless you moved your blade to my stomach you couldn't, or raised the one in your other hand, you shitting fool. 'Of course, Admiral. That's why my pantaloons are close to dampening.'

Charlzberg smiled at that and nodded, before pulling away. 'And don't forget it. You're here as a bodyguard, Spyde, but I won't hesitate to gut you should you allow me to be killed or taken.'

Any more of this and I might gut myself. 'Of course, Admiral. Can I ask—?'

Charlzberg jerked forward, both blades jabbing towards Spyde in a mock attack. Spyde offered his best attempt at a fearful cower, before continuing. 'Can I ask, why you didn't have Bosun or any of the other crew along as escort?'

Charlzberg replaced his blades and made off into the crowd once more, Spyde hot on Charlzberg's high heels.

'They're hunting food, which we talked about. You're no good for that, but I trust you in the guarding of my body.'

Spyde groaned. Charlzberg spun on him.

'There's nothing wrong with my body is there? Or the food my hunters provide?'

'No, Admiral, to both, but we did well with our last haul of loot. Why not... buy some food?' Spyde immediately regretting informing Charlzberg of their good haul. He'd have had no idea, as usual, but now... well now he might spend it on rot they didn't need. *Like a prow decoration.* 'Some lovely ham or chicken?'

Charlzberg barked his laugh before turning and continuing onward, his voice hard to hear over the harbour din.

'I know gulls, rats and cats are fine, Admiral, but the hobyahs need a good feed to keep up the pace Bosun asks of them. And Bosun himself?'

'What of it?' Charlzberg said, over his shoulder.

'He's... well... he's human, not goblinkin. He needs other foods.'

'Bosun joined my fleet knowing he was alone in his race, Spyde. If he wants to eat dandelion roots and nettle soup he should have joined a merchant cog, not a glorious galley.'

A small lapdog ran past, yapping. Spyde was sure Charlzberg squeaked, and he certainly attempted a leap into Spyde's arms before composing himself and striding on.

Spyde decided it was time to change the subject. 'Where're we heading, may I ask?'

'To spend, Spyde. We're off to spend all the money you tell me I've earned. All the lovely money I have in my pouch.'

'Lords below, keep your voice down,' Spyde said, directly into Charlzberg's torn, scabby ear. It was a wonder Charlzberg didn't turn on Spyde for that. Perhaps sense prevailed for once, Spyde mused, then it dawned on him that Charlzberg already knew of the money, to have such a pouch on him.

'Hush,' Charlzberg hissed, long after Spyde had last spoken. He held up a hand and stopped abruptly, causing two women walking behind to curse through their evasion of the halting goblins.

'Admiral?'

'We're here, Spyde.'

128

They looked up, following the white walls of the tall building before them. Up to the blue tiles of the pitched roof above. And below that again, to a sign.

Squall take me now, Spyde thought, before Charlzberg dragged him through the doors.

***

Despite the high sun, the alley was dark. And despite the noise of the street, be it people chatting and shouting, dogs barking or gulls sounding their incessant calls, the alley seemed quiet, tranquil even. No wind blew between the dirt encrusted white buildings either side. No wind to remove the wretched stench.

'Do you see it?' the Ptarmigan twins asked as one. Bosun hushed them as he crawled deeper into a nook in the alleyway. The twins offered rude gestures to the back of their human shipmate, but said no more. They looked back down the alley, to the cloud breaking scales rising from the bay beyond the bustling quayside, the twin land masses either side of the structure currently equibalanced.

A hiss within the nook was followed by a screech and a tirade of curses and grunts.

'Got it,' Bosun said. He shuffled backwards, out into the open where the siblings readied their heavy sack. Appearing fully, Bosun revealed the tabby cat he'd grabbed, fought and strangled. His thick arms were a mess of raised scratches and small puncture wounds. He spat as he threw the dead cat into the sack.

'Next,' Sister said, much to Bosun's obvious dismay. She and her brother marched off up the alley, whistling and clicking tongues to attract their prey.

''Morl's reeking corpse,' Bosun muttered, following the twins. 'If I have to eat another shitting cat...'

The twins jumped with glee. A cat strode out and purred. Bosun sighed, pounced. The next battle ensued.

After claw, tooth and hands were used to the best of both fighters' abilities, the ginger tom lay dead in Bosun's bleeding arms. He threw it into the offered sack. The twins frowned as they watched it flop atop the others.

'That was a big bastard,' Bosun said, scowling. 'A big, hard bastard. I liked him. Shame he had to die.'

'Shame he were ginger,' Brother said. His sister nodded.

'Fuck!' Bosun stomped up the alley, twins in tow. 'I forgot the pissin' admiral don't like gingers on ship. What a waste.'

'A waste?' the twins asked as one, close on Bosun's heels.

'Aye. Of time, effort and of the cat's bloody life.' He stopped short as he pushed out into the crowd and looked up and out to the scales.

'You've never seen them before, have you?' Sister asked. The twins knew Bosun didn't know which twin had asked the question, since they sounded so similar; Bosun merely shrugged and shook his head.

'Where'd you join us again?' they asked together.

'Wesson,' Bosun said, eyes flicking between the land masses suspended above the waves.

The twins looked to one another, then to Bosun. 'Wesson?'

Bosun nodded, but his eyes remained on the amphitheatre-towns.

Brother scratched his arse as he said, 'Oh, I thought you joined us on the Chriselle Coast?'

'Eh?' Bosun looked round and down to the twins, who were straining to hold the sack of cats between them. 'Put that down, you fools.' They did as they were told. 'I'm Altolnan by birth, from Wesson. But aye, you're right, I joined you on that coast, after a stint on another vessel out of Royce.'

Sister pursed her lips as her brother shrugged and replied. 'Fair one, although we would've thought you'd been here before, if you'd sailed out of Royce and about the Chriselle Coast?'

'Well, obviously not,' Bosun said, eye twitching. He paused a long while, eyes on the people moving to and fro. Without turning, he asked, 'You two ever heard of a ship called *Sessio*?'

Both twins laughed.

Bosun glared at them and they stopped.

'Everyone who sails has heard of her,' Brother said, his sister nodding. Bosun nodded too, as if he'd remembered the fact.

'Why?'

Bosun shrugged, eyes scanning the colourful crowd. 'No reason. Now come on, we need to get the food back to the ship. You two can't carry anymore.'

Nope, Sister thought, *and you ain't offering to carry it for us neither.* Her brother looked at her knowingly.

Bosun hesitated before setting off. 'Might as well dump that ginger tom before we go.'

Both twins shook their heads. Bosun's lined brow creased all the more.

'We's know how to fix it so it'll seem like Charlzberg's favourite dish,' they said together.

'He favours black cats though,' Bosun said, 'and they're rare.'

The twins grinned before Sister spoke. 'He does, yes. Now let's head back, like you say, Bosun. You'll see how we'll fix it up and you'll have to stifle a laugh when Charlzberg *mmms* and *awws* whilst eating it. Ha!' She winked at Bosun and set off, sack forgotten. Brother cursed as he realised what she'd done and Bosun cursed all the more as he scooped both goblin and sack up to catch the swiftly departing twin.

Rested on the gunwale, Bosun looked across the bay to the immense scales.

'I saw it move!' he said, turning to the Ptarmigan twins, who were sorting through their recent catch.

'Well of course ye did,' Sister said. She held up a tortoiseshell cat, wincing at the hint of ginger in its fur. Bosun looked back to the scales as Sister continued. 'It's often moving. One town rising, the other falling towards the waves. One becomes Upper Slaughter, the other Lower Slaughter.'

Brother nodded as he smeared black tar over the tortoiseshell handed to him. Ginger fur covered, he smiled and threw it on the pile.

'I know how it works,' Bosun said, 'just never thought you'd be able to see it; thought it'd be gradual, like the moving of the sun or moon.'

'That it is,' Sister agreed, 'but once in a while ye see a sudden drop and rise.'

'Be glad ye're not on either of 'em, Bosun.'

'Oh, I am, Brother, I am…' After a brief pause punctuated by the shouts of sailors and traders, Bosun asked another question. 'So, what if one of the towns drops suddenly? What if Lower Slaughter plunges into the bay?' He leaned forward, squinting, hoping to see it move again.

Sister passed her brother another cat from the sack before answering. 'Well, that's what they battle to avoid, isn't it? If one of those towns hit, they'll all drown; sacrifices and murderers be damned.'

'Yet they always seem fairly equal,' Brother said, before sniffing at a large tabby. His sister nodded at that.

'It's ironic,' Bosun said, rubbing the back of his head.

'How's that?' Sister asked, rummaging in the sack without looking.

Bosun weighed his large hands like the scales before them, dropping one and lifting the other.

'Should one drop,' he explained, 'the resulting wave would wipe out this port. The whole bloody island, perhaps.'

The twins nodded. 'And the other two islands with it, I'd expect,' Sister agreed.

'What's your point, Bosun?' Brother licked the tabby cat and grinned. 'I like tabbies.'

'My point, my shitty little friends, is that The Three created those scales, those suspended amphitheatre-towns, yet should one of them fall, should the residents fail to fight or sacrifice or do whatever sick things they need do to keep their heads and homes above water, that lump of rock will plummet into the sea. The wave following that...' Bosun filled his cheeks, held the breath and released it as he looked down to the clear waters lapping at the galley. 'Well,' he said, as a strong smell of fish struck him, 'The Three's seat of power would be no better off than the town that fell.'

The twins stopped handling dead cats long enough to look at Bosun, sniggering all the while.

Bosun turned to face them. 'What?'

Brother shook his head and took the next cat from his sister.

'That's not irony, Bosun,' Sister said, looking at the big man, 'that's the bloody point!'

Bosun screwed up his flat nose. 'What's the point?'

'It's why The Three created it. Do you not see?' Sister went on.

'Obviously not.'

Sister hurried since Bosun's words were followed by the bunching of his jaw.

'They're eternally bored,' she said, matter-of-factly. 'Immensely and completely bored—'

'Of what?'

'Life, Bosun. Life! They've been bored for centuries. They created the scales for their own entertainment. It's a game. To them, anyway.'

Bosun shook his head and looked back out to the scales. Sister continued.

'They love the fear of it. The fact that should they get it wrong, their whole empire will flood as they look on from their lofty towers.'

Bosun turned and looked upon the dark, cliff-top tower looming over the white port. He looked back to the twins. 'It's not up to them though, is it?' Bosun looked back to the scales. 'It's up to the poor folk who live, or are sent to, the Slaughters.'

'Nope.'

Bosun glanced to the stern. 'Who asked you, Tull?'

'No one, but doesn't mean I don't know the truth of it, Bosun. The Three move their pieces. They choose who they send and they influence what happens. One acts as advocate while two play it off against each other. Blood God's bell-end, Bosun, I thought this shit was common knowledge, amongst sea goers at least.'

A grunt was the only reply from the big man.

'Anyhow,' Brother said, bringing the conversation to an end. 'We best crack on with these cats before Charlzberg returns. He'll go spare if he sees the ginger tom you ended.'

'Speak of the shitter.' Sister pulled the cat from the sack. 'How'd they shift so much in there? T'was last in, near on last out? Anyhow, we need to prepare it for Cooker.'

Bosun barked a laugh. 'Cooker?' he said, shaking his head. 'Cooker boils shit to rubber and that's about it. He doesn't do much at all as far as I see it, lazy twat.'

'Cooker's a good goblin. Don't you talk bad of him, Bosun,' Tull said, rotating on his rope.

'Whatever you say, now let's see how you prepare a ginger cat so as not to look ginger. Skin it?' Bosun turned and crouched by the twins, both of whom grinned. He'd been too enthralled by the sky-scraping scales to truly take in their fixing of the tortoiseshell moggy, despite seeing them at it.

'Tar it,' they said as one.

'Eh?'

'Tar is black,' Sister said. 'Tar the cat and Charlzberg thinks it's his favourite.'

'Black cat,' Bosun whispered, face screwed up. He looked to the tar beside the twins.

'Aye,' Brother said. 'Black cat.'

'How'd he... stomach it?' Bosun felt physically sick. 'How'd he *survive* it?'

Brother laughed. 'Ever heard the saying—'

'Constitution of a goblin,' Bosun finished. The twins smiled and nodded.

Bosun turned as Cooker waddled up the galley, laughing at the conversation. 'Bosun,' he greeted. 'Wanna know a secret?'

Sighing, Bosun nodded. 'Go on, Cooker, you fat bastard.'

'Charlzberg's never seen a black cat!' The paunch-proud goblin crouched down with the others and prodded at the pile of cats. Brother begun painting the ginger tom black with thick tar.

'How's it his favourite then?'

Cooker laughed again, followed by the twins and Tull.

'He seems to like tar,' Cooker admitted, chuckling at the slack jawed Bosun, before taking an armful of limp cats, standing with a pained grunt and moving back down the galley, several hobyahs hungrily tracking his slow progress.

Dropping back against the side of the ship, Bosun rubbed hard at his face. 'I need to get off this damned galley before my mind is addled like the rest of you lot.'

The twins grinned as they continued to prepare their future meals, the groan of Bosun and the distant whistling of Cooker accompanying their work.

***

Spyde gazed up at the oak beams and various sizes, shapes and coloured bells hanging there. He marvelled at the designs, never imagining bells could come in such variety. The war galley had a small bell, but nothing like these, although there were plenty lining the walls akin to the one on the ship. The bells Spyde studied above were huge. He swore there was one as large as the weaver chamber he grew up in, larger even. His thoughts were broken by a clawed jab to the ribs.

'Pay attention,' Charlzberg said. A willowy figure of a woman glided down the centre of the bell foundry, all smiles and waves. Charlzberg returned the smiles tenfold.

'My dear, my dear,' Charlzberg said, moving to take the woman's hand. 'You grace us with your presence.'

'It is you, Admiral, that graces me,' she said, bowing and kissing the stained wig Charlzberg revealed by removing his ridiculous hat.

'It's been too long,' Charlzberg said, whilst the woman guided him to a desk supported by two silvery bells. Spyde followed a pace behind.

'What can I do for you, Admiral?' the woman purred. Spyde cringed.

'My fleet is at a stage where we require a second cannon,' Charlzberg announced, much to the surprise of Spyde, who gaped at the words.

And where will it go? Spyde thought, eyes flicking between the human and goblin before him. *And why? We've never fired the first one, for Squall's sake.*

The woman's nose twitched as she sat back in the lavish chair she'd dropped into.

Charlzberg took the seat opposite.

'And here I was, Admiral, thinking you were here to finish paying for the first one?' she said, lips retreating to a thin line after the words.

A pouch of coins landed heavily on the desk before her. The thin line on her face curled up at one side, her nose twitching once again.

'Excellent,' she said, and the purse was gone before the two goblins saw her move.

'It's all there,' Charlzberg ensured, 'plus more, as a down payment for the second cannon.'

'I am sure it is.' The woman leaned forward. 'And again, I am pleased you came to us and not the island's new cannon foundry. Too many people forget us after the creation of that place.'

'Of course,' Charlzberg agreed, coming forward to meet the woman's hands at the centre of the desk, standing on the chair to do so. 'But I remember. I remember when you created them before the market demanded it and before they were tried and trusted by humans and the like,' he went on. 'Before the dwarves muscled in with their ancient plans and wares.'

She smiled, nose twitching repeatedly, evidence of the tension regarding the latter.

They're not tried and trusted though, are they? Spyde thought, exasperated. *We've not yet tested our first and there are hardly any others on the seas. The Three may line their tower walls with them, and a small number of their personal ships, but other than that, who uses them apart from the seldom-seen dwarves? Altoln and Sirreta certainly don't, nor does Eatri or Orismar. We don't yet know the risks of these explosive horizontal bells we're to drag about behind us. At least the dwarves have made and used them for centuries. The only consolation is that this foundry uses dwarven plans, likely stolen, as far as I've heard.*

'Would it be the same cannon as before, that you desire?' the woman asked, squeezing the admiral's hands. Charlzberg hesitated at that, chewed his bottom lip.

'The cost?' she asked, nose twitching again. He nodded. 'Do not worry, Admiral, I think I have something that might interest you. And if you like it, I am confident you will be back for more. It is, perhaps, more suited to the ship you command...'

Charlzberg's face darkened. 'Ships. I command ships.'

'Of course you do, Admiral, but your flagship, the galley... well, the cannon I talk of will suit it much better than a replication of your first purchase.'

Charlzberg was nodding before she finished.

'Tell me of it?' He leaned in all the more, rising to the tips of his boots.

Spyde actually liked what she went on to describe, not to mention the affordability of it.

That was, until Charlzberg ordered two.

Chapter 23 – Compact fists

Skirting around the crowd, for fear of being trampled, Spyde led Charlzberg on a roundabout route back to the ship; the route avoided where Spyde knew the children to be, children who'd barged into Charlzberg hours before.

'Why don't I go and hunt next time, Admiral?' Spyde offered for the umpteenth time, whilst looking over his shoulder. 'It'd free Bosun up, you know, to be your bodyguard.'

'Ha!' Charlzberg scratched under his hat and wig, flat teeth bared in what could only be described as amusement.

'What?' Spyde said, a little too quickly. 'Was it something I said, Admiral?'

A ginger cat walked out into the road, sat, and proceeded to clean between its legs. Charlzberg hissed and changed direction. Spyde followed, doing his best to overtake the overly dressed goblin before they ended up in the wrong part of town.

All we need now is to run into Hillside gangers, Spyde thought, a shiver running through him.

'You don't have the skills to hunt, Spyde, we've been through this before.'

Green brow creased. 'I catch half the food whilst at sea?'

'Yes, in your web, but that's different. Where would you, would we, be if I hadn't constructed that web for you, eh?'

Pretty sure I made the net, after you insisted I did so and decided the sail was of no use. 'Of course, Admiral. We'd all be dead in the water for sure.'

'Well then.' Charlzberg grinned all the more and headed off again in a random direction, Spyde following. 'It takes a certain kind of hunter to track and kill our prey, Spyde.'

Cats? You mean enticing them with the offer of a scratch behind the ear before wringing their necks? 'I suppose it does, Admiral, aye.'

Charlzberg halted and Spyde collided with him. 'Where are we?' he said, looking up the white walls either side, to the blue tiles above. 'It all looks the same.'

Spyde silently agreed and looked for a landmark. 'I don't recognise where we've ended up.'

'My point exactly, Spyde...' Charlzberg's voice trailed off into the low keening that Spyde knew would build into a full-blown tantrum.

Squall drown me... 'You led us down here, Admiral,' Spyde dared point out. The keening grew. 'But as your navigator, I'm sure I can retrace our steps and get us back to the galley before dark.' The keening dropped away.

'Lead on,' Charlzberg ordered, removing his hat, turning it and placing it back on the right way around. 'I knew I shouldn't have followed this hat's northern peak, never leads me right. If I saw the swindler who sold me this, I'd beat him with my knife.'

Spyde set off with Charlzberg close behind.

'You're not mistaking the hat for a compass are you, Admiral?'

A pause.

'Admiral?' Spyde said, turning about. He groaned and rubbed at his face when he saw what Charlzberg was doing; the hat sank rather than span in the barrel of water at the side of the street.

The tantrum that followed was of a scale Spyde had never before witnessed.

Amazed they made it through the night, whilst hunkered down beneath a cart, Spyde breathed a sigh of relief as he saw the netted mast of the war galley ahead. Gulls laughing all about them, Spyde turned to see Charlzberg waving his cutlass at the birds, hissing and spitting all the while.

'They mock us, Spyde!' Charlzberg shrieked, jumping in the fresh morning air in an impossible attempt to slash a flying herring gull. The large bird looked down at the ridiculous sight and laughed all the more; the resulting splatter sent a white-faced Charlzberg into yet another screeching tantrum. Iron clattered across cobbles and Charlzberg dropped to the floor, folded his arms and legs and panted through his rage.

Somebody slay me, Spyde thought, picking up the cutlass before walking to Charlzberg and sitting down beside him. He sheathed the weapon at Charlzberg's side, pulled out a rotten rag and wiped the bird muck from Charlzberg's face, like a mother would a child.

'The ship's only over there, Admiral. Shall we not move on?'

'I want a flintlock pistol. Like the dwarves have. I could shoot the squawking shits. Bam! Bam! Bam bam bam! They'd be feathers and fluff which is all good stuff.'

'Not sure you'd lift one,' Spyde said before realising it. Charlzberg spun on him.

'And why not?' Charlzberg unfolded his arms and kissed his sleeved biceps, despite their unimpressive girth.

'Oh, pistol?' Spyde widened his eyes in mock surprise. 'Apologies, Admiral, I thought you meant a dwarven musket. Of course you'd lift a pistol.'

Charlzberg frowned and leaned in, uncomfortably close. 'What's a musket?'

I slipped up there, Spyde thought before answering.

'It's like a pistol, apparently, only longer, like a windlass crossbow or some such dwarven thing. I've never actually seen one, truth be told.'

Black eyes widened.

Oh shit, what have I done…?

'I want one,' Charlzberg said, brown teeth bared in a wide smile.

'I'm not sure—'

'I want one and if I don't get one I'm going to raze this island to the ground!'

Can you raze an island to the ground… when it is *the ground?* Spyde prodded his cracked lips as he thought about it.

'I'm pretty sure, Admiral,' he said eventually, 'that The Three will have something to say about you destroying their island.' *Hopefully that will put you off whatever ridiculous idea you're poorly plotting.*

'The Three with The Three!'

Spyde screwed his face up at that. *Eh?* he thought, before shaking his head and resigning himself to the fact that it was Charlzberg he was talking to and little would make sense.

'I want what I want, Spyde, and the whole of Brisance won't stop me from gaining my trophies!'

Spyde pressed his face into his grubby hands and sighed hard, despite the likely consequences. *Trophies? What the gods is he on about now?* 'Absolutely, Admiral,' Spyde said through his hands. Gulls laughed, but no response came from Charlzberg. Looking through widening fingers, Spyde saw nothing but cobbles besides him. 'Admiral?'

'Come, Spyde, we haven't all day,' Charlzberg said from a way off. Spyde looked up and saw the gaudily dressed goblin approach a group of children, all pointing and laughing at the ridiculous sight.

'Why do I bother,' Spyde muttered. He spat on the ground, climbed to his feet and ran for the group of laughing kids, who'd created a circle around Charlzberg; something within the circle started to yap like a lapdog.

Here we go again… 'Admiral, no!' *They're too much for you, you fool.*

The yapping transformed into a keening screech before Spyde could reach the group.

Compact fists came in hard and fast, connecting painfully with skin covered bone and linen covered flesh. Feet followed, both leather shod and bare, the former leaving lasting throbs that caused the victim to suck in one lungful of salt tinged air after another.

A familiar voice shouted and cursed, drawing closer at first, before fading in a different direction. Other sounds filled the void the retreating voice left. It all came so vividly, as did the ear-rushing thump of his pulse; cart wheels on cobbles, a mule laughing, gulls laughing… children laughing. Every bastard was laughing.

Charlzberg screeched, again, before gnashing his teeth; several left his mouth for good in a numbing blow that came from one of the leather shod feet.

Wrapping aching arms around his bald head, he rolled around, trying to avoid the blows that continued to fall upon his pain wracked head, face and body. He tried to block out the sound of laughter, the flashes of his own wig and hat upon children's heads – a hat he'd had to dunk Spyde to retrieve the night before. His tongue found new holes, poked at them as the tangy taste of blood assaulted the slug-like muscle. Another thump, to the back of the head, and one of the new sharp edges in Charlzberg's mouth sliced through his dehydrated tongue. Fresh blood. Fresh pain. A full-on scream that the attacking children surely envied.

More screams and shouts followed, but not from Charlzberg. Children's screams and nearby adults' outrage. Curses and grunts, barks of anger and yelps of pain. Leather and skin on cobbles, scuffing, shuffling and scuffling away from Charlzberg's sensitive, torn ears.

The flickering light between his clawless fingers darkened to near black. Those fingers parted, tentatively, revealing a hard-faced man staring back.

Charlzberg kicked his painful legs and propelled himself backwards across the cobbles, his stone scraping heels bereft of the boots he'd thought he still wore.

Blood left cracked green lips and spattered the cobbles to Charlzberg's side, decorating the grey with a red that verged on black. Looking up to the broad-chested man stood over him, Charlzberg bared broken teeth and hissed, before holding out a bloody hand so the man could pull him to his grazed feet.

I thought I was to die, Charlzberg thought, jumping despite himself as a gull laughed from overhead. His vision spun as he looked about the quayside, at the faces staring back; some angry, most amused.

Charlzberg hissed some more, spat blood and phlegm some more and stomped towards his ship, Bosun in tow. The stomping turned to a tender walk and a barked decline of offered help.

I am an Admiral. I can walk on my shitting own. I am not a kid and I am not a kid's toy, any bloody more!

Men and women parted as Bosun snarled at the lot. Even a couple of indentured goblins sniggered and moved at the last minute as the balled, bruised and largely naked admiral walked past them. His eyes lowered now, his gaze fixed on the shifting pattern of stones underfoot. Humans and gulls laughing at him was one thing, but his own kind?

I suffered enough at the hands of bastard men and boys to know their like, to know their strengths and tortures. But my own kind? My own bastard kind are no better than me. Less than me, all of them, for they weren't raised in the noble houses of men, in the keep of a lord...

'I bloody was!' Charlzberg shouted, turning on the chained goblins, now behind him. His fists were clenched so tight his claws would have dug into his palms had they not been removed by his former master's farrier.

'Come on, Admiral,' Bosun said, encouraging Charlzberg to move on. 'They're not worth it.'

Head back down, largely to hide the glistening of his black eyes, Charlzberg linked the fingers of his hands behind his neck, pulled his skinless elbows together in front of him and stomped once more, ignoring, for the first time in his awful life, the pain that came with it.

I am a sailor now, a commander, an Admiral of a bloody fleet. I lead goblins, hobyahs and men. Men! I am fearsome; no longer a child's pet; no longer a noble boy's toy. I will take no more...

Walking up the gangplank to his flagship, Charlzberg noticed the lack of eye contact he received from his crew. Even the hobyahs looked anywhere but, which was saying something, since they usually gazed at him hungrily. Stopping to look about *his* ship, Charlzberg's head raised, as did his pride.

My ship, he thought. *My fleet and my crew.*

Pain forgotten for the moment, he bared his broken teeth once more. He dropped his arms to his sides and he turned to look back at the men and women and children of the quayside, all of whom were back to their tasks and chores.

'The gulls can laugh,' he said, quietly. 'That damned mule, too. I care not now. I know what I want. I know what I need and I know who I need to emulate to do it.'

Bosun pulled up the gangplank, stowed it away and stood beside the bleeding goblin.

'Orders, Admiral?' he said, looking down on the sorry state.

'Mannino.' Charlzberg's single whispered word was lost on all but Bosun, before he crossed to and crawled under his awning.

'What did he say?' Spyde asked, coming over from the main mast where he'd been hiding.

'Didn't hear him,' Bosun surely lied.

'Looked like you did,' Spyde stared up at the man, 'judging by the look that flashed across your flat face.'

Bosun grunted at that and ruffled the black cap on Spyde's head, much to Spyde's annoyance.

Turning to walk away, Bosun mumbled something under his breath, something that made him smile, briefly; something Spyde could have sworn sounded like the name of a renowned captain he and Charlzberg had seen only yesterday.

Chapter 24 – Special Delivery

'Where's Bosun?' Spyde asked from the centre of his web, high above the deck of the galley.

The Ptarmigan twins shrugged and continued to roll their dice.

'I saw him leave in the night,' Tull said. 'He was wearing his hood.'

Spyde frowned and picked his left ear. 'What hood?'

'The black one,' Tull said, the early morning breeze catching him and turning him on the rope. 'A thin thing. Don't see the point of it really. Ain't gonna keep the night's chill off his ears. He were wearing a cloak, too.'

Spyde pursed his lips and looked out onto the quayside. The first of the traders were setting up stalls, the last of the sailors returning, staggering or swaying to their ships.

'Where'd he go?' Spyde asked, eyes on the dull, pre-dawn scene before him.

'He didn't say,' Tull said. 'And I didn't ask.'

'Fat lot of use you are.'

'How about I quit wriggling when needed and we'll see how quickly the hobyahs break chains and climb that net of yours for a snack, eh?'

Spyde looked to the oar benches below. Several hungry eyes looked back up.

'I'd feel better if Bosun were back on board,' Spyde admitted. *He was quiet all day yesterday, after the incident with the children. There's something up with him, I know that much, and I'd rather him here where I can keep an eye on him.*

It wasn't long until Spyde's wish came true and Bosun was back, and bleeding on the deck.

'Where were you last night? The admiral's been asking?' Spyde flinched as Bosun bared his teeth. His bloodied hands and grazed chin added to the intimidating aura he gave off as he stomped up deck, throwing his black hood and cloak off to the side. A hobyah growled as the thinly-woven woollen garments covered its head. Mere heartbeats later and that side of the ship was in uproar, with hobyahs howling and snarling and the cloak in tatters.

'Wasn't it past the admiral's bed time?' was all Bosun said, as he dropped down the hatch into his makeshift quarters.

Spyde glanced back from his web to Tull, who shrugged and turned slowly in the wind, squinting against the rising sun every time he came around to the East.

'Don't involve us, neither.'

Spyde looked to the Ptarmigan twins, unsure which had spoken, and saw them busying themselves with calming the now screeching hobyahs by throwing them pieces of rat and cat.

'Bosun's hurt, and somebody best take note other than me,' Spyde said, for all to hear. He closed his eyes and groaned when the one goblin he didn't want involved answered, from beneath his awning.

'Don't think I don't hear you, Spyde!'

'Then come out and fucking deal with it,' Spyde whispered. 'Oh, I am aware, Admiral. Hence my loudness. I wished for you to be present for this.' *What in the depths am I saying?*

A battered face appeared, followed by a half-naked, trembling body that turned Spyde's stomach, which was saying something considering his goblin constitution.

'You're... erm... not dressed, Admiral?' Spyde held his breath.

Charlzberg stood straight at that, clenched fists on hips. 'I shall walk naked if I choose. Real naked. This is my flagship, Spyde, you shit of a woman's bollocks!'

What does that even mean?

'Now,' Charlzberg went on, 'where is he? Where's the traitor?' He looked up and down the ship, although Spyde knew full well Charlzberg knew where Bosun was. It was the only place he could be when not on deck.

'Traitor!?' The human shout caused even the hobyahs to duck and cower. Spyde climbed higher in his web and the Ptarmigan twins climbed over the side of the ship and clung to the smallest of handholds, but it was better than being present for what was to come.

'Oh shit.' Tull wriggled, trying to turn himself away from the deck and towards the second ship of the fleet: the cannon bearer.

'How dare you,' Charlzberg said, facing the wrong way. 'Stand before me when I'm disciplining you for desertion, Bosun.'

'I've fucking had it with your shit, goblin.' Bosun climbed from the hatch, top off, unlike Charlzberg's half of nakedness, revealing blackening bruises to his ribs and multiple abrasive patches very recently clotted.

Charlzberg stood still. His only movement was to fold his arms. 'I shan't punish a man I can't see, Bosun. You must present yourself to me, not the other way... Ooh!'

Charlzberg raced to the plank before finishing his sentence, his tackle jiggling and his feet slapping the wooden deck. The hobyahs rolled with laughter at the sight. The goblins hid. Bosun followed the admiral, knuckles white.

A troop of men carted two crates precariously up the ramp onto the war galley, where Charlzberg was jumping with joy, his wounds and recent beating by children forgotten.

'My cannons, Bosun. Look!'

'Cannons?' Bosun's anger dissipated as he took in the crates, stamped with the bell foundry's coat-of-arms. He looked up the web above and caught Spyde's wide eyes.

'Did I not say?' Spyde offered a weak smile and thanked whichever god would listen when Bosun looked back to the crates.

'They look... small.'

Charlzberg scowled. 'Deck guns, Bosun. Squall's tits but do you know nothing?' His eyes never left the crates, lucky for him.

You've come close to being murdered by Bosun more times in the last few moments than any other time since we hired him. Spyde sighed. *Part of me thinks that might not be a bad thing, should it happen.* He slapped himself hard for the thought, drawing another look from Bosun. Spyde offered another smile and climbed higher.

As Charlzberg signed off on the delivery with a black cross where a name was required, Bosun started to rip apart the first crate. Once opened, he stopped grinding his teeth and bared them instead.

'You look hurt,' Charlzberg said, finally looking at Bosun.

'It's nothing.' Bosun returned Charlzberg's look. 'Tell me where you want them and I'll have them fixed on in no time, Admiral.'

Oh, shit a brick, Spyde thought, descending his web. *What in Brisance is that man up to?*

Chapter 25 – Crude compliment

'Someone's shat in the Adjunct's breakfast.' Spyde held the old telescope in one hand and clung to his net with the other. He pointed the device across the harbour, where guardsmen ran like cats from a bosun.

'What's the craic?' The Ptarmigan twins looked up from the base of the mast, but Spyde had no idea which had spoken, as usual.

Spyde kept his eye to the lens. 'The Adjunct's Guard. Someone's peppering them with arrows from a ship!'

The twins looked to one another and back to Spyde. 'They got a death wish?'

'No... They've got *Sessio*,' Spyde shouted to those below. Several of the Hobyahs looked up hungrily, sending a shudder through Spyde's scrawny limbs. He put eye back to lens and saw *Sessio's* white sails pulling her away from the dock and out into the Scales-dominated bay. 'She's away.'

'*Sessio?*'

Spyde froze. It was Bosun who'd shouted up and Spyde didn't miss the tension in the man's voice. 'Aye, *Sessio*,' Spyde confirmed whilst watching the remarkable vessel glide through the bay.

'Admiral!'

Lowering the telescope, Spyde looked down to where Bosun was stomping up deck. Upon reaching Charlzberg's awning, and without an answer from the goblin inside, Bosun dropped to all fours and much to Spyde's surprise, shoved his head through the flap. The resulting screech scattered the Ptarmigan twins and all other goblins on deck. Cooker popped up for a brief moment, but ducked back into his hole as Bosun crawled backwards, a wriggling and writhing Charlzberg in tow. Once the naked goblin was free of his den, Bosun stood, faced away and shielded his eyes from the sun.

'What's the meaning of this?' Charlzberg surged to his feet and balled his fists by his sides, revealing all, much to Spyde's disgust.

'Perhaps you should cover your jewels, Admiral,' Spyde dared. The resulting glare sent him further up his web in mock fear, eyes rolling as he climbed.

'Bosun?' Charlzberg shook with rage, a mewling whine starting to build.

'Sorry, Admiral?' Bosun turned, brow creased. 'Why are you shouting at——?'

'You dragged me out of my quarters!'

Bosun stepped back and thudded his right hand to his chest. 'Me? I'm aghast at the accusation. I was merely stood here watching *Sessio* leave the bay in haste.'

Charlzberg's whine ended and he frowned, eyes narrow.

'You know, Admiral, your renowned captain-friend's ship?'

Oh, you sly dog, Spyde thought, climbing back down his web.

Charlzberg spat. He brought his hands up defensively and hopped back when the gobbet of phlegm landed on Bosun's boot. The man clenched his teeth but said nothing.

'He's not my friend,' Charlzberg said through broken teeth after composing himself, fists once again by his sides.

'Oh... really?' Bosun's overacted shock and confusion made Spyde laugh, albeit silently.

'Yes, really!'

'Well, that's ridiculous, Admiral. He should kill to be a friend of yours. Nay, he should kill to be under your command, as any captain should.'

Charlzberg calmed at that and straightened. 'Well, quite!' He clasped his hands behind his back, pot belly and tackle thrust forward. 'Where does the mouse Mannino sail?'

Mouse? Spyde closed one eye and tried to think what Charlzberg meant. *Rat? Aye, rat, I'm sure...ish that's what he meant.*

'I don't know, Admiral.' Bosun shrugged. 'But you can bet he's on to something big, and lucrative.'

'Whatative?'

'Something that'll make him a boat load of gold. Literally.'

Charlzberg's beady eyes widened. 'Follow him!' he shouted, turning and scanning the deck for the Ptarmigan twins and the rest of his crew. 'Follow Mannino and *Sessio* you puss-filled ginger kittens!'

The deck was abuzz with goblins running back and forth. Ropes were cast off and the plank was pulled on board. Tull shouted to the rest of the fleet – the boat behind – that they were departing and Bosun proceeded to shout 'pull' after the port-side hobyahs pushed off from the quayside with their thick oars.

Charlzberg turned around, eyes moving from goblin to goblin. 'Now who The Three—'

Not here, you fool! Spyde thought, cringing and looking to the dark towers above the hillside city.

'—dragged me from my quarters?'

Bosun broke his steady shouts of 'pull' long enough to point out the deck guns he'd fixed to the gunwale to either side of the ship's prow. Eyes wide once more, a naked, bruise-covered Charlzberg charged up deck to inspect them, qualms forgotten.

'And ensure you check out the prow, Admiral,' Spyde added, grinning at the benefits he would receive for seeing Charlzberg's wish of a prow decoration through to conclusion. His only worry was whether he'd been right in gagging the kidnapped woman or not. It wasn't easy keeping up with Charlzberg's whims.

***

'Is that them?' Severun asked, glancing down the street their alley led off.

'To The Three with the lot of us if ye keep on looking at 'em, wizard.' Longoss pulled Severun to the middle of the group. 'We need 'em to be unawares.' He almost missed Severun's eyes darkening like the belly of a storm; it was only for a heartbeat and the alley lay in a patchwork of shadows despite the midday sun.

'We can't be sure if it's them or not, yet,' Coppin offered, holding placating hands up between the two men.

'We're not striking at folk unknown,' Egan said, keeping an eye on the other end of the narrow alley, hand-held crossbow at the ready. 'It's hard enough Longoss doesn't know where his old guild is, that we have to do this in the first place, but we're not attacking without reason.'

Rich coming from a witchunter, Longoss thought, although his anger came from turning down Poi Son's invitations to go to the guild itself in the past. How easy it would have been to find Poi Son now, if he knew where he was based. The bastard didn't even travel in his usual coach any longer. Turning it over in the street and torching it during a fit of rage had seen to that. Longoss took a deep breath to calm himself. *Nowt I can do about that now. Look forward, not back, that's what Coppin tells me.*

'We won't strike at just anyone,' Coppin confirmed, lowering her hands before moving one up and through her recently blackened hair. 'But since we can't find Poi Son, we've to draw him to us. Hindering his assassins hasn't worked how we'd have liked, he just sends more to kill the marks, and he's keeping his best back since there's not as many as before'

Gold flashed. 'Thanks to us.'

'And the plague,' Coppin went on, 'but ultimately we tried and failed at hindering him completely. We told you both what we knew about the mark on King Barrison, though. That has to count for something?'

Severun and Egan both nodded, safe in the knowledge their message got through to Ward Strickland. As had Severun's request, whatever that had been.

'We held up our side of the bargain there,' Coppin said. 'Now we need Poi Son to come for us again, like he did before.'

'His men, you mean,' Severun said.

Too bloody right. Longoss nodded. 'Aye, his men, and women. And lads and lasses and big fat collared rats and all manner of bastard cunts—'

The slap Longoss received across his face was clearly audible to Egan, who turned to see what happened.

'I won't be hearing that word, Longoss.' Coppin's outstretched finger caused Longoss to cross eyes. 'Ye know I can't stand it.'

Cunt cunt cunt. 'Sorry lass, ye're right. I won't say it no more.' *Cunt.*

'Ye better not.' She lowered her hand and unbuttoned the top of her linen shirt. 'Now, it's time for me to go to work.'

Gold teeth ground as Longoss nodded his head and watched Coppin walk out onto the street. It wasn't long until the wolf whistles started.

'Outstanding,' Egan said from the back.

'Pardon?' Severun said, without turning.

'We have company,' Egan explained.

Both Longoss and Severun turned and looked past Egan to the three men walking their way, spiked gauntlets glinting in the sporadic light of the alleyway, tattooed faces also visible.

'Who are they?' Severun asked, eyeing the men's wicked grins.

Longoss rolled his head and shoulders. 'They're the cunts.'

Coppin smiled at the crude compliment, if it could be called that, and traced a finger down the lad's pigeon chest.

'Ye think so?' she said, managing a giggle despite her revulsion.

'Oh aye, girl…'

Girl? Cheeky little shite.

'…I'll show ye how it's done, see?' The lad faltered as the sound of fighting came from the alley Coppin had left. A swift flick of his fingers and the group of youths around him made for the alley's entrance, all manner of knives being drawn.

'Ye're not going, are ye?' she said, purring the words and moving in close. She pressed her thinly covered breasts against the lad and whispered into his ear.

He shoved her off. 'I'm to go, aye. Stay here and I'll be back. There's things afoot ye wouldn't understand. Now stay.'

Coppin was shocked, shocked he'd so easily brushed her aside. She watched him set off for the alley, the ghost of an assassin's face hovering in her memory, laughing at her.

'Fuck off, Leese,' she said, louder than she'd intended.

'What?' The lad stopped and looked back, knife in hand.

Coppin froze.

'Did ye say 'Leese'?' He moved back towards her. Two of his companions turned back when they saw he hadn't followed. 'Answer me, lass. Did ye know Leese? Ye said her name, I heard ye.'

'There's plenty Leeses in Dockside,' Coppin said quickly, too quickly. *Coppin, ye fool…*

The lad stopped, friends now behind him. 'How did ye know the one I meant? To get so defensive so quick like?'

His eyes widened with realisation.

Coppin ran.

'Fuck,' the lad shouted. 'It's Longoss' bitch; the one that killed Leese!'

Coppin heard all three give chase.

Chapter 26 – Stab and stab and stab

Wincing at the near misses Longoss endured, Egan positioned himself to help the man.

An Orismaran's spiked fist barely missed the side of Longoss' head, and would've caught purchase if Longoss had his ears. The jab caused Longoss to roll his head left, which now sat in the path of the right hook coming at him.

Egan always found it surprising how such a small bolt could propel a grown man backwards. His aim was key, to have the missile strike the sternum of the man about to gore Longoss' face, taking him back and off balance and crashing him to the filthy floor.

The tattooed ganger whooshed out a breath as he hit the ground. Longoss kicked the man's head, likely rendering him unconscious rather than killing him, Egan noticed. Filling his cheeks, Longoss blew out the air and looked to Egan. 'Ye saved me looks,' he said, as the other two gangers came on, spiked fists jabbing and swinging. Egan baulked at how calm Longoss was.

'Do something, wizard,' Longoss said, glancing Severun's way. The closest ganger hesitated at the word, giving Longoss the opening he needed to lift his knee and throw a kick out perpendicular to his body. His foot connected with the man's chest, which surprised them both, and launched him back into his companion.

'Well done, wizard,' Longoss said, 'the mere mention of ye does the trick.'

Egan couldn't help but laugh.

'I've no room to work,' Severun protested, 'you're in the way.'

Egan reloaded his crossbow and aimed it at new voices, behind them. Several lads froze at the end of the alley. A trigger shifted and a mechanism released a tort cable which whipped its load up the alley and into the shoulder of the lead lad. He went down with a grunt and screamed like the child he practically was.

'More company,' Egan shouted. He drew his rapier and pointed it towards the approaching youths. 'They're yours, Severun.' He turned back and ran to Longoss' aid.

'Oh,' Severun said, watching the oncoming lads. 'I see.'

Coppin looked back as she ran, in time to see half a dozen flailing bodies fly out of the alley, spinning as if caught in a dust-filled zephyr. They struck the building opposite and didn't get up. In the brief moment it took to happen, her eyes refocused on the three closing lads. *Damn but they're fast.*

'Ye gonna wish ye'd left all this alone, bitch,' the lead lad shouted as he neared Coppin.

'Ye might think the same, ye little prick,' she shouted back.

Coppin's feet skidded as she came to an abrupt stop. Looking back, she smiled as her pursuers frowned in shock and confusion.

She straightened and drew her own knife. The lads slowed to a stop before her.

'Sure ye wanna do this, lass? There's no Longoss with ye now.'

The two behind smirked at that.

'Nor do ye have him to stop *me* killin' *you*.' Coppin winked at the leader. She didn't miss the quick lick of his top lip, the shift in the way he held his knife.

'I heard of the fight where Leese fell. Where many of 'em fell,' he said, his friends' smirks fading at that.

'And what did ye hear?'

'Longoss, a fire breathing demon and a green haired witch.'

Coppin smiled and ran a hand through her hair. Her fingers came away stained black.

The lad swallowed hard, the other two tensed and Coppin's hand whipped out.

The knife that thudded into the lad's throat stemmed the spurt of arterial blood until the fool pulled it out. Hot crimson liquid arced as he collapsed to the ground, a knife in each hand, one bloody and not his own.

The two who'd stood behind him faltered before they came at Coppin, a failure in their discipline; a failure in their ability to win out against one trained by Longoss.

Despite her lack of a weapon, Coppin took the lads down. She felt little joy in her bloody work, when both their weapons became her own.

'Did ye know,' she said to the last, as he choked on his own blood, 'most knife wounds are caused by the victim's own knife. Funny thing, isn't it?' she said, attempting to wipe arterial spray off her face and neck. 'Ye thought ye'd stick me with that thing,' she twanged the lodged knife, 'after sticking me with that.' He may have been passing from this world to the next, or wherever, but the lad felt the flick to his cock before he passed, of that Coppin was sure.

She sat down, right there in the middle of the street, amongst three dead lads and their dark blood. She sighed, the shakes coming on now it was over. She looked down the street to see Longoss, Severun and Egan coming her way and she allowed herself a smile, albeit a weak one.

How did he do it for so long? Coppin thought, looking about at the mess and trying not to gag at the smell. *I can appreciate the thump of my heart when it's happening, and for a short while afterwards. I can appreciate the appeal of that.* Her shoulders bobbed in the shudder of a laugh. *I can even feel the want to continue; the aggression making me want to stab and stab and stab until there's no more hurt, no more pain.* A tear mixed in with the blood on her face, then another. *But what I can't stand, what pains me more than anything else, is those last looks in their eyes. Elleth, my love, was that how you left this world, with someone looking in on that last, most vulnerable and personal moment? Is this how Blanck felt as he watched you die?*

The tears flowed as a set of thick, bloodied arms wrapped around her.

Chapter 27 – A decorative Prow

The smell of brine and the rushing of water against the galley's hull was starting to feel normal to Bosun. He wasn't inexperienced at sea, but nor was he accustomed to life as a sailor, and certainly not on a goblin war galley, despite past months. Looking out at the blackness all around, his eyes settled on the distant light they were following.

'Sessio,' Bosun whispered to himself, for there were no others near him bar the tireless hobyahs pulling on their oars. He was impressed that they continued to row, what with him offering a grunt now and then, rather than the 'pull' he usually called. *Must be my tone they associate rowing with, rather than the word itself.* He frowned as a sound reached him from the prow of the ship. He wasn't sure what decoration Spyde had added for Charlzberg, and hadn't bothered to ask or look, but it was clear there was something going on in front of him, outside the dim light his cowled lamp offered.

Grunting again for the benefit of the hobyahs, Bosun moved forward. Reaching the fore-deck, which was far, far smaller than the forecastle of the ship he'd previously spent time on, Bosun made out the silhouettes of two goblin sailors, both of which seemed to be, if he wasn't mistaken – and he wished he was…

'Pulling on their oars.' Bosun cursed and spat over the side.

The spoken words turned the jerking goblins to face the man stood behind them. Both hesitated and offered Bosun leering grins before turning back to look down at the prow's ram. Their shuddering and grunting continued anew, as did another sound. Moving forward, right eye squinted in curiosity, not to mention against the spray lifting from the cutting prow, Bosun looked to Charlzberg's new decoration. He lifted his cowled lamp high as one of the goblins, evidently racing the other to a climatic victory, gasped three times, jerked violently and sighed heavily. Bosun took an involuntary step back as he saw both the inspiration for the wretched sailors' activity and the target for the victor's grotesque explosion.

A half-naked, bound and gagged young woman stared back at him from astride the prow's barnacle-encrusted ram. It was Bosun's turn to gasp. It was his turn to move violently, although that violence had a specific aim of its own: two goblin sailors. As the disappointment of losing hindered the second goblin's… performance, the creature pitched forward, cock in hand, to meet the black waters below. The splash was barely audible over the sound of wood cutting through water; it was enough to turn the victorious goblin back to Bosun though, and to hold the hope-tinged, fearful gaze of Charlzberg's prow decoration, whose white dress was soaked through with blood and water.

It was a fist rather than a foot that knocked the second, victorious goblin overboard, and as he hit the water and disappeared with little more than a pitiful squeak, Bosun flexed his fingers and shouted back to the galley in general. 'Goblins overboard!'

He was answered by laughter; laughter and a half-hearted cheer of mockery. Grunting a laugh of his own at the ridiculous crew, before remembering the poor woman tied to the front of the ship, Bosun set his lamp down and descended carefully to the shivering decoration.

'It's alright, lass. I'll let no more harm come to you.' He drew a knife and she flinched. He cut at her bonds without explanation. Once free, the woman allowed Bosun to lift her up to the fore-deck proper. As Bosun was pulling himself back onto the fore-deck he heard her cry out in fear.

'What is the meaning of this?' The shrieking question that further startled her could only have come from one goblin. Bosun snarled, a hot anger rising, swelling, finding an outlet through the cowering woman above him.

Climbing up and standing alongside the prisoner, for that's what she was, he knew, Bosun locked eyes with Charlzberg, who was flanked by two goblin sailors, hatchets in hands. Bosun stamped his foot and both goblins returned to whatever it was they'd been doing before their admiral had summoned them with his shriek.

'Pull!' Bosun shouted, realising the oars had stopped. 'I found this poor woman tied to the front of your flagship, Admiral.'

Charlzberg's head vibrated with rage. 'Well of course you did. She's my prow decoration, you fool of a fuck!' He pulled his replacement hat - the other likely worn by a child - this way and that, before stomping towards the two humans, pathetic cutlass in hand. 'And I'll have her back there, Bosun. Back there and beautiful and bleeding!'

The woman, cold and wet, clung to Bosun's arm. Shrugging her off, he stepped between her and Charlzberg, knife away and hands out to the sides.

'Move aside,' Charlzberg said, trying to look around the bulk before him.

'She needs tending to, Admiral.' Bosun didn't move, so Charlzberg had to stop.

Through broken teeth the goblin replied. 'Step. Aside.'

'*Sessio* is close,' Bosun said through his own teeth, before adding an extra loud, 'Pull!'

Goblin eyes met human eyes, although the former left the latter sharpish and again tried to look around linen clad muscle. 'What of it,' Charlzberg said, teeth grinding, painfully – the wince confirmed it.

'We can't afford mutiny, Admiral.'

Charlzberg stepped back, jaw slack.

Bosun nodded solemnly and crouched, face to face with the goblin who, to his credit, managed to meet the glare given to him by his human officer. 'If the hobyahs knew,' Bosun whispered, leaning in to Charlzberg's torn ear, 'of a woman tied to the front of the galley, how long do you think they will row towards Tull, dangling from the stern as he is?' Charlzberg hesitated, but when he tried to speak, Bosun cut him off. 'They'll row backwards if they find out.' Charlzberg's beady, bruise-surrounded eyes widened and again Bosun spoke. 'I wouldn't tell them, Admiral. Pull! But there's those on this galley… well…'

'Go on!' Charlzberg implored Bosun to do so by sheathing his cutlass and clasping his hands together before him.

'I hate to say, Admiral, but if it weren't for the likes of me looking out for you—'

'Yes?' Charlzberg leaned in closer, until his scabby ear brushed Bosun's wet lips. Bosun snarled, out of eye-shot as he was.

'I dare say there could be mutiny,' he whispered, after moving his head back a fraction, freeing his lips of Samorl knew what. 'So—'

'Mutiny!'

'Shush, damn you!' Bosun hissed, then winced. He waited for a tirade that never came. The woman behind started whimpering. 'I'm looking out for you, Admiral, as I say. As I always do. Pull! So, let me lead here. Let me take this woman to my hole— quarters, and hide her away from the hobyahs. You can count on me, my lord Admiral.' Bosun placed a hand on the admiral's padded shoulder and pulled back enough to make eye contact once more. He nodded to hammer home the seriousness of the fabricated threat, which drew a reluctant nod from the battered and bruised goblin.

'Good man,' Bosun said aloud, standing. *Or goblin, I suppose.* He turned and grabbed the woman before pulling her past Charlzberg and off down the galley, not stopping until he reached his hole where he shoved her into the blackness below. Turning back to a stunned Charlzberg, who openly stared at him, Bosun shouted, 'Pull!' and followed the woman down. Once away from prying eyes and ears, he found the woman's shoulders in the dark and held them firm.

'I'm no Samorlian Saint, lass,' he said, 'and blind me but I don't know why I put my neck on the line for you, especially when I've a job to do, but I did, so you owe me big.' He heard her sniff with what could be the beginning of a flu, or tears, or both, and continued regardless. 'As I say, I'm no Saint, but I'm a damned sight better than those shites up top, so you do well by me and I'll do the same by you. And who knows,' he added, releasing her bobbing shoulders and leaning back onto his rolls of hessian, 'once we reach my own ship and master, you may even find your way back to a decent port with some coin in your purse. Eh?' Nothing. 'Well say something, lass?'

'Thank you,' she said, although her voice broke as soon as she spoke, the last word barely audible.

Bosun offered a breathy laugh. 'I wouldn't thank me yet. Anyhow, my name's Bosun, for now, and yours shall be Prow. I've no need for your real one. Now rummage around in the dark there, will you, I've stashed some bread and I'm pretty sure we could both do with a bite after all that nonsense.'

The sound of scrabbling hands preceded the sounds of chewing, swallowing and dry coughing.

Bosun laughed again. 'I guess you'll be wanting some of my small-beer too, eh Prow?'

Chapter 28 – Never trust a goblin

'How's tricks, lass?' Bosun lowered himself into his hole-come-quarters, eyes searching for Prow in the darkness. 'Lass?' he said again, receiving nothing in return. He settled onto his hessian rolls and fumbled in his belt pouch.

'As well as can be expected,' came a soft voice from the corner.

Bosun heard the girl shift and gasp. The quietness of it was broken by a sniff and a series of coughs.

'You don't sound well.' Bosun strained to see. He looked down and the cold steel he held struck equally cold flint, several times. A candlewick flared to life, giving light to the hole in its entirety. The immediate rotten smell of tallow struck him.

'You hurting, Prow?' A pause. 'You know, down there?' Bosun motioned low, between her legs. She drew her knees up to her chest, wrapped her arms around them and squinted at the pain it brought, shivering all the while. The candlelight was enough to see Prow nod. Her eyes remained on the wooden floor. Bosun could see her cheeks glistening in the orange light, as did her top lip. She sniffed again, twice, before rubbing her nose with the edge of the blanket that covered her back and hung over her sagging shoulders.

Bosun swallowed hard. He dripped wax onto the floor and stood the candle in it, holding it steady until it set. He looked to Prow once more, but the girl continued to stare down, at nothing, fair hair falling lank across her blue eyes.

'Was it the top of the ram, where you sat, that hurt you? Can't imagine straddling rough, wet wood in wet clothes does much for soft skin.'

She looked up, stared at Bosun, eyes hard, defiant. 'The bit I was tied to?'

Bosun nodded and offered a sad smile. 'Aye lass, where you were tied.' Another pause and Prow's eyes moved away.

'Wasn't me who tied you there though, remember that.'

Her eyes glazed over again. 'Oh, I'll remember it alright. All of it, and everything leading up to it...' her voice broke into a series of coughs. She brought the course blanket to her lips as her shoulders bobbed.

'I know you will, lass,' Bosun said, once the coughing had passed. *How old is she?* He thought, taking in her pock-marked but pretty face. *Fifteen, sixteen years? No more. And she's certainly no older than my sister was when she passed.* The thought dried Bosun's throat, causing a lump. He took a swig of the small-beer he'd poured into a clay pot earlier.

'Now...' He rummaged in a sack by his side. Prow watched as he brought forth a smaller clay pot than the one they drank from. 'A balm, of sorts,' he said, lifting the pot and turning it this way and that. 'Eatrian squill bulb and spirits, amongst other things.'

Prow frowned at the unfamiliar name, but accepted the pot all the same.

Bosun continued as she held the pot in her shaking hands.

'It'll help with, well...' he hesitated and nodded to her drawn up legs, '...you know.'

'It'll take the pain?' Prow opened the lid and screwed up her face, quickly closing it again.

Bosun rocked his head from side to side. 'Sort of.' She looked at him, eyes narrow. 'It'll stop infection and help the healing, along with a wash with salt-water each day—'

'It's soaking in that stuff that half did me in,' Prow said, putting the pot down and wrapping her arms around her knees once more.

'Listen lass, I know that, trust me I do, but that small pot cost me a pretty penny, I can tell you. For that money, it'll work, I know it. It's no magic or owt, but it's good stuff. I use it myself on cuts and such. You can't be too careful on a galley full of filthy goblin shites.' He grinned. She didn't. 'Now do as I say and you'll be right in no time. Ignore me and you'll be food for the hobyahs and no mistake.'

There was a slight nod, but Prow said nothing. She looked scared again, more than anything.

Bosun sighed. 'I'm not expecting you to apply it now or anything. You can wait until I'm back up top, which will be soon. I can already feel the bastards slowing without my presence.'

'Thank you,' Prow said, although Bosun hardly heard it. He knew what it must have taken for her to say it though, after all she'd been through, and was going through.

'Well, don't thank me yet, as I said when I first brought you down here. The balm will hurt like a slave master's whip as much as it helps, especially to start with. But it *will* help.' He smiled. 'You use as much as you can and need. A rough bastard like me can go without, despite the cost.' He grunted a laugh at that and was taken aback when the girl replied with a weak smile, transforming her plane face to reveal more of the pretty Bosun had spied. She picked up the pot again and turned it over in her trembling hands.

Bosun leaned forward. 'You still cold?'

A nod, without looking up.

'Here.' He threw her another blanket from under his hessian rolls and she caught it and wrapped it around her legs. 'Take what you need from down here, lass. I'm no monster. Well.' He laughed. She stared, eyes wide. 'A joke,' he added. 'And a poor one at that, I guess.' Bosun offered another smile and returned the subject to Prow's cold. 'I'll bring you some hot stew when Cooker's finished it. Mind you, it'll taste like crap, so don't thank me for that neither. It'll warm you though.'

Another nod from Prow, eyes on the contents of the pot, after removing the lid again. Her nose wrinkled, as did Bosun's.

'How'd the sick shites get you, lass?'

Prow's unusual-for-the-region blue eyes raised to Bosun's. More tears welled before spilling over and down her cheeks.

'If it's too hard—'

'A goblin informant called Lugg Puffitt. My man used him often. I thought I could trust him.' She wiped her eyes and nose both. It was easy to see how hard it was for her to talk about it.

Giving her a moment, Bosun busied himself by sorting some of his belongings into piles by his side. Flint and steel, whetstones of varying grains and sizes, unused candles, a reed-whistle and a pair of immaculate, sheathed daggers.

'My man died...'

Bosun looked up, left hand shifting his bits and pieces back and forth, turning and re-straightening them.

'...not long before I was taken. Not long at all.' She coughed again, violently.

'How so?' Bosun kept his voice low, sympathetic, or so he hoped.

'Murdered.' She bit back a sob, shook herself from it; tensed her jaw. A moment past and she went on, stoic, tough. 'Murdered along with his officers and soldiers, loyal men all.'

Bosun frowned. 'Soldiers?'

Prow nodded.

'This man of yours a knight or some such?'

'Not quite, although he was a king in my eyes.' She didn't elaborate so Bosun didn't ask.

'This Puffitt character...'

Prow rubbed hard at her red eyes and sniffed some more before coughing again, so Bosun stopped, left the question unanswered. She started rocking back and forth, eyes back on Bosun.

'Puffitt turned up after the Adjunct's Guard had passed, chasing...' Prow drifted off for several heartbeats, before taking a breath to continue. 'Puffitt told me he'd take me to safety. Said he'd take me to the tavern I lived and worked in.'

'I'm guessing he lied?'

Prow nodded. 'He lied to me and took me to more of his kin. He took me to the goblins of this ship, to one dressed in black who walked funny, like he was unsteady on the solid quayside.'

Bosun closed his eyes and muttered a curse aimed at Spyde in particular. He sighed long and hard before continuing. 'You don't trust goblins, lass. Everyone knows that.'

'Says you!' Prow near on shouted, face reddening as she made to surged forward. She checked herself and fell back to her scattered blankets, pain and fear playing across her blotchy face.

Bosun pursed his lips and nodded. 'Fair one, Prow, although being aboard their ship doesn't mean I trust them. It does mean they trust me though. To a certain extent, anyway.'

'Well, I wasn't exactly feeling my best when I put my trust into that little green fuck,' she said, settling as much as she could. 'I was cradling my dead lover's head in my arms when Lugg Puffitt came on by, yellow teeth flashing.'

'Fair one,' was all Bosun could say to that.

'No, none of this is fair. None of it. If anything, it's the most unfair—'

Bosun interrupted with a bark of a laugh. Prow rocked back, her right hand scrunching the blanket at her chest.

'Coming from the bloody Tri Isles, lass, I'd have thought you knew all about unfair, what with those fucking great scales The Three raised up over you.'

Prow looked to her wool covered feet.

'Why'd he die, your man? Who'd he wrong?'

Her eyes snapped back to meet his, her defiance palpable. 'What makes you think he wronged someone?'

Bosun laughed again, despite the pain it caused her. 'It's usually the way, is all. My business is in killing folk, Prow, and I'm damned and bloody good at it. Well, usually.' He thought to the dark room in the harbour and his missed mark, and his aching ribs. 'But that means I know all about killing and the reasons why, and trust me, folk don't often kill without reason, not often.'

There was near – awkward – silence for a while, apart from the sound of grunting hobyahs and the rush of water on the hull.

'My last man…' She scoffed. 'Boy, rather; jealousy, I'd say. That enough of a reason for you?'

Bosun rubbed his chin and thought about that a moment, as Prow watched on. *Motive makes sense, but…* 'This boy, *he* killed your man?' Prow nodded. Bosun pursed his lips once more. Thoughts and reasons and methods and likely and unlikely scenarios rushed about his shaved head. 'He killed your man, this boy, this ex-lover of yours. He killed your man and your man's officers… and soldiers? All because he was green with jealousy?' Bosun searched her eyes.

Prow sneered. 'I don't want to talk about it no more. It's too fresh.'

Bosun held his hands out to placate her. 'Don't worry. I'll ask no more. Tonight.' He groaned and climbed to his feet, as stooped as that made him. Prow said nothing and watched, face sour.

'I'll go see Cooker shall I? See if I can't get some of that shit stew he's boiling to death.' He started to climb out of his hole, stopped half way and looked back to Prow, whose blue eyes were glistening once more. She pulled the blankets tighter about her.

'Be sure to apply that balm whilst I'm gone, but be sure to brace yourself as it *will* hurt.'

Prow nodded.

'Oh,' Bosun said, hesitating at the top of his ladder, 'this might all go smoother if I knew your real name, rather than calling you Prow? It's been a day now and, well…'

The girl hesitated before nodding and telling him her name, voice shaking.

Bosun smiled. 'That's a pretty—'

'It was.'

Bosun's brow creased and he tilted his head, confused.

'It's Prow now, my name. The girl who came before is as good as dead.'

Taking a deep breath, Bosun nodded once before climbing out of his hole. 'Right you are, Prow,' he said from up top. 'Right you are.'

The hatch closed.

'Spyde!'

The anger in the human voice shouting his name held Spyde firm in his spot, high on his web.

'Spyde, you shite, where are you?'

'He's at the top,' came a voice from the very stern.

Curse you, Tull, Spyde thought, descending. 'I'm here, Bosun,' he dared, squinting into the dim light below.

'Get down here. Now!' Bosun was pacing, but keeping close to the base of the mast. 'Pull!'

The hobyahs surged into motion as one and Spyde, now reaching the bottom of the netted sail, realised they'd been falling asleep. *He's driving them harder than ever.*

Bosun looked up, nose and top lip pulled into a snarl.

'You called?' Spyde's voice shook.

'What's the meaning of all that noise?' Charlzberg shouted, from beneath his awning.

'Not now!' Bosun's roar of a shout silenced the ship, hobyahs and all. The rowing continued when he looked left then right, and when he looked back up, Spyde froze. Charlzberg didn't say another word.

He's taking control, Spyde thought, eyes darting about in an attempt to see the goblin crew that were surely drawing on the man who was shouting down their admiral. There wasn't another goblin in sight, bar Tull, helplessly hanging as he was and illuminated by the stern lamp.

Spyde swallowed hard again. *He sees me as the only true threat. The only one with brains enough to know his plan. But why now? When he found the woman I could understand, but now? It's been a bloody day, for Squall's sake. He taken that long to stew over it?* Panicked, Spyde made to climb. A large hand took his ankle in a tight grip and pulled. Fingers left rope and stomach rose in that gods-awful way for a heartbeat before Spyde hit the deck, hard. Bosun made no attempt whatsoever to break Spyde's fall.

'Pull!'

'Blood God and Squall curse you, Bosun!' A rush of heat flushed Spyde, anger and fear both. He surged to his feet and stared up at the man towering over him, cowled lamp in hand. Spyde surprised himself with the act of defiance, but before he could think on it, Bosun's hand lashed out quicker than Spyde could have imagined and struck him across the temple. He was back on the hard deck, head spinning and throbbing. The wind took hold of Spyde's dislodged black cap and blew it down the deck, towards a gawking, dangling Tull.

'You kidnapped and tied that girl to the prow, didn't you, you shit?' Bosun dropped low, his sneering, lamp-illuminated face close to Spyde's. 'Didn't you?' he shouted when Spyde failed to answer. Spittle from that shout flecked Spyde's face, who curled into a ball, none of the anger and fear he was feeling lending him strength to stand this time. All he could do was nod meekly and battle not to piss himself.

'Pull! I fucking thought better of you, Spyde. Of you over all the others, you fucking shit!'

Bosun stood and kicked Spyde hard. Despite knees being high, he felt the impact in his gut and coughed repeatedly.

'That's what she's doing down there, you soft twat. Coughing her guts up with Samorl knows what ailment. A cold is all, I hope, but it could be worse and if she dies...' Bosun kicked Spyde in the head. Spyde grunted and begun to cry. 'Aye, she's doing a fair bit of that too, no thanks to you and your little puss-filled pockets of shite.' Another two kicks to the knee covered gut. More coughing. More crying.

He's going to kill me... he's going to kill me...

'Enough, Bosun!'

Bosun looked up and was clearly surprised to see Charlzberg standing there, as was Spyde, truth be told; the second-hand dwarven pistol he'd bought Charlzberg was levelled at Bosun.

'Admiral?' Bosun said slowly, free hand rising as if a shield.

'Do you want me to kill you with this pistol?'

Obviously, he doesn't, you prick, Spyde thought, his cries turning to short intakes of breath that hurt his bruised chest. *Shoot him anyway!*

'Pull!'

Spyde winced at the poor choice of word, expecting a bang, but Charlzberg did fuck all. Of all the times he should have reacted, could have reacted, literally, to a spoken word... Spyde felt his bladder weaken.

Bosun stood straight and held the lamp up high, lowering his other hand, a confident air settling over him. He looked left and right, before locking eyes with a nervous Charlzberg.

'And who would have your back if you did that, Admiral? Why do you think I beat on Spyde so?' Charlzberg made to speak, but Bosun continued. 'Do you not remember our earlier conversation?' Bosun let that sink in and Spyde shuddered at the thought of what might have passed between them.

Charlzberg looked from Bosun to Spyde, who sobbed once more, curled in black on the floor. Goblin eyes met and Spyde had the hope-filled suspicion that Charlzberg was indeed about to pull the trigger.

As much as I want him to, surely he's not got the balls...

There was a flash and a loud crack, followed by an explosion of metal, wood, blood and bone as the weapon exploded in Charlzberg's hand, shredding his arm up to the elbow in the process and removing half of his hand altogether. With a guttural scream, Charlzberg fell back, clutching the blood-pumping stump with his left hand.

'Fuck!' Bosun jumped over Spyde, who rolled out of the way, eyes tight shut, before rolling back to see what happened. He launched himself to his feet, fear and pain forgotten, and ran to the thrashing, screaming goblin on the floor. He slipped on the mess before and about Charlzberg, and came skidding to a stop alongside his wailing face.

'You stupid bastard,' Bosun said, shaking his head and looking to the remnants of the old pistol. 'I told you to clean the decrepit thing.' He worked quickly, tearing cloth and binding the bloody limb whilst struggling to hold it steady.

Spyde wondered why the man bothered.

'Some help, for your admiral!' Bosun shouted.

Multiple boots and bare feet came their way. Spyde remained frozen, unsure what to do.

The Ptarmigan twins were first by their side, followed by several others that were no more use than Spyde. Cooker arrived with more cloth and a small bottle of rum which he poured unceremoniously over the bloody rags at Charlzberg's wrist and up his forearm.

Charlzberg screamed all the more before passing out.

The hobyahs stopped rowing and looked on, hungrier than ever, gnashing teeth and licking cracked lips.

Spyde looked from blood and gore to hobyahs and back. He looked to Bosun and to the massing goblin crew.

'Now's our chance!' Spyde shouted, pointing at Bosun. He quick-stepped away from the dangerous man and winced at the pain Bosun had inflicted upon him. 'That man is a mutineer. Take him!'

Either no one listened or no one dared, for not one goblin looked Spyde's way. All eyes remained on their thrashing admiral or the hungry rowers. Spyde staggered back at that, especially when the only set of eyes that met his own belonged to the very man he was accusing. Bosun smiled and Spyde shuddered, felt full on sick. He swallowed down bile then felt a warmth down his leg and it was a moment before he realised he'd pissed himself. Without another thought he jumped up, took hold of the web-like ropes he knew so well and climbed to the very top, despite the pain of his gut, chest and throbbing head. Tears welling in his eyes and piss dribbling from his foot, Spyde stared hopelessly into the blackness of the night as he heard a familiar – now dreadful – shout amongst the commotion below.

'Pull!'

'Well?' Bosun shouted for Spyde to hear. *What do you see, you little bastard.*

'Another ship, ahead of *Sessio*!' Spyde hadn't come lower than the mid-point of his net for a whole day; since Bosun turned on him. 'She has black sails?' Spyde lowered his telescope and looked down.

'Pull, you bastards!' Bosun roared. He glared at Spyde, who put eye back to lens.

'Yeah, didn't think you'd make eye contact, you shit.' Bosun strode to the stern. Once there, he addressed Tull. 'You ensure those shits down there on the other boat have that thing loaded. I wouldn't be surprised if *Sessio* made her way behind us somehow. She's tricky like that, from all accounts.'

Tull nodded and jerked about in an attempt to turn and face the boat being pulled behind.

'And thrash about on that rope like never before, Tull,' Bosun said, turning back to face the prow and the distant *Sessio*. 'I want these hobyahs pulling like a teenage boy.' *We're closing on you now, Mannino.*

Tull laughed and thrashed, but not before giving the order to the canon crew.

'Pull, you useless bastards. Pull!'

The hobyahs did just that and their pallid green skin ran wet with sweat and spray as the galley surged on towards its prey.

'What's happening, Bosun?'

Bosun looked to his hole, where Prow was starting to emerge. 'Back down, lass. No time to explain but it's all going to get nasty up here.'

Prow dropped back down as quickly as she'd appeared and Bosun was genuinely glad. *She's been through enough without witnessing what's to come.* He grunted a laugh. *And that's all I'd need, to come this far and have that lass blow it all by throwing this lot off as a distraction.* 'Speaking of distractions...

'How's the admiral, Cooker? It's been a whole bastard day since you disappeared in there with him.' Bosun looked to the awning and a fleshy goblin head popped out. Cooker stuck his thumb out, horizontally, and moved it up and down before disappearing back inside Charlzberg's den of a quarters.

'Hear that, crew?' Bosun shouted. 'Your admiral is on the mend and ready to take down his nemesis, Captain Mannino. Are you all with him?'

The goblins howled and cheered. Bosun grinned.

'What of the black ship, Bosun?'

Turning on the Ptarmigan twins, Bosun realised it was Sister who'd asked, since Brother was busying himself with his arming belt.

'You can rejoice there, lass.' Bosun grinned all the more. 'For that big bitch is with us!' Brother looked to Bosun and the eyes of both twins widened. They grinned to match Bosun's own, who turned back to the rest of the ship. 'You hear that, you little turd suckers? The black ship is with us. With us, I say!'

Another cheer and the galley surged on towards its prey.

'You're dead, Mannino,' Bosun said under his breath, as he watched the familiar black ship close with *Sessio*. *And then I can get off this shit of a boat and back to my own ship and guild. Then on to Wesson; home.* He grinned. *And perhaps I'll have Prow by my side. Now that's not such a bad thought. Not a bad thought at all.*

Chapter 29 – Black Guild, black ship

Alden-Fenn, Martial Master of the Black Guild, turned as a hollow pop drew his attention from the enemy ship they were leaving behind to the centre of his own ship's aft-castle. Eyes narrow, he took in the robed figure of a scimitar wielding, black skinned man, who set about felling sailors like they were children. Tattooed face raw from *Sessio's* opening magical salvo, Alden-Fenn flexed his black gauntleted hands and held them out to the sides, where a man on the left strapped a shield and a man on the right handed him a flanged-mace. Rolling his maille clad neck, Alden-Fenn strode forward, shoving his own men aside before swinging his mace at the intruder's back, eager to break bones or crush skull.

Despite Alden-Fenn being surprisingly swift, the robed boarder avoided the attack with apparent ease.

The boarder's scimitar swished across Alden-Fenn's shield immediately after, which was countered by a jab from the spike-topped mace. Again, *Sessio's* boarder avoided the blow. It wasn't that Alden-Fenn wasn't fast, for his speed was renowned, and not just because of his bulk. It was more that the man Alden-Fenn now faced was ridiculously fast, fast and skilled and fearless.

Master Parry, Alden-Fenn surmised. *Sessio's infamous blade master, in the flesh.*

The scimitar came across again, only to be narrowly avoided by the adroit movements of Alden-Fenn. He continuously swung and thrust his mace, considerable muscles working in a familiar way. The threat of a blow kept *Sessio's* unarmoured blade master at bay, enough to allow Alden-Fenn to defend himself at least.

An assassin attacked Master Parry from behind, but the scimitar came around fast and took the man's jaw and tongue with a wet swish. He fell away, bubbling and frothing blood doing what a scream could not.

Alden-Fenn retreated, allowing two more assassins to take his place. The curses, shouts, wet slaps of scimitar through flesh and screams of the one man boarding action continued.

'Bring her about, behind the goblin galley,' Alden-Fenn ordered, calm as ever, eyes split between the ongoing fight onboard and the swiftly approaching galley. 'Follow them in and bring me my fucking sword.'

'Aye, Master.' The man on the whipstaff pulled it to one side and the large vessel turned, pitching heavily as she did so, whilst an officer produced Alden-Fenn's longsword.

Satisfied he could now get back to the blade master cutting his men low, Alden-Fenn made to attack once more. Master Parry fell back at that, slicing a bloody path down from the aft-castle and on to the castle-surrounded main deck that resembled a courtyard more than a ship, albeit aboard a heavily augmented cog.

Alden-Fenn halted atop the steps, unwilling to pursue *Sessio's* notorious blade master into the ship's murder pit. A familiar shout from below the ship drew his attention instead, from the direction of the galley, and he made for the gunwale of his crenellated aft-castle, trusting his skilled assassins to deal with Master Parry.

'*Sessio's* coming about!' Bosun's fists clenched by his side, grin wide. 'Pull, you shits! Pull! I want us nudging those bastards with our ram. Fire those fucking guns again!'

There was another double retort and the deck guns on the prow sent iron grapeshot into *Sessio's* stern. The goblins cheered.

'If she turns, we ram?' Spyde shouted down.

'Don't talk to me, bastard,' Bosun shouted back. 'But aye, if she turns we ram and board.'

'Board *Sessio*?' Charlzberg emerged from his awning, dressed in his best clothes, sleeve pinned up to cover his half missing hand and shredded limb.

'Yes, Admiral,' Bosun said without turning. 'We send the hobyahs aboard. Pull! And let them rip into the crew whilst I slice that fucker of a captain up.'

'Mannino?' Charlzberg frowned, eyes now on the splintered back of the ship they closed on.

'Guns loaded,' a goblin shouted from the prow.

'Then fire 'em, you bell end!' Bosun laughed with glee. 'I love these guns, Admiral.'

White smoke followed the flash and bang of the small deck guns, but this time the shot didn't make its target. This time, it diverted violently to either side, splashing into the waves like iron rain.

'Bloody mages.' Bosun spat on the deck.

Charlzberg looked from *Sessio* to the spit on his ship and up to Bosun.

'Attend me, Bosun.'

Bosun waved Charlzberg away without turning.

169

'Get those guns loaded. When my ship comes about from behind, we'll take Mannino together. You'll have your revenge, Charlzberg. Pull!'

Charlzberg began to shake. He ground his remaining yellow teeth and pressed his claw-less fingers into the palm of his remaining hand. Before Bosun could react, Charlzberg shrieked, turned and ran to the galley's stern. Tull tensed and tried to pull himself into a ball as best he could whilst hanging upside down, unsure as to his admiral's intentions. He flinched when the tri-cornered hat-wearing goblin next to him screamed down at the boat towed behind.

'Fire!' Charlzberg shouted to those below, who were watching the menacing bulk of the Black Guild's ship pass across their stern, fore-, aft- and unusual side-castles rising high above them. Jumping at the sudden shrieked order, the goblins rushed to.

Fire met powder as Bosun turned, mouth gaping. He ducked instinctively. The large bronze cannon exploded into life for the very first time. The heavy ball of stone it spat forth crossed the short distance between galley and modified cog faster than the Black Guild assassin that was Bosun could scream, 'No!'

With a sound, not too dissimilar to that of a hundred trees crashing to the ground, the side of the black ship gained a hole at water level that a man could put his head and shoulders through without hindrance.

It wasn't long at all, what with her magically enhanced speed and turn, that the large cog began to list towards the galley who'd fired on her.

A large, facially tattooed man in black maille and plate appeared at the passing aft-castle's gunwale, the blade of a longsword pointing down.

'Betrayer!' Alden-Fenn shouted, eyes finding the only man on a ship full of goblins and hobyahs. *His* man.

Before Bosun could deny it, before he could do anything bar hit the deck, bolts and arrows filled the air between the two vessels. And before Bosun could do more than scrabble to and fall into his hole, the same thing happened between the galley and *Sessio's* splintered stern.

Chapter 30 – A new debt

Bodies lay scattered, many stuck with arrows, others hacked and slashed. Several groaned and whimpered, their wounds being tended by sailors; one screamed as the ship's barber-surgeon sawed through her mangled limb.

A young officer approached Alden-Fenn, an angry red line across the man's ashen face.

'Your nose may fall off you know?' Alden-Fenn quipped, the hint of a smile pulling at the corner of his mouth. 'Still, at least the man who sliced you is gone.'

'You're joking, at a time like this?' The officer frowned.

Alden-Fenn's shrug creaked as it lifted his black pouldrons. 'Who said I was joking?'

The officer raised a hand to his split nose and grimaced, pulling his blooded fingers away, eyeing them with fear.

'Report,' Alden-Fenn said, turning and watching the white sails of *Sessio* carry the guild's mark away.

Composing himself, the officer went on. 'There's a hole in the hull even you could fit through. T'was the cannon the galley pulled behind it. And after that, the goblins stopped firing on *Sessio*.'

'I'm aware of that. I wanted to know how long until we're underway?' Alden-Fenn kept his eyes on his prey.

A deep sigh came from behind him, audible over the moans and groans of his sailors, assassins and ship alike. 'A day or two, with our… remaining mage's assistance.' The officer struggled to highlight the loss. Alden-Fenn heard it in the young man's voice.

'She…'

'I know, Master. I wasn't far from her when… when it happened.'

Alden-Fenn's gut churned and it was nothing to do with the listing ship. 'That spell came from Mannino's first mate.' He touched finger to burnt cheek, the recent memory of her destruction far more painful.

'Aye, Master Hitchmogh himself,' the officer confirmed, unnecessarily.

Alden-Fenn rounded on the lad, who'd replaced a seasoned officer killed in the fighting. Alden-Fenn maintained a calm visage despite the tumultuous rage boiling within. After all, he'd lost his lover to that bastard first mate.

'Add Hitchmogh to the list. I'll pay the guild fee myself for that mark, and pleasure.'

'I'll make it so, Master, once we're in a better state.'

'Make it so now.' Alden-Fenn need not speak twice. The officer rushed below deck, blood-streaked pale face a whiter shade than before.

Looking back at the departing sails of *Sessio*, Alden-Fenn turned his attention to the equally shrinking goblin war galley.

'When we're fit to sail,' he shouted for all to hear, 'we head for Wesson; send a bird.'

A man with the barber-surgeon screamed. Alden-Fenn didn't flinch.

'And someone make note,' he continued, eyes on the galley, 'our former brother, who now calls himself Bosun, is a traitor to the Black Guild and has a mark on his head.'

Several assassins voiced their agreement to that and another officer disappeared below deck to make note and prepare a bird.

'I do you a service putting a mark on your head, *Bosun*,' Alden-Fenn said to himself. 'For if I had you in my own hands...' The martial master of the Black Guild squeezed his fists at the thought of what he'd do to the only man who'd ever dared betray him. 'Pray I never get the chance, old friend. Pray I never get the chance.'

Bosun shuddered as he sat on his hessian rolls.

'Are you alright?' Prow asked, coming forward. 'Is it over?' she added, when Bosun stared but said nothing.

Pain-filled screams and wailing shouts from above answered her question.

'The battle may be over, as Charlzberg pulls away and lets *Sessio* go, but it's just begun for us, lass.'

Prow shuddered at the fear in Bosun's eyes.

'I'm not even sure what will happen when I go up top.'

'The goblins have turned on you?' Prow's breaths quickened and she pulled her knees up before her, wrapping them in a defensive hug, the likes of which was familiar to them both now.

He grunted a bitter laugh. 'If only it were just them. I suppose you could say I turned on them though... and they responded in kind. As will he...' Bosun managed another laugh, although there was no mirth in the sound and his eyes remained vacant orbs that stared at nothing in particular.

'It sounds bad up there.'

Goblins continued to moan and wail up top, likely from the quick arrow storm that the ships had unleashed on one another whilst parting company.

'It could be worse, lass.' Bosun focused on her. 'A lot worse.'

Prow swallowed hard and dared ask, 'How so?'

Another humourless laugh. 'The dumb shit of an admiral could have missed his mark!'

Prow frowned.

Bosun fell back and closed his eyes. 'Then there'd be nothing stopping Alden-Fenn's retaliation.'

It wasn't long at all until flat but broken clenching teeth faced clenching teeth. Narrowed eyes glared at narrowed eyes. Flaring nostrils snorted as the admiral faced the mutineer.

'Drown me, but the shit is standing up to him,' Spyde whispered, his incredulous gaze moving between Charlzberg and Bosun.

'You had no right—'

'I had no right?' Bosun's knuckles whitened at his sides. 'I had no right?' he shouted, visibly shaking. Goblins surrounded him. Armed goblins. Sneering goblins. They'd massed as soon as Bosun appeared from his hole.

'This is my ship, Bosun, Squall take you. Mine! My fleet!'

'It's a fucking galley towing a boat, you little freak.'

'That bested an assassin ship—'

'Shut it, bastard,' Bosun said to Spyde, without looking to the net above. 'You,' Bosun pointed at the admiral, 'wanted me to help you take revenge on Mannino. You did, Charlzberg—'

'Admiral!' Charlzberg snapped the word, his voice more commanding than it had ever been.

Bosun sighed and rolled his eyes. 'I've no time for this,' he said. 'We need to flee. Now. We need to leave the area before Alden-Fenn rights his ship and comes for us—'

'For you, traitor.' Charlzberg sneered all the more. 'You betrayed me and now,' he licked his awful lips and grinned, 'and now your master thinks you betrayed him too.'

'I've had enough, I'm taking the fucking galley.' Bosun strode forward. He was stopped two steps later as goblin held poleaxes flanked Charlzberg. Looking behind, he saw more of the same. 'You're not serious, lads? You'd dare stop me?'

'Admiral smashed assassin ship,' one goblin said, beady eyes glinting in the sun, finger pointing at the still visible black ship.

173

'You're not Admiral, Bosun. Admiral is Admiral,' said another, from behind.

'Screw me sideways, Charlzberg, you finally and actually found your command and earned some loyalty from these shits.' Bosun couldn't help but laugh at the situation, hands now on hips, weapons pointing at him from all angles.

Charlzberg grinned all the more. 'I offer you this, Bosun—'

'What? You offer me what?'

'A bet, a wager; an accord between officers.'

'This should be good.' Bosun lifted his chin. 'Go on, hit me with it.'

'We fight, you and I. We fight for this fleet. Winner takes all.'

'Loser?'

Charlzberg's smile widened. 'Loser takes a fall.' He glanced to the side of the ship and the sea beyond.

Spyde cursed long and loud, consequences be damned. Tull and the twins did too.

Bosun laughed. 'You'll fight me for the two boats, one on one; a dual? Are you serious?'

Charlzberg's smile disappeared as quickly as the crossbow wielding goblins appeared. 'No, I'm not.' Charlzberg turned and walked away. Crossbow mechanisms clunked. Bolts flew.

'Shit!' Bosun ran.

Prow sucked in a breath as she saw the development on deck. Bosun sprinted towards her, ill-veined bolts whipping past him at odd angles as he knocked weapons aside and barrelled through the goblins wielding them. One of the goblins fell back, crossbow bolt embedded in his face.

'Out, now!' Bosun yelled, eyes on Prow.

Heart pounding, Prow did as she was told. There was no way she was going to stay aboard a goblin galley.

Goblins shouted and hobyahs howled. More bolts skipped down the deck or sailed off over the gunwales, one leaving a crossbow at a right angle and thudding a goblin sailor from the galley to splash into the sea.

Holding her hand out to Bosun, Prow allowed the man to grab it and pull her along towards the back of the ship. She held her breath, awaiting the agonising impact that would strike her at any moment.

'Hurry!' Bosun dragged her along. 'Goblins can't aim for shit and their weapons are as bad, but if we don't...' They reached the

Ptarmigan Twins by the tiller. Both hit the deck, hands over their heads. Tull covered his eyes and hung limp as Prow and Bosun leapt past him, one either side of his rope. '…jump now,' Bosun continued, mid-air, 'Squall's luck will take us.'

They landed heavily on the gun boat trailing close behind the galley. One of the goblins was trying to pull a crossbow bolt from a fallen companion, but when they saw Bosun and Prow' arrival, it didn't take long before they were voluntarily swimming.

'Cut the rope.' Bosun handed Prow a knife.

Panic taking her, she stared at the pitted blade in her hand. Bosun cursed and snatched it back, dropping the oar he'd been lifting.

'They're taking the cannon!' Tull shouted from above.

'I liked you, Tull, you bastard,' Bosun shouted, eyes on the rope he was sawing through. 'Pull!' he shouted as loud as he could. The rope frayed and snapped. The sudden deceleration of the boat was marked by the equally sudden acceleration of the galley. The hobyahs were heaving once more.

'Pull!' Bosun screamed.

Shaking, Prow looked to Bosun, who rushed to one of the oars. 'Grab the other oar, quick,' he said, pointing it out. Prow did as she was told, her quickened breaths feeding oxygen to her rushing blood.

They took and pulled on oars as hard and fast as they could, looking up, fearing the bolts that could very well be about to reach out to them. What they saw instead was more disturbing. A tri-hat wearing goblin with one arm waved, broken and yellow grin wide. Bosun frowned.

Prow breathed a sigh of relief. 'Why are they letting us go?'

Bosun swallowed hard and looked behind them, the way they were heading. His curse turned Prow's head as the goblin galley pulled away, and two manned launches from the listing, fortified cog of the Black Guild dropped into the water.

'We're fucked…' was all Bosun could manage.

Prow threw down her oar and wept.

Chapter 31 – Fight or flight

'Surely he's taken notice by now? We've been at it a week and caused him no end of trouble,' Severun said to Longoss, eyeing the destruction of the Black Guild coach, turned on its side as it was. Severun glanced at Egan and back to Longoss. He sighed before Longoss answered. Coppin could have pulled her hair out at the lot of them.

'Oh aye, wizard. He'll have known what was what all along. He's many things is Poi Son,' Longoss spat, 'but stupid ain't one of 'em.'

'Then why has he not moved on us?' Severun went on.

Coppin turned from the body she was searching, nausea bringing its bile to burn her throat. She swallowed it down. 'What do ye think all these blokes in transit were, Severun?'

Severun rolled his bottom lip and shrugged.

'Severun and I expected, well—'

'What?' Longoss interrupted Egan. 'You expected what? Poi Son to come riding for us on some black-clad beastie?'

A snort was Severun's reply as he looked to the sky.

'Of course not.' Egan rubbed his face hard before pulling the brim of his hat low. 'But we're none the wiser as to where he is, are we?'

'We're going about this wrong,' Severun said, taking a deep breath, looking to the clouds above.

Coppin stood and wavered. Egan moved to her side, offering a hand. She waved him away, steeling a glance at Longoss, who was looking the other way. *I can't be doing with him smothering me right now, now with how shitty I'm feeling.*

'Cooey!?' Longoss shouted, hands cupped around his gold-filled mouth. 'Poi Son, ye shite? Come out come out!' He spun on Severun and Egan, the lines besides his eyes creasing up as he flashed them gold. 'Any better?' he said, before stomping off down the deserted street.

Coppin nodded her thanks to Egan, for his offer of assistance, before making to follow Longoss. Severun caught her arm before she could.

'How long have you known?' Severun said in a hushed tone.

Coppin frowned and pulled her arm away, but held his gaze. Egan offered them both a tight smile and followed Longoss.

'What're ye talking about...?' Coppin's voice trailed off as she found herself holding her stomach, something she'd been doing more often of late. She licked dry lips as her breath quickened. She'd been sick of late too, unbeknown to Longoss. A presumed bug as far as she was concerned... as far as she'd been lying to herself. *Gods below...*

'I'm sorry,' Severun said. 'I thought you knew.'

She shook her head ever so slightly, before looking at the back of Longoss, who was kicking stones down the street.

'He can't know,' she whispered, Severun coming closer still. *Oh gods, he can't know...*

'I think he'd be pleased,' he said, with sincerity.

She shook her head again. 'We've never, well not since...' Coppin's shaky voice trailed off.

'Oh.' Severun's voice was barely audible as he followed Coppin's, taking in the large man now arguing with Egan. 'I apologise.'

'Don't.' She swallowed hard and straightening her back, hand falling away from her stomach. Despite her stoicism in the face of so much, the flash of a particular fleshy face in her mind's eye brought a tear. Severun placed a hand on her shoulder. Coppin looked round and up to him.

'Can you remove it?' she asked, serious, eyes boring into Severun's widened orbs.

'What?'

'The thing inside me? Can you get it out, with magic?'

Severun took a step back, removed his hand from her shoulder. He looked from her to Longoss and back, then again. 'I... I—'

'Please, Severun.' She reduced the gap between them. 'Please?'

Head shaking, Severun stammered before Longoss' bellowing voice drew their attention. When Coppin turned back to Severun, he didn't return her look.

'Coming,' Severun shouted, glancing at Coppin one last time. 'I'm sorry,' he mouthed, retreating down the street, his free hand rubbing the back of his neck whilst his white staff clacked on the ground. He seemed to be using it to walk, which she hadn't seen him do before.

After a moment or two of numbness and another shout from Longoss, Coppin followed, the devastating scene surrounding her melting away until all she could see were a split of two rooms: Mother's and the Grand Inquisitor's. With a shudder, she whispered one thing to herself, before reaching the men.

'I need to go back to Mother's.'

***

'What does it say?' Pangan dared.

Poi Son looked up from the parchment, peering over his spectacles to do so. Pangan shifted under his master's attention. After a moment's pause, Poi Son answered.

'The Eatrian assassins guild we petitioned have confirmed the contract is now in the process of being carried out.' Poi Son looked back down at the black ink, to its continuous, fluid style, but more importantly, to the detail worked into the surrounding border: an unnerving pattern of dark red symbols.

Pangan raised up onto his toes from his dark corner.

'You can't see from there, Pangan,' Poi Son said, eyes remaining on the intricate message inlaid in the blood-written border. Pangan dropped back to the flats of his leather shod feet.

'I saw red is all, in the candlelight.' The assassin took a deep breath, appreciating the scent of the beeswax candles around the room.

'Take one, if you like,' Poi Son said, studying the parchment.

Eyes wide, Pangan moved to and picked up one of the yellow candles, taking another deep breath in through his nose as he did so. 'So much nicer than tallow, Master Son.'

'Aren't they just.' The reply was absent minded, a distraction to keep Pangan from asking more questions. Pangan knew it and didn't mind. He'd asked a lot of questions since the strange contract Poi Son was fretting over appeared in his master's hands. It wasn't long until the candle's allure lost out to his curiosity though.

'Have you thought anymore on Longoss and his whore?'

Poi Son sighed and looked up. 'Why do you insist on ruining my mood, Pangan?'

Pangan shrugged. 'Apologies, Master Son. He's at large is all, and I can't help but wonder what he will do next to disrupt us—'

'The guild.'

Pangan frowned. 'Master Son?'

'It is the Black Guild he disrupts, not us, Pangan. Remember that. He makes an enemy of the guild as a whole.' Poi Son looked back to the ink and blood markings before him.

Another pause before Pangan spoke again. 'So, the other two masters are aware of his... antics?'

Poi Son crumpled the edges of the parchment, ever so slightly. Saying nothing, he merely shook his head.

Pangan folded his arms across his chest and rocked slightly, his gifted candle back on the shelf beside him. 'How are you keeping it from them, Master Son? Longoss makes such a nuisance, to say the least.'

'To say the very least, Pangan,' was Poi Son's only reply.

Pangan sighed and began to pace the room, eyes flicking from shadow to shadow. 'I'm not surprised Master Alden-Fenn doesn't know, being abroad and all, but—'

Poi Son looked up, stopping Pangan's words dead. 'Deal with Longoss yourself then,' he said, a snarl pulling at his thin lips, 'If you are so worried about them finding out.'

Hands held out, palms forward, Pangan shook his head once. 'I told you I won't take his mark and I meant it.' He lowered his hands as Poi Son looked down once more.

'Well, stop talking about him. I'm dealing with it and I'm working hard to keep it from them; from *her* in particular.'

Nodding, Pangan moved across to a black harp in the corner.

'Don't touch.'

'Wouldn't dare, Master Son.' Pangan turned full circle and headed back across the room to trace his finger down a river depicted on a map of Altoln.

The near silence stretched out longer than it had at any other point. Pangan rubbed his face, sighed and spoke once more. 'What of Terrina and her useless brother?'

'What of them?'

Pangan shrugged and studied his filthy nails. 'Why are you keeping them around?'

'They're useful.' Poi Son spoke quietly, his face a mix of changing emotions as he turned the bordered letter this way and that.

A laugh was all Pangan could manage. The laugh lifted Poi Son's eyes. The laugh was short lived.

'What amuses you about their plight, Pangan?'

'The fact that you think they're useful to us—'

'To the guild,' Poi Son corrected.

'Aye, to the guild.' Pangan sniffed. 'Blanck can't see, for starters—'

'Trust me when I say they're useful, Pangan. Trust me and leave it be for now. Understood?'

'Well no, not really, but I'll leave it be of course.' Pangan rolled his eyes as Poi Son looked back down.

Poi Son took a circular piece of glass from a drawer, thick and bulbous in the middle, thin at the edges and ringed with gold. He held the lens over the blood-ink of the parchment, despite his already magnified spectacles. He squinted in an attempt to make sense of what he saw scrawled within the blood-red border. He cursed, silently, unusually for him, as Pangan spoke once more.

'Do the other Guild Masters know about that?' Pangan lifted his chin to the agreement from the Eatrian assassins guild that Poi Son was studying, or trying to. Pangan stepped back a pace as narrowed eyes met his own.

'No, they do not,' Poi Son said slowly, dangerously. 'If they did, we'd bloody well know about it.'

Another rare curse from you, Poi Son. What's got you so rattled, apart from Longoss and his whore? Mistress Bronwen, I'd wager. Aye, Mistress Bronwen finding out you've taken a political mark and palmed it off on a foreign guild...

There was a loud knock at the door.

Shit, Pangan thought. He was pretty sure Poi Son thought the same.

Poi Son and Pangan froze, eyes remaining on one another. Both men swallowed hard; both men tensed.

There were three more solid knocks before the two men readied themselves for the worst. They'd barely prepared when the handle turned and the oak door opened.

Chapter 32 – Freeze!

Silence filled the room. None of the usual flourishes and poetic lines from Poi Son. None of the sarcastic comments and playful jibes from Bronwen. The master and mistress of the Black Guild just stood there, staring at one another. Poi Son had stood, but the desk did little to comfort him, that much was clear to Pangan, who stood frozen. Literally. Eyes darting from one superior to the other, waiting for one of them to make a move. Waiting to die.

'Is that necessary?' Poi Son gestured towards Pangan, whose breath was clouding, skin fading to white with a hint of blue, for visual effect, Pangan was sure, knowing Bronwen as he did.

Bronwen adjusted her awful robes and stowed away the off-white wand she'd been balancing between forefinger and thumb. She shrugged, shoulders lifting the greying curls atop them.

'You're giving me the silent treatment?' Poi Son made to move, but Bronwen shook her head.

The movement was so slight Pangan nearly missed it. He'd always found Bronwen's attire strange: flowing robes, salmon-, no, sick-pink today – always horrific colours – and filthy white vambraces on her forearms displaying etched numbers and symbols that made no sense to Pangan.

'How dare you, Poi!' Bronwen's tone, and stare, was vehement.

Pangan cursed in his head, although he was glad she wasn't looking at *him* whilst she spoke… and now pointed, her long-nailed finger jabbing the air between her and Poi Son, who scoffed at it all. Pangan felt numb. Realising he'd missed something said, he strained to pay attention, strained to ignore the cold that seeped into his very bones. His toes and fingers had it worse. And his eyeballs, which throbbed rather than numbed.

'How dare I?' Poi Son rounded the table, a lute string wrapped around each hand, pulled taught. It looked to be cutting into his hands, he was gripping it that tight.

The fuck you gonna do with that, at that range? Pangan would have groaned if he could.

'Yes, how dare you!' Bronwen came forward, crooked teeth revealed through her red-lipped sneer.

'You barged into my chamber, Bronwen, not the other way around.' Poi Son relaxed the grip on his cord. He stood six foot in front of Bronwen, eyes locked on hers. 'You came to me, unannounced.'

Fuck a shit! Pangan's eyes would have widened if his brow wasn't solid. His eyes moved in their sockets though. He thought that strange since they were the moistest parts of him. His eyes had moved to Poi Son, by the desk. The desk... with the contract of agreement on it, from Eatri. *Fuck a shit and more. If she sees that...* He sucked in the cloud of breath he'd expelled. *She may have come because she already—*

'I already know, Poi. There's no point trying to hide it from me.'

Poi Son frowned and, to his credit, didn't mention anything specific. He sat back onto the desk, but not before a slight shuffle which blocked Bronwen's line of sight to the letter. 'How did you find out?' Poi Son asked, resting his cord-holding hands on his thighs. Indeed, one hand had been cut by the string, and blood began to run down the wire, heading towards the other hand before gathering at the lowest point of the dip, to drip, drip, drip.

Unlike Pangan, there was no frost spell or whatever it was on Bronwen, and the woman's eyes widened enough with incredulity for her and Pangan combined.

'How do I fucking know?' she snapped. Poi Son winced at 'fucking'. 'There's been near warfare in Dockside for weeks and all since you set a mark on one of our own, and thought Alden-Fenn and I wouldn't know. All since you fucked up in gutting that stinking shit Longoss, and all, Poi *fucking* Son...' she was enjoying the repeated winces of her fellow guild master, '...since that shitting and pissing fat fucking bastard of a retard Longoss started pissing around with my... my... twatting contracts, marks, clients and fucking gods shitting assassins. You utter, fucking...' Bronwen frowned, eyes narrowed. Pangan imagined grimacing, if he could. She'd clearly, despite her furious anger, enjoyed the twitching show coming from Poi Son's face as she'd employed all the foul language she could muster, but she hadn't enjoyed it enough to miss the poorly hidden relief in Poi Son's eyes when she revealed what her problem with him was: Longoss striking back at the guild and hindering her contracts.

Poi Son noticed she'd noticed. 'I owe you an apology, and Fenn.'

Pangan's teeth began to chatter uncontrollably. *Ironically, I'll be toast if these two start...*

Bronwen was shaking her head. 'You owe me your fucking share,' she said through gritted, smoke-stained teeth.

Toast it is. Pangan closed his eyes. He wasn't a fearful man, but nor was he stupid. "Stay out of trouble, lad!" was all his old man had ever told him. Best advice he'd had from his old man. Only advice, mind, but the best. Didn't stop him gutting people for a living, but it did make him choose his contracts and choose his fights. Alas, right now he had no choice but to stand and freeze to death, unless the spell was lifted or the two egomaniacs before him tore or blasted him to atoms. *Least I'll warm up before the end, if it's the latter.* With the sound of his own heartbeat thumping in his ears, slowing he noticed, through the cold likely, but slowing despite the trouble he was in, Pangan tensed as best he could, gritted – painfully-through-the-cold – teeth as best he could, and waited for the end. And waited some more; a little longer before opening his eyes. It was only then, at the same time as he saw the scene before him, that he felt the tell-tale blood-rush before the pricking and the stabbing and the throbbing and the aching of the thaw. After all, it wasn't the first time the bitch had frozen him, albeit last time, he'd been in her bed chamber; invited, of course. His lips tingled as he smiled. Oh, what a woman she was… despite her, looks, or lack of. So, adventurous!

Poi Son glared at Pangan, hissed like a ferret and stormed from the room, through the door Bronwen had already left via.

Pangan shook his head. He shook his arms and legs too, hopped from one foot to the other and winced as the pricking pins and stabbing needles kicked in. 'What the shitting fuck just happened?'

'I'll tell you later,' came Poi Son's voice from the corridor. 'And please, Pangan,' the master assassin said, 'don't use such language in my presence, it's not becoming of you.'

You're not even in the bastard shitting room, you colossal prick!

'And as soon as you thaw completely—'

'Yes?' Pangan said, his annoyance tainting his tone.

'Go and take Terrina to see her brother. It's time.'

Pangan took a deep breath and let it out slowly, clapping hands and stamping feet as he did so. 'Why now, may I ask?'

'The icicles on your ear lobes should answer that, Pangan.'

'I don't like the sound of that; the shudder in your voice, Master Son, being the main reason.' Pangan moved towards the door.

'You shouldn't,' Poi Son said, out of eye shot, even when Pangan moved into the corridor and frowned. Poi Son's voice came from nowhere and everywhere at once.

'Reassuring.' Pangan shook his head and walked down the corridor, flicking his feet with every step to work out the last of the prickles the returned blood brought.

Here I come, Terrina. I hope you're in a better mood than our so-called betters.

Pangan left the corridor and felt one final shudder as he passed beneath the dark tapestry he hated, which hung over the steps leading down from Poi Son's chambers. The dark tapestry of a hooded figure holding a lute. The hood twitched as the assassin descended the stairs.

'Do you not want to know how it ended, Pangan?' came the disembodied voice.

'No, I fucking don't.' Pangan was down the stairs before the hidden guild master could respond. *Fuck you, Poi Son, Terrina can wait until the morning to spite you and this whole damned situation. I'm for a drink; if Poi Son and Bronwen are at war, it could be my last.*

***

The powder Pangan supplied her did little to cover the puckered pink scars criss-crossing her pale skin, framing red-rimmed eyes that had witnessed countless horrors, some of which had since been re-visited upon her.

Terrina attempted to apply more powder, watching herself in the mahogany set mirror Master Son had gifted her, here in her temporary quarters, within a safe-house.

Even the dawn gloom isn't enough to hide my sickening scars and skin.

Shifting her weight on the stool, Terrina gasped, scabs pulling as her silk dress caught. She gritted teeth and lifted the silk away from the spot that pricked at her nerves. It was far better than the linen and leather she would normally wear, but it pained her to wear such a garment, sure as she was as to how helpless it made her look, and feel.

'But I am, aren't I?' Terrina whispered, the scarred woman in the mirror saying the same thing, lips pulling, causing words to sound different, even to her. Especially to her. She hadn't missed Pangan's face when she'd first spoken, once the wounds about her face had healed somewhat. Her shoulders bobbed in forced laughter. A bitter mirth. Oh, how long her lips had taken to even partially heal, compared to the rest of her. Every time she'd attempted to bite into anything more than sop-in-wine her lips cracked, weeping and stinging with it. Even when they'd looked much better, in the mirror and to her surgeon's insistence, had they split time and again, forcing her back to sipping at a soup like so many worn, toothless hags.

Her breath shuddered from her chest and through her hoarse throat. Her slight breathing caused fluid to gather on her chest, or so the surgeon said. She was only now getting over the illness it caused. The hacking cough and wheezing flared pains she thought she'd got over.

A burning built in Terrina's chest as a tear ran from scar to scar, like a carnival water game. She wiped it away and hissed at the weak image staring back at her through sorrow filled eyes.

'You're an assassin, bitch!' she said, the curse catching and causing another of the lasting coughs to shudder painfully from her, stubborn and determined to stick around. 'I need to get out,' she managed. 'I need to...' She stared at her face, at her mask; the ghastly mask marring what had been a thing of beauty, according to many a fellow. She steeled herself, sat straighter. 'I need to cover this vile visage; it won't do to be seen so, not amongst my peers.'

'Terrina?'

She froze and looked to the reverse image of the doorway behind her. 'In here, Pangan,' she replied, stowing the pot of powder and brushing the rest from her face. She winced, not at the pain, but at the worsened image staring back. The surgeon had done his best, but oh how she hated him for the ragged, dot-lined scars he'd left behind after...

'Longoss, you fucking shite of a man.' Nose wrinkled, jaw set, Terrina dug her nails into the wood of the desk, or rather tried to. The aggression, the anger and the hate, and fear, fell away as a silhouette appeared in the doorway of the mirror. She smiled sweetly, or as sweetly as her tight lips and scarred face would allow.

'Pangan! A pleasure, as always.'

'Cut the act, lass,' Pangan said. 'You don't fool me.'

Her smile was gone before the words left Pangan's scar-less mouth.

'What do you want?' Terrina turned on the stool and even that pained her. His hand rested on the knives at his belt. They always did, whenever he came.

'Me, lass? I want for nothing.'

'Master Son?'

Pangan shook his head. Grinned. 'Blanck!'

Terrina sat stock still, stunned. She thought her brother dead. In fact, they'd told her as much. 'But...' she started.

'But nothing, lass. Do you want to see your brother or not?' Pangan's smile was genuine, Terrina knew that much.

'Does Master Son like to pluck his banjo string?' she replied, a smile of her own appearing.

Pangan laughed at the old joke and turned from the room. 'I'll wait for you outside,' he said, walking away. 'Remember to put your face on!'

Terrina's painful smile fell away, but for a moment. 'You'll not sour my mood now, you shit!' She laughed and rushed to gather her things, pains forgotten, just about. For today she would see her resurrected brother and all was well with the world; she caught sight of herself in the mirror as she flashed a glance around the room to ensure she'd not forgotten anything. *Well, almost all.*

Mere moments later, Terrina gasped at the horror before her.

Pangan winced and looked away. 'I'll leave you two to it.' Without looking back, he left the small room.

'Oh no you don't, Pangan...' Terrina's loud words stopped the man, '...not until I get answers.' Her eyes locked on the empty pits where her brother's grey orbs had once been; red and raw, wrinkled, puckered and... Bile reached the back of her throat, burning, making her gag. The sounds and smells hit her from when Longoss took his revenge on her brother, and on her. The sounds and the smells and the sights and the pains. She shuddered. She ground teeth and sneered as Pangan turned and re-entered the room.

'Very well.' Pangan closed the door and stood with his back to it, studying his fingernails.

'Look!'

Pangan looked up from the picking of said nails, looked up to a face contorted with anger. No, not anger... Terrina's face was twisted, scars pulling, others creasing, in rage. Pure, red-faced rage. Spittle flecked her bottom lip, which trembled along with the rest of her. Pangan took a deep breath and released it as a sigh.

'Look—' Terrina started.

'I *am* bloody looking, lass. Aren't I, eh? Aren't I?' He stared at Blanck, the ghost of a man he once knew, curled up on the bunk, back against daubed walls of filthy cream, a million miles from the rooms Terrina had inhabited since her and her brother's run in with their last mark, with Longoss.

Terrina sneered once more and looked back to her brother, who said nothing. 'Blanck? Brother?' Nothing but the slightest movement of his head. He rocked back and forward, arms wrapped around useless legs. 'It's me, Terrina.'

'I know.' Blanck's voice was hoarse, worse than Terrina's had been even at the height of her recent illness.

Terrina cursed long and hard, in her head. She cursed Longoss, she cursed Poi Son, but most of all she cursed herself for cursing again and again, throughout her recovery; her internment. Oh, how she'd wailed and railed and pissed and moaned about her wounds and ruined face, and all the while here was Blanck, her brother, living in a hovel with his eyes – and worse – removed.

She spun on Pangan. 'Why's he in this roach infested shit of a dive, Pangan, you prick? Why?'

Pangan's eyes narrowed. A rare sight to behold, and a damned scary one. 'Careful, lass.'

Terrina bit her lip rather than release the retort that attempted to enter the world through her wrecked lips. The pain was worth it; worth her life. Pangan was nice, as assassins went, and that made him one of the most dangerous, that she knew. And she knew a lot… or had, before Longoss turned on them.

There was an awkward pause as the two assassins watched one another. Blanck shifted, shuddered out a breath and lay flat, rolling away from his sister to face the mouldy wall.

'He can't see finery, so why surround him with it?' Pangan threw out his hands, palms forward. 'Poi Son's words, repeated by me is all,' he said.

Terrina knew Pangan wasn't scared of her, but she also knew he was no fool and wouldn't risk a fight if unnecessary: "The meanest bastard of a knight can get stuck play-fighting with horse and long-stick, his opponent on the other side of a fence. And if that can happen, the toughest assassin in Brisance can get stuck in a spur-of-the-moment tavern brawl. A fight is only worth it if there's no other way, lass. That's why I chose to be an assassin, so the other fucker doesn't have a chance to fight back and stick me through skill or by my own slip up. I've usually stuck them, you see, before they know it's coming. No pomp and ceremony. No posturing and chest puffing. A length of iron in their back or a good edge across their throat, from behind. Suits me fine." Pangan told her that years ago, and it'd stuck. She'd never followed it, wasn't her way, or Blanck's… perhaps it should have been. Pangan was nearing four decades, at least, and had not a scar to show for his years butchering folk for the guild.

And us…? she thought, turning back to her brother and stroking his back. *Well… we postured and strutted and put ourselves about like The bastard Three.* 'And look where that got us, eh Blanck?' Her voice was but a whisper, but her brother heard it, she knew.

Blanck said nothing and Terrina silently railed at the world.

Chapter 33 - Cruel to be kind

Terrina tipped the sloshing chamber pot out of the bright window, as she had been doing for the past few days and, like those other times, cared little whether there were folk below.

Someone yelled in outrage. Terrina ignored them and closed the window with a slam. The filthy glass rattled in the frame before she let go of it, crossing the room thereafter to place the pot back under her brother's bed.

'Who was that?' Blanck's voice was weak. He'd said little to her since her arrival, despite her attempts at conversation. Most of what he'd said had been questions, questions about immediate things like sounds outside and in.

'You pissed on someone, from a pot.' Terrina's attempted smile fell away when Blanck said nothing. She watched him rock some more, his back to her. His back had been to her the whole time, apart from when she helped him piss through the small pipe the cutters had inserted into... well, it didn't bear thinking about. Terrina gritted her teeth again. She'd been doing that a lot. She fantasised about sawing Longoss' cock off with a dull blade. She knew it wasn't terribly inventive, but didn't care.

'I won't kill him, you know?'

Nothing.

'Blanck, my love?'

A groan was all Blanck gave in return. Terrina watched him wrap his arms around himself all the more, rock all the more, too.

'I'll do what he did to you and more when I find him, but I won't let the stinking bastard die. No. That'd be too—'

A thud against the wall, from the adjoining room, drew her attention. Terrina frowned. 'I didn't think there was anyone else here except your watchers?'

Blanck groaned some more, whimpered, cried, shoulders bobbing. Terrina rubbed his back, her red eyes stinging as more salty tears appeared.

Another thud, followed by a third.

'Shut it, ye shit!' Terrina surged to her feet and made for the door, her hand trailing behind her after leaving Blanck's back. The door opened as her hand brushed the handle.

The rasping, dry breath that filled the following silence unnerved Terrina and she didn't like it. She'd been unnerved more of late than she had her whole life. But if she thought the breathing was bad, it wasn't until she took in the rest of the man, face and all, that she took a step back into the room, mouth as dry as the ragged breaths being forced through the desiccated nose and lip-less mouth she stared at.

Terrina sucked in a breath of her own as recognition struck her, somehow. 'It can't be?' she breathed, shaking her head. 'I thought you were dead?'

The man's voice was no more pleasant than his breathing. His red head tilted sideways to hear her, his ear-less, hairless head ironic considering the man he'd been sent to kill when this horror befell him. 'Believe… me… Terrina lass…' the former street-assassin said, the words scratching at his scar-knotted throat, 'there's many a time… I think I am dead. Then I move… and the pain reminds… me otherwise.' Each breath was a forced and conscious decision, that much was clear. It stopped his unfamiliar voice from forming words, causing him to speak slowly, carefully; painfully.

Terrina held out an arm and invited the man into Blanck's room. 'Did you know my brother was in here?' The man shook his head and shuffled past, his red stained white linens looking more like a mottled dress than a man's clothing. 'I don't think he knew you were next door, either. Did you Blanck?'

Nothing.

The burnt red blur of a man sat on the bunk next to Blanck. He raised a hand, the fingers fused, and patted Blanck's back before lifting puffy eyes Terrina's way. 'It's good… to see you, lass.'

Nodding, Terrina closed the door behind her and moved round to take in the two former killers on the bunk. 'Despite all this,' she said, finding a little strength in herself in comparison to her audience, 'it's good to see you too, Rapeel.'

'Well?' Poi Son was drawing a black bow across the strings of his favourite fiddle. The whine irked Pangan, his right eye twitching as Poi Son repeated the note once more.

'Well, they're together again.' Pangan looked about the room. It was larger than those Poi Son usually resided in, which surprised Pangan. He hadn't been to this one either, which surprised him all the more. *Is the situation that bad? Makes sense that it is, I suppose.* He filled his cheeks and released the breath he'd held. No answer came from Poi Son, so he looked away from the hooded tapestry on the wall, the only bastard thing he recognised since Poi Son had it transported with him to each building he stopped at. He met his master's eyes. 'All this time,' Pangan said, ignoring the fact that Poi Son wanted him to elaborate, 'and I never knew you had a pad above Blanck and Rapeel. I can't say I'd thought about what was up here at all really. Just another separated 'wing' of the Black Guild estate.'

Poi Son forced the bow across at an angle and Pangan grimaced, bringing hands to ears. 'Point taken,' Pangan said through gritted teeth.

Poi Son stopped, placed the bow on the desk before him – there was always a desk before him – and sat back in his high-backed chair.

'Terrina's pissed... er... I mean annoyed, at Longoss, naturally.' Pangan lowered one hand, but rubbed at his left ear with the other. The memory of the awful, instrumental sound was hard to shake. 'Well, she was annoyed at him before, but more so now.'

'And what did Terrina think of Rapeel?'

Pangan snorted. 'Disgust most likely. Sympathy too. Strange seeing the latter in her eyes, but it was there, I could see it through the spy hole.' Pangan grinned. It was brief. He sighed and continued. 'I think they'll work together, if that's what you want to hear, but it'll take them a good while to be fit for it. Flay me, Master Son,' Pangan flung his hands up and let them slap back down against his sides, 'Terrina and Blanck struggled enough against Longoss when they were at their peak, let alone a beaten Terrina with a scorched street-assassin in tow.'

Poi Son seemed to relax a little more. 'I have, items, which will ensure they are fit enough, strong and fast enough. It's their want... their *need* to do it, that I can't force. Well, not with alchemy, anyway.'

Pangan nodded. 'You give them the means, Master Son, and they'll deliver the enthusiasm, I guarantee you that. Especially when Blanck dies.'

'Is that set?' Poi Son leaned forward, hands clasped on his desk in anticipation.

Pangan winced and nodded. 'I can't say I like this, but aye, it's in motion as we speak.' He looked to the floorboards beneath him and sighed once more. *Poor lass*, he thought, guilt threatening his resolve. *Poor Blanck! That lad's been through enough. Mind you, it'll be an end to his suffering, that's for sure.* He looked back to Poi Son, who had the bow back in one hand and was reaching for the fiddle with the other. 'We shouldn't rush any of this, despite the problems we face on the streets.'

'It's not because of that, that I make haste,' Poi Son said, eyes on strings. 'It's the other obvious thing, Pangan.'

'Mistress Bronwen's visit?'

Poi Son nodded and plucked a string repeatedly, the resulting sound twanging through Pangan's head.

'I thought you didn't want to know the silent outcome of that meeting?'

'I'm not saying I do, Master Son. I wanted to know why you've sped things up is all.'

Their eyes met and Pangan's stomach lurched. Poi Son looked back to his strings.

'She didn't, did she?'

Poi Son nodded.

Pangan swore under his breath. 'Full on guild war, Master Son?'

'War, Pangan. With everything for the taking. I'm surprised she's yet to make a move.'

Pangan linked his hands behind his head. *Makes things more complicated than normal for me though, you twat.* 'Well I hope this damned and bloody contract is worth it, whenever it's carried out.'

'It will be.' Twang! 'It will be. Despite that red-haired oaf of a guardsman escaping Dockside and running to the Duke of Yewdale with a warning. Despite that, I have—

'Did you have him arrested, Pangan?' Poi Son asked, forgetting his plucking and looking up to his right-hand man.

Pangan grinned. 'Weeks ago, Master Son. Should have been to court by now and be swinging lifeless in Execution Square. I threatened the magistrates, ye see. Although it didn't take much when I said he were a fire breathing demon.'

Poi Son's eyes widened. 'Well, well, Pangan. Well, well. It's all happening now, isn't it?'

'It is, aye.' *Although I'm a boat-load less enthusiastic about it all than you are. 'Morl's arse, but this is all going to end badly. After all, the Black Guild's at war... with itself! And all because this prick wanted to teach Longoss a lesson.* With a heavy sigh and nothing more, Pangan turned and left the room, hurriedly, since his head ached, no thanks to the twanging plucker he left behind.

Terrina started as Rapeel knelt down beside her, breath scraping through his throat. 'He suffers... every moment... of every day, Terrina.'

She said nothing. Her right hand pulled at her golden locks, her eyes searching her brother's eye-less face for some hint of his former self. He'd said little. He didn't respond to her words, bar winces, grimaces and heavy sighs. He rocked ceaselessly. 'Where's Pangan?' she said, voice low. She feared it may break as she watched her brother. It didn't seem like Blanck, apart from his features, and even they...

'Busy.' Rapeel shifted and Terrina looked sidelong at him. Bile threatened to rise yet again as she studied his twisted, red skin. All creases and sores. 'I'm no looker... Terrina,' he breathed, glancing back, eyes as bloodshot red as the surrounding skin. 'But a rage burns in me that'll make up for anything I've lost, if you'll excuse the analogy.'

Terrina frowned. 'Your voice?'

Rapeel bared more of his teeth than his poor attempts at lips already showed. 'You noticed.' He looked back to Blanck, who was turning his head left and right like a bird locked in a small cage for far too long. 'It heals quickly now. Feels... better. Not how it should be, lass, but better. My skin eases, my strength returns.' He looked back at her, eyes boring into hers. 'You can have the same. You can heal quicker. You can gain the strength you need to pay that pissing bastard back. And we can do it together. For him.' A crisped clump of fused fingers shook as they pointed to Blanck. As Terrina watched the grotesque fingers, she gasped; she saw a lightness return to the skin, a hue more akin to normality. She witnessed them separating, right there before her eyes. The shaking stopped. She looked back to Rapeel's face. It remained scarred, terribly so, but the scars weren't half as bad as they'd been a moment ago.

Terrina scrambled back across the floor, ignoring the pain, a sneer pulling at her mouth, at her scars. 'What trickery is this, Rapeel? What game do you play?'

Rapeel sighed, with relief, with pleasure. He flexed his fingers in front of his face, a face positively beaming as he rose effortlessly to his feet. 'Oh Terrina,' he said, turning to her, unnerving grin ever present. His lips were better than they had been, but they failed to hide his teeth completely. She'd seen opened faces in combat that scared her less when they came back to her in the quiet of the night. 'Pangan did this for me, or rather Poi Son did through Pangan.' He dropped to a squat and sprang up again, twisted left and right at his waist, arms out wide. 'I feel... ready.'

'For what?' she said to the ear-less man.

'Revenge, lass. Revenge!' He grinned all the more, then faltered as he looked back to Blanck's prone form. Blanck had shifted onto his back, oblivious of Rapeel's transformation as he covered his groin with his hands, as he was wont to do of late.

Terrina hadn't missed the movement. It had been in her periphery, whilst staring dumbfounded at Rapeel, but she'd seen him physically move his useless legs into position before doing so. She'd noticed the winces and silent curses his lips worked at whilst doing so. So simple a movement and it pained him so much.

Rapeel crouched down again, looking from Blanck to Terrina. She kept her eyes on her brother, or what was left of him.

'You see it don't you, Terrina? You know it!'

'What?' she whispered. She did know.

'That this is the end for Blanck.'

She sucked in a breath. She watched her brother, who must have heard the words. Nothing. Not a movement nor murmur. He lay there, empty sockets facing a ceiling he couldn't see.

'It's what he wants—'

'Shut up!'

'He won't say it, but nor does he deny it, lass.' Rapeel produced a blade.

The shine from the window seemed like the brightest thing Terrina had ever seen. She cringed and pulled back, tight into the corner of the room as Rapeel moved in closer, hilt held out, offering her the weapon. 'Take it,' he hissed. His voice was much improved, but it rasped past gristle-come-lips nonetheless. 'Take it and end his misery. Take it... and break Longoss' vow!'

Terrina took her eyes from the blade and found Rapeel's. As she did, she noticed his other hand behind his back. Before she could ask what he held, he brought forth Blanck's soiled mask. Her brother's blood-tears stained the white beneath the holes where his grey eyes used to look through. Other speckles of dried blood decorated the previously immaculate mask that she knew so well. The elongated beak-like point came towards her, jerked as Rapeel offered it to her.

'Do it, Terrina. Set him free and avenge him... as both you and him. As one. Brother and sister. Friend and... lover.'

Terrina gasped again. She'd been doing that a lot in that room. Her eyes narrowed, but softened again, glazed over as Rapeel shrugged.

'Yours was a true love. Now do what you would want him to do for you and do it knowing, as he will, that you won't avenge him alone. I will be with you, lass. All the way. Until we finish this. Until we finish Longoss and his green haired bitch.'

Terrina gritted her teeth as she took her brother's mask. She ground them as Rapeel produced a second mask, this one new. The red grimacing face of the thing slipped over Rapeel's own, leaving nothing but a demon visage through which he stared at her, willing her to do the same. And she did. She pulled on her brother's bloody white mask and turned it to the lost face it once protected. To the eyeless, hopeless face she'd loved in too many ways.

Rapeel fell back as a scarred, mask-wearing Terrina slid across the floor, a flash of light on iron preceding the addition of more blood to the elongated mask that had witnessed so many deaths.

'And so it witnesses its previous wearer's demise,' Rapeel whispered, loud enough for Terrina to hear him over the gurgling, bubbling squelches of her brother's final breaths.

Terrina fell over Blanck, careless of the hot blood soaking her blonde hair red. She pulled and squeezed and tugged at his lifeless body as the flow subsided and stopped altogether. 'You promise me, Rapeel.'

'Terrina?'

'You promise me that we'll make Longoss pay for this? You give me your word like he'd give his, that Blanck will be avenged.'

'Aye lass, I promise,' Rapeel rasped. 'I promise. For you, for me and for Blanck.'

Terrina nodded, sat up, hands gripping her dead brother's shirt. She turned to Rapeel, mask to mask.

'I want whatever Pangan has given you.'

Rapeel's mask moved up and down in a grim nod, but he said nothing.

Pangan entered the room, face ashen as he took in Blanck and all his blood. 'You shall have it, Terrina love. You shall have it.' He held a small vial in his hand.

Rapeel rose to his feet and Terrina mirrored him, her new partner. She crossed to Pangan, lifted her mask... *her* mask. It made her shudder once more. She lifted her mask enough to snatch the vial and knock it back.

The pain was worse than anything else she'd endured. Anything else. And as her fast blurring vision settled on Pangan's wincing face, she felt Rapeel's arms wrap around her as her legs gave way, along with her consciousness.

Pangan walked into Poi Son's chamber above the room where Terrina had murdered her brother, and slammed the door behind him.

'I don't appreciate—'

'I don't give a fuck, Master Son. Not at this moment in time.' He glared at Poi Son. Glared with a hint of murder, a hint of his trade.

Poi Son pursed his lips and slid the contract he'd continued to study across the desk, removing and placing his spectacles down at the same time. Leaning back in his chair, he motioned for Pangan to go on.

'It's done.' Pangan breathed heavily, chest rising and falling beneath his black coat. 'I don't know what I've fed them, on your orders, but it's done. They're done.'

'They're done?' Poi Son leaned forward, eyes narrow.

Pangan spun on his master. 'Aye, they're done, Master Son. Done being them. As nasty bastards as they were, they're different now, something else entirely. What was it I fed them? And why the fuck did it take you this long to heal their wounds, if you had the ability before? And most of all, why not Blanck?'

Poi Son sat back again. 'It took some doing, coming by those vials, Pangan. Believe it or not, the guild doesn't carry such substances in stock. Well, not unless your name is Bronwen. As for Blanck… well, he wasn't worth the investment. Wasn't… *there* enough to risk trying.' Poi Son tapped a finger to his temple.

'But what is it?' Pangan's words came through clenched teeth, nostrils flaring, eyes locked in a hard stare.

Poi Son swallowed despite himself. 'Think of a flame. Think of a candle before you blow it out…'

'It flares,' Pangan said immediately, eyes narrowing.

'It flares, gutters and dies. That flare, however—'

'How long, Master Son? How long do they have?'

Poi Son took a deep breath and released it. His hand crept out, touching the edge of the contract from Eatri, touching the blood lettering around the outside that Pangan had seen him glued to since the thing arrived. 'Longer than us if this contract fails. Longer than us if Bronwen or Alden-Fenn come for us.'

Pangan rubbed his face hard with both hands, dropped them and paced, hands now clenching at his sides, near the hilts of his daggers.

'They'll take Longoss, the two of them, Pangan. I'm sure of it.'

'What then?' Pangan spun from his pacing, incredulous at Poi Son's incessant harping on about Longoss. 'The damage is done. The red-bearded guardsman made it out and informed the bloody Constable of Alton weeks ago. Mistress Bronwen wants you – us – dead. So what does it matter if those two masks down there slice Longoss from stomach to neck? What does it bloody matter?'

Poi Son rose, walked across to a corner and began plucking the strings of his tall, black harp. 'This needs re-stringing soon.'

'What!?' Pangan gaped at the man in the corner, the man talking instruments when he should have been talking war. This wasn't Poi Son, not the man Pangan knew.

'I'm going to have the strings made, Pangan. I'm going to have it re-strung with Longoss' intestines.' He flashed a dangerous look Pangan's way. 'Carry on talking to me the way you are and I'll have my lute re-strung too, and my fiddle, and my... well, you get the idea. Your intestines would go a long way, I'm sure.'

Pangan held Poi Son's stare for a time, before looking to the floor. 'Apologies, Master Son. This affair is... poor.' The word didn't do the affair justice. Poor was poor, but Pangan had nothing else at that moment, with Poi Son's eyes boring into him. His rage faded as he realised he could do nothing about it, about any of it. Well, not nothing...

'It is all poor indeed, I know that.' Poi Son moved back to his chair and dropped into it. 'Have Terrina and Rapeel strike against one of Bronwen's holds, tonight. Have them test their newfound strength and vigour before moving on to Longoss. I'm not going to sit here until that bitch storms this place, wand a wagging. We shall deliver the first blow, Pangan, and I want her to feel it keenly. If Wesson thought the Black Guild was at war before, because of Longoss' interference and the squabbling of street-assassins and gangs since the plague's touch, they were sorely mistaken, and I want the streets to know it!'

Pangan nodded, but said nothing. Where had it all fallen apart? With Longoss' betrayal? No, for he wasn't the first assassin to ever deny an order or walk away from the guild. No indeed, it was with the bloody contract Poi Son was even now keeping close to his chest. *With the bloody passing of that contract to another guild, for 'morl's sake. Another guild! What are we going to get out of all this when the damned contract is being carried out by another guild?* Pangan had no idea. It was all unravelling about him and Poi Son had him, caught in the thick of it. He sighed and nodded again. 'Where do you want them to strike?'

'I'll let you decide the details, Pangan, but make it good.'

'Oh I will,' he said. *If I'm going to do anything, I'll do it good, that's for sure. No half measures. When I act, I act. I just usually have a choice in the matter. Although I do have a choice here, of a sorts.* He hid the smile that thought produced. 'Alright, Master Son, I'll go and prepare them.' He turned to leave without waiting to be dismissed.

'Pangan.'

Nostrils flared. 'Master Son?' He didn't bother turning.

'Where *is* Alden-Fenn?'

'At sea, I believe.'

'Good,' Poi Son said. Pangan heard the tuneless plucking of strings. 'One problem at a time.'

One problem at a time? Pangan counted Longoss and Bronwen as two, and that was before all the bastards and bitches that came with them. 'Very well, Master Son. I'll report back when I have more.' It was all he could to not to spit the words.

Chapter 34 - Rowberry

Rowberry was pretty. As pretty as a human town could be, anyway. Pink, white and blue blossom trees bloomed late in the mild northern summer, whilst sheep cropped the fields flanking the walled town and river it straddled. Skylarks sang and ewes bleated continuously for lambs recently removed. The golden horse and its pale-skinned rider neared Rowberry's gates, men-at-arms watching. The man pulled up the hood of his piss-pungent robes and clutched at the satchel by his side.

A maille mitten lifted, palm forward. The palomino stopped.

Three men moved out, their black and white gambesons the livery of their liege lord, their shields the same. 'Hold, stranger,' the closest said, hand lowering to his sheathed arming sword. 'What's yer business?'

'Monk,' Cheung whispered, hand in satchel.

The sergeant screwed up his pock marked face and raised onto tiptoes. 'Eh? Speak up would ye.' He pulled back when the strong smell of urine hit him.

Cheung leaned down towards the man. 'Monk,' he said a little louder, in poor Altolnan. 'From Eatri.'

A sceptical grunt was the sergeant's reply.

'What's he about?' a conical helmed guard asked his sergeant.

'Monk, so he claims. From Eatri.'

'On a horse like that?' Conical said.

'Aye, that's what I thought.'

Hooves drummed dry earth and six eyes focused passed Cheung and his mount. Without another word, the sergeant hastily waved the self-proclaimed monk on through the gate and held up his maille mitten to the incoming riders.

Cheung attempted to listen to the questions and answers coming from behind, but gave up, taking the lucky opportunity he had been given to enter the town without further questioning.

As the shadow of the large gatehouse passed over horse and rider, Cheung leaned forward and whispered into the palomino's flicking ear. 'That was close,' he said, before rubbing the beast's neck, followed by one pat then two. Golden head tossed and rider straightened. 'Now, to find some much needed food and water.' Cheung smiled and urged his mount and friend on when he saw a worn tavern sign not far away.

***

Pangan sighed, head in hands, elbows on knees and bum on warm tiles. He sat on a Guild District roof and watched, in broad daylight, as the masked duo that was Terrina and Rapeel sauntered up the busy street below. Another duo sat with Pangan, a girl and a boy, although the boy to Pangan's left was no more than twelve years, the girl only a little older.

The boy-watcher chuckled and pointed. 'Look at that man, he near on fell over as he stumbled out of Terrina's way.'

The girl to the other side of Pangan huffed. 'You're such a boy.'

The boy frowned and Pangan smirked.

'Uh oh,' the girl said, nudging Pangan in the ribs. She pointed to four armed men escorting a richly dressed fifth. Terrina and Rapeel didn't slow as they approached the noble and his retainers, all of whom put hands to belted weapons.

Pangan hushed the boy before he could speak.

People fled, aware blood was going to be spilt. Pangan mused that the noble likely thought the two masks were targeting him. The man fell back, his guards moved forward.

Pangan watched Terrina flick her unarmed right hand out to the side, a clear indication she wanted the men – who had created a line across the street – to move aside.

'No further!' the one guard with a sword shouted, from the middle of the line. He drew that sword as the masks continued.

'This should be good,' the boy said.

The three other guards drew a falchion, an axe and a mace between them. None had shields, but all wore maille and padding. No helms.

'Veterans,' Pangan muttered, more to himself than the watchers. The way they moved, carried themselves; the way they shifted about one another, without the need to look what their companions were doing. Pangan glanced at the velvet and silk coated noble. The man looked inconvenienced, not scared.

'This won't be easy,' Pangan said, 'but it'll be a good test.'

The boy frowned and looked sidelong at Pangan. The girl sucked in a breath.

The guards had split, two to Terrina and two to Rapeel.

Dull and shiny iron and steel flashed, was thrust, swiped, slashed and dropped.

One of Rapeel's two hatchets jutted from the face of the falchion wielder, who now lay flat and dead for sure.

The guard with the mace jabbed with the lump of iron, trying to stun, knowing it to be too slow in such a fight for swinging.

'Clever,' Pangan said, head now out of his hands.

The boy winced as the swordsman's length of steel came close to piercing Rapeel's leather-clad chest.

It was then that it happened.

Pangan couldn't help but stand, step down the roof a little, eyes wide. The children gawked.

In silence, masks eerily inactive, staring, the two assassins rushed forward, through openings in the guards' positions, shrugging off the bite of sword and axe to run with incredible speed at the shocked nobleman.

The man, frozen, tense, shaking, fell in a spray of arterial blood as stiletto and hatchet found their marks simultaneously.

Without turning to even consider the two remaining guards, who were howling rage-filled threats, Terrina and Rapeel ran to and kicked their way through – with ease – the door to the tall building they'd been intent on throughout the fight, their would-be mortal sword and axe wounds seemingly forgotten.

Pangan was stunned. So were the watchers.

'How…'

'I don't know, lass,' Pangan lied, mind on the vials he'd given them both.

Screams came from within the tall building. Pangan looked down and saw the two guards running in the opposite direction. They'd stripped their comrades, and their former master, of purses. Looking back up, drawn by more screams, Pangan saw a man in simple clothes run from Bronwen's property. A flash of light on steel as a knife followed him. He fell to the ground, face smashing on cobbles. He didn't get up. Didn't even stir.

In the time Pangan would have thought it would take to get to the first floor unchallenged, a woman crashed through a shutter and fell to the ground below, head splitting and spilling its contrasting contents onto the bland stone beneath.

Another woman followed the first, her scream cut short by a similar impact. Her leg twitched, Pangan noticed, and continued to do so as he looked away.

'Who were they?' the girl breathed. She licked dry lips and hugged herself, unable to tear her eyes from the scattered bodies.

'It was a Black Guild poison pad,' Pangan said, voice dry, hoarse even. 'I need a drink,' he added, as Terrina and Rapeel emerged from the building, blooded, wounded yet calm. They walked back up the street, narrowly avoiding the bodies they'd created. They looked like masked death. Bloody masked death. When both looked up to Pangan, in unison, he shifted, almost losing his footing. He managed a nod whilst swallowing hard.

The masks nodded back and went on their way.

Pangan turned to the ashen faces of the children, saw the boy wiping tears from his face, embarrassed. Motioning for them to follow, Pangan moved to leave the rooftops, a reassuring, clasping hand on a shoulder of each of them. It was more to steady himself though, he had to admit.

Flay me, Poi Son, he thought, guiding the children away from the bloody scene. *What have we done? What have we created?*

***

The soup was good. Watercress and onion apparently, although Cheung cared not. It had been countless days since he had eaten a warm meal. He knew he had to eat slowly and not be a glutton, otherwise he'd bring it all up to waste. The road had been long, but uneventful, with nothing but gibbet trees and way stones to mark most of it. The odd inn had appeared by the side of the road, but he'd avoided them, with thoughts of the last one, and Dignaaln, haunting him whilst skirting around the dangers they presented; the mounted patrols he'd seen and narrowly avoided.

His nights had been spent off the road, without fire, and it had taken more than a couple of days to manage to wake before the palomino's morning ablutions. Much of the route had been flanked on the right by a distant forest and on the left by low hills and fields scattered with distant farms and hamlets and the odd village, their Samorlian church spires pointing to the sky like giant, dead, branchless conifers.

Cheung appreciated the open spaces he'd travelled through. It had given him time to clear his head; meditation had come to him, eventually, from within the saddle. He had learnt to trust the horse early on, which allowed him to fade from the world and find his centre once more.

Mopping up the last of his soup with stale bread, Cheung smacked his lips and sat back against the flaking daub of the wall. He could see the whole tavern from where he sat: every brazier, table and smoke filled corner. Wiping his mouth with his sleeve, Cheung's eyes settled on a man opposite him. The man's hood was up, as was Cheung's, but from the way he scooped at his own bowl with pale fingers, Cheung knew he was Eatrian.

It's not uncommon, Cheung thought, scanning the tavern again before settling once more on the hooded figure. His hand dropped to his satchel, its presence a comfort. *We're not the only two in here with hoods up, either.* A lardy man on a nearby table wore his long-tailed hood up, the embroidered mantle of it crenelated like the stone teeth of a rampart. And a young man by the door wore a leather hood up, whilst talking to a group of men.

The bowl on the far side of the room joined the table. The hooded Eatrian looked at Cheung. Shrouded eyes met. Neither moved.

Before either could make sense of it, the group by the door shifted as half a dozen men-at-arms in green and white livery entered the tavern. Their eyes darted here and there, hands working the hilts of swords, hammers and axes by their sides. The lead man, a knight for sure, wore a dog-faced bascinet, visor clipped up, the others nothing more than maille coifs and padded caps, if that. They looked hard, these men, not like the lazy gate guards, but veterans all.

With his right hand, Cheung found a bone handle in his satchel, which he used to pull the bag across his lap, bringing the second kama into range of his left hand. He slowed his breathing and sat a little straighter, watching as the bascinet wearing knight leading the group beckoned a tavern girl over. Hushed words were exchanged and a slender hand pointed towards the hooded Eatrian opposite Cheung. The hood gave a subtle shake of the head, its meaning directed at Cheung, who nodded in return and sat back. His stomach churned at what was to come. *Masters forgive me...*

Soldiers moved.

An assassin responded.

A table flipped onto a brazier, sparks reaching out to people and flames licking high and wide. Burning logs and embers caused screams and curses both. The sudden flash was followed by a darkening of the corner and Cheung watched as his fellow guild member used the confusion to his advantage; he didn't even attempt to flee.

Visor up, the knight shouted orders at his men and drew his sword, holding it with both hands, hilt and blade. He stood firm by the door as the others shoved patrons aside and rushed for the unarmed assassin. People scrambled to get across the room. Another table went over, along with stools, benches and pots of ale. A small lapdog yapped from off to the side, unseen. The tavern keeper yelled and his girls shrieked.

Reaching the moving assassin, the closest soldier reached for the Eatrian's robes to halt any attempt at an escape. The robes came free and were followed by a pale, scarred hand. The soldier dropped his falchion and fell back, both hands clutching his crushed windpipe.

'I want him dead!' the knight shouted, advancing towards the confusion. 'He mustn't escape.'

Bare feet flicked and hands flashed across angry faces. An axe missed completely, thwacking into a table. A hastily swung hammer smashed into a retreating bystander, dropping him hard to the ale soaked floor.

Cheung watched a knee break and the hammer wielder go down, face a picture of agony. The assassin held no weapons but his pale hands and feet. He struck left and right, whilst parrying incoming iron. Cheung's grip on his weapons tightened as the axe man dropped to one knee and hooked his blade around the assassin's leading leg. Before the soldier could pull, the leg flicked out, connecting with his face.

Teeth clattered across the floor and a choking groan added itself to the cacophony. People scattered as the fight moved across the tavern. Most made for the door, pushing and shoving to fit through the small opening.

Standing, Cheung moved with the crowd. To stay was to draw attention – he would have been the only one to do so. Glancing back over his shoulder, he saw the assassin dispatch another soldier, before facing the last, who was now backed by the advancing knight.

The crowd pressed in on Cheung, forcing him to the door, but he held on long enough to turn and look back one more time. Cheung saw, despite the gloom and chaos as he was pushed and pulled backwards through the door, the relief on his guild brother's face as they locked eyes. He also saw the shock and pain in those eyes as the knight stepped in and ran the assassin through.

Cursing, Cheung made for the stable. The fight drew more and more people, until Cheung was fighting against a tide of wool, linen, felt and the people it covered. He shoved on through, all elbows and fists. Curses followed, audible, about his rudeness and his smell, but no one was brave enough to do anything about it. Either that, or they were too curious as to what was drawing the crowd.

'Get me a cleric!'

Cheung grimaced as he heard the knight's voice above all others.

'I've men down,' the knight continued, at the top of his voice, 'and they're bloody heroes!'

Jumping atop a stone water trough, Cheung risked a look back over the bobbing caps and hoods flocking to the tavern. He wished he hadn't as the knight lifted a severed head. 'So ends an assassin!' he shouted, face spattered with blood.

The crowd cheered as more arrived, as if a flood.

Masters forgive me, but I thought I was the only one to be sent.

Teeth clenched with renewed determination, Cheung moved on.

Chapter 35 – Renewed resolve

Terrina's breaths sounded loud in the mask her brother had worn. She didn't like how it affected her vision, poor on the periphery, but she did like, no... *love*, how it widened the eyes of those that saw it; of those that saw it alongside the red-raw mask of Rapeel, walking alongside her. He'd done well, for a street-assassin. Nowhere near as able as Blanck was... had been. Terrina snarled. *Despite whatever it was Poi Son gave us, I feel Rapeel slowing me in a fight. But he'll get there, eventually.*

Terrina shuddered, her muscles swelling, rippling beneath her scar-patterned skin. Teeth ground, nose wrinkled. *He'll learn, or he'll be left behind.* She glanced left, looked left, the mask obscuring her glance. Framed by her brother's mask, she looked upon the red, grimacing visage of Rapeel's false face... although it looked more akin to his burnt features than her brother's mask did hers. A shiver ran up her back at the thought of Rapeel's wounds, her wounds, her late brother's wounds and death... by her own hand. Rapeel looked back, his eyes visible through the holes, visible and set as hard and cold as Terrina's own.

Terrina looked forward once more, saw a man run from their path. She smiled. A humourless thing, and for no one but herself, it being hidden and all.

Hissing, she found the hilts of her stilettos and broke into a mad dash, after the fleeing stranger. Reaching him with ease, she drove her blades into his back, dropping him to the floor where he coughed and cried together, a mangled, strangled attempt at some noise anyway; in fear more than pain, Terrina considered.

On she walked, calmed through the violent act, her steps accompanied by a double thud, the man's whimpering silenced.

Rapeel was alongside her once more. Neither bothered to sheath their blooded blades. They ploughed on, Terrina increasing their speed, scattering folk as they made their way to their rendezvous with Pangan and the watchers; impatient, Terrina wanted to ask what striking Mistress Bronwen's poison pad had to do with slashing Longoss and his green-haired bitch to pieces.

***

It felt different now, but Cheung knew he had to harden himself to it. Wiping away the blood from a fresh cut across his ankle, he rode the palomino across Rowberry's wide, house-lined bridge. His scarred face was shaded by the wide brimmed straw hat he now wore. His urine soaked robes were gone and he wore the common braes, hose and shirt seen on most of the men about him. He had a well-worn jerkin rolled and tied to the saddle and a flea infested cloak wrapped about his satchel.

He thought about the previous owner of the clothes, before pushing the brutal scene from his head. Anger wasn't something Cheung had been used to before the start of his journey. Not like he'd felt just now, at the sight of one of his guild brothers falling, anyway. At least he used it to his advantage; the stabling of the Palomino had cost him nothing, nor had the clothes.

A group of scantly-dressed girls called out to him as he rode past, commenting on his fine steed, amongst other things. He knew what they were about. It wasn't as if there weren't whores in Eatri, but Cheung had never had the inclination or curiosity of most men in that respect. He presumed the masters had seen to that long ago.

He longed for the open road once more. If he couldn't have the rooftop gardens of his home city, he would rather have the fields and woodlands of Altoln, compared to the crowded town and its crooked houses perched on a bridge.

Once across the wide river, Cheung guided the horse to a busy gatehouse. The large, central gate was open to horses and carts, the two smaller doors to either side funnelled those on foot. It was far busier than the gate he'd used to enter the town through, as had been the town this side of the river.

More guards, Cheung thought, eyeing the black and white clad men talking to a group of merchant travellers. As he approached, the closest one raised a hand without looking. The man was intent on a woman walking through one of the side doors, so Cheung made the best of it.

'Beautiful, isn't she?' Cheung said, in the trader tongue.

The man turned. 'You don't speak Altolnan?'

Cheung bit back a retort. *If I didn't, what would be the point of asking that whilst speaking it?* He shrugged instead. 'Trader tongue?'

The guard turned his head, offering his ear, frowning as he did.

'Trader,' Cheung sounded out. He glanced across as the woman from the small gate passed. The guard's eyes caught her and followed. A hand waved.

Pathetic. Cheung waved back and rode on through the gate. 'But fortuitous,' he whispered, in Altolnan.

Chapter 36 - Fun and revelations

'Ye well, lass?' Longoss took hold of Coppin's arm, felt the dampness of the linen sleeve. It wasn't a cold day, it being summer and all, but nor did it warrant such sweat. They were in a shaded alleyway after all.

Coppin nodded but didn't meet his eyes.

Longoss frowned. He glanced around the corner, watched as Severun and Egan knocked on a freshly painted red door on the well-to-do Guild District street they'd travelled to. He ducked back and looked at Coppin, who looked away.

'Lass?'

'What?' Coppin snapped.

Cheeks filled with air, Longoss shook his head, released his breath and looked back around the corner. Severun and Egan were gone, red door closing.

'Ye ready, lass?'

'Get on with it, will ye.'

'King's teeth, Coppin.' Longoss turned and took Coppin's shoulders in his big hands. 'What's the bloody matter with ye? What've I done?' He'd stooped so they were at eye level with one another. He forced her to look at him, firmly but with care.

Coppin swallowed and licked dry lips. She blinked, a lot, and sobbed as the big man pulled her close, wrapping his arms about her, his chin on her head.

'Gods, ye stink,' she said, bringing a chuckle from her own lips.

'Thanks.'

'It's true.'

'I know. There,' Longoss said, Coppin's hair tickling his chin, 'I've admitted that I stink. Now admit what vexes *you*?'

Coppin looked up, the movement pushing Longoss' head back. 'Vexes?'

Longoss shrugged, pulled his hand back to scratch at his ear-hole. 'Heard Severun saying it.'

'Doesn't suit ye, Longoss.'

He looked down, eyes narrow. 'Quit skirting the question. Tell me what—'

'Vexes me?'

Gold shone. Longoss nodded and Coppin sighed, rubbed at her eyes and turned to look back down the alley at the sound of a door slamming.

Both Coppin and Longoss jumped as a first-floor shutter left its frame and shattered against the wall opposite, falling to the ground as white smoke billowed from the hole left behind.

'That's us.' Coppin left Longoss and ran around the corner, to the red door.

Longoss sighed and followed, jaw bunching.

Egan stepped back, avoiding the slashing cleaver the brute of a man he'd thrown the glass of wine at wielded. Another swing and the brute's face reddened to match the wine stain across his shirt. His anger and frustration caused him to flail as Egan leaned this way and that, avoiding rather than parrying the hasty attacks. Egan was surprised this wasn't one of Poi Son's street-assassins, since he acted the same as many Egan had faced since setting out on the mission. The brute was dressed better, spoke better, but was still a useless thug.

As the brute roared and launched himself forward, Egan hopped to the side, rolled his rapier over and forced steel through linen, skin, muscle and heart. He felt the scrape of ribs through the hilt, through his palm and fingers. He withdrew the blade with a squelch as the large man crashed to the floor, dismantling a wooden stool in the process. He didn't move after that, apart from spasmodic twitching.

Egan opened the door Severun had gone through and a wall of white smoke filled his vision and assaulted his nose. Not wood-smoke, not oil-smoke; he didn't recognise the smell and assumed it to be Severun's work, along with the bang that had sprung him to action.

'Severun?' Egan said, in the way people do when trying to shout quietly.

'Come in.' Severun's calm voice came from the smoke whitened room.

Egan turned from the door, took a deep breath and strode in, rapier held defensively. The room was beginning to clear as a shutter-less window drew out the acrid cloud. A tall silhouette greeted Egan, accompanied by Severun's voice once more.

'It is done.'

'Just like that?' Egan frowned, doubtful.

'Just like that.' Severun's features became clear, as did the destruction of the room, of the vials and bottles and tubes and barrels; crates and chests and racks upon racks of shredded books and scrolls.

Egan's mouth hung upon. He'd forgotten the smell, the taste of the smoke. 'What was this place?'

Severun looked about, wafting his hand in front of his face. 'The Black Guild's centre for potions and spells. Very impressive indeed. Most of it arcane, of course.'

Egan saw Severun shudder at the word, despite the white shroud about them. 'And it's not Poi Son's place? I mean the thug outside was little different to one of his street-assassins, but I don't know the inner workings of the Black Guild.'

'Apparently not.' Severun moved over to a corpse, crouching and placing a hand on the unmoving chest. He pulled his lips into a tight smile. 'Not according to this here mage.'

Egan took two steps to close the gap between him, Severun and the corpse. He looked at the woman, dressed more like a handmaiden than a mage. 'Whose, if not Poi Son's?' Egan whispered, crouching alongside Severun. Their eyes met.

'Mistress Bronwen's.'

Egan frowned. 'I've heard that name.' He searched his memory, but came up blank.

'I'm not surprised.' Severun looked back to the dead woman before them. There were no visible wounds. 'The witchhunters of Wesson hunted her for decades.' There was an eerie silence between them after the words. 'So has the Wizards and Sorcery Guild.'

'And this is her?' Egan looked to the middle-aged woman, the lines on her face shallow, her features relaxed. She literally hadn't known what hit her.

Severun barked a laugh and stood. 'No, Egan. This is one of her apprentices.' He looked to Egan as the man stood. 'If this was Mistress Bronwen and I'd enacted the spell I did here...' he took a deep breath, looked about the room, out the window and back to Egan. 'This block would have been levelled, I would think.'

Egan squeezed the hilt of his rapier. *I'm not sure I believe that, but I get the point.* 'Scary thought,' he said, turning and leaving the room. He heard two sets of footsteps ascending the stairs. He made ready, then relaxed as Longoss and Coppin appeared.

'Is it done?' Longoss frowned as he looked to the brute's corpse.

Coppin cast her eyes about, knife at the ready.

Egan nodded. 'It's done, apparently. There were only two here.'

Longoss screwed his whole face up. 'That seems odd. Ye sure this is the place, Severun?'

'I'm sure.' Severun emerged from the haze of the next room. 'A guard and a mage.'

'Seems easy indeed.' Coppin sheathed her knife.

'This is Mistress Bronwen's place,' Severun said to Longoss. 'You said it was the guild's centre for magic and I've confirmed it. I doubt Mistress Bronwen operates the same way as Poi Son though, hence the lack of street-assassins and young thugs. Hence the ease of it.'

Longoss nodded slowly. 'Makes sense. She's more about political assassination, or so I hear. A drop of poison, a spell to stop ye waking, and so on.'

'You knew it was Mistress Bronwen that ran this place?' Egan asked, a little annoyed he'd not been given all the information.

Longoss shrugged. 'I know she's mistress of the guild. I didn't know for sure whether this was one of her places. Magic was never my thing.'

Egan grunted at that, only slightly satisfied with Longoss' answer. *Is this what he wanted? To move from targeting Poi Son to targeting Bronwen?*

'Least we know the boy watcher were telling the truth.' Coppin turned from the sight of the dead man. 'We can use him again.'

Egan shook his head. 'It's too risky to go back to him. We've made a statement here, to Bronwen or whoever. She'll know something is afoot when she finds our handy work and questions Poi Son about it. Don't you think?'

Severun looked to Egan. 'If she hasn't already, considering what we've been seeing on the streets; considering the places we moved against that have already been hit? The places we assumed were due to the aftermath of the plague and increased gang activity? I may have made waves in what I've been doing with you, against the Black Guild. I may have triggered something between Bronwen and Poi Son. Unintentionally, of course, and I can't be sure.'

Egan balked at that, wondering how quickly such waves would travel, be picked up on and acted on. He noticed Longoss grin gold.

'Severun may be right,' Longoss said, 'although, if Bronwen knew Poi Son had a contract on King Barrison, a political contract, there'd be less signs and more… all-out war. It's more likely Coppin and me caused the current conflict, as intended.'

They froze, all of them, at the sound of shouting coming from the street. A loud thud and another. A scream followed.

The group looked at each other.

'Are we discovered?' Coppin asked.

'Damned waves,' Egan muttered.

Severun's eyes shifted colour, shape even, much like that of a frog or toad. Static rose Coppin's long, green-black hair.

'The window!' Egan rushed into the room where white smoke clung to the ceiling like a bank of cloud. The others followed when they heard the door to the street smash open.

'It's too high to jump,' Egan said, looking at Coppin. He knew he would make it, knew Longoss would probably bounce and that Severun could likely create a bed of feathers to land in, should he so choose, but Coppin and her unborn child?

Another concussive thud outside, in the street, followed by shouts, which in turn was followed by booted feet on the stairs. Many feet.

'Just bloody go!' Coppin shouted, a hand on her stomach, Egan noticed. He noticed Severun's apparent ease at the situation too, following the shifting of his eyes.

'Hold!' a gruff voice shouted from the other room.

Longoss growled and turned, knife in hand. Coppin mirrored him. Egan gritted his teeth and spanned and loaded his small crossbow whilst Severun pushed to the front, causing Coppin's hair to lift like she was submerged in water.

At the first sign of movement in the room beyond, Egan grabbed Longoss' arm and pulled him back as Severun threw his hands high, a smile about his face; Coppin's hair dropped about her shoulders.

'Thank Samorl,' Egan breathed, relaxing as the green and white quartered livery of the Duke of Yewdale filled the far room. 'It's Morton's men!'

'Severun,' Sir Merrel said, ahead of half a dozen men-at-arms, 'I have a message.'

'I don't even want to know how they found us.' Longoss ground gold.

Egan narrowed his eyes on Sir Merrel, then looked sidelong to Severun. 'Oh, I have an idea how,' he said, fixed on the wizard and his smile. He thought back to the message he and Severun had sent from Keep's tavern, to Lord Strickland.

Severun met Egan's eyes and grinned all the more.

***

'Well, Master Son?' Pangan sat with his head in hands, elbows on knees, much like he had whilst watching Terrina and Rapeel take Bronwen's poison pad.

'Well what?' Poi Son crouched alongside Pangan, high on a roof overlooking the broken red door of the guild's, or rather Bronwen's, centre for magic, white smoke lifting from the back of the building. They'd watched a knight, mage and men-at-arms in unmistakable livery enter the building after a brief scrap with what could only have been Bronwen's watchers. There'd been a sudden and audible display of magic from both sides – posturing more than anything, Pangan thought – before the watchers departed and the soldiers entered the building, the same number remaining in the street outside, watching, alert, the mage amongst them. These were dangerous men, Pangan mused, professional soldiers the lot of them, the female mage worst of all. They made the City Guard look like village militia.

'Well, what do you think of Longoss and his chums hitting Bronwen's place? And, what do you think of the Lord High Constable of bloody Altoln's men showing up but a moment later? This is far from the Duke's city abode, Master Son.'

'It is, yes.' Poi Son pursed his lips and wrapped an instrument string around his left index finger, before unravelling it and starting again. He repeated the process several times.

'Well, Master Son?'

'I think, Pangan, we finally know who's aiding our friend Longoss.' Poi Son looked to Pangan, grinned and retreated from their position on the roof, a boy and girl following.

Pangan sighed, rubbed his face hard and followed. 'Like that's a good thing to discover,' he said to himself as he moved away. 'Least we don't need to send the masks in there now.' It was Pangan's turn to grin. *And Poi Son was pissed off with my choice for the first assault*, he thought. *If I'd had Terrina and Rapeel hit this place instead of the poison pad*, he looked back over his shoulder at the smoke lifting into the sky, *we'd have missed all the fun and revelations.*

Chapter 37 – Back to the rooftops

Pangan watched from the rooftop, face set in a scowl as white and red masks appeared in the wide doorway of a burning building. Screams came from within. A man pitched from a window three stories up, breaking and burning on the cobbles below. Pangan heard the hue and cry, locals screaming for the City Guard and for water. He watched as a man ran from a neighbouring building. When the man saw the two masks, he halted, scrabbled to turn and raced back inside, face awash with fear.

'What have we released,' Pangan whispered. The lad and lass beside him looked his way but said nothing. Their eyes moved back to the street below, where Terrina and Rapeel were untying stolen horses and mounting them, looking back to the flickering, spitting and crackling mess of the building they'd assaulted. The duo urged their mounts on. On to the next target. Poi Son had decided on multiple, swift strikes against Bronwen, rather than a single, grand assault. Longoss and his merry men, and woman, had clearly begun targeting the guild indiscriminately, not caring which guild master, or mistress, they worked against. That being the case, Poi Son knew Bronwen's third of the guild would be suffering as much as his own, or thereabouts, being that her operations were spread throughout Wesson. Still, the few holds she commanded in Dockside itself were to be struck and torched throughout the night, and damn the consequences. Poi Son's very words, as Pangan remembered them.

The attack on Bronwen's poison pad in Guild District had been all Pangan had planned, truth be told, but upon reporting back to an annoyed-to-say-the-least Poi Son, they'd moved on Bronwen's centre of magic, only to witness Longoss and his allies doing the very same.

And that was it. As far as Poi Son was concerned, there was now an opportunity to strike Bronwen everywhere. Fast and hard. Now, it wasn't outside the centuries old laws of the guild for Pangan to refuse Poi Son, to refuse a mark, but it was another thing entirely to directly refuse Poi Son in an official war within the guild, especially when Poi Son was acting so out of character; unpredictably. Pangan had thrived for years because he knew his master well. He knew Poi Son's moods and whims and knew, most importantly, his business. Pangan felt like he didn't know anything now, apart from the fact that Poi Son had potentially ripped the Black Guild asunder. It wasn't like there was never infighting, but this… well, this was as worse as it could get. It was all he could do to curb his masked assassins from wiping Bronwen's known haunts out altogether in that one night, the speed of them. When he'd ensured them that all of this was necessary before they could find and face Longoss – the reason they'd taken the vials Poi Son had procured for them, Pangan thought they'd been about to rip him to pieces. He shuddered at the recent memory.

Sighing and motioning for the young watchers to depart, Pangan took one last look at the destruction the two masked assassins delivered, before turning and following the watchers across the rooftops, on towards the next target in the escalating, ridiculous war.

***

'But we have Morton's support,' Longoss said, trying to calm Keep, who was pointing a loaded crossbow down into the cellar at Longoss.

'I don't give a rat's shit if we have King Barrison's!' Keep ground his teeth between shouts and curses. 'And do you forget what that bastard Morton did to you, eh? Have you forgotten?'

Longoss huffed. 'Of course not.' He lowered his arms to his sides, then pointed at the man aiming the crossbow at him. 'Mind, ye'd be a damned sight worse off, likely dead, if Morton hadn't fucked me over, Keep.'

Coppin, Egan and Severun watched the exchange, eyes flicking in unison from one man to the other, switching each time to the one speaking, or flinging insults.

'What's he talking about?' Coppin dared.

'Not now!' both men said at once.

Coppin scowled and folded her arms.

'There's no time for this…' Egan clamped his mouth shut as the crossbow shifted to point at him. He took a breath and looked away.

The weapon swung back to Longoss, who'd taken a step forward.

'Even if it is how you say, you'll lose, Longoss. You'll all bloody lose. Gods below.' Keep took a deep breath and unloaded and relaxed the bow. 'The whole city will lose if the Black Guild goes to—'

'It's *at* war, Keep,' Longoss said, voice steady, firm. 'Poi Son and Bronwen have already begun—'

'No thanks to you lot!' Keep shouted, knuckles white with crossbow in one hand and bolt in the other. His shoulders slumped and he leaned back against the wall, slid down it to sit there. 'You said you were going after Poi Son.'

'I said, Keep, that I were going to bring the bastards down. The lot of 'em.'

'People say such things, I didn't think I—'

'I gave me word, Keep.' They locked eyes on one another. 'Ye knew that, so ye were kidding no one but yerself if ye thought I were blowing nought but bluster about it all.'

Keep was nodding slowly. 'And so it is, the end of us all.'

'Oh please,' Coppin said.

Keep grunted a laugh. 'Coppin, lass.' He looked at her now. 'You've seen how bad it's got already, I know you have. What do you think will happen now, with so many sides involved? Poi Son, Bronwen, your little pack, the Lord High Constable of Altoln and… and,' he said, back to Longoss, 'Alden-Fenn when he's back in Wesson. Alden-Fenn, Longoss! 'Morl's ass-crack, man. Poi Son and Bronwen are the only two who keep that berserker in check; together. Together,' he said, sounding out the word as if Longoss' loss of ears demanded it. 'What now? He returns and his business mam and dad are at war with one another? Ye think, in that tiny thick head of yours, that he'll take a side? Ye think Alden-fucking-Fenn will take your side?'

Longoss swallowed hard, but nodded.

Keep burst into incredulous laughter, shaking his head all the while and staring at Longoss, Coppin, Egan and finally Severun. 'I suppose the magic man is going to whisk Alden-Fenn's shites away on a wind from is arse, whilst blowing kisses to fellow mage Bronwen, wooing her enough with glamours so Coppin here can skip up to Poi Son and place her pretty knife through his heart, eh? Eh, Longoss?'

'Ye're being stupid now.' Coppin slumped against the nearest wall, much like Keep was.

'I'm being stupid?' Keep roared, throwing himself forward onto all fours and looking down on them all with utter contempt. 'I put you bastards up, here, in my home! I risked it all so you could fuck about with Poi Son's trade. So you could piss him off enough so he'd show his ugly face. So you could cut that ugly face from his head and be done with it.' Keep lifted himself to kneeling and squeezed his head between his hands. 'I didn't put you up to invite a fucking Duke's army to march on my tavern, to relieve a fucking siege by the Black bastard Guild!' He shook with red-faced rage and fell back, laughing hysterically. 'We're all dead.'

Longoss leaned in to Egan. 'Went better than I thought, that.'

Egan hung his head and groaned.

***

'Is it accurate?' Poi Son said, eyes on his lute as he restrung it.

How is he so calm? Pangan thought, nodding. He realised Poi Son wouldn't see the nod and voiced his confirmation instead.

Poi Son nodded now, eyes on his working fingers. 'I had heard rumours, had even thought it true myself,' Poi Son said, looking up, 'but I'd never have believed, if I was honest: that Keep was stupid enough to put Longoss up. Not with a mark on his old protégé's head.'

Pangan shrugged. 'Well he has. It comes from more than one source and that's after a couple of days of quiet from Longoss and his cronies, so makes sense.'

'All of a sudden though?' Poi Son frowned.

'Aye.'

Pursing his lips, Poi Son placed the lute on its stand, crossed to his chair and sat, resting his head against the chair's high back. 'They want us to know this. Now, specifically now,' he said, eyes meeting Pangan's once more. 'They were quiet because they were planning it.'

'Reckon so, Master Son. Reckon Mistress Bronwen will know too, wherever she is.'

Poi Son started at that. It was subtle, but Pangan caught it. 'You're right, I'm sure. Nothing misses her, especially information meant for her.'

It was Pangan's turn to frown. 'You think Longoss wants her to know too?'

'I think, Pangan,' Poi Son said, leaning forward, 'that Longoss would have Alden-Fenn know if it was within his power to communicate across the sea.'

'Why?' Pangan moved closer, trailed his fingers through the dust on the sideboard, lifting it into the air. He stopped when he saw Poi Son's glare. Swallowing hard, he asked again. 'Why would Longoss want all three of you to know where he is? Especially after all the shit he's caused and continues to cause the guild, warring as it is or not.'

'Because, my dear Pangan,' Poi Son said, wincing at Pangan's choice of language, 'he wants us all to attend his show. He wants us all together in one place,' he said, wagging a finger at Pangan, 'so we do to each other what he cannot hope to do to us himself.' Poi Son smiled and sat back again, fingers folded in his lap.

Pangan raised his brow in realisation. After a moment's pause, silent but for the sound of the gulls and the street below the shuttered window he crossed to, Pangan asked what Poi Son would do.

And this is where I see your true colours, Master Son, Pangan thought, eyeing the man he'd served for a decade or more, perhaps a lot more. It wasn't as if Pangan had counted the years. He didn't even know how old he was, or had been when recruited by Poi Son. He set his jaw and awaited an answer he couldn't predict. He was glad the weight of it all wasn't on him. He didn't want to be a master, never had, so the other thing playing on his mind, the crossroads he'd reached in his life – for which he wasn't even sure he had a choice – made what Poi Son was telling him all the worse, all the harder to think about. He grimaced and passed it off as a reaction to the plan Poi Son revealed. If it could be called a plan. Suicide was more like it. Suicide capped with hubris. He laughed to himself, in his head. Hubris. The word impressed him. He'd learnt a lot over the years, off Poi Son; not to count properly, high or anything, nor to read or write, not much, anyway, but he had learnt from the man. From the master assassin. He'd learnt his trade and he'd learnt much more. He just wasn't sure whether he'd learnt loyalty; whether he'd ever learnt it in the first place or whether he'd lost it sometime in between.

Either way, Pangan thought, acknowledging Poi Son and pardoning himself so he could go and action the man's plans, *I've certainly found it now, this loyalty. Just not for you, Master Son. Not for you.*

Chapter 38 - Besieging your own

'You gonna talk to me now, Coppin,' Longoss said, 'before things get nasty?'

'They've not got nasty already?' She leaned in close with her whisper. The lamps were out in Keep's cellar, their two companions asleep. Severun snored an irritating whistle of a snore; whistling in, grating out.

'Coppin...' *Don't change the subject, lass. Not now.*

Lights weren't needed, nor were Longoss' ears, to sense the tenseness in Coppin, the shudder of her deep breath. A few whistling, grating moments passed before Coppin answered, voice low, an audible tremble present.

'I'm carrying a child.'

The whistle and grate of Severun's breathing filled the void that followed those words. It ended with a grunt. Coppin had thrown something, accurately, Longoss knew.

'It can't be mine?'

Coppin's huff was louder than her whispers. 'I worry about you sometimes, Longoss. Of course it's not yours. Would that it was.'

Longoss sucked in a breath, a shocked breath, but not a bad shock, not the kind you'd get finding a spider in your boot or an angry father in your room. No, this was a new kind of shock, or rather a rare one. He'd experienced such a rush of emotion, pleasant emotion, once before. *Elleth,* he thought, and felt guilty considering the person he now felt those same feelings for curled beside him, under the same wool blanket.

'You didn't expect me to say that, did you?'

Longoss shook his head. 'No.'

There was silence for a time, bliss, considering the snoring would start again soon.

'It doesn't have to be mine, lass, to be mine.'

'Eh?'

Longoss could hear the frown in Coppin's breathy question. He knew her that well now. Knew her better than he'd known anyone in his life. Well, almost anyone. Perhaps he'd consider Correia regarding such things, albeit a long time ago. Not now though and certainly not with such emotions. His and her relationship had been purely platonic, with a little friendship thrown in, he'd always liked to think. *Until Morton stuck his fucking beak in. Bastard.*

'Longoss?'

'Ye know what I mean, lass. The babe doesn't have to be from me, for me to be a father—'

'I'm not keeping it; not birthing the damned thing, Longoss.'

It was Longoss' turn to frown, a real eye-narrowing brow creaser. He said nothing and the pause drew on until Coppin explained.

'I asked Severun to—'

'The wizard knows?'

'Aye, and Egan.'

Longoss rolled away, looked pointlessly to the unseen ceiling above.

'Severun told me, Longoss. I didn't know, or rather didn't want to know.'

He felt her hands shift and imagined them crossing over on her stomach. He liked that image; he hated the image her talk was forcing in its way. 'And he's gonna zap it out, is he? Murder the tiny thing in a flash.'

'What would you know?' Coppin's tone dripped venom.

Fear, he thought. *Fear leads to such tones in most folk.* 'Nothing it seems. All's I know was I was dragged into this world, costing me ma her life for it and hated by me da for it. And he was me real da. My. Real. Da. Blood is as good as piss, Coppin. It's in here that makes a family.' He reached over and planted his big left hand above her left breast, felt the beating, felt the love.

Coppin sighed; cried. Longoss could hear her soft sobs. He felt her hand on his.

'I'm going to Mother's, as soon as I can. The bitch had things I could use—'

'To murder it.'

Her hand fell away. 'To stop it having the shit existence most folk in this world have.'

The silence that followed was broken by a whistle and a grate. A whistle and a grate.

'Oh for 'morl's sake.' Coppin sniffed and wiped at her face. Longoss felt the movements through his hand, which remained on her heart.

'I'd love it. I'd protect it. I give ye my—'

'Don't! Don't give yer word on something ye'll have to break it over, again.'

Longoss moved his hand away this time and felt his own eyes dampen. 'Ye're right to say that.'

220

'I know the love ye feel, Longoss.' Coppin rolled, pressed herself into Longoss' side. 'I feel it too,' she whispered, the quietest yet. Longoss only just heard it, and the next. 'But I have no love for what's inside me and that fact is killing me more than the Black Guild ever could. It's how it is though, Longoss. It's how it is and I can't help it.' She broke down completely and Longoss pulled her in closer, squeezed her gently and found the top of her head with his mouth. He kissed her and rocked her.

There's time yet, lass, he thought. *There's time yet.*

***

'Well, there it is,' Pangan said. He stood in a black alley, hooded lamp in hand. It offered enough glow to see his feet and an arm's length. He pointed within that light, pointed towards the tavern he and his companions knew oh so well. The tavern owned and run by one of their own. *Well,* Pangan thought, *a former one of our own, harbouring another former one of our own.* Pangan took a deep breath and lowered his arm. The masks behind him hadn't moved. They hadn't even uttered a word upon their arrival, nor during their journey through Dockside to the tavern. Pangan shuddered at what stood behind him and wondered how long the two he'd known so well had left in their current states. *They've certainly achieved a lot... a lot of destruction.*

'What now?' the young watcher lad said from outside the lamp's light, his voice attempting confidence but betraying trepidation, to say the least.

'We—'

Pangan was cut off as Terrina and Rapeel pushed past. There'd been no given order. No word between them. They just moved. Pangan nearly dropped the light. He swore and squinted at their backs as the duo disappeared into the gloom of the street. They'd lost or removed their cloaks it seemed, which was probably best for the fight to come.

'You didn't order that,' the hidden girl watcher said, stating the obvious.

'No. I didn't.'

'So, Master Son must have?' she asked, a shake in her voice considering what was to come.

She's likely remembering those freaky masks taking down the nobleman before destroying Bronwen's poison pad. I know I am. Pangan shuddered once more and started as someone stepped alongside him. A knife was in his free hand faster than his head turned.

'I did indeed order it,' Poi Son said, glancing sidelong at Pangan, who scowled.

'Could have told me,' Pangan managed, looking forward once again, although it was pointless in the dark. 'Did you have the street lamps doused too, Master Son?'

There was a pause. 'No,' Poi Son said, 'that will have been Bronwen.'

The girl gasped from the blackness.

Pangan looked to Poi Son once more, but before he could say anything a white flash like sheet lightning lit up the alley, those in it and the street and tavern beyond. Pangan closed his eyes. All he heard were curses, his own joining the others. An after-image of Poi Son's side profile remained etched behind his eyelids and he prayed at that point, to whomever listened, that he wasn't blinded permanently. *I couldn't cope with that man standing before me for the rest of my days.* Pangan shielded and opened his eyes at the same time.

'Was that Mistress Bronwen's magic?' Bill asked, from behind Pangan.

'No.' Poi Son rubbed at his eyes. 'No, that was the tavern I should think.'

Pangan frowned. He was shielding his eyes with his free hand as if it were a sunny day, despite it being dark once more. 'A protection of some kind?'

'Yes, Pangan,' Poi Son said. 'Courtesy of the mage Longoss has helping him.'

'This gets better and better,' Bill said to a chorus of grunted agreements, prayers and oaths from the assassins and street-assassins in the alley.

'Quiet, all of you,' Poi Son said. They obeyed.

Pangan squinted once more into the dark. 'Did you see our two out there, during the flash?' he asked anyone who might have an answer.

'No.' Poi Son.

'Yes,' the watcher girl said. Heads turned her direction: stared at the dark.

'I saw them both slipping around the side of the tavern as the light flashed, and I saw them thrown back, to the ground.'

'And?' Pangan asked, leaning her way.

'And that's it,' she said flatly. 'I can barely see you in your lamplight—'

'Shit!' Pangan dropped the light and it smashed, killing the attention drawing flames within. Everything fell to pitch and the smashing of glass and the clattering of metal on stone echoed between the tall buildings to either side.

'Pangan?' Poi Son sounded cross, confused and concerned, all in the one word.

It was too late. Before Pangan could apologise for the lamp that had illuminated their position, the first wave of arcane energy struck.

Men screamed. So did a girl.

Chapter 39 - Bangs in the night

The interior flash of light woke Severun with a start. 'They're here,' he blurted, an after image of the cellar ingrained temporarily on his retinas. Fading, the image was replaced by a darkness he cast away as quickly as the flash had come and gone. Candles and lamps flared to life around the cellar as his companions surged to their feet.

'How many?' Egan asked, arming himself as swiftly as the others, despite his myriad of weapons, concealed and otherwise.

Severun huffed. 'It doesn't work like that, Egan.' Before Severun could say more, the door above them clattered open. Severun looked up to see Keep stood there, crossbow in hands.

'Hurry!' Keep shouted. 'It looks like The Three are at war out there!' He rushed off then, Longoss sprinting up the steps to follow, Coppin close behind, knives out. Severun gave chase, as did Egan, but Longoss stopped on the top step, turned and held his hand out to Coppin.

'No you don't, lass.' Longoss blocked Coppin's path as she tried to push past, ignoring him, but for a scowl.

'He's right, Coppin my dear,' Severun said, from the bottom step.

'Stay out of it, wizard!' Coppin snapped without turning.

Longoss looked round her and met Severun's eyes. There was the slightest of nods as the big man held Coppin back. Severun swallowed hard and sighed before nodding in return.

'Longoss ye fat shit, get off—'

Longoss took Coppin's weight as she fell limp in his arms and, despite the man not needing it, Egan helped Longoss lift Coppin back down the steps, Severun making way for them.

'She'll hate us for this,' Longoss said as they lay her on her makeshift cot.

'No doubt,' Egan agreed, pulling a blanket over and up to her chin.

Longoss looked from Coppin to Severun. 'How long?'

Severun winced. 'I can't be sure, but long enough for what we need to do, I hope.'

Longoss leaned down and kissed Coppin's forehead before following Severun and Egan up the steps and out into the tavern proper.

Forgive me, Coppin, Severun thought as the trio found Keep and two of his trusted patrons, who were in on all that was happening. *Trusting them in this feels wrong.* Severun looked from one man to the other, both of them short but stocky, faces not too dissimilar to a mastiff's. He'd have thought them brothers if he hadn't been told different.

A bright white flash lit the cracks of the barred and bolted shutters and door. Severun staggered and Egan reached out, catching his arm. The will behind the assault that caused the flash felt like someone had shaken Severun's brain. He mastered himself, but a haze remained.

'My defences won't hold long,' he said, eyeing Longoss and Egan.

Keep balked at Severun. 'Ye're saying that now? Already?'

'I am!' Severun snapped, annoyed at the question. Anger flooded him, flushed through his veins like fire and he almost snapped out more than words. A hand rested on his shoulder and squeezed. Severun rounded fiercely on the owner of the hand.

'Do what you can,' Egan said, holding up his other hand to stop Keep from saying any more.

Another flash and Severun staggered once more. And again Egan caught him, lowering him this time to a chair where Severun slumped.

Longoss rushed to a shutter, tried to peek through the gap.

Breathing heavily, the air in the room stale, Severun watched Longoss and Keep's two thugs, who were looking back at him, their shaken nerves plain to see.

'Is it her?' the uglier of the two said – and that was saying a lot. 'Is it Bronwen?'

Severun sucked in a breath. *Bronwen?* 'Yes,' he said, without thinking any more. 'Yes. That makes sense.' He'd been confused at the level of power being thrown at his shielding, but hadn't wanted to say, hadn't wanted to scare them, or himself. He laughed silently. *Your staggering and snapping is doing that, you old fool.* He waved Egan off and focused, closed his eyes. 'When I say,' he said, seeing a wicked shadow in his mind's eye; a presence trying to impose itself on him. 'When I say,' he repeated, 'prepare to receive guests. I'll drop...' he took a breath and shuddered as the foreign will exerted itself and another flash lit the shutters. The pain behind his eyes was brief, but immense. He barely held on to consciousness.

'Severun?' Egan again, stepping towards him.

'I'll let but a few... through...' Severun was struggling to speak. Struggling to do anything but fight off Bronwen's assaults, both the visible, outside, and those within his head. *How is she doing this?* 'I'll-let-some-of-them-in-then-close-it-off,' he spat out, before her wicked presence struck again.

'Now!' Severun had to shout the word. Project the meaning to his companions to ensure they acted. He had to release his shielding of the tavern because Bronwen had beat him, but for a heartbeat. She'd felt him release the words in a rapid stream; she'd known it'd taken all of him right there, right then. She was weakening him with every moment that passed and he was unable to do anything about it. He didn't even know where the witch was in relation to the tavern.

In my head, that's where.

Crashing wood stole Severun's brief respite from the magical assault, Bronwen's attack hindered whilst he dropped all his magic and concentrated on blocking her out. But that concentration had been shattered like the shutters to either side, so he threw himself back into the shield as two figures tumbled into the taproom. Two figures wearing horrifying masks, one red, one white with blood-red tears.

A flash silhouetted the masked assassins. Severun's shield was back up. *They're trapped from their allies,* he managed to think but not say, one eye closed, the other flicking from one mask to the other. *They're trapped inside… with us.*

Severun fell sideways from the chair, both eyes now closed, his mind's eye entirely open, to him and to her. To Bronwen. As the distant voice of Egan screamed for Severun, and fading shouts and curses came from the lips of the others, the outside world fell away and Severun felt himself roll free from it; escape his daily bonds.

'You've realised what this will take,' Bronwen said, her soul as much of a crone in vision as he'd heard she was in person. Bronwen hissed a laugh, the sound wheezing from damaged lungs despite her corporeal form being elsewhere. 'You'll fail, Severun. Confined as you are to your laws and rules and ancient restraints your guild forces upon you.'

Severun's soul straightened, stretched out to its fullest height, width, depth, mass. He smiled through it and revealed the darkness that tainted its edges – that ever strained to reach his soul's core. 'You assume much, Mistress Bronwen.' Severun didn't project himself, didn't waste energy in such a way. He projected the words, empowered them and made her see. Made her see Him, the one whom Severun had unwittingly been keeping at bay for many months. At least for the most part. *If only I was fully me,* Severun thought, the realisation that he was not solely himself staggering his soul. He eyed, so to speak, the hesitation forming in Bronwen's fading features as she too realised it, or at least a portion of it.

'If you wish it this way,' she sent to him in the same way he'd sent his meanings to her. 'Have it!'

Severun's soul railed at the assault the arcane wielding witch directed his way, the black edges of his pulsating soul curling back as if burnt blacker still, veins of that darkness creeping in towards his core; fear laced with a knowing that he was fighting two beings, not one. A horror in knowing he was defending against her and himself both.

What if I can't hold? Severun thought throughout the attack he struggled to divert and diverge and absorb and dissipate. *What if she breaks my will... enough to... let Him in completely?*

Severun screamed, body and soul and mouth and light-leaking eyes; heart and churning stomach and throbbing, pulsating and agonising brain.

Bronwen laughed and pushed Severun harder.

Both Keep's and Egan's crossbows snapped bolts, one smaller than the other, towards the masked assassins as soon as they stood from their dramatic rolling entries. Keep's bolt scored a line across the white mask of the female, who leapt to the side: towards the uglier of Keep's two men. Longoss watched the woman move, and move fast, impossibly so. He'd seen Severun slump, eyes closing and knew him to be fighting his own battles in some wizarding way. The brutal fight breaking out before him was more to Longoss' liking, although the blood-stained white mask the woman wore stole his momentum; stole any initiative he might have used, and needed.

Egan's bolt thumped into red-mask's shoulder, a hand's breadth above the man's heart. Longoss glanced that way and knew it would have been a killing blow if the assassin hadn't moved so damned quick. That red mask came on, bolt torn free, twin hatchets lashing and slashing at Longoss in an enhanced yet familiar way.

'Rapeel?' Longoss managed, coming to his senses and deftly avoiding the bite of those wedged blades. The mask said nothing, its grimacing visage of a burned man drawing Longoss' attention as Rapeel came on and on, and on.

Egan stumbled past Longoss, barged aside by Keep who'd dived to stay clear of the female assassin, her stilettos soiled with the life of the ugliest thug lying in a spreading, steaming pool of arterial blood.

As Egan passed, Longoss used him as a well needed distraction. He'd seen Rapeel's eyes behind the mask, seen them glance at Egan as the witchunter stumbled, rapier leading the way. Longoss rushed forward, small knife jabbing towards Rapeel's bloody shoulder where the bolt wound should be paining and hindering him.

Rapeel turned in a flash, taking the plunging knife much like Longoss had taken Terrina's stiletto when... *Terrina!*

A familiar shriek turned Longoss' head whilst he dived to the side, narrowly avoiding Rapeel's trailing hatchet. Crashing hard into a splintering stool, Longoss' confusion swept him tenfold. He'd recognised Blanck's mask as soon as he'd seen it; he'd even recognised the blood red tears the assassin had shed when Longoss had taken his eyes, amongst other things, for killing Elleth. He'd never imagined it was Blanck's sister wearing the mask though. He couldn't have imagined her doing much at all after the work he'd put into carving her legs and face up. *Face. Hence the mask,* Longoss thought, grimacing as he saw Terrina drop the second ugly thug, the man's wild slashes with his scramasax doing little to hinder the woman. She turned and her frenzied eyes locked onto Longoss. Swallowing down his shock and confusion, Longoss managed a wink, intending to infuriate her, to throw her off her...

Keep fell hard, despite his prowess with the large knife he'd drawn. Longoss watched in stunned disbelief and horror as his old friend and mentor writhed on the floor, Terrina leaping over him as Egan crashed past her on a defensive retreat from Rapeel, the former street-assassin far more dangerous than he had ever been before.

Terrina sprinted at Longoss as he forced himself to his feet, breaths shuddering with the shock of it all and the exertion; his energy and speed paled in comparison to the woman's closing on him like an arrow to a butt.

All Longoss could do was throw his all into his defence as Terrina's blades came in. She shrieked as she was wont to do, twin stilettos punching out at him at odd angles, making it hard to avoid their bite. And he didn't. The pain lanced through Longoss' own shoulder – where she'd stabbed him the last time they'd met. *Again with the fucking shoulders,* he thought, before the other blade scored a line across his outstretched palm, which was lucky considering he'd expected it to slide straight through his hand. Grunting with the pain and exertion, wishing he had Sears' vial of whatever-it-was healing potion, Longoss threw himself forward and into Terrina, barrelling her to the floor where he could use his weight and superior strength, even with a stiletto embedded in him.

'Where's your bitch, Longoss?' Terrina said through the mask, voice muffled and akin to her brother's. 'I want to do to her what Blanck did to the other whore.'

Longoss roared and drove his head into the bloody mask below him. Or so he thought.

A dull thud of pain followed by lances of the same shot through his skull as his forehead met wooden floorboards. Terrina had shifted herself under him, and worked the knives she held as she did so. Longoss screamed despite his brutal stoicism.

'That's for Blanck!' Terrina screamed back, eyes wide behind the mask.

The fight was leaving Longoss, despite his gritted teeth and attempts to struggle, to roar and to best the bitch beneath him. He'd been through hell before, alongside Coppin against the gangs and assassins in Dockside, and against this very bitch and her bastard brother, not that long ago. But he'd had Sears' potion, in-between and after those arduous bouts of violence. Now? Now he was exhausted from trying to keep up with Terrina's speed and... strength, for she was stronger than her frame suggested, he realised, as they struggled with one another on the floor. His exhaustion was mental as well as physical, from the revelation of Terrina and Rapeel's return and the distracting thoughts of Coppin and the child she held within. His thoughts were stolen by Coppin and what was to become of her and her child as the brutal tumbling ended with Terrina above him, his hands on her impossibly strong stabbing wrists. Fresh lances of pain shot through him as the second stiletto slid into his side, under his ribs and up into a lung. The next breath grated and stung, stabbed at him as bad as the stilettos. Terrina screamed things at him from above, but the holes in the sides of his head failed to hear what she was saying. All he could do was focus on Coppin's face in his mind as his vision blurred and darkened. The next breath lanced and the next stabbed, followed by more of the same despite those breaths slowing. He had no idea how his friends faired with Rapeel; the sounds of shouting and smashing had faded quicker than Terrina's din of a voice.

Longoss had no idea how he himself fared in it all as the lights went out and the sharp pains dulled, fading to nothing. All he wanted to do was think of Coppin and their child as it all came to an end. *I would have loved you both.* Pure bliss overtook him at the thought.

Severun screamed at Bronwen's assaulting laugh. Each concussive bark of the dreadful sound railed against his mind and soul like the cannons of the dwarves. Loud bangs, launched from her very will, caused Severun to stagger back, which struck him all the more. To stagger was to be corporeal. His eyes flickered open and a blur and a rush of vision took him, as did the grating screams and shouts and curses in the dull room he sat slumped in. 'No,' he whispered, eyes finding the bodies of Keep's two men. Keep himself. Severun turned his head and took in Egan, who desperately fended off the red masked assassin. And on to Longoss who lay struggling beneath a slip of a woman in an old-blood stained white mask. He heard shouts, victorious shouts, from outside the tavern and realised with horror that Bronwen had not only knocked him back, but in doing so had dropped his shielding. He almost stood. Almost surged to his feet to throw himself into the fray and protect his friend.

Friend... yes. Egan Dundaven was his friend.

'No!' Severun said, his defiance finding new resolve. 'No...'

He slumped once more, eyes closing.

'No!' Severun screamed *into* Bronwen, finding her shadow as easily as he finally found his other harasser. Bronwen's presence faltered at his return, yet rolled out a wave of amusement, condescending in tone and colour and sound in a way only one of her and Severun's abilities could recognise and realise.

'You think you can best me, Severun? You're a fool if you do.' Bronwen's soul expanded, like an explosion of the filthiest, rotten will imaginable. Well, apart from the other one, the worse one; the recent realisation of that one was less staggering now and more... useful.

Severun smiled within, and without, to her, as far as she would see and feel and sense it anyway. Bronwen hesitated, or rather her soon to be devastating expansion halted.

'You are my better in these arcane things, Bronwen,' Severun projected. 'But not His!' Severun launched that last at her and at the same time lowered certain defences, completely, opening himself to an assault he'd been holding off for a long time.

Since the scroll. Since the plague.

Bronwen screamed as the gargantuan black mass of horror surged into Severun, through and out of his mind and soul and... everything, enveloping Bronwen in a terror she couldn't comprehend; in an arcane power she could not defend against, being that she had no idea it existed until right there and then. There'd been no warning. No building of suggestions and schemes and hints and nudges like Severun had suffered and forgot and remembered and fought against and accepted and denied. Unlike Severun and the gradual studying of the scroll, Bronwen was struck with the full will of the thing: the full rage and assault and malice of a great black dragon, previously held at bay and now deflected away from that which it truly desired: Severun.

Allowing it to pass through and leave him completely, one enemy consuming another, Severun smiled, his lips twitching as if a nervous tic had taken hold. Bronwen had saved him, unbeknown to her, and to Severun until that very moment. A moment where he had genuinely decided to sacrifice himself to destroy her utterly and to deny the beast that had beckoned him and controlled him, from time to time.

Eyes open once more, Severun stood effortlessly to his full height and took in the taproom with his eyes, ears and every other sense available to him. For he was back. Severun was Severun once again, whole and pure and un-accosted from a distant land.

Flexing his fingers and turning to take in both masks at once, Severun unleashed his previously restrained power in full.

Chapter 40 – Betrayal

Poi Son grunted and stumbled as Pangan manhandled him down the alley.

'I said it'd be a fucking trap,' Pangan said, dragging Poi Son from the screaming, pleading, grunts and groans; from the acrid smell of the arcane and the static that accompanied it.

'And we sprung it.' Poi Son spat after the words. The taste the impacting spell left in his mouth was foul. He hated her magic. Bronwen's. He wasn't fond of magic in general, but hers had always felt, smelt and tasted filthy. 'Like the woman herself.'

'What?' Pangan said, pulling Poi Son into a faintly illuminated doorway.

'She took my bait, Pangan.' Poi Son grinned.

'I thought we were here for Longoss and his chums?' Pangan breathed hard and his words were forced because of it.

'Oh, we are, Pangan. We are.' Poi Son retrieved an invisible-in-the-light lute string. 'But we're finishing the guild war at the same time.'

Pangan filled his cheeks and released the breath he'd held in one go. 'Could've told me.'

'I just did.'

Pangan went rigid, Poi Son could feel it in the darkness, could feel Pangan's muscles tense as he threw his hands up to the cord around his neck and fought to stop it tightening; fought to stop it closing his airway or slicing into his flesh.

Poi Son clenched his teeth as he worked. He said nothing as he arched his back and pulled on the string wrapped painfully tight around his gloved hands. Pangan's choking grunts filled his ears, that and the thud of his own quickened heartbeat. Poi Son had never understood the need to offer conversation before and whilst attempting to take someone's life. He knew plenty of assassins who would do so. He managed to breath a laugh as he fought to keep Pangan's back arched. He knew many of his own assassins who did, or had. It was a waste of time and a risk. If you want someone dead, get it done. Leave the blabbing for afterwards if you must, for the bragging or the requesting of another contract. Ironically, he knew Pangan felt and operated the same way as he. Or had.

Pangan tried to kick backwards, but missed Poi Son's knees. He tried to stamp. Again, he missed his mark and Poi Son's feet remained planted, unhindered in their superior stance. Poi Son was taller than Pangan, which helped. He could arch his back and lean further, pulling Pangan to the tips of his toes as Pangan tried to relieve the pressure and pain upon his throat.

Poi Son jerked once, twice, pulling and crossing his hands and arms, trying to finish the job as quickly as possible. After all, he didn't want his old friend to suffer unnecessarily.

Pangan's booted feet scrabbled for purchase, the scraping sounds filling the doorway and downing out – on an emotional level – the continued cries of pain and denial coming from the wounded and dying assassins further up the alley. Poi Son's men, and girl, the lot of them. But there was more at stake here. Much more. His new master... he shook his head at the word. New *employer*, had strict instructions: it had all been there in the blood-ink. The mark on Barrison wasn't enough. Dignaaln had been clear in his request and Poi Son intended to carry it out to the full. His guild depended on it. *His* guild. Not Bronwen's or Alden-Fenn's. Not Pangan's or Terrina's or Rapeel's or Bill's. No one else's but his. A clean slate, that's what had been called for and that's what Poi Son wanted, needed.

Pangan thrashed, choked and Poi Son felt the hot wet rush of arterial blood as his string finally sliced through Pangan's throat. The thrashing fell away to a judder and a shudder as Poi Son lowered the dead weight of his former right hand man to the ground. Now he could talk. Now he could risk a word or two before moving on, for now the job was done. Or rather the start of it.

'You shouldn't have placed your loyalty in Bronwen, my old friend,' Poi Son said, crouched over Pangan's leaking corpse. He strained his eyes to see the face he knew so well, locked in a grimace as it was. Poi Son stroked the man's head and shook his own. 'This would have been hard for me if you hadn't secretly backed her, Pangan. Then again,' he said, standing and looking out into the black alley, sobs and groans and moans reaching his ears once more. 'Then again, in doing so, in betraying me, Pangan, you made my betrayal of you an easy thing. Necessary it may be, but I had no love for this act.'

Poi Son laughed to himself. 'And here I am, waffling on to a corpse. What am I to do with myself?' Shaking his head at it all, Poi Son dropped the bloody string and moved off into the darkness, certain Terrina and Rapeel would see to the rest.

***

Terrina threw herself off Longoss' bloody body as a stream of blue energy reached out towards her from the standing wizard. She knew it would've hit her were it not for the gift Poi Son had bestowed upon her and Rapeel. The gift of revenge and retribution.

Launching into an arcing run, around tables, stools, benches and the body of one of the ugly bastards she'd killed, Terrina put a foot to a bench and launched herself into the air, towards the wizard who'd attempted to magic her to death. She'd seen Rapeel besting the witchunter, had seen one of his beloved hatchets moving at a speed the witchunter couldn't parry, and had seen it thwack into the man's black-clad back like a butcher chopping a carcass.

Mid-air now, Terrina kicked out at the turning wizard, who'd struggled to track her speed with his bloodshot eyes. She came in from his periphery, outstretched foot connecting with his midriff, sending him crashing into a table where he struck the side of his head.

Landing deftly on one foot before coming down into a crouch beside the dazed wizard, Terrina lashed out with her nearest stiletto, but the force of a wooden stool cracking off the side of her head knocked her to the ground beside the man before the knife found its mark. Anger flooded Terrina more than pain. She whipped her head around. Her brother's mask obscured the view of her assailant. All she caught was a glimpse of black-smudged green hair before she was battered in the face, through the mask, with something solid.

The sound of men shouting in the street followed the impact, then loud bangs and the shattering and splintering of wood.

Another impact rocked Terrina and without her vision, impaired by the skewed mask, her strength and speed meant nothing. Lashing out with blades and kicking out to match, Terrina knew she bought herself the time to drop a stiletto and right her mask in time to see green and white liveried men enter the taproom and loose heavy, windlass crossbows at Rapeel. He'd charged the newcomers and in doing so took two of the three bolts to the chest. Despite his strength and speed, the bolts punched him backwards, the back of his head striking the floor a moment before his torso and trailing legs. Terrina screamed. It was full of rage, rage enough to allow her to ignore yet another blow from a wooden stool, which she caught hold of as it came down atop her. She yanked it free of the woman who held it, turning on and lunging for her with the remaining stiletto. The green haired bitch turned to run as men shouted to her, warning her that they didn't have a clear shot. Terrina heard more men enter, clattering as they were, through the detritus of the tavern, to get to her.

'He's getting up!' one of the men-at-arms shouted. Terrina knew it to be Rapeel and couldn't help but grin beneath her mask as she took hold of the green bitch's hair, yanking her back to the floor as her stiletto slid nice and easy into her side, albeit at an awkward, hastily driven angle which had the tip punching out of the bitch's back.

As the weight of Longoss' whore dragged Terrina into a crouch, her hand gripping the hilt of her weapon, Terrina heard a guttural scream from behind, followed by more shouts and curses and the clashing of steel. She grinned again, then sucked in a breath as something struck her back, sending her tumbling over the woman she'd stabbed. She lost grip of her stiletto and growled against the pain rolling away from the new danger caused; the tumble snagging the bolt jutting from her back, snagging and pulling on it, flaring an agony within her that she'd not felt since her previous confrontation with Longoss; since the bastard had carved her and her brother up.

Another bolt struck as Terrina began to stand and it threw her forward onto her stomach. She screamed in both outrage and pain. She heard feet shuffling, men moving her way. She managed to get her feet under her and ran. She ran through a door and ran through a kitchen. She cried as she ran, pulled things from tables; plates and bottles and jars. She heard them smash and heard her pursuers curse. The pain was rolling through her, taking her, threatening to force her to the ground so she could curl up and cry and cry. Terrina barged through a door and even that hurt her shoulder, the dull impact of it. She felt slower and slower as she ran. She'd left the soldiers behind, but her run became a stumble, as one does when trying to stop a run down a steep hill. Reaching the alley behind the tavern by crashing through a shuttered window with the last of her enhanced speed and strength, Terrina thumped into the opposite wall and collapsed. She felt the stone beneath her, the dirt atop it as her senses heightened to her surroundings and to the two bolts protruding from her back; slicing up her insides as they had been her entire flight.

Terrina thought of Blanck and wept, her screams falling to pained sobs, eyes and nose streaming. The agony from the bolts was too much. She kept her back to the sky, scared of knocking the shafts on floor or wall. She heard men reach the back of the tavern, turned her head and saw them climbing through the opening she'd created with her body.

Terrina watched as two of them approached, moonlight catching the shine of maille, plate and swords. Knights, she thought, at least of the lead man anyway, his surcoat down to his plated knees. *I'm to be hauled back to his bastard liege lord.*

Crouching before her, the knight lifted the blunt visor of his helm and looked upon Terrina, a wry smile creeping across his handsome face. She sucked in a painful breath and felt it judder out into her brother's mask.

'The red bastard's dead!' a man from inside the tavern shouted. 'You got the other mask yet, Sir Merrel?'

'Yeah, he's got her out here,' the man-at-arms behind the knight confirmed.

Terrina flinched as the knight, Sir Merrel, reached out a gauntleted hand. He pulled the mask from Terrina's face and held it there, between his knee-cops as he crouched, eyes widening whilst taking in her scarred face.

'Would have been worth a fuck before she got those scars,' the man-at-arms said, crouching next to Sir Merrel, who grimaced.

'Now now, young Si, no need for that,' Sir Merrel said, his previously wry smile replaced with a sympathetic one.

It was all Terrina could do not to collapse to the floor as she held his stare. She saw two more men climbing through the window, heard one of them muttering about having the door opened for them. Then she was choking. Choking on her own blood as Sir Merrel pushed a dagger into her side, casual as you like. Terrina felt the dull press of it, the cold iron reaching inside her to steel her life. Next to the myriad of feelings and pains and agonies she endured, the blade didn't felt that bad, but she knew it to be the end of her. As she looked at the remaining sympathetic smile on Sir Merrel's face, and heard the mutterings about her and the unimpressed looks those men gave – some of which cut deeper than any blade, considering her vanity before she'd received her facial scars – Terrina took in one final breath and wheezed it out as Sir Merrel slid his blade free and cleaned it on a white cloth.

'Sleep now,' he said, standing and turning away. And Terrina did.

Chapter 41 – Effrin and Ear-less

Coppin drew in breath after breath of the rank taproom air, tainted as it was with blood and gore, sweat and piss. The sounds around her of men shouting and cursing, horns blowing and armour scraping, assaulted her senses as much as the agony in her side. She couldn't cry out, nor cry in general. All Coppin could do was suck in the next breath and press her hands to the bleeding wounds, front and back, as she'd been taught by Sears and Longoss…

'Longoss?' Copping shouted. She grimaced. Her head swam and her vision blurred as she looked about for her love. And when she found the big man's motionless body, her vision faded and she felt herself fall.

'Help me!' Effrin's heart raced as he dropped to his knees, hands outstretched over the bleeding woman. The cleric quested for the extent of her wounds, pushing away the incredulity that was Lord Severun's unconscious form laying nearby – Effrin's former guild master, who was supposed to be dead, although Effrin had heard rumours that he wasn't.

Effrin's fearful quest of the woman revealed a very painful but fixable wound in her side; through her side, from front to back. Effrin winced. He felt rather than saw someone appear beside him.

'Master Cleric?'

Effrin turned to the crossbowman. 'Fetch my supplies from the saddle. And make haste.' The man nodded and rushed away. Effrin wished he'd entered the tavern with his supplies to start with, but the unknown dangers inside, the two masked assassins Morton's men had faced, meant he'd had to enter prepared for a fight, rather than to save lives, although that's what he needed to do now. As his hands shifted across his patient's abdomen, Effrin froze. 'She's carrying a child,' he whispered, and swallowed hard. He dared not probe further for fear of harming the tiny life inside her womb. It was so very small and vulnerable – maybe even at risk from the assassin's attack – but pushing in with his power could end its mind, if not its physical life, that he knew. Effrin licked dry lips and shouted again for his supplies.

'How fair the others?' he asked of the men-at-arms crouching by those they'd come to relieve.

'Two of the big ugly bastards are dead, the inn-keeper near as damn it, as is the witchunter.' The young man spat as he said the latter. 'As for the ear-less brute over there,' he shrugged, 'fuck knows how, Master Cleric, but he's breathing.'

As the lad said the words, another of Morton's men shouted in surprise as a bloody hand shot up from the ear-less one and took hold of his maille coif, pulling him down to face gold teeth.

'Woah!' Sir Merrel shouted, rushing in from the back of the tavern, one of his men holding his sword. Sir Merrel held both gauntleted hands out to the sides to show he was no threat and approached the ear-less brute, whose eyes darted about the room like a cornered animal. He gritted those gold teeth, his breaths paining him, as was the action of holding a struggling man as big as himself – that man pulled a dagger from his belt, but at a command from Sir Merrel, he reluctantly threw it across the floor, cursing as he heard it clatter, his eyes watching the now growling man who held him firm.

'We're here to aid you,' Sir Merrel said, patting the air, 'so release my man and we'll have someone see to your... considerable wounds.' Sir Merrel balked at the bloody mess of the man, clearly realising most of the blood was indeed his.

'The fucking masks?' Ear-less said, searching the faces staring at him, some snarling, most shocked.

'Dead,' Sir Merrel confirmed, as Ear-less' eyes found the red-masked assassin's bolt-punctured body, which resembled an archer's training dummy.

'And the bitch? Terrina?' Ear-less demanded, turning back to stare at Sir Merrel.

'I ended her. Out back.' Sir Merrel lowered his arms to his sides and hung them from his plated belt with iron-clad thumbs. 'Now let my man go and let us help you.'

Effrin looked past the scene to the front door. He saw the crossbowman with his supplies and waved him over. The man had been gawking at the situation.

As the crossbowman crossed the room, Ear-less tracked him, ducked a little to look under the table that stood between him and Effrin, and howled in renewed agony. Effrin knew it to be separate from the man's wounds.

'Coppin!'

The soldier who'd been held by Ear-less was pushed back as the brute made to rise, stumbled and fell forward, crying out as he hit the floor, coughing blood by the end of it all. No one moved to assist him, likely for fear he'd turn on them. The men watched on, Sir Merrel too as Earl-less crawled across the floor leaving a dark stain like some horrific gore-trailing slug. His breathing sounded like a stuck boar's.

Effrin looked down. 'Coppin, is it? Coppin, can you hear me?' he said into the woman's ear. 'Linen on the wounds, now. And press hard,' he said to the crossbowman. The man drew linen from the pack he'd been cradling and got to it as Effrin, ignoring the sound of the crawling man, reached into the bag to clean his hands. 'Boil some water and be quick about it,' he shouted to anyone who'd listen. He heard Sir Merrel delegate the task to someone. 'And help that poor man,' Effrin added, eyes on his patient. There was a pause. He heard the shuffle of feet.

'Get off, ye bastards,' Ear-less said.

'She'll be well if you let me work,' Effrin said, loud enough for the man to hear. 'Coppin will be fine!' he reasserted. 'Now let Sir Merrel's men aid you. Let them!'

The sounds of grunts and curses and scuffling stopped.

'She carries a babe...'

Effrin barely heard the words through the sobs that accompanied them. 'I know and I can't do anything about that here and now, but unless you want her to die...' Effrin's eyes closed and he began to open himself to her; to her feelings and pain and the damage within and without, '...you'll be quiet and let me be.'

'What's your name?' Effrin heard Sir Merrel ask, quietly, soothingly.

'Longoss. And I know you know that already, Sir Merrel.' Longoss' broken voice held anger once again, to accompany the fear and grief.

'I was merely making sure you still had your wits, Longoss,' Sir Merrel said, amusement touching his tone more than the mirroring of Longoss' anger.

Effrin felt the exchange rather than heard it. 'Longoss is with us,' Effrin said and sent to Coppin all in one, ignoring the rest. 'Longoss is here and you're going to be fit and well, I promise.' He spoke the words for the big man's sake, rather than Coppin's, for she'd heard it within; within her mind, her heart and her soul. She found peace from the pain as cells bonded, flesh and skin knitted. It would take a lot from him, but Effrin couldn't in good conscience do any less for the woman, despite knowing he had others to attend to. As if reading his very thoughts and fears, for those lying dying about him, Sir Merrel gave a set of fresh orders.

'Get to packing and binding the survivors' wounds, you fools! And as soon as it's done, get them out of here and get them to the nearest infirmary.'

Effrin heard the shifting of feet on wood, the scrape of plate and the shush of maille.

'There's resistance, in parts, Sir Merrel,' a soldier said from the doorway.

'Then get the fuck out there, man, and take whoever's lulling around doing nothing. Teach the bastards what you know; what I taught you. Let them die knowing the Lord High Constable of Altoln sends his violent regards.'

Raised voices in renewed high spirits and the men ran from the tavern.

There'll be far more blood spilt this night, Effrin allowed himself to think as the worst of the damage within Coppin was repaired. She'd been lucky more than anything, or the assassin unlucky, if there was a difference. If it mattered.

'Do you need your battle mage?' Effrin asked, eyes closed. He heard Sir Merrel sigh from right behind.

'Probably, but you need her in here, don't you?'

Effrin nodded.

'Rough Paul,' Merrel shouted.

'Sir Merrel?' came a rather effeminate voice from over by the witchunter.

'Go fetch our witch—'

Effrin winced at the term.

'—and tell her Effrin needs her.'

'Understood. Oh, and Sir Merrel…' Rough Paul started.

'Go on.'

'I think the witchunter lives.'

'Then hurry the fuck up, man.'

Footsteps left the tavern and Effrin heard a shout from the lad, although it didn't sound like it'd come from a lad.

'She'll be here shortly,' Sir Merrel said. He was closer now, leaning over Effrin, likely to watch.

'Space, Sir Merrel, if you please.'

Sir Merrel shifted away. 'Of course. I'll be outside.'

Effrin nodded and opened his eyes. He shifted those eyes to the crossbowman and nodded. 'You can let go of her wounds.'

The crossbowman paused before doing as he was told. It was clear he expected blood to spring forth once more, but none came.

There was plenty about Coppin's midriff and the crossbowman's hands, and more smeared here and there, but no more leaked from her wounds.

'Clean your hands and stay with her,' Effrin said, throwing the man a cloth before moving around the table towards Longoss. He felt light headed, dizzy even, but swallowed it down, shook it off and made to crouch by the big, bleeding man, who'd allowed two pairs of hands to staunch the flow of blood. He looked deathly pale, but when Effrin tried to check his wounds, Longoss slapped him away.

'The others... first... me last,' he said between dangerously slow breaths.

Before Effrin could protest, Sir Merrel's battle mage appeared at the door, calling his name.

'There's injured about,' Effrin called back to her. 'See to them if you will.' She acknowledged and rushed to the inn-keeper, bypassing the witchunter, Effrin noticed. Longoss clearly did too. He made to speak but Effrin shoved a damp cloth under his flat nose. Longoss was out cold before a word passed between golden teeth. Effrin noticed the two men either side of Longoss relax. 'Keep the pressure on his wounds,' Effrin said. 'I've made it harder for him, to make it easier for us. But I don't like it, so don't let him or me down, understand?' Both men nodded.

'I'm not sure the inn-keeper will make it whether I continue with him or not,' the battle mage said, for Effrin to hear.

'Move on,' Effrin replied. It pained him to say it, but they needed to work on those who could be saved before those who likely could not.

'Burn my soul...'

Effrin turned, saw the battle mage crouching by Lord Severun. 'Ah, yes,' he managed, 'there is that.' He met her eyes. Wide eyes. 'Do what you can for him,' he said, nodding to her. She swallowed and nodded back, and Effrin knew exactly what warred within her. She'd been out there battling arcane mages of the Black Guild, just to be pulled in here to try and heal an arcane mage, formerly master of her own guild.

'He's fine.' She spat. 'Unconscious but fine,' she added, and with an ironic choice, crossed to the witchunter. 'As for this one,' she said quickly, no compassion in her words, 'he's already gone.'

Rough Paul started. 'I thought...' He'd immediately returned to the witchunter and had been pressing his gloved hand to the man's back: a hatchet wound that'd gaped and leaked blood before Rough Paul had pressed his hands to it.

The mage flashed Rough Paul a look Effrin didn't miss.

'Sir Merrel!' Effrin shouted.

Sir Merrel strode into the tavern and lifted his chin to Effrin.

'Have a word with your mage, Sir Merrel. For me.'

Sir Merrel frowned and turned to the woman. She scowled at Effrin, stood and barged the knight from her path through the door. Sir Merrel looked to Rough Paul, who shrugged, hands pressed to the witchunter's bloody back. It dawned on Sir Merrel and he cursed aloud, looking to Effrin.

'My apologies, Effrin, on her behalf.'

'Save it,' Effrin said. 'Just have someone who might be able to save that man do so, and fast.' Effrin turned back to Longoss' multiple wounds, drew in a deep breath, fortified himself against the loss of energy he'd suffered whilst healing Coppin and forged on, questing into Longoss as Sir Merrel shouted for his sergeant-at-arms to attend the witchunter.

Chapter 42 – And that is that

Poi Son skirted around assassins from both his and Bronwen's thirds of the guild. He had no intention of entangling himself in the fights throughout the streets and across the rooftops. Colourful flashes, bursts and beams lit the night as Bronwen's mages fought Poi Son's assassins and street-assassins. Poi Son knew he would lose most of his followers. More so, he hoped Bronwen would lose all of hers. After the night was done, all he needed do was plan for Alden-Fenn's return. He shook the thought away and stowed it in the back of his mind. For now, he needed to remain focused. Focused on surviving and, if luck was with him – and a lot of experience and skill – find Bronwen herself whilst she was no doubt distracted in dealing with the powerful mage inside the tavern; it was said the man was none other than the former master of the Wizards and Sorcery Guild, Lord Severun, back from the dead.

A scream from the next street startled Poi Son and he berated himself for his wandering mind. Focusing once more, he ducked into a black doorway, the sound of boots on stone closing. He waited until the wearer of those boots passed, then continued on his way.

'Crossbows on me!' Poi Son heard a man shout. He didn't recognise the voice, but when he peered into a broad street and saw the man, he knew he was one of his own. The swordsman ran away from Poi Son's position, three others with him, cradling crossbows as they ran. They reached a corner under a lamp and fell to the ground, lifeless. Just like that. No sounds, no hesitation, just dead.

'Bronwen,' Poi Son whispered. It was either her or one of her inner cabal, to drop four men so easily. Climbing quickly but not hastily, Poi Son reached the roof, checked his surrounds and moved towards the corner where his men lay dead.

A flash lit the sky, emanating from the tavern to his right. Poi Son knew that to be a renewed assault on Severun's shielding of the tavern. If it was indeed the wizard inside, with Longoss. Why would he help Longoss? *Ah yes*, Poi Son thought, *the Duke of Yewdale sticking his oar in because of my mark on his brother-in-law, King Barrison.*

Someone howled in pain, which stood out since the cries and screams had lessened. This final battle would have been ten times worse had the plague and Longoss' actions not taken their toll on the Black Guild. The light show from Bronwen's mages was sparse now, either from lack of her followers or lack of Poi Son's. He hoped for both, although the hope felt alien to him.

Poi Son neared the roof where he suspected Bronwen or one of her assassins to be and felt an immense pressure lift within his head. He wasn't aware, fully, of its presence until it abated. A portion of him balked at all that was happening, of all he had instigated within his guild, and without. He thought of the King, of the mark on the King and the—

Multiple boots on stone. The cacophony of it struck Poi Son and he shook away his thoughts and fears, realising how vulnerable he was. Men approached in numbers, from the south, heading towards the tavern if the echoes of it didn't deceive him. City Guard? *No*, he thought, *Yewdale's men*. Swallowing hard, Poi Son crept forward and peered over a ridge on the roof.

Bronwen! The woman's presence startled him, although he wasn't surprised the arrogant bitch was alone. She likely thought her powers allowed her some form of protection or alarm should anyone approach. But no, there she was, sat cross legged and rocking, eyes... wide open. Poi Son stared at the woman who stared at the tavern. As if called for, the slow-moving clouds shifted in such a way that the moon's silvery light beamed down and illuminated the mistress of the guild. Poi Son saw her every feature... every slack feature. Bronwen's jaw hung open, a string of saliva dangling from her bottom lip. Half of her face drooped, slack and lifeless, the other half as it should be, haggard as ever, but set in place on her cheekbone. Her hands lay by her sides in uncomfortable positions. She didn't look like she was meditating or communicating with her cabal, as Poi Son thought she might be when he came upon her. She looked... dead from within. He knew her to be alive, for her rocking motion gave that away, but apart from that... Poi Son took a deep breath, held it and climbed down to her level.

I'm creeping into a trap, he thought and feared, a determination not all his own pushing him on; the pressure in his head was there once more, although weaker than he remembered, now he seemed able to think about it. Before he could think on it too much, the will exerting itself on him settled and became comfortable, as it should be. Poi Son smiled and relaxed. He sauntered now, which wasn't like him if he'd been of a mind to consider his actions. He reached Bronwen, crouched and waved his hand before her face. Nothing. No reaction. She merely sat there, rocked and dribbled. It hurt Poi Son to see his guild partner and biggest rival so.

As the sound of men-at-arms shouting, hacking and smashing through wooden doors and shutters reached Poi Son, he casually took out a fresh instrument string and, without a word, because a job should be done, not waffled about before-hand or during, strangled the life from Mistress Bronwen of the Black Guild. As easy as that. No fighting back. No shaking or shuddering. The woman rocked as Poi Son shut off the air to her lungs. She flopped forward, string sliding around her bloody neck as she went.

Poi Son watched as the robed body tumble off the roof.

A cry went up from below. Shouts. Barked orders and a thick siege ladder struck the top of the roof, the sound of armoured men climbing it.

'And that, dear Bronwen, is that. The guild is mine. Well, almost,' Poi Son said, before turning and fleeing the scene, Alden-Fenn's brutish, tattooed face looming at the back of his mind.

Chapter 43 – Bolts, blades and strings

Poi Son watched one of his assassins, one of the last – not that there'd been many left, what with Pangan's betrayal leading to Bronwen's explosive magic in the alley opposite the tavern. Poi Son watched the man, loose fitting robes, cloak and hood, fall to a crossbow bolt which thumped him forward and off his feet. Poi Son watched from his hidden position as three men-at-arms in the Duke of Yewdale's colours reached the squirming assassin, only to hack into him with falchions and axe.

'As long as they're finishing Bronwen's lot off as well as my own,' Poi Son whispered to himself. Or so he thought.

'Master Son?'

Poi Son froze at the sound of the girl-watcher's voice. He composed himself, turned to the shadows and smiled. 'My dear. I thought I'd lost you to Bronwen's magic in the alley. Thank Samorl I was wrong.'

'But...' she sounded hesitant, scared even. 'You said you hoped—'

'Traitors, my girl. There were traitors in our midst. It is them of whom I speak. Now...' Poi Son stepped towards the girl and found her shoulders with his gloved and blooded hands. He pulled her in close and turned her to face the body of the latest assassin to fall. Yewdale's men had already moved on. 'How fair we, my young watcher?'

She hesitated before filling him in. She'd been thrown free of the blast in the alley, along with a couple of others, one of whom died immediately afterwards to another barrage of magic from the rooftops. She'd moved to another position where she knew street-assassins of Poi Son's to be mustering. Once there, she'd discovered the position was a mass of crossbow bolts and fire – of all colours. Bodies and... bits of bodies. Several fought on, taking down Bronwen's agents with numbers before moving away. She'd followed at a distance. Her voice shook as she recounted some of it, positively broke at others. Poi Son listened to it all. Carefully. Patiently. The girl was good. She told him there were few left and those were being hunted down and executed by the green and white soldiers and their mage. A demon of a woman, the girl said; which was something, considering she'd witnessed Bronwen's inner cabal fighting.

'And that's who they're finishing off now, Master Son. I heard 'em say so.'

'Bronwen's cabal?'

'Aye.'

There was a loud thud followed by a staccato burst of hollow pops as if to accentuate the girl's point.

'She must be good, this battle mage.'

'Oh aye, Master Son. Like I says, a demon of a woman.'

Nodding, Poi Son squeezed the girl's shoulders. 'And our masked friends?'

A pause, filled with not too distant screams and another burst of thuds and pops, shouts and horns, even barks and howls from neighbourhood dogs, or soldiers' hounds, Poi Son couldn't know.

He felt her shake her head to his question of Terrina and Rapeel.

'Never mind, dear. We're safe. And how shall we retreat from this defeat?' he asked.

She told him the best route away from the danger.

Poi Son choked the life from her before taking her excellent advice.

***

'Flay me to my bones, look at her neck,' Rough Paul said, lowering the lamp to illuminate and accentuate the girl's bloody wound. Two of his five companions grunted whilst the others kept their eyes on the shadows of the alleyway and the rooftops above. Rough Paul took a step back and watched as Sean crouched by the body, his heavy crossbow cradled across his lap. He scratched around in the dirt about the girl as if tracking an animal's kill. Rough Paul laughed silently at that; bitterly. It *was* an animal to have killed one so young, he mused. A man, aye… or woman, knowing the Black Guild and the assassins they'd been tracking down, but an animal all the same. Rough Paul had seen the survivors of the tavern onto carts before heading out with Sean and the others to finish the night's work.

A flash and bang caused every man, bar Sean – old timer that he was – to duck, curse or whisper a prayer. The likes of which were happening in other streets and alleys and buildings where their fellows mopped up the last of the Black Guild bastards.

'Anything, Sean?'

Sean nodded. He scratched at his grey stubble and pointed up the alley. 'That way, lad.'

'Tracks?' Rough Paul asked, squinting at the filthy ground.

'Nope.' Sean stood with a groan before heading up the alley, two younger crossbowman flanking him, their smaller bows spanned and loaded whilst Sean's remained un-spanned, his bolts secure in the leather bag at his waist.

Rough Paul followed the three crossbowmen, two men-at-arms at his back. 'How'd you know?' he asked, frowning.

'This alley is long and thin, lad. We came one way in, didn't we?'

'Aye.'

'Did we pass any fuckers with blood on their hands? Did we pass anyone?'

The bloody string used to garrotte the girl had remained about her neck, so it made sense that her murderer would be travelling with bloody hands, but no weapon.

Receiving no answer, Sean continued on his way, back-lit by Rough Paul's lamp. Another flash lit the sky like lightning and Rough Paul was amazed there were such fights remaining. He knew there were more battle mages about the area than the woman who'd been seconded to Sir Merrel's company, but the fact they faced continued resistance from a dying guild struck him as to how powerful the Black Guild had been.

Sean lifted a clenched fist. The men stopped as one, even those behind who had eyes back as much as front. The old hand stooped, wound and spanned his windlass crossbow, the lads either side of him covering him with their own crossbows. Slotting a thick bolt into the arming groove, Sean hoisted the weapon and paused.

Rough Paul held his breath and tilted his head. He listened as best he could through his padded arming cap and the maille coif that it cushioned. All he could hear was the thump of his own heartbeat rushing through his ears. He let his breath out slowly, heartbeat quickening as he saw the narrowed eyes of the old veteran crossbowman, who turned to look back past Rough Paul and the others. Rough Paul made to move, to turn, but a shake of Sean's head stayed him.

Vivid green strobes on the next street startled the group as the staccato popping that followed resonated through them. As Rough Paul winced, Sean moved. He took one large, quick step towards Rough Paul, planted his crossbow onto Rough Paul's padded shoulder, leaned into his weapon and squeezed the trigger with his thumb.

The thud and twang was second only to the snapping jerk that rocked Rough Paul as the heavy draw-weight bow propelled its missile back between the other two soldiers and off into the darkness; darkness lit but a moment ago, several times in quick succession, by the green strobes of arcane energy.

A muffled cry of surprise and pain reached every man. The other two crossbowmen turned and loosed their own bolts, despite their quarrels' trajectories passing dangerously close to their own men. Loud cracks off stone marked both impacts and as all three crossbowmen moved to re-load, Rough Paul and his counterparts chased the bolts, lamp held high.

They heard a scuffling of boots on stone. They heard grunts and curses from shadows Rough Paul's lamp or the moon above struggled to penetrate, but on they charged.

The image of the garrotted girl flashed before Rough Paul's eyes. He was thankful of his maille coif, and thankful the two with him wore the same.

If only the crossbowmen did.

Rough Paul turned at the sound of a strangled cry. He skidded to a stop and fell as he changed direction. He didn't need to see what was happening in the shadows he'd left behind to know they'd been ambushed. Dropping the lamp and pulling a dagger to accompany his arming sword, he accelerated back towards Sean and the others, barking an order for his two to follow.

Grunts, scuffles and the snapped launch of a crossbow followed by the familiar crack of an iron tipped bolt striking stone. Rough Paul slowed as he neared where the crossbowmen should have been. He cast about in the dim light of the forgotten lamp, for them, for anyone.

'Gods take us, where are they?'

'I don't know, Ten,' Rough Paul said, soft voice shaking.

'Shit, Paul… look.' Ten pointed to the floor with his falchion. The third man, Graehm, swore.

Rough Paul's blood ran cold as he looked at the two bloody strings littering the ground.

'Back to the lamp.' Ten shifted his bulk so his back was to the backs of his two friends and not the darkness. 'Paul, Graehm, on me. Now.'

Nodding and swallowing hard, Rough Paul did as Ten said, as did Graehm. The three of them moved slowly, surely, back towards the lamp, straining their eyes to see into the shadows. All had gone quiet now, in the streets surrounding them. No magical pops or shouted orders. No horns or… horns!

'Sound the fucking horn, Graehm!' Rough Paul said, palms slick on his weapons. They were nearly at the lamp when a crossbow snapped and glass shattered, taking the light with it.

Darkness took them and from that darkness came the sweetest sound of three horn blasts. Then came the curse, scuffle and choking of a dying man. No, men.

Before any aid reached him, Rough Paul stood alone, chest heaving, heartbeat filling his ears once more. He pissed himself then, whilst lunging at nothing with his blades. Slashing and stabbing, the ambient light enough to know he was attacking nought but air. Over the rasping of his breath and the thudding in his ears he swore he heard boots on stone. He strained to listen, swinging and blindly stabbing as he was.

'Paul?'

Rough Paul left the ground. He instinctively swung on the speaker of his name, but a strong hand caught his wrist. A strong, slick hand, sticky with what could only be – in Rough Paul's imagination if nothing else – blood.

'Paul, stop swinging, lad.'

'Sean?'

'Aye, it's me, and I think I stuck the bastard, though I can't see for shit to be sure.'

Rough Paul sagged. Sean took his weight. 'I thought you dead,' he whispered, eyes filling with tears despite his previous combat experience.

'I thought me dead too, lad. The others?'

It was too dark to know. Rough Paul said nothing. Nor did Sean. Before their imaginations could do anymore harm, before anything else could take them or scare them at the very least, a light appeared down the alley, towards the tavern. Loud voices accompanied that light: orders being given, names being called.

'Down here!' Sean shouted. 'We're down here!'

Rough Paul sobbed into Sean's arms as men from their company approached, lamps leading the way. Their curses and shouts of anger soon followed as the lamps revealed their dead. Two crossbowmen further up the alley, slumped against a wall, next to one another. And the two men-at-arms, Ten and Graehm, their own previously belted daggers jutting from an eye a piece. And two friends, one young, one much older, crouched and huddled between the two deathly scenes.

'I think I got him,' Sean kept saying, as their own men helped them to their feet and walked them away. 'I think I got the bastard assassin…'

Rough Paul noticed the bloody rondel dagger in Sean's white-knuckled hand and hoped his friend was right.

Chapter 44 – Ride for the hills

Pleasant pastures flanked the road Cheung travelled. He had ridden through hamlets and skirted a couple of villages, past farms and took a wide birth around a dull, squat keep. Often the palomino walked him off the road to avoid patrolling soldiers, their colourful liveries different every time. He knew various houses of Altoln had men on the hunt, few wanting an assassin to succeed in taking a king from them that, by all accounts, was loved and valued by an astonishing majority of the kingdom. Few rulers held the respect King Barrison did. Cheung smiled to himself, the moving of his lips, cheeks and eyes a bitter thing; he knew his countrymen held little regard for the ruling council of Eatri.

I know what I have to do. I do not question what I have to do. That has ever been the way of it. That is all I had ever known, until the caravan. An uncharacteristic snarl pulled at Cheung's top lip. *I lost myself there. But this solitude, on the road... it was well needed.* 'I will not fail you, masters.'

Before rider and mount crested the hill, a gull filled, smoke-stained sky gave Wesson away. Reaching the crest, the palomino stopped and pawed at the ground, Cheung taking in a city falling away to the sea, behind tall walls that looked akin to the squat keep he'd avoided, in colour if not in size.

'It rolls down the hill to waters as dirty as the sky, they say,' Cheung said to the horse. The animal threw its head back once, twice, receiving a pat on the neck for its efforts. Tipping forward, the animal knelt with its forelegs, making its intentions clear.

'We must part ways, yes.' Cheung climbed from the saddle, his understanding clear as he rubbed behind a golden ear. 'You're the most conspicuous horse I and anyone else around here have ever seen. You do right by me to insist we part company before Wesson's gates.'

The horse stood and Cheung moved about it, unbuckling harness and saddle, removing its burdens. How much he had learnt.

'You have freedom now, my friend. You have the run of this luscious land.' He hid the riding gear away from the road and came back to stand in front of the horse, his satchel slung over one shoulder and the flea-ridden cloak about his shoulders. Noses touched.

'If you are here should I return, I would thank you, but I do not expect or request it. You have shown me great loyalty and you have seen me to my destination. You have my eternal gratitude for those things. But more than that, you have allowed me to regain my focus. I am the weapon I once was, the tool to my masters' desires, and I shall succeed because of you.' The palomino released a soft whinny and stepped back, turning to look down the hill and arduous road they had travelled together.

'Go now. Run free, but run clear of these lands, as lovely as they seem. A prize like you will not run free for long. I wish you not to be captured by some greedy knight or lord, by some horse breeder intent on making his fortune off of your heritage.'

The palomino turned and looked to Cheung one last time.

'Ride for the Moot Hills and the Eastern Planes beyond. You have earned it!' Cheung shouted the last as white tail flicked and golden legs propelled the animal down and into the vale they'd come from.

Lips tight, Cheung turned away from the magnificent creature. He cast his gaze across ridge and furrowed fields and back over the city of Wesson. Scanning from right to left, he found the palace he needed to infiltrate. The towers were a lighter stone than the rest of the city, and taller than most; all but one, which he assumed was the renowned Tyndurris. He felt as if eyes were watching him from that tower, but shook it away whilst setting off down the hill.

A cold wind picked up, bringing with it fine rain.

The sort that soaks you through before you know you're wet, he thought, forging on towards his goal. Towards Wesson's Palace and the King within.

The gate was busy, and muddy from the rain that continued to fall. Water streamed from gargoyles and murder holes far above the passers-by. Carts crawled through the double gates, their contents being checked vigorously by sodden cloaked, grumpy men-at-arms of the wall and the City Guard alike, their mixed liveries indicating to Cheung how heavy Wesson's security had become. Because of him. The information he'd received from his masters about Wesson had been in depth and accurate, as only a direct insertion to the mind can be. The colours of surcoats, tabards and gambesons were as if a memory to Cheung, unlike many of those he'd seen and avoided on the roads.

Cheung walked amongst a group of Sirretan jongleurs, their garishly decorated eight-wheeled vardo following behind. He'd joined the group not far from the gatehouse itself, paying the performers all he had to swap clothes and act as if he were one of them. He strummed languidly at a lute, the musicians about him wincing at every drag of his pale, wet fingers.

'A song for you, a song for me,' the lead jongleur called to an approaching sergeant-at-arms in the colours of the City Guard. 'A song for day, a song for—'

'Night,' the sergeant finished, unimpressed. 'Yes yes, how lovely, now state your business... specifically. And make it quick.'

Cheung did his best to blend in with the others, their gaudy attire a confusion of colour and frills, of rain-darkened wool and linen and felt.

The lead jongleur bowed low, glistening flute out wide. 'We come to entertain. We come to sing and make merry. We come to feed our minds, our lungs with song... our bellies.'

'Your Altolnan is good,' the sergeant said, rubbing the back of his head. 'So, I'm sure you understood the word 'specifically'.'

A cart passed through the dry tunnel of the gatehouse, leaving three guardsmen free to flank their sergeant. He turned to them and ordered the searching of the jongleurs' tall vardo.

The performers stopped their music and some of them moved back to their mobile home, affixing worried eyes on the hands of the men rooting through their belongings. Cheung acted as they did, but kept his distance all the same.

'Why do you do this, friend?' the lead jongleur asked the sergeant, his Altolnan may have been good, but his Sirretan accent was heavy. 'Have we offended?'

A deep breath accompanied a shake of the head. 'No.' The sergeant looked past the man with the flute. 'Everyone is to be checked, and the sooner you answer my question and your wagon is searched, the sooner you can move on and find a dry tavern to ply your trade.'

Another over eager bow. 'Of course, Sergeant, of course. We have travelled far to attempt an audience with your most magnificent King. His court is renowned and we wish to impress with acrobats, fire walkers and more. We must play and prance and... paw.' The man winked as a group of women were ushered through the gatehouse, the sergeant and lead jongleur's eyes upon them and their cloying kirtles and skirts.

'Thank the rains!'

The sergeant nodded, seemingly satisfied, especially when his men claimed all was well.

'Fine, fine. On you go.'

'A gentleman this sergeant truly is, letting us pass through the gate, which is his!' The lead jongleur sang for all to hear and pointed his flute to the gates. 'He talks like a king and fights like a bear, oh what honours he must wear!'

The troupe took up the song as one, instruments coming to life in their hands as they continued the song.

The sergeant shook his head and moved on, men in tow, towards a group of riders coming down the road. He stopped as the tall vardo rolled through the mud. 'Jongleur!' he shouted, jogging to and turning the man now playing his flute. 'Have any joined your group recently?' he said as an afterthought. 'Any new faces? There'd be a reward for the truth of it.'

Cheung clenched teeth but continued to strum terribly. His eyes met the flute player's, which blinked repeatedly in the rain.

As the sergeant's eyes narrowed at the hesitation, the lead jongleur shook his head and offered another one of his bows.

'We have been together an age, Sergeant. No one joins us afresh. We all of us remain together and yet keep it fresh. We walk and we—'

'Yes, yes. Understood.' The sergeant rolled his eyes, waved his hand and turned away, muttering to himself.

As the sergeant flagged down the nearing riders, the assassin he had clearly been ordered to search for nodded his thanks to the performer putting flute to lips. The lead jongleur smiled at Cheung as they continued as a troupe, through the brief cessation of rain allowed them beneath the huge gatehouse. Once through the tunnel and into Wesson proper, another jongleur began to sing, high and loud.

> *Our troupe passes gargoyles and ancient stone*
> *We play for our fortune, be it silver or gold*
> *Singing and juggling until the crowds do come…*

'We play our tune on the road and run!' Cheung sang the words without thinking, and his stomach lurched, twisted and spun; the troupe cheered, leapt and tumbled, and to the canvas tavern of the Coach and Cart Inn they did run.

***

'He never turned up,' Longoss managed. He was drowsy, vision blurred and hearing stranger than normal. Coppin lay on the cot next to his, unconscious but purposefully so, the clerics told him. She was equally as drugged up as Longoss, but with something else to help her fall into a deep sleep which would help her recover, or so they said. Longoss wasn't sure whether the clerics in the infirmary wanted to delay the potentially horrifying news her consciousness would bring; does her baby live? He'd asked them to test, to quest. He'd asked them to bring midwives in if their magics couldn't do the trick, but they ensured him that all would be for nought if Coppin's wounds weren't allowed to mend. The cleric on the scene, Effrin, had done well. The young man's peers had told Longoss so, as had Sir Merrel. Longoss snarled at the thought of Morton's cunt-captain. Longoss had no clue as to whether any of it was true or not, or whether Sir Merrel was having Longoss told these things merely to keep him calm; to keep him from leaving his bed in a fit of rage; rage he felt surging from time to time, within. A burning sensation. A pressure that built and swelled and threatened to break free whenever Longoss thought of how wrong it had gone; how much worse it could've been.

'Poi Son,' Longoss whispered. He looked across to the tranquil form of Coppin under her white linen sheets. So peaceful. So calm and beautiful. 'He didn't come,' Longoss said again, louder.

'Who didn't?'

Longoss looked the other way, stitches pulling from the movement. Pain flared despite the drugs, but Longoss accepted it all for his failure in both protecting Coppin and destroying the Black Guild. 'Poi Son,' he said to Severun.

Severun nodded. 'He was likely about, out there,' Severun said, eyes on the sleeping witchunter opposite him. 'He was likely orchestrating it all from some rooftop or other, if what you've told us of him is anything to go by.'

Longoss sighed and lowered his head to the pillow. Such luxury. He hated it. He wanted to be out there, searching for Poi Son now that the majority, if not all, of the bastard's assassins were dead.

'You worry about one man, Longoss,' Severun said, looking to him, 'but we succeeded, my friend. We destroyed the Black Guild and thwarted whatever agenda it was playing at.'

Longoss was shaking his head before Severun finished. 'We failed, Severun. We destroyed much of it, or rather Morton's men did, and you may have cut one of the three bastard heads from the beast – and I'm impressed at that, to say the least.' Longoss looked again to Severun and shone gold. The smile faded as quick. 'But Poi Son is left. And Alden-Fenn.'

Severun grimaced. 'I've heard tell of that man.'

'There's little man in him, I'd say.'

'And that coming from you?' came another voice.

Both men looked to the door. Severun visibly tensed. Longoss tried to sit up and snarled at the combination of pain and visitor.

'Greetings, my lord Yewdale,' Severun managed.

Will Morton nodded to Severun and moved into the room, hand on the hilt of his sheathed bastard-sword. 'Severun,' he replied, pointedly dropping the former lord's former title. 'Longoss,' he added, his teeth gritted as much as the man he addressed.

'Lord Bastard,' Longoss growled.

Morton's steel pouldrons scraped as he shrugged. 'I can't say I didn't expect hostility from you, lad.'

'Hence why ye came armoured.' Longoss leaned out a little, to see around Morton; to see the two knights behind him. He accepted the pain the movement presented. 'And with yer pups up yer arse, too.' He slumped back in his bed, eyes locked on the Lord High Constable. He heard Sir Merrel grunt a laugh.

Morton managed a smile. 'Can you blame me, what with the hornets' nest we shat in? Or do you regret my acting upon that? Do you regret Sir Merrel marching into Dockside with his men and mine, losing the lives of many to put down a common enemy of ours, Longoss? Eh, lad? Do you wish, for old time's sake, I'd not bothered? Because I did bother,' he went on, before Longoss could answer. 'I did and I have to expect potential reprisals on me and my own because of it. So yes, I am armed and armoured and shadowed by men I trust. So, string me up for it.' He shrugged again and again steel scraped on steel. 'Way I see it, I've done both you and Barrison a favour here. Although, in hindsight, perhaps Sir Merrel could have arrived a touch later. Let you bleed out or the masked bitch finish butchering you before saving the day—'

'Saving the day?' Longoss winced as he shot upright, eyes wild, fists balled and knuckles white. He looked round Morton once more, to Sir Merrel. 'That what ye tell yer master, Merrel, ye prick? That ye're some fucking hero?'

It was Sir Merrel's turn to shrug. 'You're welcome,' he said, a wry smile on his handsome face.

'The Three with the lot of ye.' Longoss slumped back once more. 'It's no more than I'd have expected. Would that ye could've saved Coppin from her wounds whilst strutting around in fancy plate, acting the bastard hero.' Longoss turned to take in Coppin, before

257

staring up at the ceiling. 'Would that ye could've killed Poi Son whilst ye were at it,' he said, his former master's face appearing smug before his hazy vision.

'Perhaps we did,' Sir Merrel said, moving alongside Morton.

Longoss' head snapped to the two men. 'Tell me!' he demanded, eyes flicking from one to the other, their features blunted by the drugs that seemed to be taking him from the scene.

Sir Merrel brought his hands from behind his back – Longoss hadn't noticed them there – and revealed a rondel dagger, the blade dark with dried blood. 'One of my crossbowmen stuck Poi Son with this,' Sir Merrel said, his grin now the smuggest thing Longoss had ever seen. It wasn't like Sir Merrel, Longoss knew, but he had to assume the knight's love of Longoss was as nonexistent as Longoss' love for the knight. 'And the man claimed to have shot him too, with a bolt from a windlass, of all things.'

Morton's smile at that was genuine, his creased eyes gave that much away.

'You believe it?' Longoss pleaded.

'The crossbowman is an old hand at such things,' Sir Merrel confirmed. 'He's not a young bragger, although—'

'Yes?'

'He couldn't know what Poi Son looks like,' Sir Merrel went on, hesitating with the truth. 'Nor did he see his assailant's face in the dark alley where the fight played out.'

Longoss slumped back yet again, a frown stealing away his interest.

'How could he possible know?' Severun asked. He'd been quiet until this point, but he asked the question Longoss wanted to know.

'He can't, for sure,' Morton admitted. 'But the man they tackled killed four hard men. He garrotted two and drove the other two's own daggers into their eyes. It happened quickly and all in the same alley as a young girl found, also garrotted. The bloody strings—'

'Left behind,' Longoss whispered.

Morton and Sir Merrel nodded.

'And that's Poi Son's way?' Severun asked Longoss. The former assassin nodded. Severun looked back to Morton and his man. 'But no body?'

Sir Merrel's smile faded. 'No body.'

'That would be too easy,' Longoss managed, the drugs pulling him down. He rejoiced at the pain Poi Son must have felt at being shot and stabbed. He rejoiced and hoped, and prayed of all things, at the slow death the man must surely be experiencing, maybe even now.

Elleth, Longoss thought, a warmth flowing through him, *I think we got him. I think the bastard is dead.* The room dimmed, the sounds faded. *Now look over your sister, my love. Bring her and her babe through this, whether ye need take my life to do it or not, ye hear? Whether ye need to take a thousand lives to do it…*

Longoss' grasp on the room about him faded into unconsciousness; into a blissful emptiness and peace.

***

Cheung paid the jongleurs to get him through the gatehouse, nothing more, and they kept their end of the bargain. He thanked them, changed clothes again and moved on. The jongleurs told the truth about wanting to perform at the palace, but theirs was not an effective method of entry. For that, Cheung needed stealth and cunning… or, something a little too obvious to be of concern to the palace guards.

He travelled along large avenues, late in the day. The crowds that travelled those avenues were enough to allow his inconspicuous passage. A rain fell once more, causing rivulets to work their way through the maze of cobbles beneath his soft-soled boots. Satchel tight at his side, he moved along with the rushing folk beneath the trees, hood up, as most did whenever it rained. The palace loomed in the distance, a formidable structure hidden behind a rain-hazed veil, hiding the mark, the man; the King that Cheung sought. Tall houses and trees continued to line the avenue, which led Cheung to a small square before another impressive gatehouse, this structure of a lighter stone than the one he'd passed through to enter the city. Braziers flanked the outside of the gates, as well as the ramparts above. Palace guards huddled around the hissing flames, rain tinkling on helmets whilst waxed cloaks allowed run off to add to the puddles at their booted feet.

Cheung never expected to simply walk into Wesson Palace, but nor could he have planned his entry before seeing the place for himself. The memory-like images in his head were not enough. Subtly moving to and hiding in fast darkening shadows, the sun retreating towards the large naval buildings down the hill, Cheung crouched and watched the guards and their routines. He would find a way in, although he doubted it would be that night. What was one more day after all he'd been through and done to get this far?

***

'You did well, Severun,' Morton said, realising the filthy shite of a man lying next to Severun had passed out. 'To take Bronwen down, after all the years your guild secretly hunted her.'

Severun nodded, eyes shifting to Egan Dundaven's unmoving form, opposite. 'It was not easy, my lord, and I may have lost much in my absence from the fight within the tavern.'

'Nevertheless,' Morton said, stepping closer and drawing Severun's attention, 'you did your King a great service, you and Master Dundaven.' Morton looked across to the severely injured man. 'They tell me the hatchets the masked fuck used were soiled in sewage?'

Severun nodded once, swallowed visibly.

'I'm sure they're doing all they can for him, despite his—'

'His past doesn't come into it!' Severun said, voice raising. 'His actions since his time with me; his actions as a man, a good man, are all that matter. His actions—'

'Or yours, Severun?' Morton tilted his head, awaiting a reprisal for his interruption and comment.

Severun straightened in his bed. He breathed heavily and levelled a look at Morton that told the Duke all he needed to know of the man he'd know, although not all that well, for years.

'You've changed.' Morton's eyes narrowed. 'Something happened in that tavern, didn't it?'

A sad smile played across Severun's face. 'It did indeed, my lord. It did indeed.'

Morton looked sidelong to Sir Merrel, who shrugged. Turning back to Severun, Morton waited.

'My lord, I believe I shrugged off a presence that has been trying – and succeeding at times – to enforce its will on me since...'

'Since?' Sir Merrel asked, his intrigue equal to that of Morton's own.

'Since I purchased the scroll that caused the plague.' It pained Severun to say the words out loud. It pained yet relieved him to tell someone; anyone. Morton could see it in the man's eyes.

Morton moved to the bedside and knelt; his leather boots and harness creaked and his steel poleyn offered a dull thud as it met the

260

wooden floor. 'Tell me,' Morton whispered, leaning in. 'Tell me who, how and why, Severun.' Morton heard the shifting of boots on wood and plate on plate behind him. He waved his chamois gloved hand over his shoulder and, reluctantly he knew, Sir Merrel and Sir Fell left the room. The door closed behind them before Severun spoke.

'The plague was intended. My naivety and greed for the arcane power it offered, no matter how genuine my reasons for—'

'Severun,' Morton warned, wanting facts, not apologies or excuses.

Severun took a breath. 'It isn't a who that sent that scroll, my lord. It isn't a nation or a faction or—'

'The Three?'

Shaking his head at the reasonable suggestion, Severun continued. 'It was a dragon, my lord.' Severun stared into Morton's eyes at the revelation. He wanted it to sink in and Morton knew it, but was struggling to let it.

'A dragon?' Morton moved back, screwed up his face so his scars and lines deepened; the scar that ever pulled his lip into a snarl did it more so. His frown looked like a scowl more than anything else – he felt like a scowl was necessary. Was Severun testing him? Was he mocking him?

Severun nodded once. The fear and realisation of all that had been going on was plain for Morton to see. Not only that. There was a freedom about Severun's face. An ease despite his obvious worry for his new-found friends who lay, potentially dying, about him.

'How—' Morton began.

'The fight with Bronwen,' Severun explained. 'She was besting me, my lord. I'm not embarrassed to say. She was using her arcane against the rules and barriers my own guild has built and set in place over millennia; both within our teachings and our minds. She knew that, hence why she's always bested us as a guild, as a hunting force. We have failed to catch her because she plays by no rules to our many.' He offered a wicked smile. 'But I've played by her lack of rules before, my lord, as you well know.' His smile fell away to a look of disgust, in himself. 'We all know where that lead...'

'Severun?' Morton prompted. Too close to truths now for the wizard to digress.

'Yes...' Severun shook away his melancholy. 'I realised the shadow that pressed on my soul... for wont of a better term to explain such things to someone—'

'Go on,' Morton said, frown returning.

'Well, my lord, my defending against her assault pushed me to my limits. I had to try and draw on everything, you see. Everything. And in doing so, I finally knew...'

'Knew what?' Morton leaned in.

'I knew I was not alone. In here.' Severun tapped his head with one long finger. 'I knew the dark will trying to impose itself on me. I knew I had been unwittingly defending myself for months, or for the most part, since my purchasing of the scroll. I knew, my lord, I was fighting a battle on two fronts. So...' he smiled.

'Yes? Go on.'

'I dropped my defences to the shadow that had already been there when Bronwen attempted to destroy my defences, and me. I allowed it in... and through.' Severun positively beamed now.

Morton knew the genius of it all was lost on him, but nodded for Severun to go on, eager to find out the truth of it all; he knew he had to let Severun tell his tale to get there, so gritted his teeth and let him get on with it.

'Through,' Severun said again. 'Through me and into her. Into Bronwen. Well,' Severun grinned, 'it was my hidden assailant that destroyed the Mistress of the Black Guild, my lord, not me. Or not me alone. And in doing so—'

'You were freed,' Morton said, the simplicity of that part finding him.

'I was freed.' Severun's expression fell to one of guilt and sorrow. 'I was freed and bound in one. Bound to the horrors I unleashed on this city and its people, my lord Yewdale.' His eyes fell away to memories, Morton was sure.

'Lord Severun...'

Severun looked up at that.

'...you already felt sorrow and guilt for what you did, I knew that. I wouldn't have allowed you into my service if I thought you didn't.'

Severun smiled weakly. 'I did, but not as I do now. Not as I do... as me, my lord. The real me. The real Severun Allarance.'

Morton found himself smiling back, sympathetically. Before he knew it, he'd wrapped Severun's closest hand in his own. 'I am glad for you, my lord Severun. I am glad, but...'

'But the dragon?' Severun smiled, mouth and eyes. 'Yes,' he said, nodding. 'Let us talk of him. Let us talk of the legendary horror we call Crackador.'

Chapter 45 – Scars before the mark

Rain fell in sheets now, following the wind that swirled about the square outside Wesson Palace. The braziers flickered, spat and hissed as the guards stood about them stamped feet and clapped hands.

An orange and red inferno filled the sky to the west, lighting the underside of tumultuous clouds, which ended over the sea to allow the low sun to cast its long shadows, pointing the way for the clouds overhead; the clouds emptying their load would soon pass over and leave the city to dry overnight.

A cart creaked and groaned as it approached. Waving without cheer, the elderly driver brought it to a stop in front of the closed gates.

'Evening, lads,' the old man said, pulling his wet hood back a little so they could see his face.

Two of the four guards came forward. One spoke to the driver whilst the other uncovered and rooted through the cart's loaded sacks. He took a green apple, threw it to the other and took one for himself.

'All apples, is it?' the guard by the driver asked.

'Aye, and some rhubarb. For plates and pies and cider. Early crop though, not me best. Could've done wi' a few more weeks, but—'

'Anyone approached you on the way in?'

'How'd ye mean?'

The guard took a bite out of the apple his friend had thrown him. 'For passage,' he said, mouth full.

'Why'd they wanna do that?'

'Answer him,' said Rooter, at the back of the cart.

'No. Ent no one's approached me, 'cept more like you two, back at the main gates.'

The guard bit another chunk of the apple.

'All's clear,' Rooter said, before re-covering the load and moving back to the brazier, rubbing his green prize on his chest, under his dripping cloak.

Without a word, he guard by the driver waved him on. Gates clunked, creaked and opened.

Walking over to his companion and their brazier, the guard who'd done the talking watched the cart rock ever so slowly through. He finished the apple he'd been devouring and fed the core to the flames, which hissed in satisfaction.

'Did you not check under the cart?' he asked, looking to his friend.

Rooter laughed. 'No. Stop asking, will ye? I never do. Every damn bard song or story has someone hiding under a cart. No one's stupid enough to actually do it.' He threw his own core into the fire.

'Well they should, since no one ever checks.'

'Listen, I ain't getting down in this shit 'n' mud to check for no one to be not clingin' underneath the slowest pissin' cart I ever did see pass through those gates.' He took a breath after that. 'Poor donkey's dead on its legs, pulling that load.' Rooter clapped his hands together and shuddered as a rain drop ran down his nose. He wiped it away and turned to see his friend staring at him.

'But if there is?'

'There isn't, trust me. It's a stupid hiding place and I ain't looking stupid m'self, and getting more wet, by getting on all fours to check for nowt. I'll do the rootin', like always, but that's it. Now leave it, will ye? Unless *you* wanna look?'

A shake of the head. They both watched the cart enter the courtyard beyond as the gates started to close.

'And if Sergeant Grannit asks?'

'For 'morl's sake.'

'If there's an assassin under that there cart, and he gets in, and Grannit knows you—'

'Stop that cart!' Rooter shouted.

The donkey huffed its relief as the driver obliged, mumbling and grumbling to himself.

The two guards motioned for their friends on the far brazier to keep watch, and pressed through the nearly closed gates to the cart on the far side.

Squatting at the back wheel, Rooter glanced under and shrugged. 'Nothing,' he said, looking up to his partner, eyes squinting the rain away.

Eyebrows were raised and a helmeted head nodded back to the cart, insistent.

Following a heavy sigh, Rooter shifted his sword to the side and knelt on the wet ground, cursing colourfully as he discovered the puddle was deeper than it looked. He still couldn't see properly, so with yet more curses, Rooter resigned himself to it and dropped to all fours.

A gust of wind howled and rain fell all the more.

By the side of the cart, eyes widened before an unseen blade punched through one of them. Rooter's arms and legs went limp and he flopped to the floor with a shallow splash.

The second guard hit the ground hard as two kamas swept him from his feet, finishing him before he could shout out.

Cursing the further delay, the old driver urged the donkey on, and cursed the guards who he assumed must have passed back through the gates without telling him he was free to go.

Cheung waited with the two dead men in the evening gloom, the sun's position too low to illuminate the courtyard, nestled as it was within the Palace's high walls. Once the cart and its driver were out of sight, Cheung heaved and dragged the blood-, piss- and, in one case, shit-soiled bodies to a deeply shadowed corner, leaving blood-slick puddles in his wake. He disappeared into the sprawling palace after that, certain his mark was finally within striking distance.

Bells sounded and so did soldiers, servants and dogs. The latter barked and howled as they were led through corridors and across yards. Armour rustled and scraped and clanked and doors were barred. Knights and sergeants shouted orders and others called out warnings.

Cheung moved down a dark passageway, pulling torches from walls as he ran. He'd attempted to cross a large, empty hall as the bells started to ring loud and clear, only to find the floor dissolving as he stepped out onto it. He'd watched in confusion as the stone slabs liquefied, beginning to bob like the skin on a cooling soup. He'd turned from that path, knowing magic when he saw it.

An iron studded door stood before him as he reached the end of the torch scattered but otherwise featureless passage. Satchel gripped in one hand, he pressed his ear to the door and held his breath.

Nothing.

Turning the handle with a pale, scarred hand, Cheung eased it open and peeked through the gap.

Nothing.

He entered the oblong room and eyed the harnesses of plate armour along the walls. His heart lurched in his chest as the empty great-helms turned and eyed him back.

Mages be cursed...

Cheung ran, satchel at his side. He ran as fast as he could through the middle of the room, ignoring the scraping of metal as swords were drawn and boots stepped from flanking dais'.

265

A haze rose from the six guardians as they stepped towards him, longswords held offensively. Their armour seemed held in place by that haze to form an awkward moving mass of steel and leather.

Cheung made the door before the nearest made him. He ducked as he pulled it open, and felt a concussive shudder hammer up his arm as a large blade split oak above him. He reeled at the speed of the thing, swaying away as the hack turned into an overstretched lunge.

Taking hold of the bluntness higher up the blade, Cheung pulled hard, forcing the off-balanced animation to crash helmet first onto stone flags. Armour scattered and maille and leather flattened.

There was no respite as another length of steel came in horizontally, cleaving at Cheung's waist. He barely avoided the swing, but managed to dive over pieces of armour and through the doorway to safety.

The steel guardians fought to push through after him, hindering themselves in their single mindedness.

Scrabbling to his feet, Cheung raced on, following the sound of men shouting warnings. Turning a corner, he powered up a narrow, curving staircase before spilling out, chest heaving, onto a short corridor with a set of double doors at the end.

Two heads turned. The halberdiers they belonged to readied themselves. Cheung was sure they'd just closed those doors.

'You're not getting through,' the older of the two said. The other nodded, nostrils flaring, jaw bunching.

'I don't mean to,' Cheung said in Altolnan, between breaths. He pulled his satchel from his shoulder as the men advanced, halberds lowered towards him.

Cheung took a deep breath and slid his satchel towards the guards. A heartbeat later, as their faces turned from determination to confusion, Cheung exploded into motion. He darted forward with incredible speed, chasing his sliding satchel until he met with it, a forearm's length before the points of the lowered halberds.

Pale hands plunged into the satchel and took hold of bone.

Broad-bladed polearms thrust forward.

Two black bladed kamas left satchel as Cheung sprang up and over the weapons coming in at him. His attackers struck stone and fell forward as Cheung landed between them, black blades finding gaps in polished plate.

Landing in a crouch, blooded kamas to the sides, Cheung looked forward to the double doors he did indeed intend to pass through.

He rose to his feet and took a step forward, hearing the shift of plate too late to stop the bollock dagger from slicing across the back of his trailing calf.

Biting back a cry of pain, Cheung twisted and dropped, driving his weapons into the offending survivor, who grunted his last breath. Defiant old eyes bored into Cheung's before the light faded from them.

Cheung stood once more. He drew a single red line through his shirt and across his chest, joining two other recent additions from the courtyard. He accepted the wound on his calf as payment for the older halberdier's death, and nodded his respect of the man's final attempt to stop him.

Rolling his head and his arms, Cheung stretched one last time before approaching and pushing his way through the double doors those behind him died to protect.

As soon as Cheung passed through the doors, he heard the double clicks. More snaps than clicks. Snaps and twangs and loud cracks as two crossbow bolts smashed against and ricocheted off the plastered wall above his head. Coming back to his feet after his instinctive roll, and cursing his lack of discipline of late, Cheung launched into a light-footed run that took him, body arching and twisting and turning, through the centre of two wide-eyed halberdiers to close on the deftly reloading crossbowmen.

Their eyes were on their weapons, experience and confidence steadying their hands as they spanned the bows and begun loading bolts into grooves. The two men looked up at the shouted warning from their protectors. Their eyes widened too – one managing to drop his crossbow and reach for a dagger at his belt – before black-bladed kamas thudded wetly into shoulders. Both men went down hard, howling as they fell, blood arcing from wounds like twin fountains of crimson as Cheung made to turn right but dashed left, keeping the reacting halberdiers and their wicked polearms in his periphery.

Cheung circled the thrashing, shrieking and cursing men slipping around on the polished floor, assaulting the halberdiers with a confidence he'd not felt since his journey out of Eatri began. He was impressed how quickly the halberdiers had recovered their surprise at his speed and skill, at their surprise of the wounded men, friends likely, before them. Snarls pulled at lips and noses wrinkled. Teeth showed through peeled-back lips and as a well-trained duo, the halberdiers charged Cheung, flat-bladed halberds jabbing and swinging in quick, jerky movements — no pattern to those moves. *Hard to defend against,* Cheung managed to think, as he ran for the wall to the right of the right-hand man. He launched himself from the ground and propelled himself up, backwards and over the too-late-to-react halberdier. The long weapon the man wielded never made it up in time to stop the light-drinking blade of Cheung's trailing weapon from piercing and sinking into his eye and brain thereafter.

No shriek or agonised cry came, just a weight that pulled Cheung, along with his momentum, down and into the second halberdier, who dropped shortly after, Cheung's leading kama mirroring the action of its twin.

Cheung landed in a crouch, breaths heavy, sweat beading his scarred brow. The clatter and thud of armoured bodies striking the floor, of halberds doing the same, accompanied the thudding of Cheung's pulse in his ears, the rush of blood circulating his system. He glanced about, to the two corpses and two cursing, snarling crossbowmen, all blood covered, scared and rightfully angry at Cheung, and themselves for that matter. He knew enough of soldiers to understand that. Standing, the slice Cheung had taken in the corridor pulling at his calf now the rush of the fight fled him, he gave the severely bleeding crossbowmen a wide birth and made for the small door he'd seen one of them glance towards.

'Bastard!' the furthest man managed, voice tinged with pain.

Cheung accepted the understandable, outrage filled insult and opened the door without turning, two kamas held in one hand.

He didn't expect the gauntleted fist that greeted him; didn't expect the crunch of his nose and the spattering of hot blood across his top lip as he rocked back.

Chapter 46 – Sergeant Grannit

Sergeant Grannit backed into the corridor as the assassin came on fast and furious, despite broken nose. The palace sergeant-at-arms hadn't got where he was through hubris and bluster. He'd got and stayed there by fighting smart. By choosing his fights, the when and the where and the who, often as not. Grannit knew the man he faced was quick as a stoat and carried a deadly bite: the black blades of his cycle-like weapons drawing Grannit's eyes in a dangerous way. He also knew his thick padding, riveted maille and steel plate offered him far more protection in the confines of the corridor, where he was unflank-able and exposed only on his most dangerous side. If he was to stop this bastard, if he was to survive, he needed to use his advantage of armour and strength and take away his opponent's speed and agility.

The assassin came in low, then high, flashing in with strikes like an adder. The blades licked out like fangs, hooked at his arming sword and rondel dagger, trying to pull them out to expose him. Grannit stepped back, knowing the corridor and avoiding as many attacks by the assassin as he parried with one blade or another. He punched back with lunges where he could, but conserved his energy, knowing he'd tire first if he tried to match the Eatrian's speed and aggression. Grannit sucked in a breath as a black blade swished across the maille covering his throat. He'd hardly seen the attack in the fast dimming light – the further he backed away from the doorway to the chamber was the further he backed into the windowless corridor. He watched for gaps, forcing his eyes on the assassin's chest, letting his periphery pick up the subtle movements from shoulders through arms to weapons. If he let himself be drawn in by those black blades, or the red-spattered pale hands holding them, then he was gone; of that Grannit was sure.

The assassin knocked Grannit's sword wide. The thud and reverberation of the blade connecting with the wall opened him up enough for the assassin to flash a foot out, connecting with and staggering Grannit back through his solar plexus.

'Shitting twat.' Grannit spat at the assassin's feet and came on hard and fast, sword leading, rondel following; the tri-edged straight foot of steel designed to punch through armour would sink deep into the cloth-covered assassin, ghostly agile or not.

The assassin leapt back, but could hardly go sideways. He let Grannit come at him and Grannit knew it; he counted on it. As he overstretched with his sword, and stumbled, the assassin stepped in, black blade guiding Grannit's sword harmlessly past whilst the other hooked for the armour-less spot under Grannit's outstretched arm. The assassin twisted as he did so, seeing, Grannit knew, the danger presented by the rondel dagger. As the depth-less blade cut through wool and linen, scraping past pouldron, causing Grannit to clench teeth and roar through them with the pain, Grannit dropped sword and rondel, and the gauntleted hand holding the latter took the assassin's balls and squeezed… Grannit frowned, the confusion and realisation overcoming the pain as he sagged to the floor, black blade sucking painfully free of his under-arm and the innards it'd skewered beneath. He fell to the floor, hand grasping cloth, but no balls. Grannit felt the empty package slip his grasp as the Eatrian eunuch leapt over him and sprinted away, leaving Grannit to struggle to his feet, armpit pissing blood over polished plate and the passage-polished stone floor. Leaving him to know his failure and to know, more than likely, his own end.

'Gods but it hurts,' Grannit managed before slipping on and crashing to the blood-slick floor.

Chapter 47 – It all led to this

Nose and face throbbing, Cheung wiped at his eyes with the back of his scar-roughed, henna-faded hand. He took a breath and slowed, his walk, his heart, his thoughts. The door before him was everything, or so he hoped. He'd hoped the door after the two halberdiers had been, but alas it had not, and since then he'd travelled upstairs and down corridors galore. The map of the palace his masters placed in his head along with the original order, had been guiding him thus far. Cheung knew such a mark would prove difficult, to say the least, but the level of resistance he'd met troubled him. They knew of the mark, that much was clear. *How? Souch Sader?* He didn't know for sure, nor did it matter. The fact they knew was what mattered; to him, to the mission and to the honour of his masters. He had to see it through. He had to leave behind the doubts sown by the Caravaneers. Cheung allowed himself a rare smile at the thought of those men and women, and children. Infectious was their mirth and love of life, their passion, whether to anger or love or dance or song. Infectious. But he was an assassin of Eatri and the door before him was everything. Of course, Cheung knew there'd be the hardest resistance yet beyond that door, it only made sense. There'd be no stalking up to or jumping out on an unsuspecting mark, not this time. This would be a rush of blades and blood and adrenaline and… death. His and – or – the King of Altoln's. Cheung accepted now – more than he thought he'd accepted at any point along the road – that his life was forfeit for the mission. He accepted his masters knew so and also accepted that, unusually, they'd sent more than one of his order to attempt to see this through. No second attempts, as had happened on occasion throughout history, such as those sent against the great warlords of the Eastern Planes in centuries past, before they had become the Naga. No, this time multiple assassins, he could only assume after the one he'd seen in the tavern, had been sent at the same time. This mark must be the greatest of Cheung's time, and for that, for that honour, he was proud.

Head high and one last trick up his sleeve, so to speak, Cheung shoved through the door with a confidence he'd not felt in years. He would succeed. No Altolnan could stop him in that.

The light struck Cheung's eyes as shouts, triggered by the opening of the door, filled the room. Gruff voiced and soft voiced shouts alike; warnings and curses and threats, all in the tongue of Altoln, although three different accents were present, which caused Cheung a measure of confusion.

Polished armour, road-dusted leather, men and women and swords and a bow all greeted Cheung. As did the anger-reddened face of King Barrison, stood behind his defensive barrier of protectors young and old.

As the arrow left the elf's bow – *An elf!* – Cheung shoved the distracting thought aside and played his ace: the black blade of his left kama, following a deft flick and twist of his wrist, flew from its haft to shatter like glass on the stone flags between him and his adversaries.

All light left the chamber, as if the sun had been doused by a trillion oceans. No light shone through the grand windows. None whatsoever; ambient and direct light alike sucked from the world, as far as Cheung and, he knew, the others present were concerned.

The theoretical map of the room, of his opponents' positions, remained on Cheung's retinas, captured there like the image from a circus trickster's flash-slate, albeit captured far quicker than such a device could imagine, let alone perform.

Boots discarded after the fight with the armoured man in the corridor, Cheung dashed right, near on silently running the circumference of the room with a speed that would beggar belief, if it could be seen. Only Legg could have bested it, Cheung mused. The surety of Cheung's run lent itself, at least in part, to his faith in his ability, and the map-come-flash-image that remained of his vision. No light helped him, for there was none in the room, although that trick would fade in but heartbeats. What he saw of his path was in his mind, he knew. But those in the room didn't. His passage was but a brief wind and shush of feet and clothes, if that. And no man or woman, no matter how well trained, could react to that sound with any level of martial prowess.

Cheung neared his mark in his head. He, of course, couldn't see Barrison's expression or reaction, but he could guess at it. Shock and confusion, fear and a loss of hope, perhaps. Cheung took no pleasure in that.

Maille shushed in a metallic way, unlike Cheung's clothes and feet, and plates of steel scraped, none of them near to him or moving fast enough to stop him. Preparing his remaining kama for its final kill, for Cheung's final kill – the fear of that forced from his mind; the fear of never seeing the Caravaneers again or tending his succulents, forced away for threat of staying his hand despite his imminent death whether he succeeded or not – Cheung slowed but a fraction, bent his leading knee and leapt towards the dais that the King stood upon, kama raised and already arcing down for the kill. *I'll make it quick,* Cheung thought, as a homage to the benevolent King of Altoln. *It's all I can do—*

A thudding, concussive and, a moment later, sharp impact of something shocking hammered into Cheung's side, spinning him mid-air and striking him hard into the join between wall and floor. He heard the clatter of his kama leaving his grip. He felt the agonising pull of something protruding from his side as it snagged during his impact and subsequent collapse. Confusion accompanied the pain coursing through him; agonising pain both in his side and deep within.

The blackness of his eyelids lightened all of a sudden, so he could see the pale haze and thin red lines of blood vessels before him. Blinking, light blinding, Cheung heard voices, muffled to the rushing in his ears. He reached for the snagging in his side and found a wooden shaft there, slick with hot, wet blood. It could be nought else and the immense pain confirmed it. He tried to curl up, tried to move in any way he could to decrease the horrific pain that wracked his body.

'The elf…' Cheung managed through gritted teeth. Realisation of that, of the slight noise his run had created, therefore giving him away, struck him moments before his consciousness flickered and threatened to fade, surely leading to his inevitable, but slow death.

And more importantly, his monumental failure, after all he had been through.

All for nought, Cheung thought before the end, albeit in the weakest sense. *All for nought.*

Chapter 48 - Tumultuous and bleak

'Longoss?' Coppin looked across to the big man. His eyes were closed, but his chest was heaving as he sucked in lungful after lungful of air. His eyes flickered behind his lids and he snarled, grunted; whimpered even, whilst he slept.

'Best let him sleep,' a white robed cleric said, 'despite it being fitful to say the least.'

Coppin looked to the handsome young man. He blushed when she took him in. Her leg was showing to the thigh, wrapped around the blanket as it was, to regulate her temperature. Coppin hid it so the man could relax, more than for her own comfort.

'And how are you?' he asked, crossing the room to her.

'In pain,' she said. 'Especially when I move.'

He smiled and nodded. 'It is to be expected. You are lucky—'

'To be alive, yes. I'm sure I am.' She'd snapped at him and immediately regretted it as he rocked back at the unexpected tone. 'My apologies, Master...?'

'Morri. This is my infirmary. In Dockside. Master Effrin had you brought here, for we were the closest to, well...' Morri smiled. Coppin returned the smile. 'How's your...?'

'Tummy?'

Morri's lips pulled in tight. He nodded.

Coppin shrugged. 'It's hard to say with the pain from me side as it is.'

Nodding, Morri made a soft sound of acknowledgement. 'May I?' he said, holding out his hand. Coppin hesitated and Morri pulled his hand back. 'I can summon a female—'

'No!' Coppin said, a little too quickly. 'No, it's fine.' She took a breath and relaxed.

Morri breathed on his hands and rubbed them together. 'Apologies, but they'll be cold.' The room did indeed have a chill, despite the glowing hearth in the corner and the calm summer's night. Hands warmed, as much as blowing and rubbing can warm hands, Morri leaned forward and slid his hand beneath the blanket.

Coppin tensed then forced herself to relax.

'This may feel... uncomfortable,' he said as he pressed his fingers about her abdomen.

Sucking in a breath and clenching her teeth, Coppin thought the man needed to reassess his meaning of discomfort and replace it with pain. Not only did her stitches pull and her wound throb, but sharp pains flared within her when the cleric pressed tender areas.

'Tell me if it—'

'Hurts? Yep, it does,' she said through gritted teeth.

'Here?' Morri asked. Coppin shook her head. 'Here?' She managed a no. 'Here—'

'Yes,' she said, more a breath than a word.

Morri pressed again, brow creased.

'Yes!' Coppin said, louder.

The hand stayed there, pressing but not prodding; uncomfortable this time, not painful.

Coppin didn't know what to think. What to feel. Fear? She should do, by all rights. Fear for the potential loss of her baby… The thought of the thing sickened her. The thought of losing it didn't. And that sickened her more.

'Cheeky fucker!'

Pain shot through Coppin's wound as she jumped and tensed. She saw Morri jump too, a moment before big hands took him by his robes, hauled him off of her and literally threw him across the floor.

Morri cried out, in surprise it seemed rather than any pain.

Coppin cried out in pain and surprise, and anger.

Longoss cried out in severe pain and outrage.

'Longoss!' Coppin shouted.

'What's going on?' Severun asked, stirring from his slumber.

Boots pounded through the corridor beyond the door.

'Ye bloody fool!' Coppin said to Longoss, who was doubled over, blood spreading through the bandages he wore in several places.

Morri was quick to his feet and quick to help the man back to his bed, despite what had happened and despite the danger Coppin feared he was in.

'He were checking the babe, Longoss, ye dumb shit!'

Longoss spun on her at that, then to the cleric trying to heft him into bed. 'Truly?' he asked.

'Yes.' Morri managed the word through grunts of effort. Longoss was leaning on him fully.

'Oh, Longoss,' Coppin said, shaking her head. She heard Severun mutter something, saw him stand and move to help Morri. She also saw the cleric flinch as Severun brushed past him to take Longoss' other arm.

'Sorry,' Longoss said through gold. He was clearly in a lot of pain. A lot of self-induced pain after his actions.

'You've split most of your stitches,' Morri said as they settled Longoss onto his bed.

Longoss cursed several times, more so as two guardsmen barged in, short-swords drawn.

'You'd need more than that for me, boys,' Longoss said, eyeing the men.

'Oh, shut up!' Coppin snapped.

Morri waved the men away. They reluctantly followed the silent order.

'How's the baby?' Longoss asked Morri.

Morri flinched. He looked from Longoss to Severun and on to Coppin. 'I...'

'Spit it out, Morri,' Coppin said. She surprised them with her tone. She didn't surprise herself. *Tell me it's dead and we can be done with it,* she thought.

'I can't be sure—'

'Use magic or whatever,' Coppin said, eager for the news in ways she hated.

'He can't,' Severun answered. 'He could do more harm than good, it being so tiny and all.'

Morri was nodding before Severun finished. Morri crossed to Coppin, sat on the side of her bed and took her hands. She pulled them back and set a hard look on the man.

'Get on with it,' she said, as cold as she'd ever heard herself be.

Morri nodded. 'I cannot be sure, Coppin, but I think your baby survives. I would like to call on a midwife for her opinion, but I think—'

'Yes, thank you.' Coppin slumped back in her bed and rolled away from the prying eyes. *Thanks for ruining my recovery.* She blocked out the stream of questions coming from Longoss' gold mouth. She shuddered and wept at the thought of what was to come. She seemed to be the only one who didn't want the coming of the monster within. And in that realisation, she made her decision. Whether they helped her or not – likely not – she would head to Mother's as soon as she was fit. She would head there and search there and find the whatever-it-was that would rid her of the beast growing inside her. She would wash herself of its taint; of *him.* The Grand Inquisitor.

'Where's Coppin?'

Severun sat bolt upright. He'd been sleeping, but the panic in Longoss' voice snapped him awake. He looked around, found Coppin's empty bed. He looked around again, saw Longoss crashing out the door and into the corridor beyond. He'd been wearing linen shirt and braes and bandages, nothing else. Severun climbed to his feet as confusion gave way to a vocal challenge by the duty guardsmen. He rushed to leave the room as he heard threats, thuds and the crashing of metal on wood. Reaching the corridor, he saw Longoss bracing himself about the torso with one arm, leaning against the wall with the other, the two guardsmen laying slumped on the floor at his feet; one unconscious, the other holding his hands up, panting – blood marring his flattened nose.

'Longoss!' Severun shouted, a hint of magic worked into the name.

Longoss turned and eyed Severun warily.

'Back to bed. Now!' Heart racing, Severun held firm his air of authority and tall stance as Longoss approached, passed him and climbed back into bed. Severun called for Morri, again, a little magic laced in with the shout, before moving to Longoss' side. 'What's happened?' he asked, eyeing the empty bed beyond Longoss.

'I don't know,' Longoss admitted, shaking his head and looking up to Severun. 'I woke and she was gone.'

Where is that boy, Severun thought of Morri. 'Morri!' he shouted over his shoulder. Back to Longoss he said, 'I'm sure there's a reasonable—'

'I don't want reasonable!' Longoss shouted. 'I want Coppin. Or at least to know where she is.'

Severun made to speak, but Longoss burst into a raging torrent of accusations and threats, all aimed at Morri. 'That pretty faced cunt.'

At the worst possible time, Severun heard – over Longoss' rant – people approaching. He turned in time to see Morri enter, a messenger in the royal livery at his back. The man held a wooden tube that held more than parchment, Severun knew. He recognised the thing. He'd designed the thing. He held out his hand for that which the messenger bore, at the same time as reaching out his other and pressing it, palm first, against Longoss' face. The man collapsed to the bed and Severun felt the magical drain of the action. He remained weak, but this couldn't wait for Longoss to calm down. And he wasn't even sure the big man *would* calm until they knew exactly where Coppin was. He pushed his own worry for Coppin to the back of his mind and snatched the communication from the messenger, who dutifully stood, back straight, awaiting a response.

Morri watched with bated breath, despite the fear he'd shown at Longoss' rage. Severun glanced at him, knowing the cleric understood what Severun held, and, whilst the sounds of Morri's staff helping the downed guardsmen reached Severun, he opened the wooden tube and looked through it like one would a telescope.

Severun staggered. Morri moved to catch him but Severun had dropped to one knee before Morri took his arm. The messenger was but a heartbeat slower in his assistance of Severun, who they helped onto his bed, swinging his legs up as he dropped back against his pillows, head shaking from side to side in disbelief.

'What is it?' Morri asked, fear flecking his tone and features.

Before an answer left Severun's lips, a moan came from the other side of the room. Morri turned to look upon Egan Dundaven, who was stirring, arms moving, legs writhing and tangling in his covers. The cleric looked torn through indecision as he awaited Severun's words.

Severun watched, stunned as he was by what he'd seen and heard and felt through the magical device the royal messenger had delivered. 'We failed,' he whispered, as Morri move about Egan with haste.

'My lord?' the messenger asked, stepping closer.

'I need help here!' Morri shouted, looking to the door and back to Egan, who was thrashing.

Severun's heart pounded in his chest, in his ears. His stomach twisted and bile burnt his throat, the back of his mouth and, without warning, he turned his head and threw up between his bed and Longoss'.

'Severun!' Morri shouted, at the same time as the messenger gasped and stepped away.

Another cleric rushed into the room, a small spattering of blood on her robes from the guardsmen outside, no doubt. She was accompanied by the one with the broken nose, short-sword drawn, and two assistants. 'Master Morri?' she said, before rushing to aid Severun.

'You two, here,' Morri said, trying to pin Egan down. 'Guardsman, you're not needed,' Morri added, without looking. The man snarled at Longoss' sleeping form before storming from the room.

'We failed,' Severun said to the female cleric mopping his mouth and feeling his forehead. 'We failed,' he repeated as she attended him.

'What's wrong, Severun?' Morri said from his side of the room.

'He's dead,' Severun breathed, mind swirling and whirling and pounding at the thought, at the implications and the how and the why of it.

'Who?' Morri demanded, half listening and half concentrating on questing through to the struggling witchunter his assistants held down.

'Barrison,' Severun breathed, looking up and locking eyes with a turning Morri. 'King Barrison,' he confirmed, tears filling his eyes. 'Our King is assassinated!'

'Samorl save us,' the messenger said, unaware of the message he'd carried from the palace.

The room fell silent, but for the moans and groans of Egan Dundaven. That struck Severun, as he saw his friend in distress. He nodded, towards the man as the cleric beside him fell away, hands to her mouth. As the two holding Egan looked back across at him, eyes wide, faces ashen. As he locked eyes with the cleric held in such high regards within the guild, his former guild. 'What is it?' Severun managed, nodding again at Egan.

Morri licked dry lips, looked from Severun to Egan and back. 'It's as we feared, Severun. Our ministrations have failed. His blood remains poisoned,' Morri said, reeling from the horrific news Severun had given them.

'From the assassin's blades?' Severun forced himself to ask, mind a blaze of questions and fears about Egan and Barrison, and Coppin.

Morri nodded. 'From the sewage smeared upon them.'

'What more can you do, Morri?' Severun asked, the question seen by Morri more than heard as Egan cried out in pain.

'Nothing,' Morri said, tears filling his own eyes as the cleric next to Severun sobbed. 'Nothing,' he whispered, slumping to the stool besides Egan's bed. 'He's warded against me, somehow. By his order or... I don't know what,' Morri admitted, eyes lost in some awful place Severun – all of those present – likely wandered too. 'I can't heal him with magic—'

'And it's too late to do anything else,' Severun finished. 'It's too late to save my friend.'

Morri looked across at Severun, sorrow, regret and an anger aimed inward, plain for Severun to see.

Severun braced himself against the hurt and the pain and the shock of it all and nodded to the young man; nodded his assurance that he knew there was nothing Morri could do. That he knew it wasn't the cleric's fault.

Because it's mine, Severun thought. *It's all mine.*

Epilogue

'I never met Barrison, but I liked what I heard,' Longoss said to Severun, as they looked out from the door of the infirmary they'd spent far too long recovering within.

Severun had held Longoss back, through various means, for several days, which seemed to blur into one in the infirmary, but he was ready now – according to Morri. Severun wasn't sure if the man was ready mentally, to face what they might find out there in Dockside. As well as everything else, Severun railed at himself for not chasing after Coppin the morning they'd discovered her gone. The morning he'd learnt of Barrison's death. He heaved a sigh and glanced at Longoss, his one remaining companion.

'He was a fine king and a fine man,' Severun said, offering a tight smile. 'The likes of which I don't think…' He couldn't finish the sentence.

Longoss gripped Severun's shoulder in his big hand and squeezed. 'Let's hold onto some hope for the Black Prince, eh?'

Severun nodded, although from the times he'd met Edward, it left little in the way of hope for his coming reign. 'Quite,' Severun said, offering a smile to match Longoss' gold. He was surprised how well Longoss had healed. Of course, there'd been a great deal of magic involved, from Morri and his staff, not to mention from Effrin at the tavern, by all accounts, but the mill the former assassin had been wrung through was enough to kill most men through trauma alone. Or at least kill or fray their minds.

'Well,' Longoss said, releasing Severun's shoulder and looking back down the busy street they intended to tread together, 'at least Egan has been sent home; south.'

Severun smiled and nodded. His heart thudded an irregular beat and a coldness washed through him at the loss of his friend. For that's what Egan Dundaven had been. A man known a short while, but a friend forever. 'Yes. I made sure his body would reach his home and have an appropriate Samorlian burial, as I'm sure he would have wanted.'

'Oh, but he were a good fighter, eh?' Longoss winked at Severun, in his own way of remembrance.

Severun smiled. 'Yes he was. He likely saved more than one of us that night, in the tavern.'

'Couldn't agree more, Severun, and if it weren't for needs must, we'd be travelling with him to lay him to rest, I promise ye that.'

'I know,' Severun said. 'I know.

'Right. Shall we move on?' Severun asked, looking to his friend, who nodded his accord.

'I think so. To find Coppin and to pay respects to Keep and his tavern.

'Ye sure Lord Yewbuggerer Cunt-stubble is fine with ye accompanying me?' Longoss set off up the street.

'He didn't have any choice, Longoss,' Severun replied, easily keeping pace, what with his long legs and all. 'I told him I'd serve him for as long as he needs once Coppin was safe. And without… without Barrison to back him in my employ, and what's supposedly coming from Sirreta and The Marches, he was glad of my support.'

'Right we are then,' Longoss said, making a turn, Severun at his side; a turn towards Mother's. 'Because if the armoured prick had said no, I'd have stuck him with that bastard-sword he holds so dear, and dragged ye along anyway.'

Severun allowed himself a laugh and Longoss joined in. It was the first either had felt genuine about for some time, and with what Severun knew was coming for Wesson, it could very well be the last.

***

Stopping their weary mounts, the younger of the two Altolnan scouts looked across to his companion. 'What's wrong, Dram?'

'Those bodies, in that tree.' Dram nodded to the side of the road, opposite the inn they'd intended to use.

'The gibbet tree? That's what it's for, ye old coot.'

'I know, lad, but how long do ye think they've hung there?'

The young scout shrugged. 'Several days at the least, by the looks of them.'

'By the looks of their eyes?'

The youngster frowned and walked his horse a couple of steps towards the tree. 'I can't see their eyes, they're shut.'

'Exactly.'

He turned to Dram. 'I don't follow?'

'What circles above us?'

The lad looked up, squinting. 'Crows and rooks and the like. Buzzards even, although the crows don't look happy about that.' He grinned following his observation and looked back to his mentor.

Dram nodded, eyes locked on the gibbet tree. 'Aye, and yet their eyes are intact. Closed, but intact. Carrion birds like those above always eat the eyes, and always first.'

The lad pursed his lips and leaned forward to stare at the closed eyes of the hanging bodies, one a boy. 'What do you think it means, Dram? They spoilt?'

Shaking his head, Dram responded. 'I don't know, but—' he rocked back in his saddle, causing his mount to snort and rear, throwing him to the ground before thundering off up the road. Dram grunted, cursed and pulled himself up on his gawking friend's stirruped foot.

As the corvids and buzzards fled the scene, so too did the two scouts, on one horse. They rode up the road as fast as their exhausted mount would allow; seven pairs of eyes tracking their progress before closing as quickly as they'd opened, the bodies they belonged to swinging gently in the gibbet tree.

And Dignaaln witnessed it all.

So ends the second book from the tales of the Black Powder Wars.

Excerpt

Black Arrow
Third book from the tales of the Black Powder Wars

Chapter 1 - Beginning of the end

Brisance
Summer - 492ⁿᵈ year of the Alliance

One skip, two, three and a wide grin between red bristles.

A loud splash was followed by a colourful curse.

'Get low when ye throw,' Sears said, demonstrating his technique. 'Throw the stone, a flat stone, across like ye would bounce it from a table-top.'

Biviano grunted and scratched under his kettle-helm. 'I've never bounced a stone, a flat stone...' He dodged Sears' meaty fist. '...across a table-top,' he finished with glee.

'Watch me, ye shit.' The flat stone glided with little hops across the Park District pond. One of those hops was atop a lily pad.

Biviano's breath was long and ragged. 'I don't want to come here anymore, Sears.' Biviano walked away, or began to; frowning, he turned to Sears, who stared at nothing in particular. 'Mate, ye alright?' Biviano asked.

No response.

'Sears, ye prick, what is it?'

Sears took a beat and turned to his friend, smiling as he did, albeit weakly.

'I don't like where this is going, big guy.'

'I don't suppose ye will. Nor where I'm going.'

Biviano closed his eyes for a moment, accompanying his heavy sigh. 'Ye know what length we went to, getting ye out of there, and ye want to go back in?' And for what, Sears? A former assassin and his—'

'Don't!' Sears warned.

'I was going to say lass, ye goon, not whore.'

Sears conceded and nodded. 'Fair enough. Go on with yer mothering.'

'It's more than mothering, Sears. It's—'

'Shit!'

'It is shit, aye, but it's also—'

'Not that, Biv.' Sears reached out and grabbed a flinching Biviano by his maille-clad shoulders and turned him to the park gate. 'That! Or should I say them.'

''Morl's wrinkled scrotum, Sears. What've ye done now, eh?'

All Sears could do was frown and shake his red head. *I have no idea,* he thought, as a dozen burgundy clad magistrates' guardsmen approached, hands on sheathed and belted weapons, not cudgels.

'I take it yer here for more'n a chat and a skim of stones, eh lads?' Sears said.

The sergeant stepped forward as the armed group fanned out before the two city guardsmen.

'You can leave,' the sergeant said to Biviano, before locking eyes once more on Sears.

'Like dog shit I can, ye fat bastard. The man asked ye a question and ye'll bloody well answer it.'

'As you wish.' The sergeant's eyes remained on Sears, although one twitched at Biviano's insult. Sears and Biviano noticed the battle mage at the back of the group, also wearing the burgundy of Wesson's magistrates, and their badge of a vertical gold sword on a white field.

Sears filled his bearded cheeks before letting the breath out slowly. 'I'm under arrest, aren't I?'

The sergeant nodded.

Biviano half-drew his short-sword, but Sears stopped him with an iron grip. They looked to one another and Sears shook his head. 'Don't, Biv. They're just doing their duty, like we do.'

Biviano swallowed hard and slammed his sword back into its scabbard, turning to the sergeant as he did so.

Sears stepped forward, arms away from his sides. 'Can I ask—?'

'Do you know who this man is?' Biviano interrupted Sears and took a step toward the sergeant. Several men half-drew their weapons.

'Of course they bloody well know who I am, Biviano,' Sears said. 'That's why they're here. Can't imagine it's a case of mistaken identity with this.' He ran fingers through his red beard.

'Will you come along calmly and relinquish your sword, Master Sears?'

Sears nodded to the sergeant. 'If I must, aye.' He walked forward, but not before drawing and turning his sword so the well-worn hilt faced the magistrates' men.

The sergeant nodded his thanks and took the offered blade. He raised a hand and placed it on Sears' broad back as he guided him through the burgundy men and away from the pond; away from Biviano.

'And what of me?'

'I'll see you in the magistrates' court, ye prick,' Sears shouted, without turning.

'Aye, but for what, eh? For what? Ye bunch of shites!'

No one answered Biviano as Sears was led from the park...

Find out what happens to our beloved duo in Black Arrow, due for release 2018

Thank you for continuing to read the Black Powder Wars series, your support is what keeps me writing and the world of Brisance going.

J P Ashman

Thank you for reading:

Black Guild
Second book from the tales of the
Black Powder Wars

Reviews are more than welcome and incredibly helpful.
Please feel free to contact me on the following sites:
www.jpashman.com
Facebook
Goodreads
Twitter: @JP_Ashman

#BlackPowderWars

Also available:

Black Martlet
First short story from the tales of the
Black Powder Wars

Dragonship
Short story
(Not of the Black Powder Wars)

FALL
Sci-fi short story

J P Ashman is currently working on:

Black Arrow
Third book from the tales of the
Black Powder Wars
(Due for release 2018)

Black Prince
Fourth book from the tales of the
Black Powder Wars
(Currently being written)

Biography

Born Lancashire, England, J P Ashman is a Northern lad through and through. His parents read to him from an early age and encouraged his imagination at every turn. His Career may be in optics, as an SMC technician, but he loves to make time for writing and reading every day. Now living back in Lancashire after five years in the Cotswolds with Wifey and their little Norse Goddess Freya, he is inspired daily by everything and anything, from history to science, his reef tank to the environment.

Writing is a huge part of his life and the medieval re-enactment background and tabletop gaming lend to it; when he's not writing the genre, he's either reading or playing it. He plans to keep writing, both within his current series, and those to come, whether short stories or epic tomes.

www.ingramcontent.com/pod-product-compliance
Lightning Source LLC
Chambersburg PA
CBHW031225120726
47905CB00002B/475